Praise for *Hom*

'Moving, hopeful and heartfelt ... an ideal book group read'
AJ Pearce, author of *Dear Mrs Bird*

'I loved this warm and touching story about home, belonging, and finding your way in the world. Vivid, evocative and beautifully written, with a message of hope at its heart'
Holly Miller, author of *The Sight of You*

'Friends are where the heart is ... I very much enjoyed this thoughtful and absorbing novel'
Kate Eberlen, author of *Miss You*

'A gorgeous, thoughtful read' **Catherine Isaac, author of *The World at My Feet***

'Clever, warm and funny, Penny writes with a big heart, a light touch and supreme confidence. *Home* will be on all the best bookshelves! The ultimate comfort read'
**Veronica Henry, author of
*How to Find Love in a Book Shop***

'As heartbreaking as it is uplifting, this book wouldn't leave me. I loved it' **Katie Fforde, author of *A Wedding in the Country***

'A beautiful, heart-felt, wise, want-to-hug-the-book-when-you-finish kind of book'
Miranda Dickinson, author of *Our Story*

About the Author

Penny Parkes survived a convent education largely thanks to a ready supply of inappropriate novels and her passion for writing and languages.

She studied International Management in Bath and Germany, before gaining experience with the BBC. She then set up an independent film location agency and spent many happy years organising shoots for film, television and advertising – thereby ensuring that she was never short of travel opportunities, freelance writing projects or entertaining anecdotes.

Penny now lives in the Cotswolds with her husband, two children and an excitable dog with a fondness for Post-its. She will often be found plotting epic train journeys through the Alps, baking gluten-free goodies or attempting to reach an elusive state of organisation.

In 2017, Penny won the RNA Romantic Comedy Novel of the Year Award. This is her fifth novel.

Follow Penny on Twitter and Instagram: @CotswoldPenny

First published in Great Britain by Simon & Schuster UK Ltd, 2021
This paperback edition published in 2022

1 3 5 7 9 10 8 6 4 2

Simon & Schuster UK Ltd
1st Floor
222 Gray's Inn Road
London WC1X 8HB

Simon & Schuster Australia, Sydney
Simon & Schuster India, New Delhi

www.simonandschuster.co.uk
www.simonandschuster.com.au
www.simonandschuster.co.in

A CIP catalogue record for this book is available from the British Library

Paperback ISBN: 978-1-4711-8018-7
eBook ISBN: 978-1-4711-8017-0
Audio ISBN: 978-1-4711-8194-8

Typeset in the UK by Hewer Text UK Ltd, Edinburgh
Printed and bound in Great Britain by
CPI Group (UK) Ltd, Croydon, CR0 4YY

PENNY PARKES

Home

**SIMON &
SCHUSTER**

London · New York · Sydney · Toronto · New Delhi

For Ollie
I am so incredibly proud of you . . .

Chapter 1

Anna turned the large, cumbersome key in the lock and held her breath. This was the moment of truth every time; that first impression of her new home, however temporary. Somehow, whether by intuition or simply years of experience, Anna could always tell whether her new placement was in a happy home, or merely a glamorous shell of style over substance.

She dropped her single, efficient overnight bag at her feet and glanced around the echoing hallway of Gravesend Manor, even its name giving her a prescient shiver. Certainly nobody could accuse this rambling Victorian manor house of feeling cosy, and she had a fresh understanding of why its owners might prefer to holiday in the Caribbean sun rather than face another month of drizzle in the Oxfordshire countryside.

Her mobile buzzed in her pocket and she glanced at the screen before answering, relieved to have at least two bars of signal. 'I'm already here,' she said simply.

'And is it just as Addams Family as you thought from the photos?' laughed Emily, clearly shuffling papers as she spoke.

Anna looked around, wandering through from room to room, taking in the tapestries and polished mahogany furniture which were clearly oh-so-expensive but lent noth-ing to the welcome or comfort of the place. 'It'll be fine,' Anna said reassuringly, to herself as much as Emily – after all, she didn't have to *live* here, just keep the home fires burning until Captain and Mrs Fraser came home. 'I mean, I've walked through three different sitting rooms and I've yet to find a warm one or a comfy sofa, but it's only for a month.' She paused. 'It'll be fine.'

Emily laughed, knowing her favourite house-sitter's maxim all too well. They might rarely meet in person, but Anna's commitment and flexibility meant that she was easily the most reliable, the most sought-after house-sitter on Home Network's books. 'Do you want me to get that embroidered on a pillow for you?'

'It's easy for you to say,' Anna said, 'sitting behind your desk with a cappuccino, sending me out into the middle of nowhere without so much as a handover from the owners.' Anna walked into the kitchen, in search of the promised note that would explain her duties during her stay at Gravesend Manor.

That in itself was a little unusual; normally owners liked to meet their house-sitter in person, to hand over the keys and explain the foibles of the wonky shower, or the kitchen window that wouldn't close, or the tendency of their whippet/Siamese/ house rabbit to pine. 'It's a bit weird though, yes?' Anna asked, spotting a simple Post-it on the kitchen table urging her to 'make herself at home'. 'If they booked me to house-sit months ago, why didn't they allow time for us to meet?'

Emily sighed. 'Nowt so strange as folk. They didn't want to pay for the extra day, if you can believe that.'

Anna could easily believe that; even knowing that the captain and his wife were probably halfway to St Kitts by now, almost certainly near the front of the plane. It was all a question of priorities and some of her clients, especially the ones with inherited piles of stone, tended to view their homes as an encumbrance, an imposition on their time and their bank account.

'Besides,' Emily continued, 'their son lives nearby and he's dropping the dogs back with you tomorrow, so if you've any questions, I'm sure he'll know the answer.'

Anna bit back her immediate thought, for fear of doing herself out of a job. If the son and heir lived quite so nearby, why couldn't *he* look after his parents' home for the next month?

Still, she thought, pushing back the curtains from the French windows in the kitchen and gazing out at the rolling, manicured lawns and topiary, there were worse places to spend her time. And once the omnipresent cloak of drizzle lifted, and the plane trees in the parkland were outlined against a clear blue sky, then Anna could spend her days outside with a book and walking the two spaniels that were to be her sole charges.

'It'll be fine,' she said again on autopilot, making Emily laugh. 'And thank you, Em. I know these longer gigs are in demand, so I really appreciate you putting it my way.'

Two dogs to walk and cuddle, a crumbling manor house with more bedrooms than days of the week, and stunning views over the spires of Oxford. As job placements went, it was pretty special and Anna was determined not to let the incipient chill between her shoulder blades put her off. She dragged an Ercol chair over to the Aga and sat with her back to the glorious warmth. The ancient, clanging heating system at Gravesend might not be up to snuff, but the Aga was about to be her new best friend.

★

The next morning, Anna groaned and pulled the blankets over her head – anything to block out the insistently perky ringing of church bells at such an indecent hour. She wriggled her toes to try and improve the circulation and wondered whether a quick trip out to pick up a decent duvet might improve her stay no end. Sheets and blankets, she sighed. Whoever thought *that* was still a good idea?

It always took a few moments for Anna to find her bearings when she woke up in the mornings; an occupational hazard she'd become accustomed to. Nevertheless, it always gave her a jolt, triggering that automatic glance to her kit bag, never unpacked, just opened out for ease of access. A triumph, Emily would say, in travelling light and achieving, as espoused by women's magazines everywhere, the ultimate capsule wardrobe. Perhaps it was just easier to see it that way than to consider it an obvious outward sign of a person constantly braced for moving on?

The ringing continued and Anna admitted defeat, pulling on several jumpers over her pyjamas to combat the chill and heading directly for the fancy espresso machine she'd spotted in the kitchen. Pulling her hair back from her eyes, attempting to tame her unruly mane as she yawned her way downstairs, Anna's only thoughts were focused on the caffeine in the next room.

'Well, hel-lo, Miss Anna,' drawled an unfamiliar voice from the kitchen doorway. 'Aren't you a sight for sore eyes?'

Anna froze, suddenly all too aware of how clingy her beloved Snoopy pyjamas actually were. The man in front of her was familiar only from the multitude of silver-framed photographs decking the mantels and windowsills, charting his rise to adulthood. Andrew Fraser in the flesh. So much for 'popping in with the dogs around lunchtime' as his mother's Post-it had suggested.

One glance at the delight on his florid face at catching her unawares made Anna wonder whether that had actually been his exact intent.

He didn't say anything else for a second or two, allowing his gaze to travel over her intrusively.

Anna took a deep breath and managed the last few stairs without tripping; he wasn't the first lascivious Lothario to ever cross her path. Giving her jumper a hearty tug to cover the image of a smiling Woodstock on her bottom, she stepped forward confidently, business as usual. 'Good morning. You must be Andrew. I wasn't expecting you until later, but since you're here, perhaps we can get this coffee machine up and running while you talk me through the dogs' feed and exercise schedule?'

She walked past him into the kitchen, looking around for the promised canine companions, only to find two brown-eyed spaniels sitting soulfully outside the French windows despite the downpour.

She reached for a towel and strode over towards the doors. How the Frasers treated their dogs was entirely their own lookout, but no dog was catching pneumonia on her watch. Capability was her byword as a professional house-sitter and she saw no issue with taking the initiative.

'They're not house pets,' chided Andrew, even as he switched on the coffee machine and followed Anna's suggestion, much to her amazement. 'They're working spaniels and they're not to be mollycoddled.'

'Of course,' said Anna easily, as she pulled open the doors and deftly rubbed their wet fur dry, smoothing damp, curling tendrils away from their eyes and introducing herself in the process. The pliability and affection they both showed as she dried them suggested that Andrew and his mother might just have differing views when it came to the family dogs, especially when both spaniels instinctively curled up together on the dog bed beside the Aga.

'The black one's Angus, and the chocolate-coloured one is Betty,' Andrew volunteered, as the steam from the coffee machine clouded his glasses and pinked his cheeks.

Anna felt herself soften towards him, quietly betting to herself that he was ninety per cent bravado. She couldn't help wishing she was dressed for this meeting, or indeed had brushed her teeth, rather than piling out of bed and straight into work mode, but it couldn't be helped.

'So,' she said, sipping at the excellent espresso he placed on the kitchen countertop for her. 'Have your parents arrived safely?'

He shrugged. 'They'll let me know if there's a problem.'

Anna just nodded, learning so much about the family dynamic from that simple statement alone. 'Okay then. So I've had a chance to look around and your parents didn't leave any specific instructions. Is there anything I need to know – about the house, the dogs, the post?'

Andrew glanced over at the dogs, both slumbering contentedly in the warmth. 'No dogs on the furniture. Two meals a day. Two walks a day. The details are in the utility room. And just pile the post on my father's desk in the study.' He paused. 'No need to open any of it,' he said sharply.

'I wouldn't dream of it,' Anna replied. 'I was just offering to note the date of arrival, as some of my clients request. Sometimes they like telephone messages to be emailed over, that kind of thing . . .'

Andrew frowned. 'They're on holiday. I think the world will cope with their absence for a few weeks. Just keep the house safe, lights on in the evening, etcetera, look after the dogs. Quite the cushy number for you, I would imagine?'

Anna sipped her coffee again. Whether his parents deemed her services value for money was really not her place to discuss. She did know that her unrivalled rating on the Home Network website meant that her care and attention to detail was something her clients appreciated. Trust, responsibility, confidence – those were the watchwords of her job and she endeavoured to always do her best with each and every placement.

Different houses, different requirements, certainly different personalities to contend with, but for Anna the upside was always the same – for every residency gave her a place to call home, for a little while at least; a place just to be, where none of the details were of her choosing. The ability to move on without attachment was just as important to Anna as the carousel of changing locations was to her spirit of adventure.

'I'm very lucky,' she said simply by way of reply, a wealth of unspoken sentiments colouring her words. 'Angus and Betty will be just fine,' she said reassuringly, getting to her feet. There was no outcome from Andrew's impromptu visit that could be improved by having him here longer. 'Do let me know if your parents would like an update. Being away for weeks often sounds so much more appealing than the reality, doesn't it?'

Andrew turned on the doorstep, obviously reluctant to leave. He cleared his throat. 'And if you'd like to go out for a drink on Saturday, I can show you around Oxford?' he offered, colouring slightly.

'That's so kind,' said Anna, 'but I have a friend's wedding to attend. I'll be back to take care of the dogs though, so no worries there.'

Andrew turned away, rebuffed despite her best, most professional efforts, and Anna pushed the heavy studded door closed behind him. She sighed; the notion of domain never ceased to be confusing in this job. Still, she glanced across at Angus, who was wagging his tail tentatively against the Aga and watching her every move – at least she had a little company. And as long as there were dog biscuits in her pocket she wouldn't be short of affection either.

Chapter 2

Oxford, 2019

Anna couldn't deny that her usual polish and professionalism had deserted her. First there'd been the awkward introduction to the owners' son in her pyjamas and then, as she distractedly went through the motions all week, one rule after another had gradually fallen by the wayside, culminating in her spending last night with two incredulously delighted spaniels on her bed, not to mention a plate of fancy cheese for midnight snacking, as she read a glorious first edition from the captain's well-stocked library into the wee small hours.

A certain ambivalence about this posting seemed to be creeping in that would do her professional reputation no good at all should the Frasers rumble her flagrant disregard for their strictures. The only problem being that she simply couldn't convince herself to care.

It was just so out of character, so unusual for her to loosen her hold. But her hold on what, she asked herself, as she pulled into a fortuitous parking space near Christ Church Meadow early that morning.

For the last ten years, she'd been focused, driven really, to fill her diary with bookings and rack up the five-star reviews that were the only true measure of success for a house-sitter. This wasn't rocket science, she reminded herself – keep the house safe and clean and the pets hale and hearty. Not always an easy ride, to be sure, but certainly within the realms of possibility.

Excitable whimpering from the back of the car brought her back into the moment; there was plenty of time for soul-searching in the middle of her sleepless nights. Besides, she was already running late. Not that Kate would expect any different, she thought. Old habits, etcetera etcetera.

Opening up the boot to allow Angus and Betty to leap down and twirl around her ankles, Anna slowly breathed out. Perhaps coming back to Oxford had been a mistake. After all, she'd only taken this particular booking to be nearby for Kate and Duncan's wedding. Would it really have been so awful to miss it, or to have just popped in and out – a flying visit – without committing herself to weeks of dreaming spires and disconcerting memories?

The morning mist on Christ Church Meadow held no answers, only the crisp warmth that signalled the imminence of summer, and birdsong that carried amongst the trees echoing off the buildings nearby. The three years studying here had been the longest that Anna had ever lived in one place and some of the happiest she had ever known, yet coming back was never easy.

'Pod! Pod? Anna? Over here!'

Anna looked up, squinting through the mist as the early striations of sunlight lit up the figure striding towards them with a bounce in her step. Ever the tomboy, Kate's jeans had seen better days, her wellies gaped at the calf and an ancient college scarf was swathed around her neck. 'Didn't you hear me, you mad sod, I've been hollering for ages!'

Anna found herself caught up in the kind of effusive hug that was second nature to Kate, doled out in times of both happiness and sadness, and testament to her sheer enthusiasm for life. 'Morning,' said Anna, muffled into Kate's shoulder, blinking hard to settle herself before the inevitable Twenty Questions could begin.

'Well, don't you look like death warmed up?' Kate said, stepping back to take stock. 'Although you two are gorgeous, aren't you?' She fussed Angus and Betty, and Anna couldn't help but smile. Erratic, distracted, but sheer genius when it came to philosophical debate, Kate was the most unlikely blushing bride she could think of, and yet the love match with Duncan was almost visceral in its strength.

'So, are you excited or nervous?' Anna asked, as they fell easily into step.

Kate shrugged. 'I'm remarkably relaxed about the whole thing to be honest.' She gave a filthy laugh. 'My attention's focused more on the honeymoon. I cannot wait to just get on that plane and be somewhere warm with a cocktail in my hand.' She tucked her arm through Anna's as the dogs romped delightedly through the long grass. 'I'll even have time to read something that isn't another de Beauvoir treatise. Say, maybe a friend's manuscript?'

Anna shook her head. Four minutes thirty seconds. It was a new record even for Kate. 'One day,' she replied easily, well versed in evasion.

It niggled, of course it did, the whopping great lie that had taken on a life of its own. But still, it was somehow easier than conceding the truth.

But Kate was like a dog with a bone this morning. 'I just think that maybe some editorial input would be good. You can get too close to a manuscript, you know? Lose all objectivity . . .' She took a breath and Anna knew exactly what she was going to say before the words came out of her mouth.

'A decade is an awfully long time, Pod. I mean, it's great that you can do this house-sitting thing while you write, but you have a First from Oxford. You could literally do anything . . .'

Anna called the dogs to heel and gave them each a treat. 'I could. As could you . . .' She didn't need to ask Kate how many degrees she really needed – the girl was addicted to learning, it seemed. Or possibly hooked on the heady aroma of ancient books in the Bodleian. With Kate and her all-or-nothing approach to life, it was sometimes hard to tell.

'So seriously – you're getting married *tomorrow* and we're talking about books?'

Kate laughed. 'We always talk about books. And anyway, I'm not the one choosing my house-sits by whether they have a nice library or not.'

'True. And I may or may not have spent last night eating cheese and reading a first edition Virginia Woolf.'

'Not at the same time!' Kate exclaimed, the colour draining from her face.

'I'm not a complete heathen!' Anna replied, neglecting to mention that her only nod to etiquette had been turning pages with her right hand and eating Camembert with her left. Thinking about it now, she wondered whether she had officially taken leave of her senses – perhaps it was the first unequivocal sign of madness? Her usual deference for great literature the one enduring factor in a life where libraries had always been her solace and her sanctuary.

'We only ask because we care,' Kate boomeranged back around. 'You haven't let anyone see so much as a synopsis.'

'I promise you, when I'm finished, you'll be the first to read it,' Anna said, quietly wondering whether at some point she'd actually have to write a bloody book just to shut her friends up. There were worse motivators to put pen to paper, she conceded. And certainly they wouldn't consider her constant questing to keep moving an acceptable life plan – 'plan' in itself being too strong a word for the geographic chaos of her life.

'Now, tell me about the honeymoon at least, if I can't persuade you to be excitable about tulle and gypsophila.'

Kate frowned. 'Is that some pervy sex thing that's passed me by again?'

Anna laughed, loving the ease with which they found their feet together. 'I think it's a tiny white flower you shove in your hair.' She paused. 'Unless I'm behind the times too.'

'God, we're just useless aren't we? I mean, we're bright, educated women. Not hideously disfigured. Why do I feel so constantly out of step with the world around me?' Kate's perfect browline furrowed. 'And I always seem to come round to the fact that I just don't care enough.'

Anna faltered. 'About getting married?'

'No, no, I mean – well, maybe? I want to *be* married if that counts? I just keep thinking of the library I could fill with what we're spending on canapés and nonsense.' She grinned. 'But then I tell myself we're making memories and you can't put a price on those.' She paused. 'Although about seventy-five quid a head seems to be the going rate.'

'Blimey,' Anna said. 'Just as well I'm not getting married. I could only have six people at my wedding before going broke,' she joked. She didn't clarify that there were only six people she'd actually want to invite; it seemed a little too pity-inducing when she knew full well that Kate and Duncan's special day would be celebrated by dozens of their friends and family.

'About that, actually . . .' Kate hesitated and suddenly Anna felt exactly like the fool she undoubtedly was. Of course there was a reason that Kate had been so insistent that they meet, catch up, 'talk *properly* before I'm all dressed up like a meringue.'

'So he's definitely coming?' Anna said, taking the high road, making it easier. If not for herself.

Kate nodded. 'We could hardly not invite the groom's brother, Pod. I mean, I think he's a reprehensible human being for what he did to you, but what could I do?'

'We could kill him?' Anna suggested, laughter masking the edge to her voice. It wasn't as though she hadn't considered it.

'Nah,' said Kate. 'You'd look rubbish in orange and you'd get all twitchy if you couldn't move house every five seconds. Besides,' she breathed out, as though girding herself, 'he seems to be doing a perfectly decent job of that on his own.'

'Oh,' said Anna quietly. There was no need to explain. 'Well then, I'll smile and wave and hope that he has the good sense to stay away from the bar on your big day.'

Kate nodded. It was all any of them could wish for, really. 'Wear a killer dress though, yes? I mean, surely he should be forced to see what he's missing out on?'

Anna shook her head. 'It'll be the trusty jersey dress, as per usual. Take me as you find me.' With the added benefit that it rolled up small and didn't crease, but Kate didn't need to know that.

'Hmmm. Well, if I'm going to have to take part in some patriarchal ceremony just to get married quarters in College and a trip to the Seychelles, maybe you should tiptoe out of your comfort zone too? I could lend you something?'

'You have enough to think about,' Anna hedged.

'As a favour to me?' Kate countered. 'I mean, it's bad enough you won't be my bridesmaid. Surely I can impose *some* measure of my discomfort on you too?'

'Remind me again why you have to be uncomfortable on your wedding day?' Anna asked.

Kate pulled her into another of her heartfelt hugs. 'I'm not entirely sure. But I cannot deny that my legs look amazing in heels – who knew?'

'Apart from everyone else?' Anna teased her, tucking a wayward curl back behind her friend's ear. 'Just promise me you're not going to straighten your hair, or Duncan won't even recognise you as you walk down the aisle.'

Kate coloured slightly. 'Well I'm not going to promise to obey and nobody's giving me away like an old suitcase, if that helps?'

Anna just smiled. Words eluded her; it confused and intrigued her in equal measure that her staunchly feminist friend was taking vows at all. It had seemed like the one thing they had both always agreed on – they didn't need to belong to anyone.

'Don't judge me, Pod,' Kate whispered so quietly that Anna could barely hear her above the rustle of grass and the dogs' joyful panting. 'God help me, I love him. And I want to be his wife.' She turned to hold Anna's gaze and the conflict was written all over her face – how to choose between principles and love, ideals and convention.

'And tomorrow you will be,' Anna replied, leaning forward in a rare display of affection and kissing Kate lightly on one cheek. 'And I will be there to sign the register and raise a glass to the new Mrs Howard.' She swallowed hard; nobody said unconditional support would be easy.

Kate laughed. 'I love him, Pod, but I'm not giving up my name or my doctorate. I'll still be the Dr Porter you know and love.'

Anna nodded in relief, the lump in her throat making it hard to say anything. And really, what else could she actually say?

Tomorrow was just another day, another challenge, another rite of passage that Anna herself would never experience. And of course, there would be Max to contend with – another gem in the day to look forward to.

Chapter 3

Oxford, 2019

With both dogs nicely tired and drying by the Aga, Anna made herself a cup of coffee, still jumping at the violent spurt of steam from the slightly overstated Ferrari of coffee machines. Typically, she would just about master its quirks and foibles the day before she left. It was ever thus.

Her phone trilled beside her on the kitchen counter.

'Can you talk?' It was Emily.

'Morning. You're up bright and early,' Anna replied, deftly adding just a small swirl of cream as she hit speakerphone.

'How's it going? Any more visits from Fraser Junior?' There was a hint of concern in Emily's voice. It was highly irregular for a client's friends or family to randomly let themselves in while a house-sitter was in residence.

Anna sighed, glancing over at the kitchen table where this morning's note had been propped against the sugar bowl while she was out with Kate and the dogs. It wasn't so much that Andrew Fraser was a nuisance, but that Anna never felt that she could properly relax. Although that could also have something to do with the looming nuptials tomorrow and being back on her old stomping ground. Every knock at the door, ring of the phone, key in the lock made her jumpy and it wasn't a feeling she enjoyed; another reason she sought out anonymous isolation.

'I'm sure he'll get used to the idea of me being here soon. I mean, his parents obviously trust me enough to give me free rein in their home and with their gorgeous dogs. I'm not quite sure what his problem is really,' Anna said resignedly.

'Some people are just uncomfortable with the idea of a house-sitter, you know? I mean, it's none of his business technically, but I can't do much more to appease him from here,' Emily said.

'More?' Anna missed nothing, and she heard her friend's sharp intake of breath as she realised her misstep.

'It's nothing. I mean, nothing really. He just phoned a few times midweek. Threatened to make a formal complaint. But we've talked him down. It's not going to be a problem.'

Emily was firm with the reassurances, but for Anna it was too little too late. They both knew only too well how her livelihood depended on the quality of her reviews. She could live or die professionally by the number of little yellow stars next to her name on the website. Her stellar rating to date was a point of both pride and practicality. Anna was one of the very few house-sitters on the books to be booked up months and months in advance and she liked it that way. No time to hesitate or consider her options.

'What did he say?'

There was silence for a moment as Emily clearly considered her words carefully. 'That you were difficult to deal with and stand-offish.'

'I was stand-offish? He let himself in and wandered around upstairs while I was having a shower! What a bloody cheek.' She paused. 'Is he going to be a problem, Ems?'

'I hope not. I may have rather dropped him in it with his mother when she called. Maybe he'll listen to her? She's kind of formidable. And in the meantime, lock the bathroom door, yes? We don't want any more "accidental" interruptions.' Her tone was firm, Emily herself rather formidable when she chose to be.

Anna pushed open the French windows and, with the warmth of the Aga behind her, gazed out over the beautiful lawns and landscape that framed the manor house. The spires of Christ Church were on the horizon and the morning mist had evaporated as the temperatures climbed. Had growing up in a home like this been wasted on Andrew Fraser? It was a source of constant amazement to Anna just how much people took for granted, or considered their due.

'Listen, while I've got you, are you quite sure you won't reconsider the Anderson job? They're terribly keen to get it all sorted even though it's not until Christmas.'

'Remind me again?' Anna asked, the Rolodex of houses and names in her head whirring; a blur of Georgian townhouses, Regency villas and 'architect-designed' nouveau pads all over the world that were on the cards in the months to come. 'Was that the one with the flowers?'

'Orchids,' Emily said. 'A world of difference apparently. But they really like your profile.'

'That's lovely, but honestly, Em. I don't so much have green fingers as murderous thumbs. I can water a few spider plants and make a good fist of a veg patch but humidity-controlled conservatories are way out of my comfort zone. What if they came back to find all their prized plants limp and frazzled?'

Emily laughed. 'They don't mind that you haven't got experience; they just want someone trustworthy and responsible. They've offered a few days to get you and the orchids acclimatised?'

Anna frowned; that in itself made a pleasant change from the bungled handover she'd received here. 'Look, Ems, you know my rules. Under-promise and over-deliver. I can't in all conscience take on a job I'm ill-equipped to handle.'

'Okay, well, it doesn't hurt to ask occasionally. Just in case your principles are slipping.' Emily laughed. 'And I suppose asking you about the feature in *The Telegraph* is—'

'Wasting your breath,' Anna finished for her. She knew that house-sitting was a growth industry, catching the public's imagination in recent months in a way nobody could have foreseen. It was something about the life of the nomad that appealed to everyone perhaps, even if they weren't necessarily brave enough to take the leap themselves. Trying on a different life for size, possibly one that would never be attainable otherwise. But it wasn't all stunning architecture and luscious interiors; it took a special sort of soul to keep on moving on.

'It's only that most of my sitters are part-time. A few weeks or months a year at most. You're my one and only,' Emily said.

'That might be the case, but it doesn't mean I want my face wrapped around cod and chips, Em,' Anna said firmly.

It wasn't as though Anna lived off-grid – just because she didn't have a permanent address didn't mean she was out of the loop. She practically ran her life online, but a newspaper feature felt just too public, too exposing and unmanageable. Anna liked to keep her online presence carefully curated. With a mobile phone and an email address she could be anywhere and nobody would be any the wiser . . . emails, e-vites, text messages all reached her easily enough.

Unless, of course, someone felt the need to send you a fully embossed wedding invitation complete with scented lavender sprigs . . . Then, well *then*, she'd had a little explaining to do.

The concept of *poste restante* reducing even Kate to disbelieving silence for a moment or two.

It was almost as though the mechanics of her life confused her friends: like her ability to travel light and never, ever unpack. But it was probably for the best that they didn't understand the lack of credit card at her disposal – simply budgeting to live within her means – as apparently 'credit' required a postcode where they could track you down if needed! Even Anna's habit of picking up her mail care of a nominated Post Office could throw her friends completely.

Emily may not technically count as a friend – they'd barely met after all – but Anna talked to her more often than anyone else in her life and at least Emily knew where to find her on any given day. Explanations were unnecessary. For the most part.

'Okay. I'll let them know. And, Anna? Try and enjoy the wedding, yes? It's why you're there, after all.'

Anna hung up the phone and stared across towards her alma mater with unseeing eyes. The notion of enjoying the wedding hadn't even crossed her mind; she'd been stuck in endurance mode. Glancing at her watch, she decided to change gear. Easier said than done of course, but for the first time in a long time, it seemed worth the effort.

After an hour of bathroom ablutions the next morning involving razors, leave-in conditioners and some kind of face mask that promised to be 'cruel to be kind' – she'd actually felt her pores tightening, she thought with a shudder – Anna could remember only too well why she refused to espouse this level of grooming on a daily basis. She couldn't help but wonder how many talented female brains were limited from reaching their full potential because of hair – styling it, colouring it, removing it . . . Was hair in fact a key limiting factor in smashing the proverbial glass ceiling, she thought, and not for the first time.

A hammering at the front door stopped her in her tracks. Thoughts immediately turning to Andrew Fraser and her current state of undress, even before logic prevailed and with it the disconcerting realisation that Andrew Fraser didn't bother to knock. Tightening the belt on her dressing gown, she pushed open the window overlooking the front courtyard. 'Hello?'

'Delivery, darlin'!'

She glanced briefly at the comforting brown-liveried van on the driveway. 'Can you leave it on the doorstep?' she replied. 'Does it need a signature?'

'Well that depends, I suppose.' The delivery man stepped back in order to locate the source of her voice, smiling at the turban slipping from her still-dripping wet hair. 'If you're Anna Wilson, I can just pop it inside the porch for you, love. If you trust me to do the honours?' He waved his hand in the air as though signing a name.

'That would be great,' she replied, even as the thought crossed her mind as to how many people actually knew she was here, let alone wanted to send her a parcel. 'What is it?' she called down impulsively and the delivery man grinned.

'Not for me to say, but you know I've been doing this a few years now and my money would be on a posh frock. In tissue paper. It kind of rustles – that's always the giveaway.' He glanced at his clipboard and winked. 'Lucky girl. From the insurance value alone, that has to be one posh frock. Are you sure you just want me to leave it?'

Anna nodded, knowing she'd be down those stairs before his van had even left the drive. 'It's fine.'

She pulled the window closed, holding her breath for a second as it wobbled ominously in its Crittall frame and wondering when Veronica Fraser had last thrown it open with such abandon.

Kate. It had to be from Kate, she realised, as she dashed down the stairs and quickly pulled the rectangular dress box inside, feeling its weight, knowing its worth, and wondering why she was even surprised. Surely the fact that Kate had taken her refusal to be a bridesmaid with such calm acquiescence should have alerted her. Kate never took no for an answer, and judging by the decadent swathes of bluebell silk nestled in the tissue paper, her wedding day would be no different.

> See you in the vestry. Don't be late – we're
> doing this together or not at all! Much
> love Kx

Anna swallowed hard, touched and panicked in equal measure.

The fact that staunchly feminist Kate was getting married at all was a wonder; the fact that she refused to do it without her best friend's support should come as no revelation.

Old friends were indeed the best friends; but even old friends didn't always know the full picture. Or indeed how big an ask it was for Anna to step into even the periphery of the bridal limelight.

Her phone beeped beside her and the text message made Anna smile. Kate had thought of everything.

Get yourself in that dress and over here, Anna Wilson, or you can explain to Duncan why he's standing there like a plum at midday. Love you, darling. No excuses, okay? I'll hold your hand. Well, not during the vows obviously, although that's always an option . . . Kxx

Chapter 4

Oxford, 2019

Anna's cheeks had begun to ache with the effort of smiling long before the ceremony was over. Standing at the front of the church, even wearing the admittedly beautiful dress, was absolutely the last way she had wanted to celebrate her best friend's marriage. She'd had high hopes for a discreet pew at the back where she could snivel unapologetically into a hanky. She'd known it would be an emotional day.

'Take this. You look like you need it.'

Anna jumped, startled out of her tumbling thoughts, as organ music swelled and the happy couple shared their first kiss as man and wife before setting off down the aisle to echoing applause.

It was a voice she would recognise anywhere. Max may not have been the best man, but as the brother of the groom, he was hardly relegated to the cheap seats. The tiny, perfect, white linen handkerchief he offered was typical of her ex-boyfriend – a triumph of style over substance.

His presence was enough to halt the nascent tears in their tracks and she shook her head. 'I'm fine, thanks.'

'You look stunning in that frock,' he persisted. 'A perfect elfin beauty.'

There was a compliment in there somewhere, of course, but Max of all people should know how much she hated comments about her size. In her mind, petite had become a byword for weak; 'feminine' code for delicate. She wanted to be seen as strong and accomplished – in mind and in body – not 'elfin' or 'dainty'.

She turned to face him, half wondering how she would react to seeing him up close and personal for the first time in years. She took a breath and waited for the inevitable landslide of emotion and then paused. Nothing. She felt precisely nothing. A shiver of mild annoyance at best.

She gave him a relieved smile, no doubt confusing him no end. 'Well, it's Kate and Duncan's special day. Even I could see the logic in a posh frock. I drew the line at heels.'

They fell into step as they turned to follow the happy couple out of the church, pews emptying at speed as all the guests surged ahead of them.

'I'm so glad you're here,' said Max quietly. 'I'd rather like to apologise. Belatedly, I know. But I behaved appallingly.'

'You did,' Anna agreed.

He hesitated, presumably unprepared for her to offer no resistance. 'Well, yes, right – breaking up the way we did, when maybe I'd implied that we had a future together. But we were so young and I wasn't ready for commitment . . .'

'Oh, Max. You really haven't a clue, have you?'

'Well, yes, obviously. I was there too, Anna. I saw how upset you were.' The colour was rising up Max's neck, a sure sign he felt off balance.

Anna stopped walking and turned to face him. 'I was "upset" as you put it, Max, because you stole the basis for my dissertation,' she said calmly. 'You couldn't think of something for yourself, because you were permanently hung-over and lazy, so you took my idea and submitted it. Early. Not a last-minute panic, but early. I believe you'd call that premeditated. Or is it "with malice aforethought"? You're the lawyer.'

'But our break-up? When I left—?'

She shrugged, this conversation proving surprisingly cathartic. 'You already broke my heart when you claimed my work as your own. And then made it worse, frankly, by making an utter hash of a brilliant idea.' She turned to walk away and he caught her arm.

'It's always about the books and the theories with you, isn't it?' he said nastily, clearly piqued by her revelation and abandoning all pretence of contrition.

'Books never let you down,' Anna said simply, removing his hand from her arm with the best look of utter disdain she could muster, ignoring her racing heart at the ferocity of his words. For a man like Max, the golden boy, to dent his pride was the only way for him to register emotion. If only she'd realised that years ago.

She swept away from him, swallowed into the crowd, pressing her hand against her chest and forcing herself to breathe. No matter her protestations, Kate had been absolutely right: if you needed to be strong, looking fabulous while you did it was an excellent head start.

'Anna! You're here!'

She felt herself being subsumed into friendship groups of old, friends who had simply fallen off her radar one by one as she moved from place to place.

'You sly vixen, where on earth have you been hiding?'

'Glorious dress!'

'Can you believe it? Kate and Duncan are married!'

'How the devil are you?'

The words bounced around her. Effusive greetings and rhetorical questions punctuated by the string quartet's allegros.

'Hi,' she said simply, being pulled into yet another embrace. Had she been to more weddings, more family gatherings, then perhaps she wouldn't have worried as much. These were hardly the soul-searching conversations they'd shared as students, awake until dawn, finding their feet in the transition to the adult world. This was small talk. And small talk she could do.

In fact, over the years, Anna had become adept at painting a picture of her life: her nomadic profession cast in a rosy glow of stunning architecture and travel opportunities. The odd funny anecdote about Park Lane Persian pussycats with foie gras addictions and suicidal tendencies and she was good to go.

'You're so lucky,' breathed Sarah, one of Kate's childhood friends. 'You can follow your feet and never get bored.' She cast a glance at her florid husband who was waxing lyrical about the state of pork futures and sighed. 'And are all the houses just glorious? I'll bet they are, aren't they? I mean, you'd hardly pay for a house-sitter for some crappy flat in Clerkenwell.'

Anna shook her head. 'You'd be surprised. Sometimes it's more about the pets. For me as well. I try and keep an open mind, but if there's a beautiful Irish wolfhound or one of those miniature wire-haired dachshunds in the mix, then all my desires for waterfall showers and slipper baths tend to come in a poor second.'

'Do you ever have a snoop?' Sarah whispered, slightly the worse for wear on raspberry Bellinis and agog with curiosity.

'Nope,' said Anna firmly. That wasn't even a matter to joke about.

'Really?' said Kate, stepping into their conversation and tucking her arm around Anna's waist. 'Aren't you even tempted? Just a teensy bit?'

'Really, truly not,' Anna replied in earnest, forgetting for a moment that this was a social occasion, a time for tall tales and fun. 'I can't think of anything worse, can you? They're entrusting me with their home and their pets, stepping into their lives for weeks sometimes. I couldn't do it.'

'I would,' said Kate firmly. 'I couldn't resist. It would be like a history project, piecing together how their life worked, whose photos are out on the mantelpiece and whose are hidden away.'

Anna could feel that they were veering into dangerous territory. She certainly didn't want to get caught up talking about the non-disclosure agreements she was asked to sign from time to time. The high-profile husbands who no longer shared the marital bedroom, the variety and quantity of prescription meds in a headlining barrister's medicine cabinet – really the list went on . . . It was no coincidence that the keyword search used most frequently on the website was 'discretion' and according to her reviews, discretion was something that Anna offered in spades. Most likely because even when she came to an event like this – and that in itself was once in a blue moon – she made a point of driving home.

One glass of champagne was always her limit.

One glass of anything. Always.

'Of course, the same doesn't apply to their books!' she joked. 'I can never resist a good library.'

She could have kicked herself. How to kill a chat. She knew all too well that nobody wanted to talk about first editions or leather-bound classics anymore. They wanted scandal and dirt and the feeling of knowing something that they shouldn't. The scoop.

There was a momentary awkward pause and then Sarah laughed. 'Me too, Anna. I may never judge you by your shoes, but I can't help getting the measure of a person from their bookshelf. Now, Kate did tell me that you'd been working on some secret manuscript. And that this whole house-sitting fandango was your way of planning your life around books. Is that true, then? Are you going to tell us what it's about?'

'Oh good luck with that!' Kate cut in. 'I've been asking her for years and she's annoyingly tight-lipped about the whole project.'

Sarah reached into her clutch bag and pulled out a business card. 'Well, when you do want to talk about it, call me. I'm not a commissioning editor yet, but I will be one day.'

Anna glanced down at the card, careful to conceal the surprise on her face. Assistant Editor at Papyrus Publishing was no small achievement in itself. 'Thank you, Sarah,' she said simply instead. 'But please don't hold your breath.'

'I knew you two would get along!' crowed Kate happily, snaffling a canapé from the circulating tray. 'And if anyone can persuade you to talk about your novel it's Sarah. Don't let the whole ditsy thing distract you; she has killer literary instincts. She'll be running Papyrus one day, I promise you.'

'From your lips to God's ears,' said Sarah with a smile. A smile that slipped firmly off her face as she realised what her husband was doing on the other side of the room.

Anna followed her gaze to see half of the men in the marquee lining up shots and Kate's face drop accordingly.

'Leave it with me,' Sarah said, laying a hand on Kate's arm reassuringly. 'I won't let the rugby club antics ruin your day.'

She sighed and held up her hand, her own freshly minted wedding ring catching the light. 'It's too late for us, Anna, but think long and hard before you get one of these. Mine's turning me into a total killjoy. I didn't realise that being a wife meant being his mother too.'

As she walked away, Anna felt Kate tense beside her. Even with her own loving family as a template for married life, it seemed that her best friend was taking a leap of faith. She glanced over and saw Kate's parents ecstatically entertaining their own friends, their eyes returning constantly to their beautiful daughter on her special day.

When it came to having a template to follow, Anna knew that hers was a cautionary tale at best. How on earth did she know what choices to make when she had no clear idea of the destination? How fitting, then, that she chose to spend time trying on different lives for size . . .

Kate sniffed and leaned in to hug her tightly. 'I'm so glad you're here, Pod,' she said, slightly emotional and with her bridal tiara no longer perfectly central. 'It really wouldn't have been the same without you. And I'm so bloody glad that dress fit too! Can you even imagine?'

Anna leaned into the embrace, trying not to let herself feel jealous. Not of Kate for being the first in their group to take the plunge, but of Duncan. He got to live with Kate, dig in for box set marathons with her, travel with her . . . All the things that Anna had truly treasured in her friendship with Kate over the years, she was now committed to sharing with Duncan. Officially.

Duncan was no longer a passing fancy; he was permanently part of the picture. And as much as Anna loved him and his bumbling, affectionate ways, she couldn't deny that it changed the dynamic when he was there.

'If it all goes to shit, I'm moving in with you by the way,' mumbled Kate into her hair, still holding on tightly, having apparently now bypassed ecstatic with the second flute of champagne and swung round to poignant and overemotional.

'Wherever I am,' Anna agreed. 'There'll always be a place for you.'

Kate pulled back, one hand on each shoulder, and looked straight into her eyes unflinchingly. 'But you are happy, aren't you, Pod? All this hoofing around, never in the same place twice? I want you to be happy.'

Anna nodded, the assurances Kate was looking for sticking in her throat. 'It's going to be fine,' she said in the end, falling back on her standby motto for life.

'Will you know it when you see it, do you think?' Kate asked, tilting her head to one side as she considered her own question, the tiny pearl tiara listing still further.

'Will I know what?' Anna asked, wondering if her friend could actually read her mind.

'The place you want to stay,' said Kate. 'The place you want to call home?'

Chapter 5

Oxford, 2019

In Anna's experience of grand parties and celebrations, limited though it was, things always took a turn for the worse once the port and cheese came out. Whether it was that frozen moment of indecision about which direction the decanter should be passed (left, she was almost certain it was left) or whether she might accidentally cut the 'nose' off the brie with the wrong knife . . . Either way, she felt exposed.

Smiling weakly as she hefted the cut glass clockwise to the chap on her left, she watched the cloying, sticky port slosh up the side, climbing down slowly.

'No port for you, Anna?' he asked, eyeing the veritable forest of pristine glasses in front of her. One for each course.

'I'm driving,' she said simply, hoping that, now they were officially grown-ups, that line might carry enough weight to see off further questioning.

He raised a rakish eyebrow. 'And I can't tempt you to an impromptu overnight?'

Anna shook her head, trying not to laugh at the brazen cheek of the man. He'd barely made the effort to make conversation through dinner, unless one counted regaling her with tales of his prowess on the rugby field and a brief but intense quiz about whether she made 'a decent living with this house-sitting malarkey'. As seduction techniques went, it was one she was all too familiar with.

'Come on,' he said confidingly. 'Let's grab a bottle of fizz and explore the maze.'

'The maze?' Of course there was a bloody maze, thought Anna irritably. Along with the ice sculptures and the vintage Morgan and the party favours scattered liberally (expensively) across every table. In fact, if she didn't have direct line of sight to the bride, couldn't see with her own two eyes that this was in fact Kate's wedding, her Kate, bluestocking, overachieving Kate's wedding then she wouldn't have believed it.

All too easily she was struck again by the notion of loss. Of their friendship slipping through her fingers as coupley dinner parties and talk of mortgages and nurseries and school fees filled Kate's life in the space where Anna had been. She swallowed hard.

To love someone was to risk losing them, she'd always known that.

Had always seen that.

But with Kate, with their student house on the Cowley Road in Oxford, Anna had felt brave enough to take the risk and open her heart, if not her baggage.

Emotional and material.

'You okay there, Anna?'

What *was* his name? Anna shrugged away her dinner companion's lingering touch to her arm with irritation. Annoyed with herself that after two hours of admittedly one-sided conversation, she couldn't quite recall that salient fact. 'I might head off actually.'

She was tired. Tired of smiling. Tired of pretending to be someone she wasn't, sitting here in her silk dress, surrounded by acquaintances, all of whom were desperate to prove their success and net worth to each other. It was as though the decade since graduation had barely changed the landscape at all, merely the budget.

'Wilson, Wilson . . . I knew that name rang a bell. Do you know, Anna, I think I met your father in court the other week? Grey-haired chap?'

Anna froze. Her legs suddenly unable to support her as she sank back into her gilded chair. It wasn't that it was impossible; after all, who knew where he was? Who even knew what he looked like . . . But the notion of him standing in the dock being questioned by this young upstart was enough to make the single glass of champagne in Anna's stomach turn to acid.

'Yes. He was rather inspirational, actually. Not many barristers so open-minded in their approach. I was just there for my six, but impressive stuff.' He leaned in closer. 'I might hit you up for a personal introduction, darling.'

Anna breathed out slowly. Wilson was a common enough name. No need to illuminate Rupert – *that's* what he was called – that the Graham Wilson on her birth certificate would never knowingly have been on the right side of the law.

It was possibly the only gift she'd received of any value from her parents: an ambiguous name.

Anna Wilson could be anyone, from anywhere; equally unremarkable in the Benefits Centre as the quadrangles of Oxford University. Posh Annas were aplenty, as were their grafting counterparts born without the proverbial silver spoon.

'Not my father, I'm afraid,' she said quietly, watching the interest in his eyes fade, clearly wondering how quickly he could shift his attention to the girl on his left, to make sure that his night wasn't a complete bust.

She caught Kate's eye across the marquee and blew her a kiss, knowing that she was hampered by acres of tulle and the top table stretching away from her on either side. All she could think about was getting back to the manor, taking off this dress and snuggling into bed with Angus and Betty. She wouldn't be sleeping alone tonight and there'd be none of the awkward disappointment that she would undoubtedly have encountered with Rupert the next morning.

Really, she thought, as she edged her way discreetly between the tables, there was very little in her life that couldn't be improved by a decent cup of coffee, an engrossing book and a little canine companionship. Even if it occasionally broke her heart a little to say goodbye to her furry friends, knowing that she was just a temporary fixture in their lives was nothing new.

'Pod! Wait up!'

Anna stalled the engine of her ancient Mini at the sight illuminated by her headlights. She pushed open the door and stepped out in her bare feet. 'You can't run away; you're the bride,' she said to Kate, who was walking towards her as fast as her fancy red-soled bridal shoes would allow.

'I'm not running away. You are,' Kate called, as the distance between them closed. 'Again.'

Anna smiled and drew her into a hug. 'I'm just ready for my bed, that's all.'

Kate frowned, the emotion of the day, coupled with barely a bite to eat as she'd been so on parade and no shortage of fizz, made her normally lightning-fast acuity somewhat sluggish. 'Why?' she managed in the end. 'I'm only getting married once, Pod, no matter what my mother might say about starter marriages. Stay and celebrate with me?'

Say what you like about Kate, she knew exactly which buttons to press to make Anna feel guilty.

'You can't just rush off to yet another house that isn't even home. I never know where you are. Nobody does.' Her eyes darkened. 'I'm beginning to wonder whether you're actually even writing a novel. Nobody serious about getting published would have been quite so blasé about Sarah's interest. She's a big deal, you know. I mean, I know she looks so quietly sweet, but she has a core of literary steel. Like a ninja.' Kate wobbled slightly as her questionable ninja hand skills challenged her already precarious balance.

'What are you doing, Pod?' Kate asked. 'If I promise not to judge, will you tell me?'

Anna nodded. 'Just as soon as I know, you'll be the first person I tell.'

Kate narrowed her gaze. 'So there isn't a plan? It's all a bit aimless?' Kate looked utterly confused. She was a planner, a goal-setter, a woman of many lists. That anyone could be so cavalier about their future clearly was beyond her comprehension. 'But. But, why?'

Anna shrugged. 'You should see the houses I get to live in, though, Kate. They're the stuff of dreams. Whole rooms full of books, vast kitchens, sitting rooms fresh from an Austen novel. Modern homes with sweeps of granite and glass one week and Georgian townhouses the next. Every single one is unique and every single one is a home like nothing I could ever dream of. I get to live there, Kate.' Her voice had taken on the slightly softer, supplicating tone that came so naturally when she wanted to persuade someone that she was right, but Kate was having none of it.

'But they're other people's homes, darling. Not yours. You're just passing through. It's not your life. It's not even your furniture, or your books, or sodding bedsheets. It's smoke and mirrors, Pod, and it's stopping you finding your own path.'

'Maybe this is my path,' Anna said loudly. 'Did you ever stop to think of that? Maybe I have no frame of reference for how I want my life to be.' She glanced back into the marquee, at the smiling faces of Kate's family and friends celebrating together. 'Maybe the idea of putting down roots feels like an anchor to me, dragging me down, unless I keep moving.'

She stopped, biting off her next words before she could say any more, reveal any more. 'Katie-Kate, I am just fine bumbling around. I'm being paid to live in luxury houses and see how the other half live. It is not a bad choice. It's just not your choice.' She nodded towards the marquee where Duncan was now standing outlined in the swagged doorway. 'I am over the moon, utterly delighted, thrilled for you and Duncan. You are a gorgeous couple and I wish you every happiness in the world. Watching you take your vows meant the world to me, so please don't read anything into me leaving other than that I'm very tired and very sober and I have zero desire to be fondled by the rugby team on the dance floor.' She smiled. 'And we both know that's where this evening is heading.'

Kate stepped forward and hugged her tightly. 'Sorry. I didn't mean to get all bridezilla on you there. I think this tiara is literally killing my brain cells the longer I wear it.' She smiled. 'I just worry about you. I guess I just don't understand how you can be so incredibly self-sufficient, and despite all my bloody credentials and qualifications, I still need all this to validate my choices.'

'I know, right? I mean, who knew that you, my fiercely feminist friend, still needed doves and a string quartet to affirm your love?' Anna swept one hand dramatically back against her forehead in a swoon and in moments they were both laughing together like drains.

'I love you, Anna Wilson, you know that, right?' Kate waved her hand in the air. 'And one little band of gold and a few words in church won't change that. But listen, promise me – don't be an island, okay?'

Anna slipped back behind the wheel as Kate returned to Duncan. How could she ever explain that independence wasn't a choice for her, it was a necessity? She had only herself to turn to and only herself to please.

As she drove through the dark Oxfordshire lanes towards the manor house, the absolute silence of the night in contrast to the bubbling, exuberant crowd she had left behind was not as comforting as she had hoped.

For a fleeting moment, Anna could only wish she had the fortitude to turn around, the irony not escaping her that honesty and vulnerability required a lot more strength than keeping her friends at arm's length; almost as though she'd been doing it for so long that her metaphorical elbow was locked into place. Bending was no longer an option.

Chapter 6

Oxford, 2019

Oxford at night was a masterpiece of light and shadows. As the engine idled at the T-junction, Anna couldn't help but pause, taking in the spires and towers that punctuated the skyline even from a distance. She adored the town, loved her friends – though even she would acknowledge that they might not actually know this, based on her remote behaviour since they had all moved out of their shared student house.

And, like the skyline in front of her, Anna herself was a mass of contradictions – old and new competing for space, for breathing room.

She pushed the silken, billowing fabric of her dress aside to reach the handbrake, grateful that Kate had given her the push she so clearly needed to step up today, yet somewhat unnerved by the feeling that she was on the cusp of tumbling down the rabbit hole again. She had dived into their life as students here together with such naivety, allowing herself to feel a part of something without holding back, without measure, for the very first time.

She glanced up as the lights changed and swung the wheel to the left on autopilot, instinctively returning to the Cowley Road.

She couldn't have been the only one who had wished it would last for ever – who had reeled at the exhortations to 'keep in touch' even as her housemates' taxis and trains whisked them away to pastures new?

She pulled up to the kerb outside number forty-four and sighed, assailed by memories of happier times. Proximity had always been the only measure of commitment that counted for Anna – those who mattered stayed, or so she firmly believed.

Seeing everyone tonight, seeing how the bonds of friendship had ebbed and grown, morphing with their changing lives, she felt a shiver of regret. She had done what she always did when she was unsure – she'd pulled back, pulled away, a self-imposed boundary drawn harsh in the landscape of their friendships. It wasn't that she begrudged them leaving, but that she doubted their relationships could survive the change.

'You should have more faith,' Kate had told her over and over, refusing to be fobbed off, refusing to be sidelined, possibly knowing more than most how the dismantling of their household, their temporary family, might make Anna feel.

Well then, thought Anna, her mind flickering back to the bride and groom and the affectionate, laughing speeches, to the effusive greetings and welcome she herself had received, maybe it wasn't too late? She glanced down at the passenger seat, at the bridal bouquet she had caught despite every evasive measure she could think of. Almost as though Kate had been aiming it directly at her.

Perhaps she would go back for the brunch tomorrow – the morning after the night before? Perhaps she would dip a toe in the water, and maybe, just maybe have a proper conversation with Sarah about how publishing actually worked.

Maybe that alone would be enough of a push to get her back on track: her dreams of being a published author neglected for far too long. Even if all those dreams tended to focus on the image of holding her novel in her hand, seeing it in the window of a bookshop, seeing her name in print. That goal had always been crystal clear – but as to the contents of those three hundred pages? Anna would be the first to admit that she had given that important detail embarrassingly little attention of late.

Twenty minutes later, the gravel made a satisfying crunch as she pulled the Mini to a halt outside Gravesend Manor. A chill breeze lifted the tendrils of hair at the nape of her neck as she stepped out into the darkness, kicking herself for not leaving a light switched on to come home to, wondering whether it would really have been so awful to relax with a glass of wine and stay over rather than returning to this daunting Victorian pile alone.

She pushed open the front door, shoes in one hand and the hem of her dress hooked over her arm to avoid tripping over the acres of fabric. Angus and Betty hustled towards her excitedly, their bottoms wiggling as their tails wagged in effusive greeting. Dropping her shoes, she crouched down to fuss them, as they clambered all over her for attention and affection. 'Oh you are gorgeous. Are you pleased to see me, are you?'

'Well, I know I am.'

Anna fell back onto her bottom with a thud, even as the dogs took it to be part of the game and scrambled onto her legs, snuffling happily. She didn't need to glance at her watch to know it was long past midnight, or at the key in the door to know she'd locked up. There was no way on God's earth that Andrew Fraser should be standing in the kitchen doorway, tie unravelled, hair dishevelled, and a half-empty glass of wine in his hand.

'You need to go home, Andrew,' she said firmly, trying to swallow the quiver in her voice that would betray the sudden sense of foreboding that winded her with its intensity.

'Home? Home? Are you taking the piss?' Andrew said, not moving, only his eyes raking over her legs. 'If this place is anyone's home, Anna my love, it's mine.'

He was across the hall in six large strides, suddenly towering over her. He gave a short, abrupt whistle and the two dogs instantly stilled, sitting at his heels and leaving Anna free to stand up. He held out his hand – an aid that was only necessary because he was standing so incredibly close to her.

Nevertheless, Anna scrambled to her feet without his help. There was no way she was going to buy into whatever story Andrew Fraser was running in his mind. The flash of angry disappointment in his eyes told its own tale.

'Come and have a drink with me, Anna. Since you're living in my house for *free*, it's really the very least you can do.' He clasped her upper arm tightly and propelled her towards the kitchen, giving her no choice. The resentment was bubbling away beneath the surface of his every word and Anna's tired brain struggled to compute – was he implying that she owed him rent? In whatever form that might take?

She pulled her arm away, noticing the angry red welt that had mottled her skin and feeling her own temper fraying in response.

'You know they wanted to charge me rent to live at home? My own parents! Said that I was an adult and should contribute to the "cost of living" if I never planned to leave.' For a man in his thirties, Andrew sounded remarkably like a petulant child denied chocolate cake for breakfast. 'Well, I showed them. If I'm going to pay rent,' he spat, 'I'm not going to do it to live at home with Ma and Pa, am I?'

Anna flinched. It was presumably better not to say that she assumed that very outcome was exactly his parents' intention. She saw all too many spoiled, entitled 'adults', stunted in their maturity by never having to lift a finger, work a day, have a plan – still sulkily inhabiting their childhood mansion rather than trade it for the lowly bedsit they could probably afford from their own earning potential.

Spoiled. Not just overindulged, but spoiled like rotten fruit, their youthful potential dimmed by a lack of necessity and drive.

Anna herself found it particularly hard to stomach; even more so when the man-child in question was staring at her with such a cocktail of longing and loathing.

She stepped back, making sure that one of the Frasers' sturdy kitchen chairs was between them. 'This is probably a conversation we could have during the day,' she said. 'Let's catch up tomorrow.'

Never engage; never justify – lessons from the fostered years would never leave her. Be pleasant, be polite, beyond reproach – unless of course there was no choice.

She silently pleaded with Andrew Fraser to keep his cool and his options open. He was maybe two steps away from some seriously poor decisions – as though letting himself into his parents' house in the middle of the night, drunk, to accost the house-sitter wasn't bad enough.

He pulled the chair between them aside, making Anna's heart thud into her throat, before planting his backside down, thighs spread. He tilted his head back, appraising her through heavy lids, weighted down by alcohol and frustration.

Her gaze flashed to the open front door, to the discarded shoes and clutch bag where her mobile phone remained stubbornly, inexorably, out of reach.

'And are you enjoying your time as Lady of the Manor?' he asked switching pace, almost pleasant, were the question not coming hot on the heels of his obvious distaste for the arrangement. 'Is it fun trying on other people's lives for size?'

Just rude then; not stupid.

'What makes someone who looks like you' – his eyes travelled over her again intrusively – 'want to live like that? Why isn't there a Mr Anna and lots of baby Annas and a white picket fence, I wonder?'

He reached forward and caught her wrist, reflexes fast and smooth for a man his size, despite the flush of wine to his cheeks. His abrupt lunge made the dogs flinch, as though they had been on the receiving end of those reflexes more than once.

'So tell me, Anna Wilson.' He tugged hard until she fell against him and she stiffened briefly in protest, but the muscle memory was already there. Her gaze was blank, vacant almost, as though she had already left the proverbial building. She didn't tug her arm away, make a sudden lurch for her phone – God knows screaming would make no difference. She just felt the fight leave her body and blinked at him hollow-eyed.

He grunted his disapproval. Clearly one of those men for whom the verbal riposte was part of the fun. Did he want to see her fear? Hear her beg for him to let go?

Anna allowed her arm to soften in his grasp, her expression carefully neutral. He didn't need to know that she was mentally cataloguing the contents of her overnight bag upstairs, assessing its necessity.

Simply walking away was often the better part of valour and certainly a tried and tested method.

He ran his slightly sweaty hand over her bare shoulder, snagging at the fabric of the spaghetti straps as he did so, his pupils dilating. 'So, Anna. Is this just part of the service then, keeping the family happy?' he leered.

She removed his hand and dropped it with disdain. 'I think we both know the answer to that, Andrew.' She paused. 'There's a window for you leave now, without any repercussions or hard feelings.'

She stepped back, but his hand shot out and caught her again. 'I'm fairly sure the night's not over yet, Anna. And as for repercussions – who are they going to believe?'

Anna's stomach lurched; a part of her had still been hoping that she was over-reacting, slipping into past patterns, that she was no more vulnerable here than at any other time since reaching the magical marker of her eighteenth birthday. The difference being that now, she had no need to keep the peace.

'Whatever you're considering is a very bad idea, Andrew. Your mum and dad trusted me to look after their house and their dogs. That's all. Don't read anything more into it, okay?'

Man-child that he was, Andrew didn't even seem to know what to do. Faced with an easy choice, he seemed determined to make life difficult. 'You can't leave and I don't intend to,' he said, standing up and towering over her. 'I think you just need a little persuasion.'

An acidic burn hit the back of Anna's throat as she considered her options. Fighting back against a man his size would not end well for her.

'I'm going to make coffee,' she said, peeling his fingers from her wrist and walking decisively towards the machine. All the while the tattoo in her head was running: calm, slow, steady, calm, slow, steady . . . She clocked her handbag, still listing sideways on the hall floor, car keys and shoes beside it.

Six or seven paces for Andrew; ten or twelve for her. 'Do you want a cup too?'

He frowned, caught off guard, clearly expecting a more dramatic reaction to his latent threats. A slow smile spread across his face as the thought occurred to him. 'I knew we were on the same page, lovely Anna. Must be lonely, moving around all the time?'

Anna pressed the button on the coffee grinder hard, watching with satisfaction as the beans were reduced to fine powder.

Lesson 101 for all baristas – if you think chilli in your eye is painful, have you ever experienced finely ground espresso beans? It's a mistake you'll only make once.

She turned to him, trying to soothe her racing heart and the cloying sensation of déjà vu. She breathed out to calm herself and forced a smile onto her face even as she unscrewed the lid.

Chapter 7

Oxford, 2019

Pulling into a lay-by before she joined the dual carriageway, Anna's hands were shaking so hard she could barely hold the steering wheel. She pushed open the car door and heaved violently onto the concrete, her eyes watering. Cool and calm could only take you so far and then the adrenaline had to carry you forward, as she knew only too well.

She wiped her mouth on the silk of her skirt, already ruined by coffee grounds and blood. Her blood, she realised, from the throbbing pain in her eyebrow where Andrew's flailing elbow had caught her and split the skin. Still, it was a small price to pay.

She closed the car door and pushed down the tiny plastic knob, the satisfying crunch as the central locking engaged giving her a disproportionate amount of security. She picked up her phone and breathed out slowly, even as the sour adrenaline burned from her system, to be replaced by a hiccupping relief.

Who could she call?

Where could she actually go at two in the morning, looking like this?

She hesitated before clicking on the pitifully small menu of her 'favourite' contacts. Emily. It could only really be Emily.

A flicker of unease niggled at the prospect of explaining that she'd abandoned her post, abandoned the dogs in her care, walked away – damn it – run away without even a thought for the eviscerating review that would no doubt follow. She hesitated and pressed dial.

An echoing recorded message filled the car. So much for this being the twenty-four-hour hotline. She took a breath to leave a message, feeling the sob building in her throat and jabbed at the buttons to disconnect.

Disconnect.

Disconnected.

The words spiked into Anna's subconscious.

How very appropriate, she thought, a slightly hysterical surge of laughter catching her unawares.

She turned the key in the ignition and breathed out slowly. This was a story for daylight and distance. Every mile she put between herself and Andrew Fraser giving her another ounce of resolve and refuge.

Pulling out onto the dual carriageway, Anna knew exactly where she was going, wondered why she had even hesitated. If it was refuge she was seeking then the second tiny silver key on her key ring was the only answer.

Anna rattled the creaking garage-style door up over her head and sighed. Three o'clock chimed from some distant spire and she shivered in her ridiculous dress.

Stepping inside, she pulled the corrugated metal down behind her, flicking the only light switch so that the single, bare flickering bulb lit up her domain.

One could hardly call it home.

A series of racking lined both walls of the self-storage locker, filled with plastic boxes, all catalogued and labelled. Most of them were barely half full and Anna knew from experience that her entire worldly goods could fit in the back of the Mini. Even including the petite and slightly ratty 'bedroom' armchair that crouched in the corner.

She dumped her handbag on the side and sat down with a sigh that seemed to come from the very soles of her filthy bare feet. She'd grabbed her bag and her keys – that was all. Her overnight bag and her shoes were simply casualties of the evening that she would have to live without; collateral damage from Andrew Fraser's sense of entitlement and arrogance.

She plugged her phone into the charger that was already dangling on the shelf beside her. The apps that she relied upon to organise her life were ill-equipped to deal with nights like this – this was when you called on a friend, or a neighbour, a sister perhaps, should you be lucky enough to have any of those to hand.

Airbnb.

HotelsByDay.

Youth Hostels Association.

All of which had been pressed into service before to keep the cogs of Anna's nomadic life running smoothly. She liked the anonymity. She liked that she could rustle up a bed for the night without explanations or niceties or seven different phone calls each taking longer than the last to simply find a sofa bed to crash on.

Swipe.

Tap.

A token payment and she was sorted.

Not at 3 a.m. though. And certainly not looking like this. Questions would be asked.

The only part of Andrew Fraser that was injured was his pride, but she had no desire to spend her evening drinking putrid coffee from a plastic cup and justifying her actions to the authorities.

She reached forward and pulled an old T-shirt from a box, splashing a little bottled water onto the fabric and holding it to her head, wincing as she made contact.

Emily would know what to do, she reassured herself, as she dropped into an unsettled sleep, huddled in an old jumper and startling awake sporadically as the waking nightmare of the evening relived itself over and over again.

'But I don't understand,' Emily repeated, as the line crackled slightly every time Anna turned to pace in a different direction. In a storage locker barely ten feet long, it didn't really help their conversation run smoothly. 'Why on earth didn't you call the police?'

'And spend hours in an interview room playing he said, she said?' Anna asked drily. A few hours' sleep, a little distance and having shed the infernal silk dress like a second skin and Anna was feeling far more cavalier than she had the night before. There was little point in dwelling on what might have happened; the fact was that she'd had a close call – that was all. Andrew Fraser would move on with his life after a trip to the dry cleaners with his coffee-stained suit and, outside some fairly stern words from his mother no doubt for "upsetting" the house-sitter, his gilded existence would carry on as normal.

'I just need to make sure that he can't sabotage my online ratings with a poisonous review,' Anna continued.

'I can't believe we're talking about your bloody star rating at a time like this!' Emily exclaimed. 'I'm all for being professional, Anna, but let's not forget that behind every profile is a real person with real feelings. In this case – you.' She paused, almost audibly dialling down her outrage on Anna's behalf. 'Are you actually okay?'

Anna's fingers feathered over the split brow and she winced. 'I've been better,' she confessed. 'But I'll be fine. Can you check that someone's around to look after Betty and Angus? Even Andrew Fraser can't be that useless, but I'd feel better knowing . . .'

Emily sighed. 'I'll call. But I cannot promise to be polite, and to be frank with you, I'm going to strike the Frasers off our books. I might be wrong, but I'm not sending anyone else into that house while their vile son has a key.'

Anna nodded, even knowing that Emily couldn't see her. Words, for a moment, were just out of reach.

'About that,' she managed after an awkward pause. 'I'm going to need a new placement. I was supposed to be at the Frasers' all month.'

'Oh, Anna, can't you take a break? Go home, get rested, get settled?'

There was little point explaining her true circumstances without causing alarm. What bothered other people sometimes bemused Anna herself. All her kit was safe and this was the first night in five years she'd been forced to resort to sleeping in the knackered old armchair. And even that scenario had not been of her doing. She pulled up her diary on her smartphone, Emily's voice echoing on speakerphone. 'I'm not due in the Cotswolds until the end of August. That's nearly four weeks, Em. Can you put something together for me?'

A tapping of keys staccatoed down the line. 'The likelihood of one placement, at this short notice—'

'I know. But I'm happy to move around week by week. Maybe there's something exotic just waiting for me? That Antigua placement last year was a last-minute job wasn't it?'

Emily snorted. 'Only because there was a freaking hurricane.'

'Weather's weather.' Anna shrugged. 'Someone had to look after those poor dogs.'

'I'm so sorry, Anna. All I've got are couple's placements, or even longer-term jobs than you're available for. I don't suppose you've got a mate who'd like to join you?'

Anna frowned. The only person she'd consider a job-share with was already winging her way to the Seychelles in a post-bridal haze. 'Just me,' she said.

'Shame,' Emily sighed. 'There's a few plum assignments coming up that I just can't fill. I've half a mind to take some time away from the office myself. There's one here on an island – day skipper qualifications a must. Can you sail?'

'Nope,' said Anna.

'What about the whole reptile thing? Are you still staunchly against?'

Anna thought back to the last, rather savage, iguana in her care. 'Never again.' She shuddered.

'Horses?' Emily offered, scrolling through her database. 'Didn't you say you could ride?'

'No horses,' Anna said firmly. 'A month of lessons at the local riding school when I was twelve do not qualify me for equine care.'

As Emily chattered on about how tricky it might be at this time of year to pull something together – something of the standard Anna was used to – her mind began to wander. How could she communicate the urgency of the situation? This wasn't a time to be worrying about waterfall showers and orthopaedic mattresses, stunning views or adorable dogs. She needed a place to call home for the next four weeks and ideally she needed it now.

'Tell me about the horsey job,' she said begrudgingly, even knowing that some of her colleagues would kill for anything approaching the Pony Club dream.

Emily smothered a gasp. Anna's rules had always been hard and fast the whole time she'd worked for Home Network. She'd clearly only mentioned the job to illustrate the difficulty of a last-minute placement. 'Are you sure? I mean, I'm sure you could do an admirable job, but you always said—'

'Em,' said Anna firmly. 'This isn't a time to be picky.' She quashed all her principles screaming to be heard – never commit to something out of your depth. Beggars couldn't really be choosers, she cautioned herself, even as her own rules of engagement were in danger of being ignored. 'As long as there isn't a yard full of thoroughbred racehorses demanding a daily gallop, how hard can it be?'

'That one is actually a couple's placement anyway,' Emily said in her most soothing voice, 'so you don't need to compromise yourself just yet. Give me a few hours to look around?'

Anna paused and looked around herself, at the tiny cell-like room where she'd gone to ground. 'Okay, but I'll need to sort something out for tonight. I'm not going back to the manor for anyone.'

'Anna? Are you really okay?' Emily asked. 'You didn't even tell me where you are. Shall I hop in the car and visit?'

'No,' said Anna abruptly. 'I mean, no, don't be daft. I'm fine. Best thing you can do, Ems, is find me somewhere bucolic and beautiful to bide my time until Chipping Norton.'

'Okay,' Emily said warily, not quite trusting the reassurance or upbeat delivery of Anna's request. 'Have a think though,

Anna. Maybe a couple's placement with a mate wouldn't be the end of the world after such a horrid time at the Frasers. Safety in numbers and all that?'

'Point taken, but it's still just me,' Anna replied with a sigh, knowing that Emily's heart was in the right place, even if she didn't seem to grasp the situation. 'So maybe we could just check that there's no lecherous key-holders with the next job instead?'

She hung up and closed her eyes, wondering if people knew how much easier their lives were simply by being a part of a family, a team, a community even. She was all for savouring her independence, but just sometimes she wondered whether a little compromise might go a long way; a little vulnerability in admitting how lonely it was to travel the world in luxury and at someone else's expense. She'd take whatever was on offer right now, though, and she knew it: choice being one luxury, as so often before, that she couldn't afford.

'First World problems,' she scoffed to herself as she gently cradled her swollen brow, mindful that she was lucky in so many ways.

Chapter 8

St Pauls, Bristol, 1998

Anna stood in the hallway, confused and unsure. She gripped her legs together tightly, desperate for a wee, one sock down around her ankle and her school uniform snug to the point of discomfort. She looked at the doors around her, all tightly closed, conversations humming behind each one.

No loo.

'Stay here, darlin', won't you?' Jackie, the social worker, had said, plonking Anna's belongings down beside her. There was no sign of the pretty overnight bag she'd so treasured, the one with the unicorns that sparkled different colours; now everything she owned was bundled into this one black bin-liner.

Learning about similes had been a mistake, Anna decided crossly, glaring at the bin-liner, feeling like trash.

'I'm nine, not stupid,' she wanted to shout at the kindly yet patronising people who offered her a sticker and then discussed her life behind her back. Jackie was Anna's third social worker in nearly two years. Losing Irene hadn't been so bad; her breath stank of coffee and the hairy mole on her cheek made Anna feel kind of sick. But she missed Mandy – even with her short skirts and clackety nails, Mandy had always taken the time to explain what was happening, why Anna was being moved yet again. Sometimes she would even give her a hug and point out that in every Disney movie, the heroine always won out in the end, even without any parents to help her.

Mandy made sense.

And certainly watching *The Little Mermaid* over and over again was a comfort that Anna could rely on.

But apparently Mandy hadn't been 'social worker material' – even if Anna had no idea what that actually meant. Was it the sneaky Haribo, or the proper kindness – the sort you could actually believe in? Or was it that her short skirts were, really truly, made from the wrong stuff?

Anna had never felt so helpless or so lost.

Not even when her mum first left, because at least then, Anna had fully believed she was coming back.

She didn't really believe that now.

Perhaps, late at night, eyes clamped shut, she might offer up a little prayer the way Miss Jennings had taught them in Year Two. Promising to be no trouble, to be good . . .

The problem was that, even now, Anna had no idea what she'd actually done to make her mother so angry, so cross, that leaving Anna at school one day and never coming back had been the punishment.

Even overhearing her form teacher talking in the corridors, saying that Anna was 'in the system now' didn't really help, when you were four foot nothing and the only system you really knew about was the one with planets and stars that revolved around the sun.

And it wasn't as though the 'home' she'd been staying in was horrible. It did smell different and there was nowhere quiet, but after years of just her and her mum, it had been nice sometimes, just to know she wasn't the only one.

For a long time, Anna hadn't known that. She'd gone to school every day – or at least every day that her mum could be persuaded out of bed to take her – and she pretended.

She'd been good at it.

'A right little actress,' her mum would say with that funny look on her face.

Anna squirmed, feeling a little panicky now. Jackie hadn't come back and she really, *really* needed a wee.

She tapped on the door nearest to her, tentatively turning the handle, only to be confronted by an empty office and a janitor emptying the bins, headphones on and oblivious.

Closing the door, Anna couldn't work out which was worse: not being here when Jackie came back or wetting herself. The thought of either made that odd prickling feeling under her hair start up again.

This is so unfair, Anna thought, gritting her teeth together, before deciding that she'd rather be punished than embarrassed and running down the corridor, looking left and right for the little shape of the lady with the triangle dress.

She got there just in time, but couldn't reach the high lock on the cubicle door. She could never reach anything. And it wasn't something you got used to. But she *had* got used to jumping and climbing to get what she needed. Small and wiry – scrawny, her mum said, which made her sound like a rotten chicken – she'd long since decided it was better to be feisty than feeble.

Asking for help was no longer in her vocabulary.

She'd be just fine, thank you very much, even without her mum and her grotty friends with their stinky cigarettes and those horrible pills in the brown bottle.

Her mum would shake the bottle like a maraca, call them her 'forgetful medicine'.

But what Anna could never understand was, why you would want to forget *everything*? Forget to eat, or take Anna to school, or one day even to put her cigarette out . . .

Anna managed a smile as she sat on the loo, legs dangling in blissful relief, remembering how lovely that fireman had been, letting her wear his hat and climb up into Dennis the fire engine, with his name in big letters on the front.

That was just before Anna's mum had decided she'd had enough. Enough time with Anna, enough time being a mum.

She'd shouted a lot the night before.

It was two years ago now and Anna still flinched at the memory of her angry, scary voice screeching down the phone, 'She's your fucking daughter too, Graham.'

Anna hadn't even realised that she could talk to her dad on the phone. Or that his grown-up name was Graham. To her, in the hazy memories of her childhood, he'd just been 'Dad' – teller of stories, flipper of pancakes and giver of hugs every time she fell over. With him, she remembered feeling precious, safe and protected – and he never called her scrawny. That was important too, because it was one thing being on your own in the world, Anna thought, but it was so much harder doing it when you were always, always the smallest kid in class.

She often wondered, if she had one wish, whether she'd actually choose to be tall, rather than back with her parents. Parents, as she knew all too well, weren't always for ever. But being tall would last a lifetime.

Anna knew her dad wasn't actually dead, although that's what her mum had said to begin with, as she ripped his clothes from the wardrobe and stuffed them out the open window with such force that she cracked the pane of glass.

And so began a litany of reasons she gave that Anna's dad didn't want her, didn't love her, didn't care. But the one that stuck with Anna most, probably because she'd been reading *The Famous Five* at the time, was that Anna's dad was nothing more than a 'common criminal'.

She had never been sure what that meant exactly, even if she understood the two words on their own perfectly well. Perhaps he was a little bit like the Fantastic Mr Fox, but without the waistcoat and pocket watch?

Back by her bin-liner – she'd had a moment's panic that the Janitor would have thrown it away – she waited again, impatiently. It was dark and she was hungry but Jackie had been so enthusiastic about this meeting that Anna hoped it meant something good.

When the door across the hallway opened and Jackie called Anna inside 'to meet someone special', she felt mainly relief that she hadn't been standing there in soggy knickers. Clasping her bin-liner tightly, taking no chances, she stepped into the room and felt that echoing thump of disappointment she knew all too well.

Not, in fact, her dad.

Or even her mum.

Just a nice lady with tightly curled grey hair and dog hair on her navy-blue trousers. Sure, she seemed nice, but then what did it really matter? Wherever she went – and even at nine Anna was shrewd enough to know this – it would only be for a little while. Nobody could adopt her; she already had a mum and dad. They just didn't want to be with her.

'Hello,' said Anna politely.

'Hello yourself,' said the lady, her smiling eyes taking in everything about the tiny scrappy bundle that was Anna Wilson, aged nine and three quarters. 'Jackie tells me you like dogs? Is that right?'

Anna nodded warily.

'I have three dogs – Benji, Jasper and Nitwit – would you like to see some pictures?' the lady said, holding out a small bundle of smooth, glossy photographs.

Was she just bragging, Anna wondered. She herself, obviously, had no dogs, and here was this lady with no name who had three!

'I'm Anna,' Anna said, and the lady gave a tinkly laugh that sounded like a windchime.

'Of course you are. And I've forgotten my manners in all the excitement. I'm Marjorie. And, if you'd like to, Jackie has arranged for you to come and live at my house. With me.' She laughed again, a little more nervously this time. 'And the dogs obviously. I suspect that's the bigger incentive.'

Anna had no idea what an incentive was, but she understood what this meeting was about. Girls at the home had meetings like this all the time; some of them she never saw again – off to enjoy their happy ever after – but some of them came back, tired, quiet and tearful.

'Would you like to see a picture of my house?' Marjorie said, looking questioningly at Jackie, possibly unnerved by Anna's lack of reaction. She flicked through the photographs and the three funny-looking dogs disappeared to be replaced by a small, fat bungalow that was painted a funny dull green colour so it looked like a bogey.

Anna looked up at Jackie, trying to work out what they wanted her to say.

'Aren't you a lucky girl?' Jackie said, prompting her. 'Fancy getting to have your very own bedroom *and* three dogs to play with?'

'Thank you,' said Anna dutifully, realising this was the bit where she was supposed to be grateful.

'Do you like gardening?' Marjorie asked hopefully. 'There's a little vegetable patch round the back where we can grow our own food. Won't that be fun for us to do together?'

Anna nodded. 'That sounds lovely,' she said, trying not to let her words sound as hollow as she felt.

'What do you enjoy doing, Anna?' Marjorie asked, not taken in for an instant.

'I like books,' blurted Anna. 'Stories mainly.'

'Then you and I are going to be just fine,' Marjorie said, visibly relaxing.

Jackie stood up, looking at her watch, all business. 'Well then, no time like the present to get you settled in, Anna. Grab your stuff, darlin', and we'll drive over to Marjorie's house.'

'Just like that?' Anna asked, looking from Jackie to Marjorie, thrown off balance. 'I'm not going back to the home?'

Jackie shook her head, a smile tightening the skin across her cheekbones. 'You've got a new home now, Anna. So you'll want to meet Bernard and Jerry—'

'Benji and Jasper, you mean?' Anna said, confused. 'And Nitwit?'

Jackie's smile tightened perceptibly more. 'Of course.'

Jackie drove like she talked, sharp punctuated bursts that made Anna feel queasy. She was past hungry now and simply nauseated. She clutched her bin-liner beside her on the back seat, hoping she hadn't forgotten anything back on her bed at the home, listening to Marjorie and Jackie's conversation, awkward, and probably with all the interesting bits missed out, she guessed, for her benefit.

The sooner people realised that nine was just a number and that Anna saw and heard so much more than they realised, she thought, then the easier life would be. Maybe one day, they might even let her say what she wanted?

It wasn't that grown-ups made bad choices – not all grown-ups anyway – they just weren't *her* choices. And she hated that.

If she was going to be on her own in the world, and she had almost resigned herself to the fact that she was, then at least she, like Ariel in *The Little Mermaid*, would get to make her own choices. It wasn't a hug, or a bedtime story, but at least it was something.

They pulled up outside Marjorie's house; even in the street lights it was just as squat and bogey-like as in the picture.

'Aren't you a lucky girl?' said Jackie again with added pep.

As Anna was ushered from the back seat and in through the front door, she ran those words like a mantra through her head; anything to offset the disillusionment that was sticking in her throat and making her want to cry.

The bungalow smelled funny and the carpet was swirly and brown. Even the barking cacophony of greeting from behind the kitchen door felt new and dangerous. She liked dogs. At least she thought she did.

She looked up at Jackie and forced herself to smile. 'Thank you,' she said.

Chapter 9

Redditch, 1998

'You understand, though, that this home placement is just temporary,' Jackie said, biting into a slice of Genoa cake and spraying crumbs everywhere. 'For now, at least.'

Anna sat beside her, strangely hypnotised by her rhythmic chewing – disgusted, but fascinated. Somehow, Jackie had never seemed like the kind of person who actually ate anything; she was all pointy corners and fake smiles.

Anna sighed, missing Mandy.

Mandy would have noticed the tear tracks on Anna's face from the drive over, would have noticed the way Anna was twisting her paper napkin into tighter and tighter corkscrews in her lap. In short, Mandy would have noticed that something wasn't quite right.

Temporary or not – and weren't her placements *always* temporary? – Anna felt that horrible pressure in her chest building again, as though the tears were just waiting for the right moment to flow. She wasn't sad though; she was angry.

But she would *not* cry in front of Jackie.

No way.

She looked around Marjorie's sitting room, at the book-shelves and the photographs, trying to imagine living here, her attention caught by some weird and wonderful masks hanging along one wall. Not to mention a carving of a monkey sitting squarely in one corner, at least half as tall as Anna herself, and so lifelike that she almost forgot how deter-mined she was to be cross and waved at him.

'That's Myrtle,' said Marjorie, leaning in, 'and I traded her in Zimbabwe for three football shirts and some notebooks.' She said it as though it was the kind of thing a person did every day and, just for a moment, Anna was side-tracked from her furious indignation at being brought here, without even being asked if she wanted to be.

'She's carved from a wood called ebony, so that's why she's such a lovely dark colour,' Marjorie continued, deliberately ignoring Jackie's sigh at the detour in her planned conversa-tion. 'There's a beautiful picture book here somewhere about all the animals I met in Africa—'

'Yes, well, that's lovely,' Jackie said. 'But I'll need to be off in minute and I want to make sure that you're settled. Both of you.' She gave Marjorie one of her stern looks but, much to Anna's growing delight, it seemed to have little or no effect.

'I'll tell you what,' Marjorie said instead, 'why don't you take a look at these and then maybe I can persuade you to eat a little something?'

She opened a huge, heavy photograph album onto the table beside Anna and opened it up to show photographs of lions and elephants and zebras. Except in some of the photo-graphs you could see Marjorie as well. Like she was actually *there*! Anna could almost feel her eyes widening and she looked at the lady in front of her, in her boring navy trousers and knitted top, in a whole new light.

She jumped as the book slammed closed, barely missing her fingers.

'Plenty of time for that later, Anna. Maybe something nice for the two of you to do together when I leave? Aren't you a lucky girl?' She smiled, but, as always with Jackie, it was a mouth smile, not a smile that sparkled into your eyes, like Mandy's had.

'I'm going to get you some nice cold milk and some Cheddars, Anna,' Marjorie said firmly, 'because not everybody likes Genoa cake.'

Anna had never actually tried Genoa cake, but after watching Jackie eat some, she knew it was very likely that she never would now. That fat sultana hanging on to the front of Jackie's jumper alone made her shudder.

There was a brief scuffle in the kitchen before Marjorie emerged again, carrying a strange plastic jug with a button on the top and a plate of tiny round biscuits that smelled delicious. Anna's tummy let out a traitorous rumble: there was no point saying she wasn't hungry; she was always hungry.

But she was also equal parts grumpy and intrigued.

She was angry with Jackie. She was always angry with Jackie. However many times Anna had asked to see her mum, talk to her mum, even just on the phone, Jackie always said no. Always said that Anna would thank her one day, whatever that meant. Thank yous were big in Jackie's world and Anna was always left feeling rude and ungrateful.

She hadn't chosen to be here. Temporary or not. And she just wished that people would talk to her properly. Did temporary mean a week, a month?

A month with Marjorie.

She watched as Marjorie pressed the button on the orange jug and tilted it, filling a glass with fresh, cold milk.

'Try them together,' nodded Marjorie, sliding the cheesy biscuits across the table towards her.

Marjorie's smile was a twinkly smile, Anna noticed, as she tentatively took a bite and then a sip. 'Thank you,' she said, trying hard not to wolf the whole plateful down and not to dribble milk on her chin. It was nice, she decided, to say thank you for something she actually wanted.

It seemed to Anna as though both she and Marjorie breathed a little easier once Jackie had left the building, the forced cheerfulness and her bossy insistence on Anna's good fortune making them both stand a little straighter and mind their Ps and Qs.

'You know,' said Marjorie as they waved at the headlights receding into the darkness, 'I'm not sure that Jackie is always quite right.'

Anna turned and blinked at her in surprise, realising that, without her tall shoes, Marjorie was barely a foot taller than she was. That was nice too, she decided.

'I mean,' said Marjorie as they still continued to look out at the driveway, street lights illuminating the quiet cul-de-sac, 'I rather think that *I* might be the lucky one.' She tentatively rested a hand on Anna's shoulder, pulling away before Anna could even respond or react.

Marjorie reached into her trouser pocket and pulled out three small biscuits in the shape of tiny cartoon dog bones. She held them out to Anna, warm to the touch and slightly crumbly from being carried around all day. 'Now, do you want to meet the boys?'

Anna hesitated; the barking when she arrived had made all the tiny hairs prickle on the back of her neck. She didn't think she was afraid, but she was certainly nervous. Holding the biscuits in her palm, she simply nodded, breathing out slowly. It was all too obvious from the look on Marjorie's face that 'the boys' were her pride and joy.

'Good girl,' said Marjorie. 'Now remember, you're the boss, okay?'

The biscuits grew damp and Anna had to resist the overwhelming urge to stand behind Marjorie as she opened the kitchen door.

'Nitwit – come!' said Marjorie in a firm voice that made Anna want to laugh for some reason, especially when she saw the ridiculous tufty little dog that wiggled out through the scarcely open doorway. 'Sit.'

The sight of his adorable little face, eyes wide with excitement, his fluffy tail wagging so hard that his bottom fidgeted on the spot, was more than Anna could take, and her giggle erupted with such force, it took them all by surprise.

Marjorie laughed too, as much at the astonishment on Anna's face, it seemed. 'He is a little funny-looking, isn't he? And look, he has one blue eye and one brown eye, did you notice? Now gently give him one of the biscuits and you'll have a friend for life.'

She guided Anna's hand forward. 'Gently,' she said firmly, whether to Nitwit or Anna it wasn't quite clear. The snuffling of his whiskers against her fingers felt new and strange, but not at all scary. Nitwit took the biscuit with such softness that Anna couldn't help but laugh again.

Moments later Nitwit was nuzzling against her, looking up at her with his crazy, happy eyes, and Anna knew that Marjorie had been right: they were friends now.

'I think,' Anna said seriously, 'that I like dogs.'

'Me too,' said Marjorie, smiling. 'They're awfully good at listening you know. And they never think you're silly for worrying or getting cross,' she paused, 'or dancing round the kitchen when your favourite song comes on the radio.'

Anna nodded sagely, her forehead wrinkling in concern. 'I don't think I have a favourite song.'

'Well that's easy enough to fix – and we can have some fun finding out. While we get to know each other, I'm betting we find out a few things about ourselves as well.' She shrugged. 'I don't have a favourite movie, or a favourite meal, or even a favourite cheese—'

Anna frowned. 'That's silly – nobody has a favourite cheese.'

'How do you know?' countered Marjorie with another friendly smile. 'Now, are you ready to meet Jasper? He's big, but he's a bit slow. Jasper! Come!'

Anna shook her head in disbelief; she'd never met a grown-up who talked like Marjorie. Scratch that, she'd never met a *person* who talked like Marjorie, as though life was an adventure there for the taking, a quest to discover new favourites.

Jasper, on the other hand, looked as though his idea of an adventure was a long nap in the sunshine; his fur was golden yellow and smooth and he ambled towards Anna with cool indifference. It was as though he expected more from her than just another biscuit. Feeling bold, Anna reached out and stroked his head. 'Good boy,' she said before holding out his biscuit.

His tail gave one satisfied thump against her leg, but then he leaned gently against her, his loyalty now clear.

'Benji! Come!'

The skittering of claws on the lino floor made Anna catch her breath. Jasper was wise, Nitwit was bonkers, but Benji it seemed had the energy of all three – he looped around the sitting room, cornering without grace or style, giving excited yips as he wound himself up into a frenzy.

'Benji,' Marjorie said warningly.

Benji dropped to the floor, edging towards Anna on his belly, before rolling over and presenting her with his tummy. 'What's he doing?' Anna said, pulling back in confusion.

Marjorie hitched up her trousers and sat down on the floor. 'He just wants you to scratch his tummy. He's just a baby really. See?' As she put her hand on his tummy, Benji's tail thwacked back and forth happily.

'Doesn't he want his biscuit?' Anna asked, the last one now clammy in her hand.

'Let's see shall we? Benji? Shake hands.'

To Anna's speechless delight, Benji wriggled around until he was sitting in front of her, nearly eye to eye, and then solemnly offered his paw to her in greeting. After tentatively shaking hands, Anna offered him the biscuit, surprised when he looked to Marjorie for her approval.

'Good boy, Benji,' Marjorie said.

Benji took the biscuit from her hand, snuffling slightly for crumbs and tickling her palm, and in that moment Anna fell in love a little. Nitwit was still searching for more treats around her feet, Jasper was leaning against her and Benji just looked at her with his soulful brown eyes.

In that moment, Anna felt like a part of something in a way she hadn't for years.

They were just dogs, she reminded herself, but somehow that didn't matter. With them beside her, she didn't feel quite so alone anymore.

She pressed her hand over her mouth, embarrassed to be crying when Marjorie had been so kind to her. 'I'm not sad,' she managed, laughing a little as Benji leaned in to lick her cheek, with a rough yet gentle thoroughness.

'It's been a big day,' said Marjorie gently, 'and these daft boys have been so excited to meet you.' She reached up from her position on the floor beside the dogs and squeezed Anna's hand. '*I've* been so excited to meet you. And if we have a few tears and a few wobbles along the way, well, that's what being part of a family is like. It won't all be sunshine and flowers, Anna, but at the end of the day, for as long as we can, we'll have each other—'

'—and the boys,' Anna finished for her, sliding down onto the floor, where Nitwit immediately climbed onto her lap, watching her every move.

'And the boys,' Marjorie agreed. 'You know, Anna, I've lived all over the whole wide world and if there's one thing I've learned it's this: you can live in a lovely house anywhere, but having a dog makes it a home.'

Anna nodded, her fingers already seeking out Nitwit's soft ginger fur for comfort.

'Thank you. For inviting me,' Anna said quietly, and this time the words came straight from her heart. And, as the dogs settled around her, their breath warm, their eyes never leaving her, Anna decided she would remember this moment for ever.

Chapter 10

Redditch, 1999

A month with Marjorie quickly became six and Jackie's visits became less frequent, the dark cloud of unease she seemed to carry along with her clipboard nevertheless lingering for a while, even after the sickly scent of Shalimar had long since been aired from every room.

Marjorie liked to air things – bed linen thrown back, windows flung wide, thoughts and feelings scattered like punctuation throughout their days.

Jackie's visits felt like a trial – like those Anna had seen on the television – as though every word from her mouth would be picked over and judged, used as a reason to take her away from Nitwit, Benji and Jasper. Away from Marjorie and the bedroom she'd come to love, not to mention the wonderful evenings they spent, curled up together on the sofa with a book, transported away to Narnia or Mallory Towers or even Africa. Times when Anna felt her limbs soften and her mind transported, hours flying by without a thought but for the lives on those pages.

'You know,' Marjorie said one day, as they stood side by side, rubbing butter into flour to make a crumble topping for the gooseberries they'd plucked only that morning, warm and plump, from the bushes in the garden, 'this summer with you has been one of the happiest times in my life.' She dropped a kiss on the top of Anna's hair. 'We were too busy travelling to have children of our own, Tony and I. It was a choice we made, but I'm not sure it was the right one.'

She stopped, her fingers coated in flour, the butter already melting in the heat of the day. 'I missed out on lots of experiences when I was younger, Anna. Sometimes because I was scared and didn't realise it was okay to ask for help, and sometimes because I just wasn't brave enough to speak up and say what I really wanted.'

'Like the tea cosy lady?' Anna replied, her brow furrowed in concentration as she tried to imagine Marjorie ever being afraid, or shy.

Marjorie smiled. 'Like the tea cosy lady.' The beautifully knitted figure whose skirts wrapped around the earthenware teapot was a source of fascination to Anna, not least because of the tiny banner that read 'Votes for Women' in miniature black stitches. Her expression was fierce, yet softly crafted from wool, and the word 'suffragette' seemed to carry a deeper meaning that spoke to Anna, beyond the song in *Mary Poppins*, beyond the stories of bravery that Marjorie recounted.

Was it okay, Anna wondered late at night, to admit to yourself that you too had been suffering? Not from anything brutal like the stories that filled the history books she now adored, but somehow deeper inside? A pain with such sharp edges that even to think of her life before – before, when she'd known who she was and where she was supposed to be – made her want to curl in on herself and smother it.

Yet somehow Marjorie knew.

She knew when the tears began to fall in the middle of the night, or when a memory was so sudden and so strong that it knocked the breath from Anna's chest. She knew that a story, or a hug, or a walk with the dogs was sometimes better than asking over and over again those questions for which neither of them had an answer.

Marjorie knew, and turned a blind eye when Nitwit began to sleep on the end of Anna's bed, creeping up during the night to lie curled in her arms.

Somehow knowing that other girls, other women – those suffragettes (not the knitted ones!) – had stood up and fought, made Anna determined. Determined to be strong. Determined to find a life that was hers alone, to share only as she chose. 'You must always, always have a say in your own life,' Marjorie would tell her, as she poured their morning tea, one hand, as ever, supporting the wobbly head.

Suffragette. Serviette. Courgette . . .

New words Anna habitually tucked away for another day. New words, new tastes. Avocados and plums, cherries and raspberries.

Anna had made herself sick that first week at Marjorie's, unable to believe that the bowl of fruit on the kitchen table was hers for the asking. Or that she could 'help herself'. No sharing, no stiff white cardboard toast to fill her rumbling tummy. Anna had gobbled so many apples and so many tiny black grapes that her stomach had groaned in protest and Marjorie had flushed with embarrassment that she hadn't thought to ration these sweet, juicy treats.

'Grab me a spoon, Anna. It's too hot for crumble – look!' She held up her delicate hands and laughed, the mixture far from crumbly, but bound together into a single smooth, yellow clod. 'The butter's too soft; we'll have to make shortbread.'

Anna smiled; she liked it when this happened now. Even Marjorie's frequent comment that 'all plans were made to be changed' didn't carry the swooping wave of fear that it used to. It hadn't for a while now; a few false starts to be sure, but gradually Anna was beginning to see that not all change was a bad thing. 'It'll be fine,' Marjorie would laugh. And, by and large, it was.

'If we make shortbread, can we dip them in chocolate?' Anna ventured, jumping on board with this new and unexpected plan.

'We can dip them in chocolate with orange zest,' Marjorie agreed. 'And then we can make the gooseberries into a fool.'

Anna flinched, almost subconsciously, as she still did whenever there was name-calling or swearing. 'Why?'

Realising her mistake, Marjorie stopped what she was doing. 'A fool is a delicious pudding, made from fruit and custard and cream – I think it might become your new favourite.'

Anna frowned. Words had so many meanings it sometimes made her question her own memories. Perhaps so much of what had happened in her life was because she herself had misunderstood? Had there been a word or a plan that she'd mistaken one day, to cause her whole family to fall apart?

Marjorie, however, was no fool and immediately saw the wistful expression filling Anna's eyes, could hazard a guess at the stories she told herself sometimes, when her bottom lip was caught between her teeth, and her whole, tiny body became taut with confusion.

'Taste this, darling,' she said instead, scooping a little of the shortbread mixture from the bowl, distraction the one tool that rarely failed.

Anna shook her head. 'It's not cooked yet.'

'What can I tell you?' Marjorie asked, popping a spoonful of the mixture into her mouth with obvious pleasure. 'Sometimes things are nicer when they're not the way you expect, or the way you think they're supposed to be.'

Life in Marjorie's house was certainly nothing like Anna had supposed it would be, that first day in the dusk; green and squat and ugly. For even amongst the ugliness of life, there was fun and laughter.

When Jasper sickened and died, Anna had thought her heart would surely break, yet the fragile cherry sapling they planted over his ashes soon grew strong and each tiny pink bud brought with it a memory of the joy they had shared together.

At least that's what Marjorie said.

Anna had simply added his soulful brown eyes to the roll call of loss she carried deep within her.

Yet, with each passing month, Anna found herself walking a little taller, a little prouder. By the time she sat her grammar school exams, she had already found an affinity for words that brought with it a sense of satisfaction and achievement. Books filled her with joy, but numbers fought back, yet her determination only grew.

Small, slight, devoid of witty stories and caring not one jot about fashion or boys, Anna's sole focus was on building her own strength. She ran with the dogs, she watched the news, and increasingly Marjorie would lean across the kitchen table and entrust her with a task: pop to the corner shop for some milk; phone up the cinema for the film times; work out the connecting trains to get to London.

Each task felt like another step forward, an honour really, to be entrusted with Marjorie's supple brown purse, or a weighty handful of pound coins.

And, in turn, Marjorie showed her how to ask for what she wanted. 'Being bolshy will get you nowhere,' she would caution, 'and it's always better if you understand what you want *before* the conversation begins.' Hesitating, then, 'Some people like to bend your words, Anna, convince you that you want something different – it's okay to listen, they might even be right – but know your own mind. You're the only one who has to live with the consequences.' She spoke those words with such feeling that even Anna, in her short socks and pigtails, knew they must come from painful personal experience.

Having an opinion, for the first time in Anna's life, became something to be celebrated. Assuming she could explain why.

'But *why* is an apple better than a banana? There's no right or wrong answer – just tell me what you think.'

And as she grew, even if only a little, they would catch the bus into town to buy clothes. New clothes. Never-worn-before clothes, that soon smelled of Fairy washing powder and the garden where they blew on the line in the sunshine.

Somehow even the smallest task became an adventure: new words gave way to new ideas, new foods to new cities and galleries. Anna felt filled with possibility. She hadn't even known that painting pictures could be a job. Or writing books. Or even taking photographs.

'Find a job you love and you'll never work a day in your life,' Marjorie would laugh, never short of a fortune cookie saying. But she made a point that Anna had never considered before: life didn't have to be hard and painful. It could also be filled with joy and beauty and, dare she even think it, love.

Chapter 11

Redditch, 1999

Tempting fate. That was what they called it in the movies.

The letters had arrived together, in a bundle of junk mail about pizzas and making your lawn green and stripy.

Anna holding her breath as she tore open the envelope, looking up at Marjorie, only to see the same expression of hope and apprehension mirrored on her face.

She hadn't been able to read past the word *Congratulations* before her eyes had blurred.

One of one hundred and twenty.

All that hard work and studying had opened up a new world of possibilities, starting with a place at King James Grammar School.

She'd barely noticed Marjorie slipping her own envelope into her trouser pocket to read later, so caught up was Anna in the unexpected, twirling excitement of her own achievement.

'I am so, so proud of you, my darling, wonderful girl,' Marjorie had said, eyes swimming with tears. '*You* did this, Anna Wilson. This is *your* moment. The adventure starts here.'

Pulled into a tight, almost suffocating hug, Anna had been blown away by Marjorie's reaction. Such emotion, such pride. It almost felt too much.

But of course, it was the weight of the other letter, the other words that Marjorie had apparently half anticipated that caused tears of happiness to mingle with the grief she knew was coming.

There had been a lump.

Just a tiny bump really.

Nothing to worry about.

Or so Marjorie had said.

Until suddenly, there *was* something to worry about, and the waft of Shalimar filled the sitting room again as Jackie and her clipboard returned, talking about 'options' and 'best interests'.

Marjorie and Anna were somehow silenced in the onslaught of nurses, and doctors, and social workers filled with good intentions.

By then the stories and the fruit from the garden, even Anna's good news about her grammar school place, were not enough to eclipse the truth.

'A whole new adventure,' Marjorie said, hands clasped tightly around Anna's, the dogs perturbed by the comings and goings, whiney and clingy.

How Anna longed to cling on too. If she never let go, if she never acknowledged the words that now filled their days. Words she had never heard before, which now buzzed around her head even as she slept.

Chemotherapy. Radiation. Macmillan.

'Don't forget to gather new words, try new things and be brave, my darling girl,' Marjorie said, swallowing hard as the tears clouded her words. 'Life is what you make it and you only get one, so there's no harm in going somewhere new is there?' She paused. 'Even here was somewhere new once.'

Anna nodded, desperately seeking to reassure with a smile. 'The bogey house,' she said, making Marjorie laugh despite herself.

'I'll refrain from jokes about the rich pickings we've had here, then, shall I?' Marjorie managed, pulling Anna into her arms.

'Please don't make me go,' Anna whispered into her shoulder, the scarf covering Marjorie's head tickling against her cheek, unable to stop the tears from falling, her hands from clasping ever tighter.

'You've been the greatest gift in my life,' Marjorie said. 'Promise me, Anna darling, promise me you'll keep looking. Build your life, build your family, find your home.'

'I promise,' said Anna.

Chapter 12

Dittisham, 2019

It was always a source of wonder to Anna the disproportionate difference that a shower and a clean set of clothes could make.

A fresh start.

Literally.

Indeed, as she drove south towards the coast a few days later, it was Anna's soul that was rumpled and tattered, not her appearance. Gingerly she touched the swelling around her eyebrow, disguised beneath layers of adeptly applied concealer – as first impressions went, battered and bruised was hardly a look that inspired trust or confidence.

Sleep, of course, had been elusive and the long nights at the Premier Inn had reminded her all too clearly that a hotel room was a lonely place to be at 3 a.m., with no distraction from her taunting thoughts, or in this case, the intrusive image of Andrew Fraser's florid, leering face.

The small hours of the morning often played host to all those old feelings of powerlessness, of impotence, that Anna worked so hard to avoid. The frustration of being dependent upon other people's choices, not to mention their agendas, had been such a huge part of her childhood that she wondered whether its legacy would ever truly leave her.

She may not have the stability in her life that people like Kate and Emily enjoyed, but her life and her choices were her own.

Until this week.

Until one entitled fool had thrown her best-laid plans into disarray, and with them Anna's composure and hard-won self-assurance.

Still, at least she had somewhere to go now and it actually felt really good to know that she was stepping in to help this new client at the eleventh hour. The same client who was inadvertently helping her.

Saving her, if you felt like being dramatic about it.

And, as she concentrated on the road, on only a few hours of snatched sleep and with her brow pounding into a tormenting headache, Anna gave herself permission to do just that. Just for a moment. Before she arrived and she needed to be on parade.

Trustworthy, reliable, confident.

The perfect house-sitter.

Several hours later, Anna pulled over into a grassy lay-by at the side of the road. Well, technically she supposed it was a road, but there was barely room for her tiny Mini between the steep banks either side. Should she happen upon a car coming the other way, it was surely each man for himself? Sheer anticipation of this eventuality had sweat prickling her chest and her arms taut on the steering wheel.

She slowly breathed out, pulling on the handbrake, taking a moment to settle herself.

The map on her phone screen showed the coast only a mile or so ahead, but all Anna could see, down in the trench of this country lane, was mossy rocks, overhanging trees and the rolling pastures beyond. Not quite Hardy country, but a few miles further over and it would hardly take a stretch of the imagination to see Tess herself wending her way through identical fields and valleys.

The map disappeared, replaced by a photo of Emily, smiling in front of the Home Network logo, and an insistent trilling that was impossible to ignore.

'Are you nearly there yet?' Emily asked.

'God knows,' Anna said, only the sound of seagulls through her open window giving her any confidence she was even heading in the right direction.

'Trust the directions,' Emily replied, as she always did. 'By all accounts, Dittisham is a glorious place and the weather forecast is amazing for the next week. You can just walk on the beach and put your face in the sun. Catch your breath a bit?'

'Well, that does sound wonderful,' Anna agreed, smiling despite herself. 'Although the prospect of boats and birds makes me a little nervous—'

'It's only one very small bird,' Emily cut in. 'And you're not *living* on the boat. There just happens to *be* a boat there if you'd like to use it.'

'I know, I know. And I'm not being a brat. I'm so grateful to you for sorting this, Em. Truly. Finding these new placements at short notice has got to be a nuisance.'

'Nah – you're fine. It's quite nice to have someone available for the people who call up in a last-minute flap.' She paused. 'Look, before you keep leapfrogging around the country, I need you to be completely honest with me for a minute – *are* you okay? I mean, really, truly okay. Not the whole it'll-be-fine fob-off?'

Anna hesitated. 'I am fine, though. Really. I mean, I'm angry. Furious, if we're being specific. Who wouldn't be? But once my eyebrow heals over . . .'

'I just don't want you to be there all alone, double-checking the doors are locked every five minutes . . .' Emily's enquiry was tentative, knowing all too well that Anna regretted sharing that particular titbit about her past. 'Although nobody would blame you if you were—'

'I can't say the thought hadn't crossed my mind too,' Anna said reluctantly. 'But you know, that's fine, right? I would have thought a house-sitter with a touch of OCD was a boon. So, I check their house is all locked up. And if I check it again then, you know, where's the harm?' Anna's jokiness was no real disguise and they both knew it.

'Okay. Point taken. But you do see, Anna, that anybody – I mean *anybody* – would have a tricky time adjusting after what happened with that Fraser bloke. Split eyebrow or not, it's going to take a little time to heal. Maybe moving around so much isn't a good idea? Come stay with me? Or take an *actual* holiday?'

Anna laughed. 'I thought every day as a house-sitter was a holiday?'

Emily all but growled. 'I already apologised for that ad campaign.'

'You did and, honestly, I am grateful, Em. Maybe a little sea air will blow the cobwebs away?'

For a moment, Anna allowed herself to believe in that possibility. But didn't there come a point, for every person with an eidetic memory, where they had long since given up on forgetting as even an option? Acceptance was a more real-istic alternative.

And she wasn't there yet.

'Look, I get to stay in a house by the sea with a Great Dane and a parrot—'

'A ring-necked parakeet.'

'Quite. So, it'll be fine. A new adventure,' Anna said firmly, essentially shutting down the conversation. 'Now all I have to do is find the bloody place.'

'Tiny village, massive house. I'm guessing you follow the smell of money,' Emily joked. 'And in all seriousness, could you please report back on what an 'architect-designed house' actually means. I mean, aren't all houses designed by architects, or is there some rogue market in barmen sketching out houses on napkins that I don't know about?'

Anna snorted. 'I'm on it. And, just reading the email again this morning, this dog, Chewie? He really only eats raw food? I mean, I actually have to dice up steak and stuff?' She gave a shudder of revulsion at the thought of doing that early in the morning. 'No wonder he eats the furniture. I mean, I'm guessing, why else would you call a dog Chewie?'

'I think it's short for Chewbacca. Seriously, the bird's called Leia, so there's definitely something going on.'

'This just keeps getting better,' Anna said. 'Is the boat called Han Solo?'

'Who knows? Maybe? I know they're not that old, just minted. And fresh out of London. So you'll hardly be roughing it. Besides, they're off to her sister's wedding at their place in Italy, so they're hardly going to be bored on the beach and breathing down your neck. You can relax.'

Anna blew out her cheeks, suddenly paralysed by the kind of bone-gnawing exhaustion that crept up on her from time to time. The very idea of meeting this couple, making a good first impression, being the confident, capable person they needed her to be, was simply overwhelming.

'I'd best get going then,' she said, trying to ignore the bitter taste of envy that still caught her off guard.

What a way to live.

'And Anna? Maybe you could invite a friend, or I could come and join you for a bit? If I can't persuade you to take some time off, then at least think about a little company.' Her voice softened. 'Nothing wrong with asking for help, you know. It's a lot to process.'

Anna said her goodbyes and ended the call as firmly and politely as she could. It wasn't the idea of Emily's company that made her feel so uncomfortable, so much as *anyone* staying with her right now. She simply didn't have the energy to be on parade, making conversation twenty-four seven. She rested her head on the steering wheel and closed her eyes, counting slowly to one hundred, before turning the key in the ignition and setting off downhill towards the sea, windows down and the echoing sound of gulls growing ever louder.

Okay. So, on first impressions, 'architect-designed' seemed to mean either a house that was imposing and completely out of keeping with its surroundings, or possibly modern, innovative and really rather flash. Pulling to a halt and staring up at the stark-white and glazed behemoth in front of her, The Cove would apparently fit the bill either way.

As would its owners. Anna buried a smirk as she reached around for her overnight bag and caught sight of the couple pulling open the front door to greet her like a *Hello* magazine photo call. High heels, make-up, perfect blow-dry. And him in his white, white jeans, like the bloke in the Persil advert.

'Hi! Hello there – before you hop out, could you possibly tuck your little car – so adorable – just around the side there?'

Fingers waggled, tennis bracelets sparkled, disdain that the Mini might sully the aesthetic written all across Mrs Lyndell's face.

'No problem,' said Anna, wincing as the Mini started up again with a sputter of smoke from the exhaust. It was only really when she saw her choices through other people's eyes that she felt embarrassed. Stuff just didn't matter to her and, so long as her Mini got her from A to B, she couldn't see the point in replacing it with something newer. Shinier. Soulless. She patted the Mini's round dials apologetically, just in case it could read her thoughts, wondering whether she had officially lost the plot.

Striding over towards her, the man of the house knotted his soft, clearly cashmere, jersey around his shoulders a little tighter. 'Hi. Hi, Anna. I'm Oliver, this is Liza. We're so grateful you could come at such short notice. Come in, come in.' He reached out a hand to take her bag, waiting expectantly for another.

'I travel light,' Anna explained, scooping up her handbag and slamming the car door closed.

A flicker of intrigue crossed Oliver's face as he sized her up. 'A skill of the job, I imagine. Liza, darling, lessons to be learned here, I think.'

They stepped into the echoing white entrance hall, soaring a full three storeys high, light pouring in from a glazed wall that swept up from the ground on the far side. Beside the door was stacked a veritable indulgence of luggage, logoed and immaculate. Six, no seven, suitcases.

And one suit carrier, which Oliver picked up playfully. 'This one's mine,' he joked with Anna, before quelling under his wife's furious gaze. This was an argument that was clearly already well under way.

'It's a wedding not a pool party and I'm assuming you want me to look nice?' she countered, pointedly giving Anna's outfit a once-over that seemed to suggest that travelling light could only result in such sartorial failure as to be an embarrassment.

'You have a beautiful home,' Anna said, diplomatically changing the subject. 'May I?' She was drawn towards the glazed wall, framing as it did the perfect sea view, a swathe of blue ombré that seamlessly blended into the sky.

'It's breathtaking, isn't it?' Oliver said. 'And honestly, Chewie and Leia will be no problem. If you stick to the food and the walks and everything that Liza has written down for you, you'll still have plenty of time to enjoy the village and the harbour. Have you been here before?'

Anna shook her head. 'It's so tucked away, I'm not sure I knew it existed.'

Liza wandered over to join them. 'The trick to places like this is to catch them when they're up and coming. Daddy did that over in Sandbanks, Dorset, you know, and made a killing.' She sighed. 'Of course then you have to wait for them to up and come.' She scowled across the garden at the only neighbouring house in sight, a small bungalow in local stone with a large satellite dish balanced incongruously on the weathered slate roof.

'Now, I don't know how familiar you are with pedigree dogs, but Chewie has a very delicate system. No treats except the chicken livers in the fridge, and only his meals.' She sighed again. 'At least Sonja had the presence of mind to get that all sorted before she swanned off to her sister's. So thoughtless, I mean really, we've had this trip planned for months.'

As if the very situation had offended her all over again, Liza stormed off.

'Sonja?' Anna ventured, hoping that Oliver might see fit to fill in the gaps.

'Our housekeeper. She's broken her ankle sadly. Can't be helped.' He paused, checking that his wife was out of earshot. 'But actually do be careful on the marble floors in the bathrooms, won't you?' He looked out at the view again. 'To be honest, I rather envy you a week of peace and quiet here. Chewie loves a good leg-stretch on the beach of a morning and then he's done for the day. Do use the boat too, won't you? I'd like to think that somebody's having a good time.'

Moments before, she had found herself judging him, but the dejected look of compliance in his every gesture provoked a strange kind of pity.

'I'm not much of a sailor,' Anna said apologetically.

'The sailboat in the marina is Liza's and Liza doesn't share. Anyway, it's my little rowboat you'll have the most fun with.' He pointed down to the bottom of the garden, where a small wooden jetty extended out over the water and a fat red rowboat bobbed happily on the swell.

'It's lovely,' Anna said simply, wondering at these two souls and how their lives had collided, or perhaps, more saliently, how Oliver's had been subsumed into Liza's.

'Anna! An-na!' Liza called impatiently from somewhere in the middle of this stylised, oversized beach house. 'Are you coming to meet Chewie or not?'

'Oh-oh. Trouble,' came a chirping voice from Anna's left, and she couldn't help but smile when she saw the bobbing yellow bird, a small collar of red feathers making her tilting head look a little like a helmet. Perched on the branch of a living tree in an enclosure bigger than Anna's car, the little bird whistled. 'Kisses?' she asked, hopping forward to say hello.

Oliver grinned and, uninhibited, began making kissing noises, which Leia mimicked happily.

'An-na!' called Liza again.

'Come on,' said Oliver. 'Come and meet the lad and then I'm afraid we'll need to leave you to it.' He glanced at his watch, a classic Cartier. 'Bye, baby,' he said to the little bird sadly.

'Bye, baby,' she echoed, bobbing her head and even Anna, despite her avian suspicions, couldn't help but smile.

Chapter 13

With Liza's volley of last-minute instructions still rattling in her head — her own name bastardised to the apparently more palatable Ah-na — it was almost a relief to wave them off on their trip. Anna smoothed down her hair from where Liza had tugged at her ponytail distastefully. 'Try not to use the pool too much, it's such a pain to clean the filters.'

There was a strange pleasure in knowing that, whether someone like Liza conceded it or not, there was a need in her life for someone like Anna. Like Sonja. It was surely necessary, after all, to have someone to look down on, in order to be *that* confident and so utterly convinced of one's own superiority? That inner certainty was perhaps cast in the DNA of some people and, as ever, Anna found herself simultaneously awed and irked by this self-assurance that would always, always elude her. This absolute belief that theirs was the opinion that mattered, and that their wishes and desires should therefore eclipse all others.

But, how?

How did one even *begin* to quiet one's inner anxieties, ignore those unspoken but unassailable doubts, so ingrained as to become lore?

Anna had no idea. Sometimes it was easier simply to watch and marvel, and try not to become obsessed with the wheres and whyfors that so intrigued her.

And yet – however disparaging the looks, the comments, and however begrudging Liza's welcome – Anna was now here, living in the luxury of The Cove for the next week. The sun was shining, rippling across the frosted tips of the sea, and she had a new place to explore and, presuming she promised not to shed(!), then a beautiful indoor pool in which to swim. She had sweet little Leia to entertain her, who even now seemed to be working through the harmonies of 'Bye Bye Baby' with such innocent pleasure that it was hard not to be enchanted.

If she could just persuade Chewie that she wasn't in fact the devil incarnate, then it could almost be the holiday that Emily had prescribed. She whistled once more to try and get Chewie's attention and then went looking. The heavy, meaty smell hit the back of her throat as soon as she walked into the vast kitchen, the Great Dane seemingly proud of his deposit in the middle of the marble floor. He eyed Anna boldly, challenging her.

She threw open the French doors, gulping in fresh air, questioning yet again the sanity of this raw food diet. 'Get out, you bad dog!' she cursed, hoping that it wouldn't come to a battle of wills or strength; he probably weighed more than she did.

'Bad dog!' echoed Leia from next door, before pealing into laughter. 'Good baby! Bad dog!'

Anna stepped forward, refusing to blink, growling under her breath. 'Get. Out.'

Chewie dithered for a moment, clearly so used to being the alpha in this household that he was unsure how to respond.

Anna stepped closer again, until she could feel his hot breath on her chest. 'Listen, Scooby Doo – just accept that I'm in charge here or it's going to be a very long week.' She stared him out, her own eyes beginning to water, but refusing to blink first and lose the only battle that mattered.

He wobbled for a moment longer then dropped his head and trotted obligingly out into the garden, cocking his leg up against one of the sculptures on the lawn on his way.

Anna breathed a sigh of relief, grateful that the garden was apparently completely secure, and she could leave him out there for a moment while she dealt with the kitchen floor.

As was her habit, Anna took her time finding her bearings. It was part of the promise of a new place, a new adventure, to tease out the first tour of the house. Why rush, after all, from room to room when each new vista, each bookshelf, each silver-framed photograph could be savoured and scrutinised?

This was not, she always justified to herself, snooping.

She just needed to get the lay of the land, as it were, prefer-ably in daylight, and in a house this big, she liked to make sure there were no surprises. Heated tongs left on, windows wide open, alarm clocks set for 5 a.m. – this was not her first rodeo and she was forever amazed by how carelessly people were content to leave their houses. And somehow the more deca-dent the home, the less care and respect it was afforded.

Case in point, the array of sodden towels on the bed in the master suite.

Without Sonja to pick up the pieces, who exactly was supposed to handle the mouldering heap?

As ever, a house-sitter's role involved walking the line between privacy and duty of care.

Anna, of course, picked up the towels.

Four bedroom suites later, each with their own spacious bathroom, dressing room, and sweeping view, it was hard not to begrudge her own quarters downstairs. Sonja's quarters, to be precise, the entire square footage of which would fit into one of the ensuite bathrooms with room to spare. A small, rectangular window looking out at the wall of the pool house, should you be inclined to stand on tiptoe. One tiny, crispy blue towel awaiting her at the foot of her bed, compared to the bountiful array of silver-grey softness stacked in every bathroom.

Anna frowned, the temptation to move up to one of these bedrooms overwhelming.

Chewie's bed in the sitting room was better appointed than her own.

Would it be so wrong?

And then she thought of Liza's expression, her obvious distrust of a stranger in her home, and professionalism prevailed.

Sure, wouldn't it be night-time anyway?

There were fresh sheets on her bed, food in the fridge and, with the doors securely locked, a cocoon of anonymity around her – just one house amongst many. What did it actually matter where she slept?

Later that evening, as the view from the Eames armchair in the sitting room darkened and the lights on the boats in the harbour flickered like fireflies, Anna sat spellbound. Even the slightly ominous presence of the cavernous, empty house behind her was an irrelevance. The whoosh of the tide coming in was the only sound she could hear, still not enough to drown out the thoughts in her head.

With only a stack of pristine *Architectural Digest* magazines to read, Anna lay one finger across her bruised brow-bone and considered her options.

Here, and at Gravesend Manor, there had been an unwelcome shift in her role. To these people, she was simply staff. No better, or more valued, it seemed, than the woman who broke her ankle scrubbing their floor. Of no more importance than a woman to be coerced and bullied.

She wasn't kidding herself that hers was a prestige career choice, but freedom and flexibility had always been the draw of this life. Yet somehow now, without her diary planned out months in advance, that same freedom felt rudderless. Hollow. The next few weeks a yawning void, without boundaries or purpose.

Already the week here felt like a place holder, as though she were treading water until she could get back on track. But back on track to *where*, she could almost hear Kate's voice protesting.

First World problems, she reminded herself, stroking Chewie's head on her lap and trying to force herself to relax into this lap of luxury.

Docile and affectionate after their showdown in the kitchen, Chewie hadn't left her side and she'd even got used to Leia's habit of suddenly and loudly muttering 'tick-tock-tick-tock' over and over again in the background.

Reaching for her journal, she flicked back through the last few pages. Bermuda. Orkney. Thailand. Tenby. Holland Park. Her words and sketches painted a picture that projected each placement afresh into her mind's eye. Her random aesthetic collages made her smile. Illustrated sugar packets and the eye of a peacock feather, simple portals to the past on a single page.

And, of course, her words; each line carefully, eloquently, considered to rouse the senses.

Every one of her journals became her treasure. Soft, battered leather with cream pages, her writing a work of art.

Personal. Perceptive. Perfect.

Yet the last entry made her hesitate; so filled with optimism and excitement for Kate's wedding.

And not a word since.

At least, no words she would sully these pages with, for sometimes it was better to forget.

She closed the journal and tucked it away. If good editing could make a writer's words soar, then surely she could be forgiven for editing her own story from time to time.

She breathed out slowly and picked up her phone instead, flicking through emails and typing deftly in the half-light.

Words on a screen always felt liberatingly transient to Anna. No need for fine-tuning, fine penmanship or, indeed, self-censorship. A temporary repository for ugly, half-formed thoughts. No commitment required.

As her typing slowed, the purge of words dwindling to a trickle, she sat back, exhausted.

Tomorrow, she decided, she would find a bookshop. With a book in her hand, she could feel at home anywhere; tried and tested to soften even the most jarring of relocations.

A sudden hammering on the front door spiked both her adrenaline and her heart rate, Chewie barking loudly and careering around the room, claws skittering on the polished oak boards. Frozen in the chair, Anna clung to the belief that without the Lyndells' car outside, her visitor might yet give up and go away.

The hammering continued without pause. On and on, if anything building in intensity.

Tentatively getting to her feet, trying to shake off the bitter taste that filled her mouth, Anna peeked through the window, only catching a glimpse of a large imposing figure outside.

'I can see you in there. Answer the door, for God's sake!' he shouted, his voice gravelled and urgent.

Anna breathed out slowly, wondering how the hell she managed to get into these situations. Once could be excused as a mistake; twice in one week should surely be taken as a sign.

'If you think I'm opening the door to somebody yelling in the dark, you're mistaken,' Anna called back.

She watched as the figure outside seemed to slump, perching against one of the staddle stones outside. 'Point taken. I'm sorry.' He stared at a crumpled letter in his hands, no longer threatening, merely sad and frustrated. He was far younger than she had realised.

Against all her better judgement, Anna still found herself walking into the hall and pulling open the door. 'I'm really not sure I can help you, but if you need me to call somebody for you, I can,' she said.

He looked up, eyes tired and a day's worth of stubble darkening his chin; he could barely be twenty-five. Despite herself Anna felt a quickening of intrigue.

He held up the letter, an official-looking crest at the top of the page. 'This can't go on, you know. It's harassment. And you're making my grandparents ill with the worry.'

'I don't live here; I'm just the house-sitter,' Anna said apologetically.

'Oh, right. Right, okay then,' he said, making as though to stand up and leave, yet going nowhere. 'My grandparents live in the bungalow down there. A blight on the Lyndells' view apparently.' He shook his head. 'Forty-three years in their house, and suddenly they don't feel safe in their own home. They've been pestered to sell up, threatened with all sorts of supposed building code violations – for God's sake, when that place was built there were no building codes!' He sighed. 'I know, I know. You're just the house-sitter. Not your problem.'

Anna shook her head. 'I didn't say that. Are they okay, your grandparents? You said they were unwell?'

He shrugged. 'They're old and they're frightened – it's not a winning combination.'

He finally garnered the impetus to stand up and turned, looking at Anna properly for the first time. 'I'm sorry if I frightened *you*. I'm Henry. And I don't make a habit of hammering down doors in the middle of the night, I promise you.'

'Anna,' she replied, holding out her hand, pleasantly surprised by the warmth and firmness of his handshake, finding that she actually believed him.

'So, you're just here looking after the house? Trying to rein in that spoiled dog?' he hesitated. 'They're friends of yours? The Lyndells?'

Anna shook her head. 'It's my job, actually. House-sitting. Well, pet-sitting too, obviously.' Somehow she felt the urge to share more with this tousled stranger on the doorstep, but sanity prevailed. 'Goodnight, Henry,' she said softly, closing the door and leaning back against it, deep in thought.

After a few moments, she walked through and lay down on the sofa, staring out over the sea, Chewie insinuating himself into the gap beside her.

How was it possible that Henry's strength, to her at least, seemed to come from his very willingness to be vulnerable, and yet Andrew Fraser, for all his brutality, now seemed small and weak?

It was a question that circled in her mind, over and over, until the sky grew warm and orange and another day began.

Chapter 14

Dittisham, 2019

Anna sat cross-legged outside Leia's birdcage the next morning, unable to pluck up the nerve to let her fly free. She'd checked the doors and windows, several times actually, but somehow the risk still felt too great, no matter what Oliver had said.

'Smi-le,' Leia chided her, hopping over to where the branch poked through the narrow silver bars. Tentatively, Anna opened the little door and held out her hand, trying not to be squeamish about the tiny talons that reached out and gripped her fingers. Glossy, black and fragile, but still sharp and strong in their own way. Leia bobbed her head and hummed a little tune to herself, stretching out and seemingly revelling in a different view.

'You're really very sweet, you know that?' Anna said to the little yellow bird, fascinated up close by the eponymous ring of red feathers that circled her throat. Her simple innocence so endearing and reassuring; it was the perfect antidote to the chaos of the last few days.

'Good baby,' Leia agreed. Yet another flurry of increasingly insistent voicemails lit up Anna's phone, startling them both. So much for her time here being her own.

The urgency of Liza's predicament was in no doubt, but still the tone left a sour taste. 'Just get the shoes from my study and get them couriered here. Today.' Not a please or a thank you in sight.

Anna felt herself physically bristle with resentment, yet what could she do?

It was hardly her fault that Liza had been so wrapped up in packing her own wardrobe that she'd forgotten the bride's shoes. Custom-made. Eye-wateringly expensive if the lacquered red sole was any guide. She laughed in disbelief for a moment, trying to imagine herself in that same situation, twisting herself like a pretzel in abject apology for any inconvenience, her speech littered with 'just's and general self-effacement.

And so, of course, her morning had become about packaging up the shoes and writing out labels and phoning around for the best avenue of delivery. Flustered by the incessant demands for an update, Anna reluctantly returned the little bird to her aviary and switched her phone to silent, begrudgingly putting aside her pyjamas and pulling on a pair of jeans and some Converse. Translatable clothes. And for all that Liza had scoffed at Anna's limited luggage, Anna knew deep down that she herself could blend in anywhere.

Even without custom-made shoes.

Standing in the hallway, Chewie circling her legs and barking in frustration that his morning walk had been delayed, Leia calling over and over from her aviary, 'What'ya doing? What'ya doing?', Anna felt the lack of sleep begin to catch up with her – hands full, poised to leave, yet still she felt that old compulsion just to check, to be certain that every door and window was closed. Not just closed, but locked. Kettle unplugged, coffee machine ditto. Even the humming of the satellite TV box gave her pause. She clasped the front door keys so tightly in her hand that she flinched, clammy sweat prickling her hairline, a breath away from tears, even as she ran a slow-motion replay in her head of checking each and every door and window.

Breathing out forcefully, she muttered under her breath. 'Trust yourself, Anna. The house is fine.' Opening the front door and stepping outside, Chewie nearly pulled her off her feet. His exuberance and his sheer size made him a handful at the best of times, but he was in no mood for patience. 'Post Office first, then beach,' she told him, somewhat pointlessly. After all, she could hardly take the Louboutins for a seaside stroll when they were required in Florence so urgently.

Pulling the front door closed and testing it, then testing it once again, Anna tried hard to focus, to give herself the confidence, and indeed relief, of stepping away with a clear mind. A visual memory of the door safely closed. 'The door is locked, I've locked the door, this door is locked.' Anna turned and nearly tripped over a small basket on the doorstep.

Crouching down to pick it up, Chewie pulled her off balance in his single-minded desperation to be away.

'Sit!' she said firmly, brushing the gravel from her grazed palms and checking to see that the precious parcel was unharmed. 'Chewie, sit!'

He shuffled back onto his haunches on the gravel, mouthing off with a volley of whimpers and yelps. Yet Anna was intrigued by the basket, by the note inside and by the thought that had clearly gone into putting it together.

She glanced at the signature – Ruth – wondering who had seen fit to leave freshly baked scones and a jar of homemade jam with her name on it. Unfolding the note, it all made sense.

Anna - please forgive Henry disturbing you last night, he's a good boy, and so protective of me and Arthur. We would love to see you for tea one day, if you feel like company.

P.S. Chewie will do almost anything for a little bit of cheese ... (although maybe don't mention that to her Ladyship.)

Ruth

She glanced down towards the bungalow and smiled. Such a genuine offer of kindness was rare in Anna's world and, checking that the scones were safely packed away in their Tupperware container, she tucked the basket out of sight for her return, her morning dramatically improved by one thoughtful, generous gesture and the prospect of a cup of tea with a neighbour.

Having walked down the steep hill at the ridiculous pace dictated by Chewie, Anna could barely take in any of the beautiful pastel cottages and sea views, her hand almost raw from the lead pulling her forward. Seemingly everyone she passed had an eye out for Chewie, glaring at her as they skirted away out of his range. Waves of hostility threw her off balance once more, serving only to confuse, especially after the kindness of the gift basket.

'You really have quite the reputation, Chewie,' she grumbled, her arms beginning to ache and her temper to fray. Just once, she'd like a little equilibrium in the universe.

She apologised to a mother with two small children when Chewie surged towards them, making them squeal. 'I'm so sorry,' she said, quashing the urge to shout after them. 'He's not mine – I'm just looking after him!'

'You are quite the piece of work,' she cursed the dog under her breath, catching hold of a lamp post and wincing, as she attempted to anchor him and catch her breath.

She looked around where the lane levelled out, trying to get her bearings, and hesitating before approaching the doorway of what appeared to be a village shop, pub and Post Office all in one. Small groups were clustered on the terrace drinking coffee and chatting, their children and dogs milling around happily.

For a moment, watching them all, Anna felt that momentary give – a release of tension – from having landed somewhere welcoming, somewhere friendly. Even if the dog was a hell-hound and her clients were equally petulant and demanding, they were hundreds of miles away and, with the sun on her face and the prospect of a beach walk and then scones, Anna felt her day might be looking up. She turned and snapped a photo on her phone to send to Kate later, a harbour view to counter all those sickening palm trees and white sands.

Her stomach rumbled at the enticing aroma coming from within; hot, buttery, salty pasties calling her name.

'You can't bring that dog in here,' a sharp voice cut through her reverie, making her jump.

Anna looked around, to see a florid-faced woman behind the Post Office counter glaring at Chewie.

'But—' Anna began, looking around at all the other dogs.

'Oh, we allow *dogs*, before you start. We just don't allow *that* dog.'

The sense of injustice hit Anna hard, before common sense reasserted itself. It wasn't Anna herself being rejected, ejected, discriminated against, whatever her default setting may suggest. It was Chewie – larger than life and twice as disobedient.

'I just need to send a parcel. An urgent parcel—' Anna began, wondering if she dared tie the dog up outside for the few minutes it would take, trying to second-guess Liza's exacting priorities: her dog or her sister's wedding?

The woman behind the counter stepped around, hovering just out of reach, eyeing Chewie warily. 'Friend of the Lyndells are you?' she said coldly.

'I'm just the house-sitter,' Anna said, as she had last night, distancing herself and speculating at the reputation that clearly preceded owner and dog alike.

'Right,' said the woman, giving her the once-over, her gaze lingering on Anna's battered tote bag and well-worn Converse. 'You don't look much like her, to be fair.'

'Just the hired help,' Anna said, shrugging. 'But grateful to be in this beautiful village for a week, to be honest. I'd never heard of Dittisham before—'

The woman snorted with laughter and shook her head. 'Yes, well, that's obvious.'

Nothing about this exchange was obvious to Anna though, and she hesitated for a moment before responding. 'Well, it's nice to explore somewhere new.' Chewie tugged at the lead again, skittering backwards in his quest to get going, to get to the beach and run free. 'Oh for the love of God, would you Just – sit – down,' Anna said firmly, brooking no nonsense, all her frustrations and confusion channelled into those three final, forceful words.

Chewie sat, nonplussed.

A round of applause echoed throughout the store and from out on the terrace, taking her by surprise.

'Been a long time coming, that!'

'Well done, my luver!'

To Anna's immense surprise, the woman in front of her transformed from prickly to affable in a moment, chortling in delight at the downcast expression on the dog's face as he sat beside Anna, almost reaching her shoulder. 'Now *that's* more like it. I wondered for a minute, a slip of a girl like you in charge of that brute. Runs amok around here he does, but do they care? I'm Molly, by the way.' She walked over and held her hand out for the package, eyebrows lifting at the Florentine address. 'This'll be expensive.'

'And overnight,' Anna said, hoping there was enough money on her debit card. Praying that Liza would, as promised, reimburse her. 'And I'm Anna.'

Molly weighed the package and eyed Anna's proffered bank card thoughtfully. 'We'll just pop it on their tab shall we, my love? Sixty-two quid is just chump change to them folks.'

'Sixty-two?' Anna breathed in sharply, sickened, tucking her card away quickly, grateful for Molly's intuition.

Every penny she had was accounted for. Not that she actually *had* a lot of monthly expenses, beyond her phone, her car and the storage locker. And she'd learned quickly that being thrifty with her daily stipend slowly inflated her savings account, because having a little money on hand would always, always give her more comfort than anything she could possibly buy, and sixty-two pounds could buy a lot of peace of mind.

Sixty-two pounds on postage was obscene by any measure.

Yet presumably pocket change to Liza Lyndell.

Parcel duly dispatched, Molly's demeanour softened by the minute.

'I won't come in,' said Anna, still standing in the doorway, 'but I don't suppose I could buy some cheese? If you could find it for me?'

Molly hollered with laughter. 'Ah, well then, you've been talking to Ruth? I'll grab you some cheddar and you can put your purse away, Anna. Anyone who's willing to take on that ridiculous dog just to get a week at the seaside earns my respect a little. And I'll even make you a coffee to take to the beach – my apology for being so . . . Well, let's just say that when it comes to the Lyndells you won't find much love lost around here. But that doesn't excuse my being rude to you.'

Taking the block of cheddar gratefully, Anna smiled. 'Sometimes the owners are lovely, when I house-sit, sometimes – well, sometimes not so much. The whole job is a bit of a lottery to be honest.' For a moment her thoughts flickered to Angus and Betty, the glorious spaniels she'd abandoned at Gravesend Manor. 'Sometimes the pets make the whole job worthwhile and sometimes it's just the view.'

Molly nodded. 'Well, you're welcome here any time, if you leave the hound at home.'

Anna smiled. 'Thank you, Molly. I'm looking forward to exploring and I need to find a bookshop. Sooner rather than later.'

Molly sucked air through her teeth and shook her head. 'Then you'll be needing to head into Dartmouth for that, my love. Not much call for books around here, we've all got too much to do.' She nodded towards a single shelf in the far corner. 'Unless there's something in our Book Exchange that catches your eye?'

Anna hesitated again, eyeing up a sulking Chewie versus the desire to have a literary companion for the night. 'I'll pop back later,' she said, begrudging the dog his absence of manners that now stood between her and escapism. 'Exploring has to be the plan for this morning. Find out all that Dittisham has to offer.'

Again, with the sniggering.

'Anna, was it? Allow me to let you in on a little secret – only the grockles, the tourists, call it "Dit-i-sham".' She deliberately emphasised each syllable with a mocking posh accent. 'Anyone who lives here, or comes regular, well then to us, it's just Ditsum. Okay?'

'Sure,' Anna replied, hesitating, convinced that both Oliver and Liza had enunciated all three syllables, despite being residents.

Molly grinned. 'And I see you've rumbled us. So maybe don't correct Lady Muck, will you? It's a small pleasure when she's throwing her weight around, but we do have a laugh.'

Anna smiled despite herself; it was rare that she felt a part of something, even something as trivial as this.

'Oh, and Anna? If you're popping over to see Ruth and Arthur, snip some of them delphiniums from the garden at The Cove – nobody'll miss 'em and it would make them both ever so happy. They planted that whole lower garden you know, before they sold it off to the Lyndells. Ruth and Arthur weren't getting any younger and I think they just gave in in the end. Badgered them into it, they did, those Lyndells. Shame though – loved her garden, did Ruth.'

Anna nodded; she could understand why.

A garden was something she could only ever dream of, inspired by the books of her childhood; Secret Gardens, Midnight Gardens, Kipling's Glory all had a lot to answer for in the gardens of Anna's imagination.

Yet, as she walked along the harbour towards the beach, her spirits were lifted by the simple image of a dormouse and a familiar refrain of delphiniums and geraniums in hues of red and blue that refused to leave her head.

Chapter 15

Dittisham, 'Ditsum', 2019

Oliver had been right, Anna realised, as Chewie exhausted himself running huge loops of the beach, springing in and out of the waves: he was an altogether nicer dog after his walk. Not exactly a pleasant companion, but at least no longer a teenager in revolt, his awkward limbs and impulses seemingly out of his own control.

Resolving to get up even earlier the next day to get the beach all to themselves, she used small cubes of cheddar to excellent effect with each command, popping a piece into her own mouth first, each and every time. Through every gate, she made him wait while she walked ahead, never missing the opportunity to stare him down if only from a few inches above his nose. No matter how uncomfortable it made her feel, being the boss was the only way to get through the week ahead with her body and mind intact.

A mile or so along the coastal path, she turned and looked back, Dittisham – Ditsum, she now heard in her head, with a smile – laid out in nature's shades of green and blue, the pastel buildings of pink and white and yellow creating the picture postcard view. As Chewie finally deigned to settle down beside her, she allowed herself to breathe: the surprise visit last night, the awkward diplomacy in the Post Office, not to mention the furore with the shoes, had all been deeply unsettling.

Not because Anna had been truly bothered so much by Henry's distress or by Liza's demands, as by her own reaction. Her Pavlovian response to smooth things over, to absolve herself and to make sure that she, Anna Wilson, was as genial and agreeable as possible. To everyone, it seemed, except herself.

'Spoiled little sod,' she said to Chewie as he gnawed on some boules of sheep shit he'd unearthed from somewhere. She looked down at her palms, red raw and spackled with dark gravel. But did he appreciate it, she wondered. Did anyone, who had life delivered on a silver platter, appreciate *any* of it?

'Anna! Anna? I thought that must be you.'

She looked down across the water and saw Henry waving from a large wooden skiff, running several lines from the back and with a large bucket of iridescent, blue-grey mackerel already on board. Without the vast jumper of the night before, he cut a slight figure, yet his clinging, damp T-shirt revealed a certain wiry strength.

'You must be doing something right, if you've worn out that bloody dog,' he called, his words slightly snatched away by the breeze. 'I'm so sorry about last night—'

Anna shook her head. 'Don't worry about it. I'm going to see your grandparents later to say thank you for the scones.'

He looked immediately chastened. 'Yeah. They weren't impressed with me last night either.' The boat rocked, a sudden swell splashing over the bow, but Henry simply adjusted his weight, unfazed. 'Can I make it up to you, maybe?

Come to the pub with me one night and meet some locals? I'd hate to think of you leaving Ditsum thinking we were all oafs and idiots.' The flush that spread up his neck was sweetly endearing; he really was terribly young.

'Maybe,' she hedged.

'Come on – a night out will be fun. And you won't have to even talk to me if you don't want to – there's live music . . .' He looked up at her hopefully.

'Well, you'd have to take me as I am,' she said, hesitating when she saw the effect of her ill-chosen words on the stead-ily increasing flush of his neck. 'I mean, I've brought jeans, jeans and jeans, so if your pub's a little fancy—'

For a moment, she felt a disconcerting swell of longing for her beautiful, indispensable jersey dress abandoned at Gravesend Manor, before shrugging it off. 'I'm not known for my grace or sartorial flair.'

He grinned, taking her caveats as a yes. 'Molly said you were a good sort. But be warned, she'll try and get you dancing.'

'Ah, now, and you'd almost convinced me to come along,' Anna laughed, teasing him.

He dithered for a second, and Anna almost took pity on him – she forgot sometimes that her own flippancy could unnerve other people quite so thoroughly.

'Come out fishing with me now?' he countered, surprising her with his resilience. 'Chewie'll be fine in a boat, won't he? He glanced around the deck of the wooden skiff, holding up a red life jacket. 'He can wear this—'

Anna laughed and shook her head. 'You're a little bit crazy, you know that?' But she couldn't deny a magnetic pull to the very idea of something carefree and careless. Just for once. For herself. Because being responsible all the time was beginning to feel more than a little exhausting.

'There are worse things to be than crazy,' Henry said seriously. He slowly pulled in the lines and rowed over towards a small jetty a little way along the promontory. 'You can climb down here, it's not steep.'

There was surely a kind of madness in taking a Great Dane out fishing?

She thought for a moment of all the risks she never took, the fun she shied away from, and looked out across the sea – small boats dotting the horizon and the gulls' raucous cries still somehow carrying the promise of summer indulgence. What was the point of this nomadic life if she didn't take pleasure in the unique experiences that crossed her path?

Tugging on Chewie's lead, Anna slithered down the grass bank. Henry leapt out and scooped the enormous dog into his arms before Chewie could really appreciate what was happening. 'Hold her steady,' Henry said to Anna as he deftly hopped back on board. He clipped Chewie into the life jacket and laughed. 'Now that's a look!' He held out his hand to Anna. 'Climb in and then I'll push us off – this rig weighs a tonne.'

Perpetually alert to any allusion to her own size or weakness, Anna dug in her heels. Flexing her arms and trying not to wince as she put pressure on her sore palms, she ignored his request and pushed them away from the jetty, hopping nimbly aboard just before it floated out of reach.

'Cool,' Henry said simply, shaking his head. 'You're feisty, aren't you? I get that.' He held up his arm, as though flexing his 'guns', yet showing only sinew and a quiet, subtle strength.

Rather than flaring up at his comment, Anna found herself softening towards him. 'Small can be strong,' Anna said. 'I'm at least eighty per cent Jack Russell, I reckon.'

'Little dog with big ideas?'

'Something like that. Determined, anyway. And something Chewie has clearly never had to concern himself with.' Anna ran a reassuring hand over the huge dog, sitting proudly in the stern, watching every flicker in the water with absolute concentration.

'My gran calls it a runner's build; the kids at school called me Steve Rogers.'

'Didn't he turn into Captain America and save the world?' Anna queried, confused.

Henry laughed and held up his hands. 'Hey, I never said they were bright!'

'Have you noticed though,' Anna said, nodding, 'that tall girls are never feisty? They're strapping or athletic.'

'Yeah, but strapping kind of makes me think of a cart-horse, so' – he grinned – 'on balance I reckon you win.'

Anna sat back and tilted her face to the sun, running her fingers through the ice-clear water as they moved out into deeper channels. Whatever she'd expected when she'd pulled into the driveway at The Cove yesterday, it hadn't been this.

'Anna, look!' Henry said, one hand holding tightly to Chewie's collar just in case. 'Quickly!'

He pointed up above them, at a small dark shape climbing up into the sky, flashes of yellow between each flap of its dark pointed wings. Henry glanced over at her briefly to check she had seen, his face alight. 'It's a peregrine falcon. And it's hunting – look.'

Anna squinted against the sunlight, the reflections from the water making it hard to see, even as Henry gave an excitable running commentary. 'See, see, how it's picking up speed,' he said in awe, as the bird began to dive, beating its wings so quickly now that it seemed to drop like a pebble from the heavens. 'Faster than a Ferrari,' Henry murmured, just as the falcon pulled its wings back sharply, slowing with intent, just as Anna realised the focus of its efforts. She winced as those bright yellow talons flashed forth and literally plucked the small swift from the air.

'Oh God,' she gasped. 'That's just so – brutal,' she breathed, just as Henry said, 'Beautiful.'

They looked at each other in confusion, even as the falcon bore its prize away.

'It's just nature,' Henry said apologetically. 'It's majestic though, right, seeing all that power, that grace – small but determined,' he joked, uncertain how to garner the reaction he'd been expecting. 'It's incredibly rare to see that, you know. Special,' he insisted.

Anna nodded. 'I can imagine. It's just a lot to take in – it all happened so fast.' She looked around them, up into the sky. 'Now I know what I'm looking for, I won't spook so easily.'

Henry frowned at her, still clearly trying to get a read on this girl in his boat. 'Ah well, the last I saw was six months ago, but you know – you're welcome to stay . . .'

'I think maybe I like nature more when it's David Attenborough narrating the carnage,' Anna said apologetically.

'City girl, huh?' Henry nodded as though that explained everything.

Anna shrugged. 'Kind of an everywhere but nowhere girl, really.'

'Cool,' said Henry again. 'That sounds exciting. I never really left South Hams until I finished school, what with Mum being so ill and my gran having her hands full.' He looked awkward for a moment, that slight flush warming his neck again. 'And now I've made my choices, built my life here so . . .'

'And your mum?' Anna asked.

'Yeah, she died,' Henry said, the bluntness still not disguising the obvious pain it caused him to say that. 'So, you know, I'm lucky really – to grow up here, with my grandparents.'

Perhaps it was the word 'lucky' – that disingenuous praise that had been bandied about for Anna's entire life – or perhaps it was the sudden set to his jaw that spoke of so many emotions unspoken, but Anna found herself leaning forward confidentially.

'I grew up in foster care – some good times, some bad – but I understand, Henry, that sometimes "lucky" doesn't really feel that way, does it?'

His eyes widened as he looked at her, suddenly so vulnerable, so very young, all the bravado stripped away. 'But you're – you're so . . .' He grinned awkwardly. 'Well, maybe you're feisty for a reason then, Anna. But to me, you seem lovely. Normal, you know?'

She smiled, knowing all too well what a compliment that was. She pointed to a family of mallards, bobbing along the edge of the coastline, dipping occasionally with their tail feathers in the air. 'You see those ducks, swimming?'

'Sure.' He grinned again. 'I get it – so you're all paddly under the surface? Is that what you're telling me?'

'Something like that,' Anna said. 'And you know, Henry, seeing that peregrine falcon really *was* amazing. The kind of thing I feel *truly* lucky to have seen.' *A kind of borrowed magic*, she thought, but didn't say.

'Even if you were secretly feeling sorry for the swift?'

'Well, you were already rooting for the falcon – it's nice to shout out for the underdog sometimes,' Anna insisted.

'Cool,' said Henry again. 'You won't hear any complaints from me on that front.'

Chapter 16

Dittisham, 2019

Later that afternoon, Anna sank back into the sofa and closed her eyes, still feeling as though she were moving on the water. Chewie's head was heavy on her lap as she took a moment to admire the view from the sitting room window at The Cove, attempting to chart her earlier route along the coastline and out to sea. Her skin tingled, having caught the sun on the skiff, and her limbs ached pleasantly from a little fresh air and exercise. Even Liza's constant phone calls were barely a blip of annoyance.

Yet still, she startled, as her phone vibrated beside her.

Anna took a calming breath, prepared to be professional, before smiling when she saw Kate's number on the screen; fleetingly relieved that Kate had chosen to call now – now that Anna was a little more herself than she had been a day or two earlier.

'Aren't you supposed to be having oodles of sex and staring into the sunset?' she said, by way of greeting, tapping the screen until Kate's laugh filled the room, even from the middle of the Indian Ocean.

'Dear God, Anna. What were we thinking coming to a couples-only resort? It's like they're all in competition with each other to prove how in love they are! Quite frankly, it's a bit of a mood killer. All the soul-gazing and hand-holding over supper alone is enough to put you off your octopus curry.'

'Tell me you're joking,' Anna began.

'About the snogging or the octopus?' Kate cut in. 'We could be having so much *fun* here, you and me. The people-watching potential is insane. There's probably an anthropology dissertation in it somewhere. The posturing and naivety alone! Not that I would *ever* judge.'

'Of course you wouldn't,' Anna agreed with a smile. 'And much as I'm delighted that you wish I was on your honeymoon, I'm not sure Duncan would agree.'

The exhalation carried across the oceans between them. 'Ah he wouldn't mind. There's feck all to do here once you've marvelled at the petals on your bed and the pretty little beach. We walked round the island six times yesterday just for a change of scene.'

Anna paused, this conversation jarring so comprehensively with everything she'd ever heard about honeymoons, or perhaps what people had chosen to share. 'I'm sure he'll think of a way to keep you entertained. He's a resourceful chap, your husband.'

'He is,' Kate said drily. 'He's persuaded the houseboy to take him out bonefishing.'

'No!' Anna said, a little bit shocked despite herself. So much for romance eclipsing all the detritus in your mind. She hesitated. 'And you – you didn't want to go along?'

'Hmm now let me see – up at dawn, two hours in a tiny boat to a different tiny island to stand in the shallows trying to catch something that looks a lot like Professor Welham, and will probably taste like mud – and presumably bones.'

'That'll be a no, then?'

'Quite. But if you'll believe me, I wasn't actually phoning to moan – First World problems and all that – I wanted to see how *you* were faring? Was it just awful? Be honest.'

Anna stilled, her mind running circles and trying not to trip over itself. How on earth did Kate know? *Kate*, who Anna had wanted to call so very badly, who had been Anna's obvious touchstone to reach for after that awful, hideous night in Oxford, but who had been strictly off limits on her romantic holiday of a lifetime.

'Well,' Anna began, and then stopped. What could she possibly say about how very close Kate's wedding night had been to becoming a truly degrading experience? Rather than simply terrifying and humiliating.

'I mean, I know he promised to be on his best behaviour and all that, but Max does have form being a twat with a drink in his hand, right?' Kate continued, before Anna could formulate a sensible response. 'Duncan suggested he apologise, but really, what could he possibly say to make amends? Other than admitting that he's a deeply flawed, deeply insecure individual who never bothered to develop a personality and still relies on good looks and charm to excuse his lamentable lack of intellectual prowess.'

Anna was silenced, not only by the left turn she hadn't seen coming, but also the vehemence of Kate's disapproval of her new brother-in-law. In a funny way, the disloyalty to Max was just the reassurance that Anna needed that she herself was still a priority to Kate.

'Say what you think, why don't you,' Anna laughed, relieved that she didn't have to talk about Andrew Fraser while the what-ifs and maybes were still so fresh in her mind and her brow-bone still throbbed painfully lest she forget for a moment.

'Well!' said Kate. 'He may be easy on the eye but he makes my brain hurt with all that squandered privilege. What did you ever see in him, Pod?'

'All that squandered privilege probably,' said Anna honestly. 'It was kind of intriguing, you know? Or maybe you don't. But seeing someone who has literally everything handed to them on a plate, yet seemed to care so very little; it was kind of fascinating.'

'You see – that's why we study chimps, not date them,' Kate snorted.

'He wasn't a chimp though, was he?' Anna said, thinking back. 'He was polished and confident and incredibly fortunate. And he noticed me.'

'You say that as though nobody else ever did! All those nerdy hearts breaking all over Oxford, Anna. Did you seriously never see that?'

Anna shrugged, aware that Kate couldn't see her, yet unable to formulate a sensible reply. It certainly didn't tally with her own recollections. Recollections that still had the power to make her skin crawl with impotent fury.

The only thing that was crystal clear in Anna's memory was that Max was a thief. Anna's value to him had been in her work, her ideas. It was never about falling in love with her.

Adept at taking a hint even across the oceans, Kate yawned. 'So come on then, what's it like being back in Oxford anyway? Is it strange and nostalgic, or are you so taken with the place that you're tempted to stay?' She gave a half-laugh of awkwardness. 'I can't deny I'm hoping for the latter but presume you're still a permanent flight risk?'

Easy ground. Anna relaxed a little. 'Actually, I've already moved. I'm down by the sea, in a vast house full of pointy corners and no books. But there's a sweet parakeet and a mental Great Dane so, you know, it all balances out.'

'Jesus! I can't keep up with you,' Kate protested. 'I honestly don't know how you do it, Pod. Just the thought of always packing, always living out of a bag . . .'

'It's hardly a bother – you know me, travel light,' Anna cut in.

'I know, I know. But the thing that worries me, us actually, is that you seem to travel light emotionally as well. You're never in one place long enough to put down roots, make friends. Maybe date a little.'

'But that's why old friends are the best,' Anna reminded her quietly, the words hitting painfully close to home. Even amongst the decadent luxury of The Cove, it took an enormous strength of will not to feel a little bit lonely. Even with Chewie snoring loudly beside her.

'Sarah was so impressed with you by the way,' Kate said, taking another about-turn. 'I mean, you and I both know you were being all weird and evasive about your writing, like usual, but she just put it down to "creative reticence". So, you know, you *could* pick up the phone any time and she'd take your call. Called you intriguing.'

'Ah well, that's me: a riddle wrapped in a mystery inside an enigma.' Levity had long since become Anna's default setting when emotions overcame her.

'Alright, Churchill,' Kate laughed. 'But I think it was more that she felt you probably had something to say. Something special actually. She thinks you might have a unique voice – I mean, she has a point, you've seen life from all angles, right?'

'Are we calling my misbegotten youth research now, then?' Anna said, deeply touched, but nevertheless uncomfortable.

'You're fascinating—' Kate began earnestly.

'All the boys say so,' Anna cut in, smoky voice and attitude drowning out the prickling feelings of discomfort.

'Don't be flippant with me – I know your wily ways, Anna Wilson.' Kate was taking no nonsense. And that was probably another reason why old friends were the best friends: they knew your shit and called you on it.

'So, where to next then, while I'm stuck suffering on Love Island?' Kate said, the irony heavy in her voice.

Anna laughed. 'You poor soul. Maybe have a massage to deal with the stress?'

'Don't dodge the question. Somebody needs to know where you are.'

Still reeling from Sarah's beautiful comments, Kate's warm compassion was nearly Anna's undoing. 'Look, this month *is* a little out of the ordinary. It's all ad hoc, and kind of disconcerting, if I'm honest,' Anna replied.

'So, while it looks like chaos normally, it's actually *planned* chaos?'

'Something like that . . .' Anna managed, her hand pressed firmly to her heart, breathing slowly out to allay a sudden urge to overshare. 'So tell me about the honeymoon suite? Is it terribly romantic waking up to the sounds of the ocean?'

Kate laughed. 'Mate, I have to tell you, this romance business is *hard* work – I'm still picking rose petals out of my—'

Anna winced and tried not to listen.

Oversharing was not an issue that Kate worried about. Apparently.

Chapter 17

Dittisham, 2019

Buoyed by her wonderful chat with Kate, Anna felt almost renewed, singing along to the radio as she prepared her supper, uninhibited by her inability to hold a note or indeed accurately identify a lyric. Leia burbled happily from her aviary, but Anna could have sworn she saw Chewie roll his eyes in disbelief.

'Hey, buster, your yowling is hardly in tune, you know,' Anna pointed out, waving the weighty chef's knife in her hand for emphasis.

It was amazing how cathartic a bit of slicing and dicing had been, and now the kitchen counter was adorned by a veritable rainbow of stir-fry ingredients, all julienned and ready to go. Quick, easy suppers for the rest of the week.

It was almost a shame though, Anna realised, to apply her usual whistle-stop efficiency to catering when she had this amazing kitchen at her disposal. Chances are, it cost more than any flat Anna herself could even contemplate affording, but rather than being ostentatious, it felt professional, sleek and entirely enjoyable.

Sipping a chilled Seedlip from the glass-fronted fridge dedicated entirely to an array of drinks, both soft and vintage, she looked around, leaning back against the marble counter-tops and surveying her domain. Well, her domain-of-the-day, she smiled.

She imagined the long beechwood table laid up for a casual kitchen supper, her own friends clustered around, crystal flutes in hand . . . Well, maybe not crystal for a casual supper, but there didn't seem to be much call for IKEA's finest tumblers in Liza's kitchen. She imagined huge platters of rocket and parmesan, drizzled with the treacly balsamic vinegar she'd found in the larder. Maybe a crackling rolled loin of pork with crispy sage? Or more realistically a vast lasagne – wasn't the company more important than the menu after all?

And here Anna would be, relaxed, at home – the perfect hostess. In her sleek, professional kitchen . . .

Answerable to no one.

It was a thought that had been bubbling in her subcon-scious for days now since she'd fled from Gravesend Manor. Yet, in all honesty, Anna could no longer deny that, with each layer of her entrenched defences that was sloughed away, she felt not only more raw, but also more alive than she had in years. As though she had nothing to lose by making the diffi-cult decisions. As though she had options beyond a nomadic call to evasion.

She'd even plucked up the courage to venture onto Rightmove earlier, to click on the lozenge that said 'To Rent', stymied only by the pop-up message innocently asking for a location or postcode to search. A little more thought was clearly required.

'Dare to dream,' she murmured to Chewie, who was lying at her feet determined to catch anything interesting that fell to the floor. But, really, how realistic was the dream anyway

– and not simply because this house wasn't hers, but because Liza's kitchen table seated at least sixteen people.

Anna wasn't sure that she *knew* sixteen people.

Possibly, if one called in fleeting friendships and acquaintances, she could make it to a round dozen.

Still, it was hardly a pressing issue: she had always counted quality over quantity when it came to friends. And her hit-and-run approach to the people she met on her travels was hardly conducive to lasting friendships either.

That didn't stop the longing for a kitchen table supper though and – Anna cranked up the radio – she could allow herself a little fun pretending.

Singing into the spatula as she tossed tenderstem broccoli and ribbons of red and yellow peppers together, Anna danced around the kitchen, around the dog, around the sixteen Perspex chairs. Her talent for self-sufficiency may have begun as a salve to her childhood of uncertainty, but as an adult it was a gift. She could find happiness anywhere; all she needed was a good book, a cheesy song on the radio and a little peace of mind. And it was no coincidence that her peace of mind had dramatically improved since her phone ran out of juice, and for as long as it took to recharge next door, then she would make the most of it. No call to duty. No temptation to check her Home Network bookings. Or her ratings.

Her time was her own.

A knock on the front door lurched her out of her improvised homage to Madonna and brought a flush to her cheeks, as she glanced around to check whether she'd been caught in the act. 'Fat lot of good you are,' she said to Chewie, who apparently couldn't give two fucks who was knocking on the door, his focus still welded to the strips of chicken sizzling in the wok.

'It's only me!' called Henry from outside.

Wiping her hands on a linen tea-towel – far too nice to be a tea-towel – to avoid any oil stains on the brass door handle, Anna jogged through to the hallway. 'This is a nice surprise,' she said, watching his face light up.

'Oh well – even better.' He smiled. 'I thought you might enjoy a little barbeque on the beach? There's a bunch of us getting together and you'd get to meet everyone.' He shrugged. 'Well, you don't have to meet everyone, but I thought we might have fun?'

There was a hint of flirtation in his invitation. A hint that he quickly smothered. 'My grandparents might come down too – it's the more the merrier really.'

'Sounds lovely,' Anna said, surprised by how genuinely she meant it. 'I just need to get myself sorted. I was just making a stir-fry.'

'Cool,' said Henry. 'I can help you eat it if you like – it'll be hours 'til the hog roast is done and I'm starving.'

And just like that, he walked through to the kitchen and picked up the spatula.

Like they were, well, friends or something.

Anna eyed the table as she followed him through. Sixteen empty chairs looked back.

Hair plastered to her forehead, plastic beaker of cider in her hand and the flickering flames of the bonfire lighting up the laughter and conversation on the beach in the darkness, Anna danced like nobody was watching. All around her, bodies moved to the beat, caught up in themselves and the music. The sand was damp and cold, squishy between her bare toes, but she hadn't felt so warm, or so alive, in months.

Sure, it was no Full Moon party in Thailand, but the food

and the company eclipsed the chill in the air now the sun had long since set.

This was what freedom felt like. This was the joy she remembered.

A timely reminder as to why she lived the way she did: dancing on the beach was her office, she thought to herself with a hiccupping laugh, carefree and happy.

The cider sloshed over her wrist and she discreetly tipped the rest away. She was having too much fun to explain herself tonight.

The first sip she'd taken to be polite, slipping down like apple juice.

And then, well, then she wasn't really sure how many times her cup had been refilled because of the dancing, the banter, the general merriment. But that didn't mean she had to drink it to have a good time.

Sometimes, it was just easier that way.

She looked around her, trying to fix this moment in her memory. This feeling.

The last few years everything had run like clockwork – country by country, continent by continent – and yet all those months of unimpeded travel now blurred together. The experiences somehow melded into an indistinguishable litany of glorious bedrooms and heart-stopping vistas that, in hindsight, all seemed somehow beige.

But, *now*, after these last few days, where seemingly everything had been destined to go wrong, challenges thrown up at every corner? When the logical response would be to take a hint from the universe, maybe even heed Kate's advice that it was time to move on from moving on?

On the contrary, these last few days had been the first time in a long time that Anna had actually felt fully present. For better and worse, it had been full technicolour living.

It was as though that night at Gravesend Manor had shocked her out of her stupor – perhaps it had been the fear, or the memories? Or simply enough adrenaline to charge her system and restart her heart.

She twirled to the music, arms swaying, her body alive to every sensation.

Closing her eyes, she smiled, grateful to Henry for this invitation. Grateful to her own body for remembering why she lived the way she did. There was nothing wrong with a little pleasure-seeking when you were young – quite literally footloose and fancy-free.

'Anna! Anna! Come and say hi to my grandparents.' Henry strode across the sand towards her, jolting her from her reverie, his shoulders somehow broader and more powerful in the firelight.

'Sure,' said Anna, sweeping her hair back from her face and looking up at him with a smile. One of the very few perks of being this short was the ability to look up at a man; one of the ongoing challenges of her life was finding a man worth looking up to.

'I'm so glad you're down here with the young folk,' said Henry's gran, introducing herself by pulling Anna into an enormous, lung-emptying hug. 'I'm Ruth. And I'll wager you could use a night off.' She gave Anna a knowing look, as though she knew all too well how demanding the Lyndells could be. 'And my Henry said you saw the peregrine hunt? Now, isn't that something special?'

'Ah nonsense, the lass travels all over the world, Ruthie. One little falcon getting himself some dinner isn't going to rate much.' Fisherman's jumper, white beard, twinkling eyes that were one part Henry, one part mischief.

'And you must be Arthur,' Anna replied. 'And at the risk of

disagreeing with you within moments of meeting, I have to tell you that you're quite, quite wrong.'

Arthur guffawed, clapping her on the shoulder so hard her teeth rattled. 'Oh Henry, my lad, I can see why you like this one.'

Henry stared firmly down at the sand, unwilling to meet Anna's inquisitive look. 'I am so, so sorry,' he murmured, the humour and resignation obvious in his voice.

Anna grinned. 'He's been brilliant actually, showing me round and helping me settle in.' She paused. 'It's nice to have some local knowledge.'

Ruth nodded. 'Well, he had some making up to do, after scaring you half to death that first night.' She tucked her arm through Anna's, her face turning instinctively to the warmth of the bonfire. 'But does he have it right, love? Are you constantly on the move, looking after people's houses and pets and whatnot?'

Anna nodded. 'It's not for everyone, but it works for me.' She shrugged, honesty prevailing. 'Well, most of the time.'

'And do you not ever get homesick? Long for a little continuity over glamour?' Ruth persisted. 'A nice relationship maybe?'

'Well, it's not all glamour, I can tell you,' Anna hedged, a prescient whisper of where this conversation was heading cooling the back of her neck. 'Once you've wrangled alpacas out of your bed, or given a Maine Coon his medicine twice a day, you remember it's a job not a holiday.'

Ruth's face softened. 'Oh love, I'm not saying you don't earn your keep. I was just wondering how you manage for a social life. Nights like tonight? With your friends? Or your young man?' This time there was no escaping the fact that Ruth was sounding her out. 'Henry's a lovely boy, but he's had enough heartache in his life, Anna,' she said gently, giving her arm a squeeze.

Anna nodded. 'No heartache on the agenda, I promise,' she said.

'And with Oscar as well, he—'

'Now who's for a dance?' Arthur interrupted them, giving Ruth a firm pat on the backside. 'We've still got it, haven't we, Ruthie? Show these youngsters a thing or two?' He dropped a kiss onto the top of her head. 'Happily married for forty years now, Anna,' he said proudly.

Ruth swatted at him with a laugh. 'Now if that isn't an oxymoron, I don't know what is.'

'Who are you calling a moron, woman?' he said, pulling her into his arms.

They bickered even as they danced, Anna noticed, but the love between them was so real as to be almost tangible.

'They're lovely,' Anna said to Henry, who stood close beside her, watching them dance.

'They're embarrassing as all hell, but yeah, they're pretty cool actually. And they've just always been there for me, no matter how many times I've made life harder for them. They've been really supportive about all my choices. No matter how left-field.'

He stepped fractionally closer until Anna could feel his warm breath on her shoulder. 'When my mum was ill they showed me what parenting really means – they literally nursed her right to the end.' His voice cracked a little, the grief still visibly raw. 'I want that one day.'

Anna turned to look up at him again, her hand instinctively reaching out for his, touched by a sense that his trust, his confidences, bonded them together somehow. More than virtual strangers hand in hand on a beach.

'Not the dying young part, obviously.' He gave a strangled laugh.

'Obviously,' Anna replied.

'Just, you know, the absolute devotion . . .' he said quietly. 'Bickering and all.'

From where Anna was standing, warm and safe beside him, she could see his point. To be anchored, both literally and metaphorically, in a place like this with family around you? What could be better – even in the toughest of times?

Chapter 18

Dittisham, 2019

The next morning, Anna blew her hair from her forehead, her skin already warm and tight with salty air, the day ahead promising to be every bit as hot and humid as the soporific weatherman had promised the night before.

Hence the early walk.

And a chance to gather her thoughts before the crowds descended for a day at the beach, driven by some primal urge to capitalise on a few hours of sunshine before the British summer could revert to type.

Chewie looped the beach without his usual enthusiasm, tongue lolling, as he half-heartedly chased the seagulls staking claim on the treasure left by the ebbing tide. The haze of the early-morning sun cast faint ethereal shadows on the sand, as it climbed beyond the headland to the east, and Anna breathed out slowly, the nightmares of her interrupted sleep finally receding little by little in tandem with the waves.

It was Henry's fault really, she reasoned: his awe for that doubtless beautiful, but equally murderous peregrine; his grief over his mother's death somehow assuaged by a gentle acceptance of life and death; and his thoughtful, affectionate touch on the beach last night. And throughout it all, decency. So many questions in his young life were seemingly without answers, but the big ones – the ones that shaped a childhood, a personality – were apparently absolute. He had been loved. He was loved. And here, in 'Ditsum', he would always have a place to call home.

The guilt from a lingering, callous thought lay heavy on Anna's conscience. For how many times in her life had she wondered – dare she say it? *wished* – that her own life would have been so much improved had her mother died rather than simply abandoned her?

Too many.

But sometimes the truth *was* uncomfortable, right?

Somehow, by her very absence, Anna's mother had created greater ripples than her presence might ever have done.

She breathed out slowly, willing the thoughts from her exhausted mind and, for a moment, she allowed herself to revel in the splendid isolation. Not a soul in sight and a view to be savoured, before wondering – as she so often did these days – what it might be like to share the experience. Not necessarily with a boyfriend, but with *someone*.

Someone without four legs and his nose buried deep into a tangled heap of glistening seaweed.

Chewie yelped and leapt back from his investigations, as a small but disgruntled crab scuttled away from the swathes of seaweed. The ridiculous dog skidded backwards in alarm, before running over to Anna and thrusting his wounded nose into her crotch. She was so busy comforting him that at first she didn't notice that they were no longer alone on the beach, didn't notice the young father walking along the tideline, singing softly, his feet in the water and a baby papoose strapped to his chest, his attention entirely on the tiny bundle within, arms and legs stuck out like a starfish.

It was the lilting refrain that caught her attention, the Beatles track an old favourite of hers and entirely appropriate for this beautiful morning as it carried across the sand.

'Here comes the sun . . .'

Anna caught herself in a wave of unexpected emotion. There was something so simple, so pure, about his devotion. His absolute focus. The easy familiarity which spoke of hours dedicated to this new soul. She couldn't help but watch, all the while feeling a little as though she were intruding, yet somehow unable to look away.

'Anna?'

She blinked, thrown from her reflections, and completely blindsided, half wondering whether her thoughts had summoned him here. 'Henry?'

He left the water's edge and quickly closed the gap between them, leaving neat, distinct footprints in the wet sand. 'I thought I was the only one mad enough to be out and about this early.' He looked incredibly awkward for a moment, before obvious pride reasserted itself. 'This is Oscar.'

Anna smiled. The dozing baby, although older than she'd realised from afar, certainly suited his name; indeed he already had the look of a little old man about him – a neatly buttoned cardigan and navy chinos gave the impression he was heading off to teach a little physics or history after his stroll.

'He's very sweet,' she said hesitantly, wondering how Oscar fitted into Henry's life, and equally unsure how to ask.

'He's mine,' Henry blurted. 'I mean, he's my son.'

Anna found herself simply nodding; the bond between them was almost primitive – there had really been no doubt – and yet still she found herself surprised.

Hurt, even.

They may only have shared a small glimpse of their histories, but this omission felt like a glaring oversight.

'I'm so sorry I didn't tell you,' Henry said, one hand automatically holding his sleeping son close. 'And I don't know why I didn't really. But here he is – six months of boundless energy and rampant insomnia – and the best decision I ever made.'

'Decision?' Anna said, pulling her gaze away from Oscar and looking at Henry properly for the first time. 'Sorry – you don't have to answer that. And honestly, no apology needed.'

He reached out, missing her hand by only an inch or two. 'I disagree. And it sounds a little bit mad, but there's not many boundaries round here. Everyone knows everything and I can promise you, they're never short of an opinion. So, it was just – well, it was really lovely to have a conversation with someone who didn't.'

Anna smiled, watching as his hands strayed to cradle Oscar's dangling feet. 'I can see that. It must be all-encompassing having a new baby.' She broke off, unable to ignore the niggle of discomfort that she had misread their new-found intimacy so completely.

Her own duplicity conveniently forgotten.

This sense of connection – or even a desire to connect – didn't happen often as Anna made her way around the world, dipping in and out of other lives. Yet when it did, she had become well versed in the art of reframing her own behaviour to be a little more acceptable than it probably was: fast friendships, intense relationships, a taste of vulnerability so much easier with an expiration date.

Even if she was the only one who knew that.

'We're not together,' Henry said intently. 'Oscar's mum and me, if that's what you're thinking.'

Anna blinked, a little shocked that the thought hadn't even entered her mind. And she didn't actually like what that might say about her. 'Ok-ay.'

Could it be that her own interest in Henry was so fleeting as to make his circumstances irrelevant?

The weight of unspoken hurt in her throat suggested not, and for all its discomfort, it was also a relief. A relief caught on the tail by a more galling realisation: that her entire being was focused on the slumbering Oscar. On the weight of his lashes on those pinked, plump cheeks. On the rhythmic clasping of his miniature hands into fists. On the absolute contentment and trust as he leaned into the comfort of his father's chest.

'He's wonderful,' she said simply, Henry's pleasure at her reaction written all over his face.

'I think so,' he said. 'But then I am rather biased.' He shifted slightly, readjusting the papoose, moving fractionally closer to Anna, a waft of baby powder and warmth catching in the air. 'I've always wanted to be a dad.'

Instinctively Anna held out her hand, watching in fascination as Oscar's hand curled around her finger and held fast. 'How . . .' she began, before wondering where to even begin with all the things she suddenly, *desperately*, wanted to know.

Henry, eager to please, and slightly missing the point, saved the awkward silence. 'I've known Lily since I was six. We've been best friends, well, almost for ever when you think about it but we never went out. And honestly, I think that's why we knew we could make it work when this one took us a bit by surprise.' He shifted slightly. 'A few dodgy ciders and we're still not sure why that one night seemed like such a good idea. But now we have Oscar. And me and Lily – we've always liked each other, you know? Like, properly respected each other as people. A proper mate.'

Mate. A simple word with so many connotations, but Anna was struck hard by Henry's convictions that it was the friendship, more than any whirlwind romance, that would sustain them.

She nodded, still trying to alight on the question she actually wanted to ask. 'But how – how did you know you were ready? I mean, where does a person even *begin* in being a parent?' She gave an awkward laugh. 'A good parent, I mean?'

Henry hesitated, seemingly realising that there were so many layers to Anna's questions. 'My mum and dad did everything by the book, right? But she still died. And our family never really got over that.' He paused, correcting himself. '*I* never really got over that.' He gave Anna a goofy smile. 'But like I said, I've truly always wanted to be a dad, and I reckon there's more than one way to be a family. Me and Lily, we're making it work. We'll carry on making it work, co-parenting this little wombat because we both love him more than anything else in the whole world. It's not perfect. But then, what is? But we're better parents than many. We're young. We're not in a relationship but we support each other and split our time with Oscar. So really, it all comes down to putting him first, you know?'

Anna nodded. She did know that. She'd never experienced that herself, but on so many levels it really was that simple.

'Are you okay?' Henry asked, after a moment. 'I haven't upset you?'

'You have absolutely not upset me,' Anna replied, her finger still caught in the warm, sticky clasp of Oscar's fist. 'You have impressed me, though.' She shrugged. 'I guess I'm a little in awe of anyone who can make that commitment, even more so of anyone who has the resilience to see it through.'

The lie was ready on her lips, so easily trotted out over the years. A twist of the truth to imply some biological impediment to having children, but Henry's gentle honesty disarmed her. 'I guess I'm too afraid of history repeating itself to risk it. If I turned out to be anything like the disaster that my own parents . . .' She broke off, frowning. There was sharing and then there was baring her soul – she was unused to either.

'Ah, the dodgy parent gene,' Henry said knowingly, nodding his head in recognition. 'My mate Josh worries about that all the time.'

Anna looked up at him crossly, her surprise and exposure making her tense.

'I don't think you're alone in having that concern, is all I'm saying,' Henry said softly, reaching out and rubbing her arm. His touch was kindness personified, yet still Anna felt herself contract. 'Have you never thought that you might be the pendulum that swings so far the other way simply *because* of the childhood you had? Because you, Anna Wilson, strike me as a very lovely person, who might yet make a very lovely mum one day.' He nodded down towards Oscar's hand entwined with hers and gave a rueful smile.

'But again,' he said, 'I think I might be slightly biased on that front too.' His smile was filled with teasing affection. 'Have you never really thought that having a family might yet be worth throwing caution to the wind and giving it a go?'

Anna breathed in slowly, fighting her instincts to rebuff, or rewrite her own history.

'Once. I thought so once.' She nodded to herself as she spoke. 'But the timing wasn't right. And the boy wasn't right. And loving him wasn't enough to build a life on together, because he wasn't actually very nice.' She offered a watery, apologetic smile. 'But I truly thought that *I* might be enough, on my own, if I was completely and utterly committed to that little soul, to making it work. Like you have.'

Henry stayed silent, patiently letting her work through what she wanted to say. Yet another sign that he was probably a much nicer human being than she was.

'But I . . .' The pain, it seemed, never really went away. She hesitated; swallowed the memory of the blue lines on the pregnancy test, swallowed the hopes and dreams that had toyed with her so briefly all those years ago. The insurmountable doubts. 'It didn't work out. Life intervened.'

'One false start doesn't mean you give up altogether though, Anna. Not if it's something that's important to you,' Henry said.

'Oh, I don't know,' Anna replied. 'Maybe it was a lucky escape. For the baby. For me?' She'd said the same words before, but still didn't quite believe them. Even the thought of that time, years ago, still had the capacity to wind her. It was better not to open that particular Pandora's box of pain. 'It's actually been easier since I just closed the door on that kind of life. And it's not for everyone, right? We don't all get a happy ever after, just from willing it so.'

'I don't believe you,' Henry said, his eyes never leaving her face. 'And I don't think fear is a good enough reason not to follow your heart.'

Anna laughed, a small yelp of mirth at his endearing naivety. She would never see this wonderfully earnest young man once this week was over and a reckless disregard for her own habitual discretion swept over her.

'Oh, Henry, you darling boy. Fear is an excellent motivator for almost everything. To do something. To avoid something. To plan your life around the line of least resistance.'

He stilled, even as Oscar stirred, awoken by her outburst.

'I get that you've been afraid, Anna. I do. Honestly. But you only answer to *you* now, right? If you make the wrong call, you can change path. There isn't only one way to do anything.'

She frowned, the words jumbling into an order that jarred with her own reality. Her whole life she'd been telling herself the same story: there was a template for being a proper family, a proper writer, a proper partner . . . Henry was right in part, but the sentiment was misguided: there *was* a right way, and a wrong way.

And Anna, who had fought so hard to outstrip the trajectory expected for people like her, with childhoods like hers, was determined to make the right choices. The perfect choices. Or simply not make them at all.

Chapter 19

Dittisham, 2019

Henry and Anna walked along the beach, settling Oscar back into his snuffling doze and giving Chewie the chance to run gentle loops through the shallow waters. Occasionally their arms would brush together and Anna felt herself grow increasingly aware of his proximity, yet theirs was a comfortable silence as they let the waves and the vocal 'kryks' of the resident seagulls fill the need for words.

Every now and again, Oscar would jerk in his dreams, little arms and legs shooting out rigid, making Anna jump, yet Henry took it all in his stride. The very definition of a hands-on dad, he cradled the sleeping baby against him, and occasionally dropped a kiss onto Oscar's downy head.

'You're very sweet with him,' Anna said when he glanced up and caught her watching.

He shrugged. 'Why wouldn't I be? He's fabulous. Hard work, but everything I ever wanted.' He gave her another goofy grin. 'Although I might not have been so generous at 3 a.m. on the fifth nappy change. But to my mind, you always get out of a relationship what you're prepared to put in. So, you strip the sheets and sing a lullaby and remind yourself that this little fella is entirely reliant on you. On his mum. And you make the best world for him that you possibly can.'

Anna blinked hard, her emotions apparently so readily on call this last week. Imagine what a life little Oscar would have with parents that adored him so unconditionally; with parents who were committed to making it work, even outside the boundaries of a traditional nuclear family. With parents who seemingly didn't actually care about how that might look to the world at large.

They wanted to raise their son here, with love, with friends and family around him.

Home: an ever-fixed mark that would give him constancy and a sense of belonging.

How could that possibly be wrong?

And in that moment, as the sun broke through over the haze above the headland and the waves sparkled and glistened, Anna began to wonder whether she had been horribly mistaken for a very, very long time.

'Aren't you scared of getting it wrong though? All that responsibility?' she ventured, her own fears and insecurities still colouring her every experience.

'A bit. I mean, who wouldn't be? These little buggers are slippery.' He grinned. 'But I'm not doing this on my own, Anna. I know Lily and I aren't together, but we're part of something here, and on the days it gets a bit much, I can guarantee that my gran is there with open arms to pinch this little fella for a few hours, or even park him with Molly at the Post Office. All five of her kids have left home so she's always up for a little cuddle.' He blushed. 'With Oscar, I mean.'

He stopped for a moment and turned to look at her, the sun behind him blurring his features into shadow but the intensity in his words no less diluted. 'I think if a person waits for everything in life to be perfect, then they will always be waiting. And life throws curveballs anyway – so what was perfect one minute can be broken the next.' His voice cracked a little. 'I had a wonderful, amazing, loving mum. And then she was gone. Life's too short to be on hold, Anna.' He reached out and took her hand, squeezing it gently as he held her gaze. 'If you take one thing away from your stay here, I really wish it would be that.'

She prickled slightly. She knew pity when she heard it and it never felt good.

'A little caution is no bad thing, when you've seen what life can throw at you,' she said, hating the self-righteous justification that sprang so readily to her lips. Wanting Henry to step back, to stop looking at her as though he could read her mind and most of all to stop the deluge of uncomfortable questions that were scrolling through her mind like the credits on a movie.

He let go.

And instantly she wished he hadn't. Contrary as ever.

'So tell me. Tell me how your life is better for being cautious, for waiting, not doing. I'm not being arsey, Anna, I promise; I'm just genuinely intrigued. Because you talked about writing and about travelling, and your friend Kate, but you never say where you're heading, or what exactly it is you're waiting for.'

Anna stared at Oscar, willing him to wake, to throw a spanner into the conversation and save her from Henry's well-meaning but entirely intrusive questions. 'You don't really know me,' she said instead.

'No. You're right. I don't. But I'd like to.' He smoothed Oscar's cardigan, gathered at the shoulders by the papoose, and then looked at Anna with such open regard, such devastating honesty, that Anna felt her irritation ebb away.

'And I'm not being cagey,' she said. 'Honestly. It's just that I don't really like being quizzed.'

'Okay,' he said simply. 'I didn't think I was quizzing you, so much as finding out what your plans were. But I'll stop. Hey, Anna – I'll stop. The very last thing I want is to make you uncomfortable.' He gave an awkward smile. 'You might not know this about me, but almost everyone in my life has always been in my life. I don't range far. So making a *new* friend – well, I don't have much practice with that . . .'

His cheeks were flushed and she could tell that she'd made him feel uncomfortable now too. Tit for tat. An easy, habitual deflection, but a hollow victory.

In fact, none of her usual coping mechanisms felt all that comforting right now. It was as though that one night with Andrew Fraser had morphed her life into some kind of snow globe, where even the slightest movement or deviation threw up a blizzard of emotions and unanswered questions. And that, in itself, hurt more than the physical bruises she'd been smothering with arnica.

How many other bruises had she been smothering too, she wondered. The invisible kind, where arnica and ibuprofen would never be enough.

'I have this thing about doing things right,' Anna said slowly. 'And I know, even as I say that, that I sound like a control freak, but actually it's almost the opposite.' She breathed out slowly, even the familiar comfort from knowing that she would be moving on soon not quite enough to make this particular truth palatable.

But if not now, then when?

If not here, on this beautiful beach with this kind, generous man who wanted to be her friend, then where?

She'd not been short of stunning locations over the years, or indeed offers of company. But genuine offers of friendship had been in short supply.

'I've been on pause for a decade,' she confessed. 'I was driven to get myself to Oxford, to prove to myself that I could, as much as anything. And then, when I left – a little older, a little wiser, a little more broken if I'm honest, I had absolutely no idea what to do next.'

'My grandpa would have a word or two to say about that,' Henry said, nodding. 'He likes a nice concrete goal to work towards. He's not fussy: work, life, money, getting a budgie . . . He just reckons that the most demotivating thing in life is to be aimless.'

Aimless.

The word spoke volumes to Anna, as all of her aspirations suddenly felt vague and wishy-washy.

'I mean, look at your clients. The Lyndells,' Henry continued. 'All that money, but are they actually happy with their lot? I remember when they first moved down here. They were building their company and they were so filled with excitement and possibilities. But once they sold it, they lost all sense of purpose.'

'And decency?' Anna frowned.

'Ah, no, you've got me there – Liza was always a bit, erm, particular. But they seem so lost now, they put all their focus into random shit that doesn't matter, just to feel important.'

Anna nodded. She could see how easily that might happen. How the veneer of confidence and perfection might actually be papering over the holes. How their big plans of cashing in might not have provided the happily ever after they were hoping for. Their beautiful home, a sterile carapace and insufficient antidote to their unhappiness.

'Hindsight is always twenty-twenty though, isn't that what they say?' Anna shrugged. 'No point trying to change the past. I just try and focus on not cocking up in the future too. Just trying to get it right, you know?'

'And what would happen if you got it wrong? Life?' Henry said gently. 'Would it really be so bad to take a few chances, make a few commitments? You do know that you can always change your mind, right? You said something on the boat the other day and it really stuck with me – about being afraid of settling down somewhere and realising you'd got it wrong.' He gave her a little nudge. 'You do know that you aren't obliged to *stay* there. I've heard tell that there's a whole industry based on people moving house . . .' He smiled. 'Go on. Be brave. And if you get it wrong, you are absolutely allowed to have another go.'

'Oh shush,' Anna said, smiling despite herself. Getting it wrong never really felt like an option for her. Part of this exhausting commitment to the moral high ground meant that failure could not be an option. There would be no divorce, no failed manuscript rejected all over town, no nasty break-ups, or crying children.

It was admittedly twisted logic, but it made sense to Anna within the framework of her life so far.

'I'm beginning to wonder whether perfectionism is the last socially acceptable form of addiction,' she said, thinking out loud. 'But it's not easy to give up.'

'I can imagine,' Henry said. 'I don't imagine it's an ethos you could ditch overnight, either. Could you maybe start with a small change? Something important enough to care about, but where it really, truly wouldn't be the end of the world if it went tits up. Something you want in your life but that you've been avoiding for fear of getting it wrong.'

Anna nodded. For someone so young, Henry made an awful lot of sense. And seeing him this morning, with Oscar strapped to his chest, he had somehow gained a gravitas and authenticity that had been lacking as they'd larked about on his boat, on the beach.

Her mind skittered through the possibilities, and as she thought about her writing, her friendships and the possibility of a place to call home, she realised that one unnerving theme had developed: so many of her big decisions of late hadn't ever been hers at all. She'd been letting life happen to her, unengaged in the process, and buffeted by prevailing winds.

'You know something, Henry, it is so much harder to ask for what you want out of life, if you have absolutely no idea what that is. I mean, beyond the vague and generic. I want to be happy. I want to be healthy and safe. But doesn't everyone?'

'Probably,' he agreed. 'But not everyone wants to be a writer. Or to spend their lives globetrotting.'

'So I could go back to actually submitting my travel articles, rather than just thinking about it?'

'Are you asking me, or telling me?' Henry grinned. 'One of my gran's best rejoinders there, by the way.'

Anna laughed. 'For what it's worth, I think I'm a little bit in love with your grandparents. And their fisherman's therapy.'

'They are the best,' he agreed. 'Another favourite of hers: there's no reward without a little risk – but who are you betting on if not yourself?'

'Shit.' Anna shook her head. 'Imagine if I'd had a cuppa with your gran ten years ago. I could have saved myself a decade of soul-searching.'

'Yeah, that pesky decade of fun and travel and exploring the world – who wouldn't want to avoid that?' Henry laughed. 'But that doesn't mean you can't put it to work for you.'

Anna resisted the urge to stick out her tongue, but she felt a small lift in the weight that sat so squarely on her shoulders. Time you enjoyed wasting could never really qualify as wasted time, after all. If only she weren't always, always, so hard on herself.

All she had ever really wanted, it seemed, was to find answers. And yet, the more she travelled, and the more lives she temporarily borrowed, the more it served only to throw up more questions. Ten years of trying on lives for size and she was none the wiser about what she, Anna Wilson, actually wanted in her life.

And it felt as though a few decisions on that front were now long overdue.

'Can I make a suggestion?' Henry said, the colour rising up his neck again as he fidgeted. 'Start small. Make a small change. A small plan.'

'Like what?'

'Like staying in touch with me when you leave – I mean, I'm guessing that's not something you normally do, right?'

Anna wrinkled her nose. He made a valid point. So many connections over the years. So many moments of small truths. All of them left behind.

'Staying in touch?' she said.

He nodded. 'You know, almost as though we were friends.'

Even before her whirling mind could consider what that might look like, Anna felt her face crease into a smile.

'I think I would like that,' she said.

Chapter 20

Swindon, 2001

Anna looked around her bedroom – a monstrous confection of pink kitsch – and wondered whether she was in fact, as Jackie had often chastised her, just plain rude and ungrateful.

A bedroom of her own.

No sharing, no negotiating, no demarcations of where she was allowed to put her belongings. No need even to say goodbye.

A room designed, apparently, with only her in mind.

And therein lay the rub: how could Kara and Ian possibly know her, even a little bit, if they thought this would be something she would like? No bookshelves, but a heap of glossy 'teen' magazines. No radio, but a hot-pink stereo with a stack of pop CDs. And, possibly worst of all, the wardrobe already filled with girly, flouncy skirts and dresses in shades of pastel and white.

Mary Janes in patent black leather.

Anna held tightly to the bag in her arms, her jeans and T-shirts, her few novels, suddenly feeling even more precious – a last semblance of who she truly was.

And perhaps it *was* a little strange for a girl her age to prefer Beethoven to Busted, or *White Teeth* to *Harry Potter*. But then, she had never pretended otherwise.

It was just a very confusing place to be – this room – since she'd met Kara and Ian several times. They'd talked, laughed, discussed how her life with them would be.

And none of those plans had included tulle or twinkles.

Anna lay back on the bed, throwing a sequined pillow across the room in frustration, and trying to find a comfortable spot. This was to be her third placement in as many years and, whatever Kara and Ian had promised, Anna could only see this new situation as temporary too.

She wasn't a likeable child. Fact. She knew that she irritated people with her quiet resilience; she would share her belongings but never her thoughts. In her mind, she'd already given away the very last measure of privacy and pride, and she determined that her feelings, at least, would remain her own.

And so she read, or perhaps devoured, novels that were well beyond her age, to challenge herself, yes, but also to see what life would be like when she too was a grown-up and could make her own decisions. Books were, at times, her only constant, her only companion, and Anna treasured the few volumes she had with an intensity that bemused those who took care of her.

After Marjorie, there'd been Gail. Gail and Mike with their petulant daughter, Lucy. Anna was to be the longed-for sibling, the child that 'completed' their family, and yet apparently nobody had sent Lucy that memo. Angry, slow-witted, bitterly resentful, Anna's every academic achievement irked her and laid the groundwork for some hateful tirade; insults that Anna had never even heard in the foster homes poured out of the mouth of this perfect blonde cherub, her pink cheeks contorted with jealousy.

It was never going to last.

And so, to Tina and Dave – the last hope for Anna to stay on at her grammar school, the last placement within the catchment. And there, Anna had learned very quickly to trust her own instincts, her own gut. Deep down, she'd known that there was something a bit 'off' about Dave even on their very first meeting, but Jackie had been clear on her options and, for a girl like Anna, her school had become her happy place. A place where her passions and endeavours had been encouraged, not ridiculed. A place where Marjorie's words of wisdom made sense, like the pieces of a jigsaw fitting together to make a picture of her own choosing.

When Dave's wandering eye became a daily, cringeworthy occurrence, and the incipient threat of wandering hands grew more hazardous by the day, Anna had locked herself away. His avuncular promise to 'tuck you in later' turned her stomach every night as she went to bed, locking her door and checking over and over again that it was secure, with increasing anxiety, even as the handle turned and jiggled late into the night.

When Tina announced she was going away for a few days 'for work' and Anna saw the look of delighted anticipation on Dave's face, his moist, fat tongue flicking out to touch his lips, then suddenly a grammar school education didn't seem like a price worth paying.

Anna had never been so pleased to have Jackie on speed dial, even accepting with good grace her sigh of annoyance as she drove over to collect Anna once again.

'Anna? Anna love? Are you okay in there?' Kara tapped plaintively at the bedroom door. A door with no lock.

'I've made us some supper and we thought, as a treat, we'd eat in front of the telly? What do you think?'

Anna stood up and opened the door, all too familiar with the longing expression on Kara's face. It was like looking in a mirror. Eyes wide, supplicating, wondering what it would take to earn affection.

'Thank you, Kara. That sounds lovely,' Anna said.

Kara hesitated, waving her hand towards the wardrobe. 'I know some of it might not be to your taste, but Jackie said you didn't have much.' She offered a wavering smile. 'It can all go back, if you'd rather go shopping together? We can make a day of it.'

Anna felt torn. So much thought, so much effort, however misguided. And if these were the clothes that Kara had chosen, then surely that spoke volumes about the kind of 'daughter' she was looking for?

'Maybe we can do a little of both?' she suggested tentatively. 'I'll mainly be in school uniform and casual clothes, won't I?' The thought of having more seemed almost alien. After all, how many days in the week were there? Uniform, pyjamas; jeans and sneakers for the weekend. Anything more felt decadent to the point of extravagance.

Kara clapped her hands. 'Of course, but did you see these?' She bounded into the room and with huge ceremony reached into the chest of drawers, emerging with a pair of bright velour tracksuit trousers laid out across her hands like an offering, 'Juicy' studded across the backside. 'I've always wanted to have some of these but I think my tush is past it.'

'Wow!' said Anna, curling up inside a little, willing herself to find the necessary enthusiasm. Blatant lies made her feel disingenuous, she'd decided last week, as she'd copied the definition into her notebook in her careful cursive script: *slightly dishonest and insincere.* Yet the desire to fit in, to blend into each new placement like a chameleon was still strong, almost overpowering.

It wasn't enough to long for her mother, a person she barely even remembered without an inexplicable chill of apprehension, but now, everywhere she went, Anna tried desperately to recreate the life she'd so briefly discovered with Marjorie; a life where her opinion mattered and her childhood was simply an apprenticeship for the grand adventures and successes she could strive for in her own life. Soon. In six short years.

'Do you like them?' Kara pushed.

'I never dreamed I'd own a pair like that,' Anna said, nodding, not a word of a lie.

It was probably the springy velour trackpants that shattered all Anna's resolutions that this time would be different. This time, she'd promised herself quietly in Jackie's car on the way over, she wouldn't be a chameleon, blending to fit. She could be herself, couldn't she? Admit to her own interests and ambitions, talk about the travels and adventures she longed for?

But somehow, with the generosity of that gift, which seemed to embody Kara's desperate eagerness to connect, Anna felt herself weakening. Surely fitting in, pleasing Kara, was more important than that feeling of freedom Anna so rarely felt, when she could actually be herself?

If she even knew what that looked like anymore: she felt like a glass of orange squash, diluted down to a pale imitation of herself.

But maybe it was worth it, because no matter what life threw her way, there was always that hope, however small, that she had finally landed somewhere she could stay.

Even when the common-sense voice in her head urged caution, anticipating a more pessimistic – dare she say it – realistic outcome.

Everything and everyone in Anna's life was temporary. Until Anna's mother showed up – one way or another – foster care was the only option on the table.

Anna knew it; Kara knew it. And yet still she made no secret of her wish to adopt. 'Just to be sure,' she would say with a smile, as she plaited Anna's hair into long, heavy braids that weighed down her small frame and made her scalp ache.

Strangely though, after only a few weeks, it was Ian who called time on Anna's ruse.

'Now, you two, I've been thinking about this a lot and it's time we had a frank conversation,' he said, pouring gravy over his chicken and passing the boat – a gravy boat! – over to Anna. He looked at his wife sternly, affection and concern mingled into one. 'Our Anna isn't to become your mini-me. She's twelve, not thirty, and whilst I'm glad you two have had fun with the yoga and the outings this summer, school's about to start and there'll be lots of clubs and activities to join. So, I think we need to talk about what *Anna* really enjoys doing.'

Kara blushed but didn't look surprised, almost as though this wasn't the first time Ian had shared his concern.

Anna shook her head, spilling gravy from her fork and instinctively flinching, looking around for a cloth.

Ian simply handed her his napkin reassuringly. 'It's only gravy, love,' he said kindly. 'So tell us – and there's no need to be polite – what do *you* enjoy?'

Anna shrugged, unaccustomed to the spotlight and confused as to her role. 'I'm fine,' she said earnestly. 'I don't really know what I like.' She speared an enormous roast potato, still getting used to the fact that every night, without fail, they sat down to a lovely meal. No more white toast with sugar to fill her gnawing stomach. No more lying awake, daydreaming about hot salty chips at the seaside.

She looked around their house – always immaculate, bright scatter cushions and huge prints hanging on the pure white walls. Their only concession to clutter had seemingly been Anna herself.

'I like books,' she offered, 'but I'm guessing you knew that?' She smiled nervously. It was a source of confusion to Kara that Anna would rather spend her allowance on paperbacks than party clothes. Not to mention a standing joke that Anna would arrive at the local library clutching all three of their library cards for maximum book-borrowing capacity. It was only of late that she'd stopped selecting books by weight – reassured that she could come back again whenever she liked.

Ian laughed, nodding towards the newly installed book-shelves. 'Yes, I'm not sure what tipped us off about that one. But seriously, it's going to be a fresh start at Hinchworth, and the chance to make lots of new friends. And sometimes those friends are the ones you meet in class, but often they're the ones who share your hobbies and interests. You might join the same clubs or teams . . .?' His voice petered out, concern etched on his face as he took in Anna's unexpected reaction.

Colour draining from her tanned cheeks, making the freckles stand out on her face as though drawn by marker, her eyes darting back and forth uncertainly between Kara and Ian.

School was something she'd simply chosen not to think about, a talent she'd developed for when things bothered her. Leaving the grammar school had been so much harder than she'd realised, especially when Jackie had taken her for a tour of Hinchworth.

'Excellent,' said Ofsted.

Terrifying, thought Anna.

The school was vast, with endless corridors that smelled of wrinkled apples, sweat and bleach. Huge classrooms with rows of desks, enough for thirty children. In each class. The library was tiny and musty; the computer suite boastfully gleaming in its expensive newness. There were locker rooms and sports fields and a huge swathe of concrete that surrounded the buildings and cut them off from their surroundings: rows and rows of battered, tattered council houses.

'The bus will drop you inside the grounds,' Jackie had said matter-of-factly. 'Best not to go wandering around here.'

So those were the choices that had rattled around in Anna's head until she'd called time: a school she loved and the constant threat of Dave's unwanted attentions, or the life with Kara and Ian as their treasured companion, and the prospect of Hinchworth on Monday.

Not only Hinchworth, the building, but Hinchworth's thousand-odd pupils judging her, watching her, wondering whether to be her friend. And everybody knew that the smartest kid in class was a target. Should she maybe go in fighting from the front? Maybe they wouldn't even be surprised – she was a kid in care – maybe fighting came with the territory?

'You can be yourself, here, Anna. And at school,' Ian insisted, knowing better than to reach for her hand, wounded too many times by the flash of fear and discomfort in her eyes.

'It's true,' Kara said, slightly guiltily. 'The friends you make at school will be a big part of your life. It's all about . . .'

'Authenticity,' finished Ian with a crinkly-eyed smile.

Anna simply nodded, determined to look up that word as soon as dinner was finished. She wasn't sure, but it felt as though Ian was calling her a fraud.

Chapter 21

That fraudulent feeling was only endorsed by the start of term at Hinchworth, her new uniform itchy and uncomfortable, name tapes rubbing at the back of her neck and tight leather shoes squeezing her toes after weeks in flip-flops and trainers.

She'd looked up the word – authenticity – and she could see that, from *Ian's* point of view at least, it was a worthy goal.

But then Ian didn't have to spend his day with hundreds of twelve-year-olds, each posturing and fraudulent in their own way, trying to be something they weren't in order to fit in. Anna withdrew a little more into herself with each passing lesson, at first astounded and then despondent at the lack of interest or respect each teacher was afforded.

'We don't stream in year eight,' the head of year had told them proudly when they looked around. 'It discourages a growth mindset.'

From where Anna was sitting, in the chaos of a maths class-room where half the kids still had no idea what a prime number was, and the other half couldn't apparently stay in their chairs, it seemed to discourage a learning mindset too.

She'd raised her hand precisely once.

The sea of furious faces that pivoted to stare her down was like nothing she'd ever experienced. Lowering her hand, along with her expectations, Anna decided that being fraudulent about who she was, and what she could do, might at least give her the gift of invisibility too.

Orange squash; getting weaker.

One day soon, she would just be a glass of water.

But at least it wouldn't be thrown in her face.

Anna learned to seek refuge in the library. Too many conversations about eyeliner and planned trips to New Look were exhausting. Too much bragging from Hannah King – the only girl in the year with a boyfriend. A boyfriend in the year above, at that.

A boyfriend who made Anna's skin crawl with the disdainful way he treated Hannah, as though she were an object not a person. His face was inflamed by acne and he smelled oppressively of Lynx body spray, yet Hannah hung smugly from his arm like a prom queen in the movies.

Anna wanted to pull her away, beg Hannah to value herself just a little more.

But she didn't.

Staying below the radar somehow eclipsed all the morality and pride that Marjorie had drilled into her.

So the library it was.

'Hi,' said a quiet voice from behind a row of Penguin Classics. 'You seeking refuge from the masses too?'

Anna looked around anxiously, knowing full well that the Lower School weren't allowed library access during break.

'Relax, if old Brockworth comes back, I'll just say you're with me.' Emerging from the stacks with a Chupa Chups lollipop poking from one corner of her mouth and her

arms full of books, Anna's eyes widened when she saw
Lucy Graham: Head Girl, Oxbridge applicant and the
source of much hero worship amongst the tiny (and necessarily undercover) nerd population at Hinchworth
Comprehensive.

'Hi,' said Anna, offering a weak smile, embarrassed by the
warm flush that coloured her neck, trying not to stare at the
beautiful girl in front of her, wanting to ask how it was that
Lucy could just 'own' herself so completely.

'You know, year eight is utterly foul, and I'd be lying if I
said year nine was any better.' She gave a dramatic shudder.
'All that one-upmanship and hormones. But trust me when I
say that it all gets a little better once you've taken your options.
At least everyone in the classroom has chosen to be there, and
in maths and English – at least it's streamed to filter out the
idiot factor.'

Anna snorted with laughter, her cheeks pinking even more
at the honking sound.

Lucy just grinned. 'You know you've been thinking it. Is it
just awful moving here from a grammar school?' She said the
words as though invoking the Holy Grail. 'I always wanted to try
out but my folks weren't keen.' Beneath those words was a multitude of pain and disappointment and Anna felt herself relax.

'How did you—?'

'Head Girl's privilege – you'd be amazed what I hear in the
staffroom,' Lucy replied with a grin.

'Are you enjoying these?' Anna asked, feeling a little braver.
She picked up *Pride and Prejudice* and skim-read the cover.

Lucy shrugged. 'I think I may have analysed them to death
by now. I can tell you all about the pathetic fallacy and anaph-
ora and dramatic irony, but I'll be damned if I can remember
whether I enjoyed it.'

Anna nodded. 'Jane Austen gets on my nerves – she's hardly all that.'

'Is that right?' Lucy laughed.

'Give me Anne Brontë any day. *The Tenant of Wildfell Hall* is just so much meatier, don't you think?' Anna said, forgetting herself for a moment.

'I do, as a matter of fact,' Lucy said, sitting down and leaning forward with interest, a poetry compendium in her hand. 'And what do you make of Emily Dickinson?'

Anna shrugged. 'I love the one about hope being the thing with feathers,' she sighed, 'because it's beautiful and spot on, like she really knows how it feels.' She paused, frowned. 'But then *everybody* knows that one.'

'They do,' conceded Lucy. 'But that doesn't make it any less wonderful.'

'I like Maya Angelou,' Anna said quietly. 'And I know it's not even a poem written for girls like me, but every time I read "Still I Rise" I get goosebumps down my back and tears in my eyes.' It was the first open and honest moment that Anna had dared to share at Hinchworth and she held her breath for a moment, her face breaking into a smile of recognition as Lucy replied with a wistful sigh,

'And that last refrain – Chills. Every time.'

There was a second of stillness, the light from the tall sash windows catching the dust motes circling lazily in the air, and Anna was once again reminded how books could be the very antidote to loneliness and confusion, loss or frustration.

'Anna, do you think you might like me to be your Big Sister here at school? Everyone gets paired up with somebody higher up the school and, well, to be honest I've been dreading it, knowing I'll get some mouth-breathing idiot to tag around with. And what is *with* the body spray obsession? But you and me, we could have fun, yes?'

Anna simply nodded, blown away a little by Lucy's suggestion, longing to ask why, yet somehow understanding that it was this conversation, this moment of connection. And that made it all the sweeter.

'I don't know all the poets,' she said obliquely instead.

'Nobody does,' Lucy said, shaking her head. 'But we might have fun talking about them together. You must be bored shitless going over *Of Mice and Men* line by line.'

Anna giggled; she couldn't help herself. It wasn't that Lucy was swearing – in the library of all places – it was because she could suddenly see all too clearly that Lucy had once been where she was now, in year eight, listening to a beautiful text being murdered into stultifying, mangled chunks.

'It gets easier,' Lucy promised once again, checking her watch and picking up the teetering pile of textbooks and folders: English, history, psychology. A world of promise.

'See you later, Anna-Banana,' said Lucy with a smile, tousling Anna's hair as she left, a bloom of happiness and optimism in her wake.

'Don't you look a picture?' said Ian that evening, as he took in the sight of Anna, textbooks and notepads strewn all over the dining table. 'Maybe we really should sort out that desk for your bedroom if we ever want to eat at the table again?' He was smiling and for a moment, Anna could have sworn she saw a flicker of pride on his face.

'Can we really?' Anna asked. 'And I don't mind having the bookcase upstairs too if it's taking up too much space.'

He shook his head. 'Neither you nor the bookcase are taking up too much space, Anna. I just thought you might need somewhere quiet to study your,' he picked up the book that Anna had taken out of the library that afternoon, '*Poems of Emily Dickinson.*'

Anna nodded. 'I'd like that, but . . .' She paused for a moment. 'I quite like working down here too.'

'I like the company,' Kara called through from the kitchen. 'Leave her alone, Ian, there'll be time enough for her to barricade herself in her room when she's a teenager!'

Ian laughed. 'Four months and counting. Are you going to be utterly vile?' he asked, mock-seriously. 'Just that a heads-up would be appreciated, so I can build my man shed in the garden.'

Kara walked through and flicked at her husband with a tea-towel. 'Of course she won't be vile, will you, Anna? More likely we'll end up with a reverse curfew for this one.'

'A what?' Anna looked up, intrigued.

Kara shrugged happily. 'Oh you know, "You can have your book back, but first you have to go to this party for two hours!" or something like that.'

Ian and Anna caught each other's gaze and laughed, shaking their heads, a new solidarity building between them that made Anna so happy.

'Or maybe,' Kara continued, 'this new friend of yours will lead you astray for me?'

'What's this, now?' Ian said, pulling off his tie and sitting down at the table.

Anna coloured again, as she had telling Kara earlier. She hadn't planned to say anything at all, but apparently the pleasure of that chance encounter in the library had been 'written all over her face' when she walked in the door.

'I made a friend, I think. She's called Lucy,' Anna said quietly, noticing the look of relief that passed between Kara and Ian.

'Brilliant. Did you join a club?' Ian asked, unable to disguise the hope in his voice that she might finally be settling in.

Anna shook her head. 'She was in the library. But we got to talk about how full of herself Jane Austen is and everyone loves her, but Anne Brontë gets ignored all the time. And poetry.' She caught her breath, reeling off the list. 'And Oxford applications too.'

Kara looked a little bemused. 'Well that's lovely, sweetheart, but isn't it a bit, well, soon for all that?'

'Lucy's in the sixth form, so it's probably all she's thinking about at the moment.'

Ian shook his head. 'Now, why am I not surprised? Only you, Anna. Only you.'

Anna paused, unsure how to take his comment. 'We have lots in common. Like you said, it is so much easier to talk to people when they care about the same things. And she's going to be my Big Sister at school – like a mentor or something . . .'

'That's wonderful,' said Kara. 'And maybe she'd like to come round one day? I could bake something?'

Ian and Anna exchanged indulgent looks at Kara's enthusiasm once again. 'She might not want to do that,' said Anna apologetically.

It was all she could do to finish her homework, and dinner took an age. For once, Anna wasn't starved of conversation and she counted down the hours until bedtime, until she could be alone with her thoughts and replay her day over and over again in her head.

Lying on her bed in the dark, Anna felt all mixed up. There had been such a pure and innocent joy in talking about books with Lucy and yet, still, her mind returned to the wicked flash of fun in Lucy's eye, her readiness to laugh, the swear words she scattered so liberally in her conversation and the way her hair fell so smoothly into waves all down her back.

She glanced over at the teen magazines still sitting in the corner, barely flicked through, wondering if they might yet contain answers she'd never needed before.

She couldn't be sure what this elusive yet all-encompassing feeling was, let alone name it. Was this what it felt like to make a true friend, or was it simply the relief of finding someone who shared her interests?

Chapter 22

Swindon, 2001

It was hard to explain how meeting Lucy Graham changed Anna's perspective on Hinchworth Comprehensive. It wasn't simply that lunchtimes now held an unfamiliar allure, or that she jumped out of bed in the morning with genuine enthusiasm for the first time in months. No, on some level, it was the reassurance of seeing that, grammar school or no, cream could always rise.

Leaving King James had been such a bitter blow that Anna had buried her hurt, anger and frustration, unwilling to acknowledge how deeply its loss affected her. Not willing to give Dave the satisfaction of seeing her cry.

And no matter how welcoming and kind Kara and Ian had been – always, always going above and beyond to get her settled – on some level she now realised that she had resented them for taking her away from her grammar school and the prospect of a different future. A better future, where her own hard work and effort might finally give her the security she craved.

Blame was childish, she knew that. Yet for a while there it had felt good to be angry. Not just with lecherous Dave, but conversely with Kara and Ian for being so unerringly, constantly nice. And of course, there were her greatest hits, to be returned to time and time again: her mum and dad.

Being angry always felt better than being a victim; it had become an old friend in times of upheaval. Anger gave her a sense of choice and ownership, as her life changed around her yet again without any say-so or approval from Anna herself.

Yet only a fool would stay furious in the light of the life in which she had currently landed. Two foster parents, who not only appeared to like each other, but also treated her with affection and encouragement. A school that could offer up Lucy Graham as an example of what was possible with enough hard work and application. There was even the promise of a puppy – once they could all decide which breed might suit them best.

There were definitely worse ways to start the week.

'Hi,' said Anna, still, as ever, a little shy when approaching the sixth formers in the library. 'Do you mind if I join you?'

Kevin and Gus, Lucy's English lit classmates, were about to say something scathing, but Lucy thumped them firmly. 'Pull up a chair, Anna, and then you can put these two eejits to shame with your knowledge of all things Eliot.' She grinned and scooched over so there was room for Anna to slide in beside her.

Heart racing, palms a little sweaty, Anna did just that, blocking out the gurning faces of the two boys opposite. 'Too lazy for their own good,' Lucy had whispered when she'd first introduced them. 'But annoyingly clever when they can be arsed.' In short, the worst kind of wastefulness.

But Anna was already learning: nobody liked a prig, or a know-it-all.

Lucy got by with aplomb thanks to her natural effervescence and just a hint of flirtation. Although surely it was against the uniform code to wear a skirt *that* short, even if you did have the legs to pull it off?

Anna discreetly rolled over the waistband of her skirt, and pushed back her sleeves. She could do nothing about her height or her hair, but maybe there was no harm in emulating Lucy, who seemed to have life sorted aged seventeen and three-quarters, just a little?

'I haven't read any Eliot.' She shrugged.

She had.

'So I wouldn't know what to tell you.'

She did. But what was the point with these two leering buffoons in the way? It was different when it was just her and Lucy, chatting easily about all things literature, with only a sense of a kindred spirit and not a hint of judgement.

Lucy narrowed her gaze and stared at Anna, making her feel all kinds of uncomfortable. 'Hmm. Well, let's say I believe you. D'you reckon you could read my essay anyway? Feels like I'm missing something.'

'Me?' suggested Gus, grabbing at his crotch provocatively, his broad Glaswegian accent somehow making everything he said sound menacing.

'Fuck off, Gus. You're not my type,' Lucy said lightly, turning to open her folder for Anna.

'Come on, Lucy. What the feck are you doing with this little scrote anyway?' Kevin chimed in, apparently not to be outdone on the massive wanker front, even if his delivery was that of a mamma's boy play-acting 'hard'.

Lucy rolled her eyes. 'Don't worry, Anna. At some point their balls will drop and they won't be such colossal cunts to live with.'

Anna started back in surprise. She was all for learning new words – quite a lot of new words – at Hinchworth but there were still some that she knew, deep down, were not good words, or words to be repeated. They definitely weren't going in her notebook, put it that way.

The two boys grabbed their backpacks and stormed off, leaving Lucy holding up one finger to speed them on their way. 'Now that's better.' She sighed happily, throwing her arm around Anna's slight shoulders and giving her a squeeze.

Anna nodded, mute for a moment, at the overwhelming pleasure she felt, sitting here on a rainy Monday lunchtime, with Lucy Graham's arm around her.

'Now, before you tell me all about your thoughts on Eliot's imagery and cadence – and no, Anna-Banana, I do not believe that you haven't read "The Waste Land" upside down and inside out.' She grinned conspiratorially. 'Let's get down to business – are we talking black Lab or cockapoo?'

Anna laughed and tugged a copy of *Dog Breeds of England* out of her school bag. 'What do you think about collies?' she asked earnestly. 'It says here that collies and poodles are the cleverest breeds. You can teach them all sorts.'

'Cleverer than Gus and Kevin anyway.' Lucy smiled, picking up the book to scan the page, her arm still leaning on Anna's shoulders. 'Have you never had a dog before? I think it's a brand loyalty situation oftentimes.'

'Sort of,' Anna replied. 'I lived with a lady who had a golden retriever and a Heinz 57 for a while.'

'A what now?' Lucy said, her brow furrowing and her eyes crinkling with amusement.

Anna could barely look away, flustered. 'Oh, you know, when it's a real mixture of different breeds and you can't really tell which. Like the Heinz sauces?'

'You really are a dark horse, you know that, Anna Wilson? Fancy laptop, crappy bag? Great haircut, gnarly, bitten nails, girl. And your brain? Well, you just put me to shame with some of your insights, you know that?' Lucy lifted her arm away and for a moment Anna felt a chill of loss where the heat of approval had lain.

So many answers she could have offered. Some frank, some embarrassing. It was still a source of conflicted shame that Social Services had provided her with said laptop as a nod to her academic prowess, and a sop to moving away from King James. Tutors had been offered. Support nothing short of awkward, as apparently it was 'policy' for the gifted amongst the 'looked-after children.' But that didn't sit easily with Anna; surely it was the children who struggled, who were slipping through the cracks that would benefit most from a little extra help? She had everything she needed between her own two ears.

But, still, the laptop *was* cool. And had probably won her more friends at Hinchworth than anything else she owned or had done.

'You know,' Lucy said quietly, dropping her voice until her words were just a whisper on Anna's neck, 'if there's anything you want to talk about – school stuff, home stuff – I'm always here.'

'Thank you,' Anna said, thrown a little by the intimacy. 'But I'm remarkably boring.'

'Oh, I doubt that,' said Lucy with feeling. 'I doubt that very much.'

'But what could I have said?' Anna sighed crossly later that day, sitting at the dining table reading T. S. Eliot for the umpteenth time. Obviously, because she enjoyed it, but also because she'd noticed that Lucy had another essay due next week. And this was something she could do to say thank you for the daily lunchtime respite in the library.

'What did you *want* to say?' asked Kara, wiping her hands on a tea-towel bearing the legend 'I cook therefore I am'.

Anna shrugged, her new default reaction to everything, which was in danger of giving her a crick in the neck. 'Well, I'm not sure "My dad's in prison and my mum fucked off and left me" is a real conversation starter,' she burst out crossly.

'Anna!' said Kara, shocked. 'I can't dispute the fact, but the language!'

'Sorry,' Anna muttered, not really meaning it. Swear words lent themselves so well to expressing all the pent-up, pissed-off feelings she carried around like an old, annoying friend you couldn't shake off.

'You could say that you live with foster parents? You could say that you've had a tricky time and you're enjoying starting over?' Kara gave a nervous smile as though she might have been overreaching. 'You could just say nothing?' She twisted the tea-towel between her fingers as she perched on a chair beside Anna.

'Why are you looking at me funny?' Anna scowled.

'Because I'm wondering if I'm brave enough to make a suggestion that might help,' Kara said honestly. 'Because you're not the only one making adjustments.'

'O-*kay*.'

'Well, I wondered if it would make it easier, when you're talking to friends, or here at home, well – I wondered if you'd like to call us Mum and Dad?' Kara said, the words tumbling over each other in a rush to get them out.

Anna was speechless.

The look on Kara's face was enough to tell Anna how important this was, certainly not a moment for mindless reactions or rudeness.

'I don't know,' she said honestly, going to reach for Kara's hand but then unable to breach that final few inches. 'It's just, I kind of already have a mum, and a dad. I mean, I know I never see them, but they're the reason you can't adopt me, right?' She paused. 'Ian said something about hurdles? I'm guessing they're the hurdle?'

Kara nodded.

It was one of the things Anna liked so much about them: neither Kara nor Ian ever talked to her as though she was a baby. They shared things – good and bad – and they asked her opinion. Like with the puppy. Anna knew that Kara wanted a little scruffy terrier, but they'd left the choice to her. Which seemed kind of bold, when you reasoned how long a dog might live, against how long Anna might get to stay in one place.

'I could try it,' Anna suggested. 'I just don't know if it might feel weird.'

Kara nodded, a little choked up by her honesty. 'No pressure from me, sweetheart. Just thought it might normalise things a little for you.'

'You know,' Anna said, squirming in her seat, but aware that Kara somehow needed more from her, 'maybe I don't have to call you Mum and Dad for you to know how much I like it here, how much I like *you*.'

Kara gave a little sob and then pulled Anna into a clumsy hug, the damp tea-towel pressed between them.

The radio in the kitchen burbled away in the background, some Irish bloke bemoaning that his life was a rollercoaster and he just had to ride it.

Anna could identify.

For all the ups and downs of late, she had started to finally buy into the idea that Jackie was right and that she was, in fact, a very lucky girl.

But, still, a lucky girl in a state of constant uncertainty.

Until she got some answers, no matter how hurtful, she wondered whether she would ever be able to let go of her mother, or of the hope that one day she might come back and claim her. Or perhaps, even, just know for sure that it was over. Talking to Lucy of late, Anna had begun to see her mother in a whole new light – and the older she became, the more she was certain of one thing: her mother's actions were entirely selfish. Neither here nor fully gone. No adoption on the table for Anna, yet no contact with her mother either. Never knowing when Jenny Wilson might appear in her life and turn everything upside down.

A life in limbo, in fact.

'Would you be cross,' Anna asked quietly from the middle of the hug, 'if I asked Jackie to arrange a meeting with my mother?'

Chapter 23

Swindon, 2001

It might have been a knee-jerk request, but Anna's mention of her mother sat heavily upon the household all over the weekend and into the following week. Unacknowledged to the point that Anna began to wonder whether she'd actually spoken aloud, the discomfort and awkwardness persisted, conversations suddenly shallow and superficial.

She hadn't meant to hurt Kara. Or Ian.

But obviously she had, and therein lay the conflict, because Anna really did want to see her mother, to ask her the hard questions, to drill down for the truth. She'd become more and more convinced that the only way forward, for her, was through. And she was prepared to go through all the pain and uncertainty all over again if it meant she'd get some form of closure.

The image of Lucy's carefree confidence was her constant touchstone.

But there was no way she could even conceive of herself being so together at seventeen without some form of change – overnight it seemed that answers were the only currency that mattered. With Kara and Ian holding the proverbial purse strings though, she was stuck, bound by their generosity in giving her a home, inviting her into their lives. How could she possibly make them understand that she would be more 'theirs' if she wasn't so torn in different directions?

It was also, she realised, the first time she'd asked for anything since moving in with them and, sure, it was a biggie right off the bat. It was also an honest and genuine request and their reaction confused her.

'Ian,' Anna began tentatively, twisting her spoon in the bowl of homemade rhubarb crumble that had become her favourite dessert. 'Did Kara mention to you about my mum, about me wanting to see my mum?'

His face clenched a little, the colour blanching from his lips, his laden spoon frozen in mid-air.

'She did. We talked about it. It's not a good idea.'

Three short sentences that made a mockery of the relationship they had begun to build. None of the usual consideration, open conversation or treating her like an individual. Right there, clamped down, as though Anna wasn't a person at all.

The gleam of the rhubarb in her bowl took on a fleshy pink resemblance and Anna felt a wave of such intense nausea sweep through her body that it was as though she were on a boat out in choppy seas. Could she – was it possible that she had misjudged these people too?

'But—' she began, wanting to explain about how she could properly settle if only she knew why she was here, living with Kara and Ian – who wanted her to call them Mum and Dad – in the first place.

'Enough,' said Ian quietly but with such force that Anna felt winded. 'You'll upset Kara. Anna, for God's sake, don't you care that you're upsetting Kara at all?' He pushed his chair away from the table and walked through to the kitchen where his wife was making a pot of tea to bring through, as was her custom after every meal. He caressed her taut shoulders and whispered something into her ear that made her turn to look up at him adoringly, her tired smile outlined against the darkness of the kitchen window and the world beyond.

They stood for a moment, joined together and, watching them, Anna felt a little piece of herself let go. She released any hope that she might one day be theirs, for they already had each other. And apparently her feelings would always, always come second to that. How did the proverb go? The children of lovers are orphans? Well, she already felt superfluous in her own parents' lives; she truly didn't need that reinforced by these people, however well meaning they were.

So, technically, she decided, pushing away the now repugnant bowl of pink, she had nothing left to lose.

She stood up and walked through to the kitchen, twelve years old, only just over four feet tall yet filled with barely concealed fury at the world.

'I want to meet my mother. My real mother,' she threw in cruelly. 'So are you going to phone Jackie to organise it, or shall I?'

Anna touched her fingers to the burn on her ear, wincing at the sudden stab of pain. It had seemed so important to look nice for today. Without Kara to help her, the heated tongs had been unwieldy – slippery and so very, very hot. Without Kara, she'd dithered about what to wear, blindsided by the array of clothes in her wardrobe, unsure what went together, tags still swinging.

Kara and Ian had simply left the house as soon as Jackie arrived, eyes averted, shoulders tense.

She might only be a child, but did they think she was stupid? Did they think that pushing her out would make her want to come back in? Every day since that horrible evening had been worse than the one before: stilted, polite but utterly cold, as though in asking for what she wanted rather than playing their chameleon game, she had rebutted their offer of acceptance.

Weren't they supposed to be the grown-ups? Two months of the cold shoulder surpassed even the shittiest of kids at Hinchworth.

But still, she supposed, looking at the clock again, her eyes flickering to the tiny notepad where she'd jotted down the questions she wanted to ask – Jackie's idea – in case she got flummoxed.

There'd been no secret about how difficult it had been to track down Jenny Wilson in Dublin, or indeed of how reluctant she had been to commit to this day. Months in the making. In the waiting. Jackie had carefully, considerately, told her this, 'because she was old enough to understand that happily ever afters were only for fairy tales'.

Ya think? Anna had wanted to reply, but she didn't; instead she'd merely repeated her requests for answers and a sense of whether there was anything left from the first seven years of her life.

'She's late,' Jackie said, patting Anna's hand with her own; padded and clammy, it hardly felt real. Shalimar stung the back of Anna's nostrils. 'And it's still okay if you've changed your mind?'

Anna shook her head. Sitting like this, looking out of the window across the street, smart clothes unforgiving and stiff, she reminded herself that on the other side of this conversation was the rest of her life.

A life like Lucy Graham's maybe? With an offer of a place at Oxford and a shining confidence that lit up the dull greyness of Hinchworth. Even if Lucy had *inexplicably* decided that Gus was the kind of person she wanted to kiss. Urgh.

'I'm fine,' said Anna, continuing to stare down the empty street, heart racing at the occasional passing of a neighbour's car. When finally another bus pulled up across the road she held her breath, increasingly panicked that she wouldn't recognise her own mother when she saw her.

She needn't have worried.

The bus pulled away leaving only two teenage boys on the pavement, lobbing chocolate wrappers at each other and laughing as they tussled. Carefree.

Or so it seemed.

Anna was getting good at looking past the smoke and mirrors. She might have failed with Dave, ignoring her gut, and yes, Kara and Ian had disappointed in such a fundamental way that for a while there she'd felt untethered from herself and her own instincts, but she would learn. She would get better. For what else was there?

'Are you okay, poppet?' Jackie said, the extra warmth in her voice a well-worn sign that things were not going well.

'She's just late, right?' Anna said, doubting herself all over again.

The clock didn't lie though. Half an hour, maybe, could be nothing. An hour might have warranted a text to Jackie. But after two hours and four buses?

'She's not coming, is she?' Anna asked, looking up at Jackie for answers, never before feeling so small or as vulnerable as she did in that moment. She just wanted a conversation – she wasn't interested in guilt or blame or even the promise of a future. She just wanted to *know*.

Angry tears leaked from between her lashes, carrying with them dark streaks of Maybelline.

'Oh, poppet. We all knew it was a gamble. She's just not – well, she's not the most reliable, your mum, is she, darling? Kind of why you're here.' Her words were soft, well meaning, but they left Anna cold. Didn't anybody understand that she wasn't asking for much?

She just wanted to know.

And this wasn't the kind of thing she could look up in the library.

'I don't want to stay here,' Anna said, her jaw pulsing with unspoken emotions. 'Kara and Ian. They don't want me. They want somebody who likes pink, and who agrees with them about everything and who doesn't have an independent thought in their head!' she burst out.

Jackie nodded, considering her words. 'I think you've just described a lot of parents.' She attempted a smile to show she was joking around, that everything would be okay.

'No,' Anna insisted. 'I don't want to stay here. And you can't make me.'

For a moment she thought of Lucy in the library tomorrow, waiting for her, an essay in her hand, that easy smile of welcome, and she hesitated. But it wasn't enough reason to stay – even though common sense told her that she was incredibly privileged here, her heart yearned for something more.

A family where she could belong, just as she was.

No contortions, no selling of her soul required.

And maybe, just maybe, somewhere where she was wanted and valued, just as she was.

She thought about going into school especially, just to say goodbye, to hear Lucy's heartfelt promise to keep in touch.

Three little words that could mean so much, yet often translate to so little.

'Of course,' Anna could almost hear herself reply, already all too familiar with the concept of an empty promise. Really, what was the point?

She shook her head. 'I'll get my things,' she said to a shocked Jackie, who was clearly scrambling to adapt to this sudden change of affairs.

'Wait, Anna, this is madness,' Jackie said, catching her hand. 'Sit down, love. Let's talk this through.'

Anna sat, obedience apparently still her default setting.

'Jackie. Nobody is ever going to adopt me, right? My parents are still alive. They don't actually want me, but they don't want anyone else to have me either, yes? They won't let go of their – what did you call it?'

'Legal paternity,' Jackie said resignedly, as though she could now see where Anna was heading with this. This bright, precocious twelve-year-old who seemed to see far beyond the little that Social Services had chosen to share.

'So people like Kara and Ian – they want a little girl to adopt, yes? Somebody to call them Mum and Dad and be one of their family? For keeps.'

'I suppose,' said Jackie, 'but they—'

'—settled for me?' Anna supplied matter-of-factly. 'And Dave? At the last place? He didn't want to be my dad, did he?'

Jackie shook her head. 'No, darling, he did not. And you know how sorry we all were that he slipped through the vetting process.'

Anna shrugged. 'I've been reading about sociopathic behaviour,' she said. 'The worst people are always the best at hiding it, did you know that?'

'You might be right, Anna, but that doesn't mean you should be thinking that everyone around you is like that!' Jackie protested, clearly upset and shocked by Anna's reading material.

'So, I should just *trust* people?' Anna said quietly. 'Trust my mum not to leave me, my dad not to be such a fucking useless criminal that he can't stay out of prison for five minutes? Or maybe trust my foster dad not to want to touch me up when his wife goes out of town?

'Or maybe I should be trusting Kara and Ian to love me and take care of me, even when they've made it perfectly clear that I am, at best, a disposable daughter, a substitute for the baby they can't make together?'

Anna's voice had risen higher and louder with each statement, and she now shook with the exertion of venting her rage.

'So, Jackie, tell me – who am I supposed to be trusting now?'

Jackie held on to her hand, her concern and, yes, affection for Anna etched on her face.

'Could you trust *me*, Anna? We've come a long way, you and I. And I know – I know – that I'm the necessary evil in your life and you didn't choose to have me in it. But I've got your back, Anna Wilson. And, do you know what – you may be small of stature but you're big where it counts.' She tapped her heart and her head. 'And I, for one, am not going to let you down.'

'Okay then,' said Anna, suddenly unwilling to release Jackie's hand, as though it were a life raft. 'Another fresh start it is then?' her voice trembled with the uncertainty of where she might land next. 'Another new adventure?' Marjorie's words and the memory of her belief in Anna brought a wobbly smile to her face.

'I think it might be for the best,' Jackie reluctantly agreed.

Chapter 24

Dittisham, 2019

Anna walked across the lawn at The Cove, drawn to the idea of Oliver's bobbing red rowing boat, even as she shied away from the reality. Being out on the water was a double-edged sword – she loved the sense of freedom and possibility, but loathed with a passion the surrender of control. Henry's deft handling of his skiff had been eye-opening. Because in her mind, sailing had never been so much a skill one could acquire as an act of faith.

Kicking off her shoes and rolling up her jeans, she walked to the end of the tiny jetty and dangled her feet in the water.

Close enough.

Faith was something that seemed to feature pretty heavily in Henry's life and it confused her and fascinated her in equal measure. Because, for Henry, his faith wasn't about church on a Sunday and living by Commandments with a capital C – it was about believing in the very best of human nature and the possibility of happy endings. Faith in his ability to build a family in a way that suited him. Faith in lasting friendships and loving respect for his grandparents.

Faith in her.

And based on what? Nothing more than a few conversations and his own convictions.

The very idea of keeping in touch only showed how little he really knew her. How little he realised about her life and the plethora of similar empty promises she'd heard over the years. How she went out of her way to avoid making them herself, even when her soul was craving a connection.

She thought for a moment of a girl called Lucy Graham and the pain of saying goodbye to the laughter and rapport that had sustained her during some truly awful times. Yet still not enough to endure. She frowned, trying to remember whether she had even tried, or whether she'd simply walked away, making the decision herself to avoid the inevitable heartbreak later.

She could blame her nomadic life.

She could blame other people.

But when it came down to it, there was an element of self-protection that Anna couldn't ignore.

She had the life she chose. She also had the friendships she chose. Or the lack thereof.

She was hardly blameless, hardly a tumbleweed.

And she could hide so many of her idiosyncrasies under the aegis of her role as a house-sitter, but she wasn't a fool – she knew that whilst this erratic life of hers came with certain gratuities, hidden benefits beyond a roof over her head, there had always been trade-offs.

In this case, Liza. Liza, who appeared to have mistaken the role of house-sitter for that of personal assistant.

And Anna, being Anna, had yet to alight on the perfect way to say no without irritating her client or wringing herself with recriminations for having dared to speak her mind.

Yet to Henry, it had been immediately obvious that the trade Anna had been making all these years was so much greater: her own life, her own plans, her own desires all on hold. Slipping so seamlessly, as always, into the role of the ultimate pretzel. Bending to fit, diluting herself.

Start small.

Easier said than done, but as the waves lapped at her ankles and the hamster wheel in her mind inexorably turned, Anna allowed herself to ask what it was that she needed.

She allowed herself to consider, however uncomfortably, how she might take back a little control of her own destiny. Getting to Oxford had been so huge as a goal, it had blinkered her every choice for years. Beyond that, she genuinely had nothing aside from the vague, naive ambition to be published, and it now seemed as though her life had been held in aspic, just waiting for her next considered chess move.

It had been a long time coming and yet now – from the cruelty of one man and the genuine friendship of another – it seemed as though her eyes were finally opening.

She picked up the phone. 'Em, it's me.'

'She lives!' Emily said, the joke only managing to mask her obvious concern just a little. 'I'm so sorry that Liza's being so demanding.'

'I'm not sure Liza even sees it that way, to be honest,' Anna said frankly, having almost forgotten the irritable message she'd left for Emily a few days ago.

Her stay at The Cove had been, in part, a struggle of constant frustration, the sun bright and the sea beckoning her with a siren call, yet Liza's interminable demands keeping her tethered to home base far more than she would like. Only the thought of those omnipotent star ratings on the Home Network profiles had kept Anna's increasingly short fuse in check, if she were honest.

That and the company of Henry.

'Look,' Anna said, realising that speaking up now might actually help someone else in her position later, 'I'm only thinking that it might be a good idea to mention to clients upfront that we are house-sitters. There to take care of the house and the animals – not be their personal assistants while they're away. You know, avoid any confusion and ill feeling.'

'I know, I do. And you're not the only person to mention it. It seems to be a thing this summer more than ever before. I don't know if clients are just becoming more entitled, or whether we've all been so polite and helpful for so long that we've created a rod for our own backs . . .'

Anna blinked. She could relate.

'Listen, that's not actually why I was calling. I wanted to talk to you about cancelling my next placement.' Anna looked down in surprise at a sharp pain, to see that her nails had formed perfect crescents in her skin, so tightly was her hand clasped into a fist.

Asking for what she wanted shouldn't really be this hard.

'Oh thank goodness,' Emily said. 'I can't pretend I'm not hugely relieved. I mean, you've been through so much these last few weeks.' She gave a nervous laugh. 'I was thinking I might have to stage an intervention one day soon.'

Her words petered out as Anna remained silent at the other end of the phone line.

Had her unravelling been so easy for everyone to see? Everyone, it seemed, but Anna herself. Sure, she normally prided herself on being even-tempered and easy-going. And, with the benefit of hindsight, she was aware that her message to Emily, ranting about Liza Lyndell, had been neither. Yet she hadn't quite accepted how tightly wound she was, unable to let go, or move on. Either from that night at Gravesend Manor, or the quicksand her life had become, anchoring her in the past, no matter how far and wide she travelled.

She thought of her conversation with Henry on the beach. The very notion of asking for what she actually wanted so alien by now, the dread of being considered 'demanding' far outweighing any small desires of her own. She frowned, actually furious with herself as she realised how her ingrained habit of pliability persisted.

'I'm sorry, I wasn't clear. I just need a different placement, somewhere more vibrant. A beautiful city with lots of book-shops and libraries and museums would tick an awful lot of boxes,' she said. She needed culture, diversion and distraction. The pretty cottage in Rye with roses round the door was not going to cut it.

'Ooh, okay. Libraries. Got it.' Emily paused, and Anna could almost hear the cogs turning as her friend scrambled to readjust. 'Have you research to do for your book then?' Emily asked, her whole demeanour more relaxed, relieved even. 'Leave it with me, I'll see what I can do – Edinburgh, Bath, Cambridge, somewhere like that do you?'

'Perfect,' breathed Anna, as ever comforted by even the proximity of the academic life she had loved so much and a little surprised by Emily's easy acceptance. Was the concern about being difficult all in her head?

She tilted her face back to the sun.

Small change; big difference.

One tiny element of control in her own destiny.

One eye-opening realisation that she had been kidding herself for years: footloose and fancy-free did not necessar-ily translate as liberty or autonomy, when the constraints were carried with you, in your own mind. By your own actions.

Chewie stuffed his face into her lap, desperate for attention, and she scruffed him absent-mindedly behind the ears, feeling good, time elastic with the ebb and flow of the water and the cacophony of seagulls overhead.

Her phone pinged and she took a calming breath to see what Liza had in store for her next, yet it was Emily's icon that flashed onto the screen.

Week in Bath – stone's throw from the Royal Crescent – so you can fill your literary boots AND let your hair down. Least demanding clients I have ever met. Almost jealous. Will send details. E x

'Bloody hell,' Anna exclaimed, gaining Chewie's immediate attention. She was astonished by Emily's speed and efficiency, and delighted by the result. 'Geroff, you daft hound, stop licking my face!' Anna laughed, batting him away.

'A week in Bath! Can you even imagine, hey Chewie? All those antique markets and bookshops. I mean, we can ignore Jane Austen, right, although I'll bet she's bloody everywhere with her bonnets and bonhomie.'

She breathed out slowly. Happily. Prepared to concede that Henry had a point.

Small change, big difference.

And a week in Bath to consider her next move.

Chapter 25

Bath, 2019

With Leia's plaintive rendition of 'Bye Bye Baby' still echoing in her ears several hours later, Anna felt her spirits lift as she crested the hill and saw the city of Bath laid out below her. There was something immediately and instinctively appealing to her about the precision and order of this Georgian city; the way the crescents of soft Bath-stone terraces layered their way up the steep hillsides, flowering out in concentric symmetry around The Circus. And The Circus itself was Anna's destination, if only she could navigate the one-way system and various bus gates that seemed to thwart every logical avenue of approach.

The honeyed stone caught the early-evening sunlight and warmed the whole city to a golden hue of welcome and a smile quietly lit up Anna's face, even as she tackled another particularly tricky hill start, the Mini furiously protesting the gradient and oblivious to the charm. The notion of a circular terrace of Georgian houses was appealing enough, yet the whimsy surely lay in the name – The Circus . . .

Anna could only hope that the entertainment inherent in the name was largely of the metaphorical variety – she'd had enough entertainment getting away from The Cove to last her a lifetime. Liza and Oliver's return had been several hours early and unnecessarily dramatic, but then who would have expected anything else?

Slipping away, her services no longer needed, was par for the course.

Being pulled into the middle of a marital dispute was hardly new.

But for Anna, standing there, bag and car keys in hand, to be on the receiving end of a parting tirade from Liza, Ruth's jar of homemade jam in her hand as proof of Anna's apparent duplicity, had been a bridge too far.

Anna had called upon every last ounce of professionalism she had and worked hard to keep her cool. Rather than flare, she simply listed the tasks that had been handled and updated her client on Chewie and Leia. Rather than bite back, she simply counted down the moments until she could leave. Rather than tear strips off this clearly unstable woman, whose insecurities seemed to be warping her every interaction with the world, Anna focused on the tiny gold stars on the Home Network website and met every criticism with grace and diplomacy.

As always, knowing she was leaving made everything so much easier.

Although leaving Henry and Oscar the night before had been so much harder than she'd imagined.

'Let the girl go, Liza,' Oliver had interrupted eventually, bundling a few crumpled banknotes into Anna's hand by way of a tip. 'And thank you, Anna. Truly appreciate all your hard work this week.'

It was only when Anna had finally got to the car that she realised all four banknotes were salmon pink. Maybe Oliver knew exactly how demanding his wife had been?

★

Flat 2.

Hardly the most beguiling of addresses, yet Anna stood in the entryway of the building where Brock Street met The Circus – the architectural punctuation point below the question mark of The Royal Crescent – and breathed in. The air was warm, slightly humid, and the excited chatter of Italian schoolchildren milling around in packs made the atmosphere feel almost frivolous and holiday-like.

The aroma of sautéed garlic and freshly baked baguettes wafted across the street from the tiny French bistro opposite and Anna's stomach rumbled appreciatively. She'd already decided to take Emily's advice to heart this week and embrace the role of holiday-maker and tourist, eschewing her usual desire to seamlessly blend in like a local. Indeed, she could almost visualise the pages of her journal she would fill while she was here.

It was a welcome return of her inspiration.

'You're here! How divine – and just in time for lunch.' The invitation was extended even before the door was fully open and caught Anna on the hop, gusts of Chopin drifting down the stairs and out into the street.

'Hi,' she said, holding out her hand in greeting. 'I'm Anna.'

'Of course you are,' said the graceful dowager before her, hair perfectly coiffured in vibrant shades of silver and gunmetal grey, which somehow gave her the appearance of vitality rather than age. 'Now, quick, quick. Let's get your parking permit sorted before those bastard traffic wardens shake you down.' She looked left and right as though hunting her prey and Anna immediately pitied the traffic warden who had the temerity to ticket Eleanor Harvey.

'I've paid and displayed so there's no rush,' Anna said easily.

'Ugh. Robbers.' She thrust a laminated card into Anna's hand. 'Get that on display and then we can have a little glass of something to say hello.'

There would be brooking no argument with her new client it seemed and 'a little glass of something' was apparently neither the first of the day nor optional.

'Richard!' Eleanor bellowed through the lofty communal entrance hall. 'She's here already. Lay another place for lunch.'

Making short work of the stairs and pushing open the door to the first-floor flat, Eleanor revealed the sweeping high ceilings and elevated sash windows that made Anna's heart swoop with joy.

Somehow, she hadn't equated the banal moniker of 'Flat 2' with the prime location within a Georgian house. Her face lit up as she took in the cornicing, the fireplace central to the sitting room and the light – oh the light that danced through the windows and illuminated the whole space, giving it a timeless, rose-hued quality. And then there were the books. Floor to ceiling.

'Wow,' she breathed, words mainly eluding her. But then she could work on that. She could already imagine filling the pages of her journal with descriptions of this stunning room. A balm to her very soul.

'Good girl,' Eleanor laughed. 'That's exactly the reaction we like. Now pop your bag down there, and we'll get you settled in after lunch. Hope you're not one of those faddy feeders – we've got bread, cheese, and some of that lovely Parma ham. Wafer-thin, the way it should be.' Eleanor looked at her expectantly, defying her to announce that she was gluten-free, vegan or some similar transgression.

'Perfect,' Anna said. 'And thank you for inviting me to join you. I know I'm a little early, but I thought it would take an age to park.'

'Rosé or white?' called Richard – or so she assumed – from the adjoining room.

'Might I have a glass of water first?' Anna prevaricated, catching Eleanor's tiny slump of disappointment. 'It's been a long drive up from the coast and I'll confess to being incredibly thirsty.'

Eleanor nodded. 'Of course.'

Opening the door into the kitchen allowed the light to flow directly from front to back of the apartment, and gave Anna her first view behind the scenes of Brock Street: the garden must have extended seventy feet to the south of the building, delineated by the same stone walls of the houses, and the strip of manicured lawn surrounded by flowering shrubs and borders. An oasis in the heart of the city.

'Can't take any credit for the garden, I'm afraid,' Richard said with a smile, reaching out to shake her hand. 'Belongs to the family in the maisonette below. Green-fingered chap – retired, you know. Still, we get to enjoy the view.' He gestured to the tiny wrought-iron balcony outside the kitchen window where two folding chairs hovered above a precipitous drop. 'Mind your head when you clamber out, won't you?' he added solicitously. 'Best spot you'll ever find for morning coffee.'

He smiled affectionately at his wife. 'Unless you're heading for Rome, in which case, I imagine we won't be lacking.' Checking his watch and then glancing up at the station clock above the kitchen table for confirmation. 'Three hours, darling, until the car comes, so shall we crack on and we can fill in young Anna here as we eat?'

'Of course, of course, but you must meet Norbert first or he'll lose his mind.' Eleanor stepped back and opened another door from the hallway, a rush of ginger fur and pent up excitement spilling through as she did so.

Anna crouched down, immediately enchanted. Norbert the Norfolk terrier was miniature perfection, apart from enormous ears that made him look a little like a Wookiee.

'Hello, Norbert. Aren't you gorgeous?' Anna said, as the little dog tumbled around her hands and into her legs, his tail wagging so hard in delight that his body moved too.

'Not exactly show standard, but the love of my life,' said Eleanor without inhibition. 'Present company excepted, of course.' She shot Richard a smile, but it was clear from his indulgent acceptance that his place in the pecking order was well established.

'And then you'll find Ulysses somewhere around, but he's not so much shy as aloof,' Eleanor warned.

'Ulysses is the cat?' Anna clarified, as Norbert gave her a very thorough once-over, no doubt smelling both Leia and Chewie on her clothes.

'Technically he's a cat,' Richard laughed, 'but realistically he's Satan. Honestly, Anna, just put out his food and empty the litter tray. He's not much company unless he wants something.'

'Richard!' Eleanor chastised him, shaking her head. 'He's just sensitive.'

'Hmm, well if Attila the Hun was sensitive too then I imagine you might be right. Now, less chat, more lunch, darling, unless you've gone off the idea of the Eternal City?'

Tucked around the tiny fold-out table in the kitchen, Anna felt immediately at home. There was food, conversation, laughter and a sense of welcome she hadn't experienced for a while. House-sitting could be a rum gig, she acknowledged to herself, as much a lottery as anything else. And, yes, the past few weeks had hardly run to plan, but this – this she could get on board with.

Listening to Eleanor and Richard banter back and forth – teasingly, rudely, affectionately – it was easy to see how the years of marriage had been kind to them. Hearing that Norbert had been named by Harry-Potter-loving grandchildren added another dimension to their otherwise civilised life.

And, no matter how small this city kitchen, it was fitted to perfection – magazine-worthy granite worktops, limed oak cabinets and a sense that these people knew exactly who they were and what they liked. This idea was only compounded by the snack foods alongside the Instagram-ready arrays of tagliatelle, grissini and extra-virgin olive oil on the open shelves, by the shameless jars of maraschino cherries, brandy snaps and Cadbury Mini Rolls.

'Are you going to Rome for a special occasion?' Anna asked, nibbling on pimento olives and sipping her sparkling water.

Eleanor blushed a little. 'Well, it's actually a work trip.'

'She's too modest,' Richard cut in. 'She's actually the keynote speaker at the university convocation – rather an aficionado in her field, aren't you, darling? And true, Anna, you might say that nobody else could be bothered to dedicate their life to studying the Divine Aesthetes of Ancient Rome, but that's where you'd be wrong. Quite the crowded field and yet still my Eleanor stands out.'

Eleanor swatted his compliments away. 'Any jokes about winning the scarecrow award will be harshly received, Richard.'

'I have been warned,' he chortled to Anna, filling up his wife's glass, pride etched on every inch of his face amongst a lifetime of wrinkles and sunspots, hair receding yet still a distinguished gentleman.

'So, do you have any plans for your week in Bath, Anna?' Eleanor said, shaking her head at her husband in loving reproval. 'You'll find that you can take Norbert almost everywhere except the museums. Ridiculous really, when they let all those children in.'

Richard caught Anna's eye and smiled. 'You're getting a sense of the priorities around here already, but truly, Bath is a wonderful town to explore with a dog at your heels.'

'I have big plans for making plans,' Anna said firmly, as much to remind herself of this commitment.

There was a loud thump on the ceiling and a volley of shouting, the vocabulary of which widened even Anna's eyes. Then followed an angrily slammed door and hammering feet down the stairs.

'And that would be our other neighbours,' Eleanor said tiredly, suddenly looking her age. 'It's all hours, I'm afraid. And I'd like to say that you get used to it, but . . .'

Richard frowned. 'They're no trouble, other than the noise. Shouting mainly.' He glanced at his wife as though silently conferring how much to share, and Anna's heart sank. Just for a moment, a fleeting moment, she genuinely thought she had landed on her feet. Her disappointment must surely have been almost palpable.

'There's a daughter, Callie. Sweet girl. Very bright. But clashes terribly with her mum's new beau.' She sighed. 'You might find Callie calls round from time to time. Don't be put off by her, well, by her appearance. She's a sweetheart and the sooner her mother sees sense about that ghastly man, the happier the whole building will be.'

'You don't need to get involved though, Anna. We've told Callie that we're going away. And it probably sounds worse than it is in our kitchen because it's directly underneath their sitting room. You'll be fine at night. It never bothers us in our bedroom does it, Ellie?'

Anna watched Eleanor's expression carefully. It was clear that there were different interpretations of the word 'bother' at play in this conversation. It was, in fact, clear that the whole situation with Callie *bothered* Eleanor Harvey very much indeed. Yet still she stuck to her husband's covenant. 'It's true, you don't hear a thing in our bedroom.'

Chapter 26

Bath, 2019

It was true: you could hardly hear a thing in the bedroom, but that didn't stop the echoes of the arguments resounding in Anna's head as she struggled to fall asleep later that night.

There was a joy to be had, certainly, from being in the heart of the city; not least the camaraderie from seeing so many lights dotted through the darkness, still shining in the wee small hours.

She wasn't the only one burning the midnight oil, although she doubted how many others had lost track of time with a leather-bound copy of *Paradise Lost*. Ungainly reading until you found your rhythm for sure, yet there was still enough of the magic in Milton's prose to hold her captive and hopefully distract her from her circling thoughts.

'You really are a useless waste of space.'

That was the line that had stayed with her, closely followed by yet another slamming door, which reverberated even through the thick Georgian walls down into the Harveys' apartment.

Her imagination, as ever, prepared to fill in the gaps.

Hence the Milton.

Yet, shouting neighbours aside, Anna knew that she owed Emily an enormous debt of thanks. This placement couldn't be more perfect: a compact one-bedroom a stone's throw from The Circus and The Royal Crescent, a sunny orientation and a book collection to rival those of her dreams. Not to mention that Eleanor and Richard were so keen for her to enjoy her stay that they had filled not only the fridge, but also a notebook with suggestions of their favourite haunts.

Kind, caring people, a beautiful and affectionate Norfolk terrier, and a cat that may or may not have been possessed by the devil. Anna couldn't help but smile, even as Ulysses yowled from the front window in protest at being abandoned by his mistress. The scratches on Anna's hand were a testament to his refusal to accept substitutes.

Norbert's approbation had been easier to achieve: stroking his silky ears and welcoming him onto the bed, where he immediately curled into his habitual spot, seemed to have done the trick.

So, on balance, a few slammed doors were a small price to pay.

You really are a useless waste of space.

The disparaging scorn in every syllable, however, refused to release its hold even hours later. Who was the poor girl on the receiving end of this tirade? And please – *please* – let there be somebody looking out for her, somebody she could talk to at least.

An image of Jackie flashed into Anna's mind, bringing with it the memory of Shalimar and that pinched look of concern that seemed to be a constant fixture whenever Anna's name was mentioned. Yet, for all her stand-offish authority, Jackie had always been there, on the end of the phone, in person, fighting her corner.

She felt a moment's shame that it was entirely possible she'd never said thank you.

Too late now, she sighed.

Jackie had retired three months before Anna turned eighteen, disappearing off her radar completely and absolutely, as though she'd never been there at all.

There was a loud thump in the stairwell behind Anna's head and she started, unable to stop the scenarios running in her ever-vivid imagination. She climbed out of bed, leaving Norbert snoring gently, and wrapped a cardigan tightly around herself.

'Hello?' she called. 'Is anybody there?'

Flicking on lights as she walked through the apartment, Anna tentatively opened the front door. Sitting in the stairwell outside her door was an extraordinary girl – mid to late teens, but dressed like a gentleman from the 1940s, with white and black brogues and baggy chalk-stripe trousers. Her hair was a lurid shade of violet and her face was pale and drawn, dark circles beneath deep indigo eyes.

'Shit. Did I wake you?' the girl said, her voice pure West Country. 'You're Anna, right? Eleanor said I should be considerate.' She paused. 'I forgot.'

'So, I'm guessing that you must be—'

'Yeah. I'm Callie. The nuisance upstairs?' She stood up to shake Anna's hand, her manners incongruous with her appearance, unfolding her gangly limbs and betraying her youth in the embarrassed smile she gave.

Ulysses yowled piteously from behind Anna's ankles, his tail fluffed up to epic proportions, skittishly avoiding physical contact.

'The cat hates me,' Anna said, almost conversationally.

'Ah, that cat hates everybody except Eleanor,' Callie reassured her. 'I wouldn't take it to heart.'

They hesitated there, in the half-lit darkness of the stairwell, neither, it seemed, quite certain what was expected of them in this exchange. Anna half wondered, from what Eleanor and Richard had said, whether the care and feeding of the girl upstairs was also included in her brief of housesitting Flat 2.

'You hungry?' Anna said without overthinking the situation. 'Supper seems hours ago and there's enough food in this fridge for an army.'

No need to mention she already knew that Callie had missed out on her own supper upstairs, the arguments flaring before they could even sit down to eat.

'Food would be good,' Callie replied, almost apologetically. 'And maybe I could borrow Richard's fleece? It's suddenly a bit nippy.'

A bit nippy. So said the girl with the violet hair and the one, two, three somewhat brutal piercings that adorned (or possibly marred) her beautiful face.

Anna stepped back and opened the door a little wider, holding Ulysses back with her foot.

'I won't hold you up though. A piece of toast and I'm good to go.' She paused. 'Maybe a little sugar on top if that's okay?'

It was like a kind of shibboleth – an acknowledgement that Callie, like Anna, knew how to fill an empty stomach when times were tight. Anna had to restrain herself from enveloping this fragile girl, and her mass of contradictions, into her arms.

'We might even stretch to a little cinnamon if you're feeling reckless,' Anna offered, pausing a beat. 'Always worked for me.'

Callie's eyes flickered up to hold hers, an unspoken understanding passing between them.

Even in this Georgian splendour there was anger and strife and, yes, even a poverty of sorts. But Anna had been down in this hole before, and the least she could do – if only for tonight – was offer to show this girl a way out.

Before she could even edit herself, she blurted out, 'Nobody is a waste of space. You know that, right? We all have something to offer, even if the people around us don't recognise it.'

Callie stilled, any pretence dropping with her shoulders as she turned to look at Anna, as though looking deeply through her, assessing her motives.

'I know,' she said with such conviction that Anna felt herself relax just a little. This girl might be slight, but she clearly knew her own mind and was certainly no easy victim.

With the pot of tea refilled and crumb-strewn plates scattering the kitchen table, Anna nursed her cup and listened.

Not in that polite way she'd honed so well over the years, with the instinctive head tilt and enquiring gaze, encouraging her clients to talk, to share. But in an almost physical way, leaning in and turning every short admission over and over in her mind, looking for the words unspoken.

Callie was a master of subtext and understatement. Her rounded, eloquent vowels may have been at odds with the story she was telling – her story – but the emotion in every sinew of her being was all too real.

She glanced up at the ceiling – plaster and floorboards separating her from the source of her unease. 'I don't know who he thinks he is. Honestly, Anna – the gall of the man. He'd barely been dating my mum for six weeks before he's moved in and then, what are we, four months later? He's laying down the law with me too.' She shook her head. 'I mean, my mum's alright, you know? But she's always been . . .' She held up her hands expressively as though words eluded her.

They didn't.

Anna could see that Callie knew only too well how to describe her mother, yet held back out of what, habit? Courtesy? Maybe even love?

'Has she always been like this with boyfriends?' Anna asked.

Callie nodded. 'It's like she forgets she has a say, or an opinion, as soon as there's a bloke on the scene. It's all or nothing – these poxy losers elevated to gods in her eyes, while they sponge off her and take the piss.' Callie sighed, exasperated.

'And, you know, maybe I *am* over-reacting: it's not as though Liam hits me, or touches me up, is it?' She turned pained eyes towards Anna, looking for support for this wonky theory.

'I've been here less than twenty-four hours, Callie,' Anna said gently. 'And I've heard what I've heard. And I happen to know that Eleanor's worried too and she doesn't strike me as the flappy type.'

Callie barked with laughter. 'No, flappy is one word you could never apply to Eleanor.'

'So then, tell me,' Anna pushed. 'I'll be gone in a week. No reprisals, no shame of oversharing for all eternity. What's Liam's problem? With you, I mean – I'm guessing he may have a few issues of his own.'

A smile of recognition, a flicker of complicity in her eyes. 'In a nutshell? He's a controlling cu—' She wrinkled her nose. 'Sorry. Twat.'

Anna shrugged. 'Don't mind me. I've heard worse and it takes a lot to shock me. Controlling like coercive?'

'Controlling like insecure and out for what he can get,' Callie said matter-of-factly. 'He lost his job – he was a plumber

I think – and then he moved in with Mum. I know it looks like a flash address but it's social housing – we're not loaded or anything. But he just wormed his way in, all helpful to begin with. "Let me cook tonight, darlin'" and all that. But in, like, weeks he was just sponging off my mum and then lecturing me every chance he got. Arsehole.'

Anna frowned, trying to get a clearer picture of what Callie was deliberately avoiding putting into words.

'And I can see what you're thinking,' Callie said tersely. 'Happens every day, right? Mum gets a new boyfriend, kid feels pushed out? But with him, it's a daily battle of wills.' She rocked her empty mug between her hands, biting at her lip. 'He thinks I should leave school and "contribute to the household" – says education is a waste of time and I'm welching off him and my mum when I could be earning rather than "flouncing around with books".' She scoffed at the thought. 'Yeah, 'cause clearly his four GCSEs have set him up for life!'

'She's your mum – you're not the one welching,' Anna protested, preaching to the choir, but flaring at the injustice of his accusations. 'How old are you, anyway? Sixteen?'

'Seventeen next month,' Callie replied sadly. 'About to start my A levels. So basically more than a year 'til I can tell him to go fu—, I mean, get lost.'

Anna shook her head. 'Stop editing yourself, Callie. You're fine as you are – scary piercings and potty mouth included. Although . . .' She squinted closer. 'I have to ask what the hell you've got there, stuck through your ear?'

Callie grinned and her face lit up. 'Ah, well, that's a plumber's nut, innit? Just my little way of pissing him off, you know. Not becoming for a lady to have piercings.'

'Or purple hair?' Anna offered, getting a sense of how Callie had evolved into this eclectic mismatch of style statements.

'Or dress like a bloke,' Callie confirmed, still grinning. 'Look, I do know it's childish but sometimes it's nice just to have a voice he can't shout down, you know?'

'I do, actually,' said Anna with feeling. 'Do you know what you want to study?'

Callie nodded, assurance lifting her chin and her gaze.

Safe ground.

'English, French and biology.' She failed to hide the delighted smile. 'I got nines for all three at GCSE, so I think I can make a pretty decent fist of it. Then university. English probably. I have zero intention of ending up like my mum.' She paused, cogs almost visibly whirring. 'And what about you, Anna? Didn't Eleanor say you're a writer? You have to know that totally slays.' Callie leaned forward, intrigued.

'One day, someday, maybe,' Anna replied. 'For now, I'm a house-sitter full-time.'

'So, you've time to write,' Callie finished for her, almost determined to stick with the illusion.

'Not always,' Anna hedged. 'Not often, actually.'

Honesty deserved honesty.

Unfazed, and with the boundless enthusiasm of youth, Callie simply nodded. 'Maybe I could help?' she said cheekily. 'I is good wiv words.'

'I is too,' Anna laughed. 'Until I try and write them down.'

Chapter 27

Bath, 2019

Her own words stayed with her through the night, even as Ulysses prowled and yowled, and Callie lay snoring gently on the sofa.

What *happened* to the ideas that still pinpricked her thoughts and daily actions when she tried to translate them onto the page? They became elusive and clumsy, skittering away from capture like butterflies from a net. Any of their originality or insight got lost as she tried to coax them into sentences, paragraphs, plotlines.

And, on the rare occasions those ideas complied, bent a little to her will, just enough to give the illusion of control?

It didn't last.

It couldn't last, because somehow they still escaped her bidding, even on the page; *somehow*, they were vocal in their own direction and form.

Disconcerting and disheartening, not to be the master of your own prose.

Kate had suggested it was time to let go of her globe trotting, experience-seeking job, but in the small hours of the morning, Anna formulated a counter-proposal: it was time to let go of the dream.

For dreaming was surely a young person's game, a hint of naivety necessary for the fantasy to survive? Talking to Callie that evening, hearing the certainty and conviction in her voice had made Anna feel somehow *less*. *Less* equipped to take a chance on herself and her creativity, certainly, but also *less* for not having the motivation to even give writing professionally a shot. A real shot.

Callie herself, so animated, so reminiscent of a girl called Lucy Graham as she enthused. Lucy, who hadn't troubled Anna's thoughts for years, was suddenly in her head again, vocal and driven and opinionated without any of the realities of adulthood denting her teenage ambitions.

Anna curled around Norbert, weaving her fingers into his fur and wondering when she'd quite so comprehensively lost her nerve. Had it been around the time she stopped emulating Lucy? Or at least her chutzpah and self-belief? Although that approach alone had given Anna the courage to apply to Oxford, to carry her through the interviews and assessments, and then ultimately buoy her through that first week of university when she'd felt such an imposter that without Lucy to emulate, she would surely have drowned.

Anna frowned in the darkness, still remembering that jolt of disconnect when, in her second term, she'd discovered that her whole methodology had been built on a lie: Lucy Graham had flunked it. Straight Bs had carried her off to some university on the south coast, and away from everything she'd been working towards. Away from Anna.

And so, the pale imitation had curled into a corner of the Bodleian, her Jesus College scarf protecting her from the draught, tipped from her axis and more confused than ever.

The memory was so clear in Anna's mind that she could almost feel the chill in the air and the echoing sounds of the

Bod, that musty aroma of ancient books heavy in her chest once again.

Could it simply be that Lucy had had everything to gain and Anna had absolutely nothing to lose? A gamble for both, yet somehow Anna's phony confidence had trumped Lucy's convictions.

And what kind of message did *that* send?

It had been around that time that Anna started questioning everything and everyone. Their motivations, their authenticity, consumed her as she tried to get a handle on how the world actually worked outside the classroom.

Introvert. Extrovert. Outspoken versus quiet resolve.

It wasn't so much that she had lost her blueprint, her idol, as that she felt rudderless. Everyone learned by example, yet Anna's life had hardly offered up a surfeit of role models. Learning how to be – who to be – had become a full-time preoccupation for a while. And still, even now, Anna wasn't convinced she knew the answers.

She was still blindsided by those with innate confidence and authority, confused by those who simply took up more space in the world, without easement or apology.

Owning the room? Anna felt that she could barely afford to rent it.

Sweaty and grumpy after a night's tossing and turning, Anna awoke to the smell of coffee. Tugging an oversized jumper over her pyjamas, she walked into the kitchen to find Callie engrossed in Sylvia Plath, a half-empty cafetière steaming beside her.

'A little light reading?' Anna said by way of greeting, pouring herself a cup of coffee and hoping it was strong.

Callie looked sheepish. 'Eleanor lets me borrow her books. She has all the good stuff and it's nice, you know, to dive into something without having to write about it, analyse it and snuff the joy and spontaneity away.' She tapped the cover. 'Not that there's a lot of joy in *The Bell Jar*.' She grinned.

'More a how-to guide, if I recall,' Anna said yawning, before her gaze snapped into focus. 'You're not feeling, you know – I mean, you'd say if you were feeling *that* bad, right?'

Callie shook her head. 'I'm not going to top myself if that's what you're asking. Wouldn't give Liam the satisfaction.'

'Okay,' Anna said, wondering if that was a good enough reason to stand down the instinctive surge of concern. 'But maybe I should talk to your mum?'

'No need,' Callie said abruptly, standing up and putting her coffee cup in the sink. 'I have to go to school now, anyway. Please, Anna. Don't get too involved. You said yourself you'll be gone by Friday.' She shrugged. 'But I did truly appreciate our chat last night, and the sofa.'

She walked over to the door. 'That cat is the devil, by the way. I woke up this morning to find him sitting on my head. I'm not convinced he wasn't trying to smother me.' She offered a shaky smile. 'Maybe see you later?' And with that, she was gone.

Anna sank down into the vacated chair – the comfy one with the view right down the garden to Royal Avenue and the bandstand beyond. Was Callie's life really any of her business? And, having been specifically asked not to speak to her mother, was it really a step too far to ignore that request? She frowned, kicking herself for asking – better to ask forgiveness than permission – wasn't that how the saying went?

She sipped the coffee and, as so often, when pop-philosophy 'popped' into her head, she smiled, thinking of Marjorie, who'd never met an aspirational quote she hadn't liked. Marjorie, who had instilled in her a sense of adventure, the courage to go somewhere new, and a deep and abiding love of dogs.

'Norbert?' Anna called, wondering at the kind of terrier that so enjoyed a lie-in. 'What do you say we go out for breakfast?'

It was easy to see why this café was Eleanor and Richard's favourite spot: the vintage glazed windows flooded the whole area with light and the shiny-leaved rubber plants softened the hard corners of the rustic wooden floor and tables.

Norbert trotted sweetly through the maze of tables and chairs and hopped onto a small upholstered armchair in the window. It seemed he was a regular.

Anna felt her shoulders settle and her breath came easier. She hadn't quite anticipated the pull of Bath's steep hills and her calves were only grateful that she'd limbered up in Dittisham. She certainly didn't need to seek out a gym while she was here.

The café was mostly empty, a few tables dotted here and there with pairs of women deep in conversation over poached eggs and coffee. And no matter how adorable Norbert looked sitting opposite her with a look of trusting expectation, Anna couldn't help but wish that Kate were here instead.

A few funny texts – mostly disparaging the other honeymooners – and the odd snatched conversation had hardly been enough to fill the void, and Anna had to work hard at times to remember that not only was she happy for her friend, but that she also truly liked Duncan. Duncan, who had quietly but consistently stolen away Kate's heart as well as her time.

Instead she took a breath and tapped out a text to Henry. It was a promise she'd had little intention of keeping, but staying in touch with him by text was almost too easy. A simple text much less personal than a call and hardly demanding. So much so, that the little quack every time one of his photos or messages landed had begun to make her smile, even before she'd opened it. Anna snapped a photo of Norbert – her breakfast date – and hit send before she could overanalyse herself. Small steps.

'So,' she said, turning her phone face down on the table, 'what do you say, Norbert? Bacon?'

His ears pricked up instantly and Anna laughed. 'Okay, so I see where this is heading. I order my breakfast, you eat it?'

'Actually, he normally has his own,' a deep, resonant voice said from a few feet away.

She turned, taken by surprise, and watched as a tall, somewhat erratic man folded himself into the armchair at the adjacent table. Did the concept of personal space not extend to this bloke, she thought crossly, checking that there were in fact twenty other tables he could have chosen without sitting right on top of them.

Was he like one of those twats who liked to swim as close as possible when you were doing laps? Maybe he wasn't British and hadn't received the memo that crowding a person was poor form unless absolutely unavoidable.

He laughed and his hazel eyes were filled with apology. 'And now you're thinking that I'm one of those monsters with no concept of personal space, aren't you? It's just – well – this is my regular table. Just as that one is Richard's. I guess we're both creatures of habit.' He reached out and stroked Norbert's tufty ears, looking momentarily ill at ease. 'I could move, if I'm making you uncomfortable?'

Anna shook her head, reminding herself that she was stepping temporarily into someone else's life; she hardly got to call the terms.

'You just took me by surprise that's all.'

'I'm Jack.' He held out his hand to shake in greeting. 'And I'll leave you in peace.' He nodded at the notebook and pen that lay open in front of her.

She smiled. 'I'm Anna. And don't worry. I only arrived yesterday so today is about finding my feet a little.'

'Anna.' Jack nodded, as though committing her name to memory. He held up his noise-cancelling headphones by way of a promise of privacy and nodded at Norbert. 'I can promise you though, that if the lad doesn't get his own bacon – a sausage too, if you're feeling generous – then you'll get sod all work done over his nagging.' He grinned once more and then settled his headphones over his conker-brown hair and turned away.

Anna had intended to write a list of all the things she wanted to do and see in Bath, but in that moment, an old familiar feeling came over her: it seemed vital that she record every nuance of this coffee shop, of the wave in Jack's hair, of the sounds and aromas emanating from the open-plan kitchen in the corner. As her pen scratched across page after page of disjointed thoughts and impressions, Anna could feel the release in her soul.

She carried so much and shared so little.

Writing had always been the one outlet she could trust.

Trust not to betray her confidences, but sadly not to be loyal – fickle talent that she had.

Catching herself staring at Jack's profile, she wondered whether it was simply a lack of application on her part. Within moments of plugging in, he seemed engrossed in the lines of coloured code he was creating on the MacBook. Oblivious, even, to the world around him.

He looked up and caught her eye, smiled, then returned to his work.

Not oblivious then. Anna blushed, embarrassed to have been caught watching.

Order placed, Norbert placated, Anna was soon deeply absorbed in her own spontaneous project. There was something about the light in this coffee shop that illuminated the warmer hues and cast deeper shadows; the juxtaposition beguiling and inspirational.

It had been a very long time since Anna had attempted anything new, but where was the harm in a short story of no consequence? Might it not in fact give her the permission she needed not to censor her writing at every pause?

Turning the page to a blank sheet, she began to write.

A fresh notebook was the ultimate blank canvas – no pressure to memorialise her travels and impressions as she did in her journals, yet still with more weight and bearing than a simple email, dashed off in haste.

And, as always, the first page was actually the easiest for her, before her critical inner voice had time to chime in, or her imagination run on into wilds of darkness.

Her phone beeped beside her and she glanced down at the screen, Kate's latest photo showing a half-empty cocktail glass and a backgammon board against a tropical night sky.

Tell us you're doing something interesting? We spent the day learning about a giant nut. Coco de mer. Oh yes, ask me anything – I am now an unwilling expert . . . It was that or learning to dance the Moutia.

Anna replied, grinning. Only her academically minded friend could be suffering so in the luxury of the Seychelles retreat.

I'm writing in a coffee shop with a Norfolk terrier, a foxy code-writer and a lot of bacon.

> Oh. My. God. I don't know which part of that to unpack first. Bacon, I remember you . . . So many questions . . . But mainly, I guess, I'm just thrilled that you're writing. I won't disturb. Speak later.

And then she was gone, a blur of Kate's warmth remaining.

Anna didn't need sixteen acquaintances to fill those sterile Perspex chairs at The Cove; she had already won the lottery with Kate.

So, with Kate's voice echoing in her head, Anna picked up her pen once more, determined.

It took three more pages for the concept to dissolve under Anna's stewardship. The characters morphed into edgier, more brittle, versions of themselves, the putative plotline no longer gentle and appealing but underscored by a note of impending tragedy.

Frustrated and annoyed with herself for falling into the same old patterns, she tore the pages from the notebook and ripped them in two. In that moment, she didn't care about the look of concern from the next table or the inevitable disappointment in Kate's next message. She was too angry, too caught up in revisiting her own past to even care.

Chapter 28

Coventry, 2004

It was certainly one way to make an impact on your child's sixteenth birthday.

Not necessarily the Sweet Sixteen, moments-to-always-be-remembered, type impact, yet definitely unforgettable.

Anna held the envelope in her hands and turned it over and over, trying to decipher how she felt.

The only other card, signed by every resident of the group home, stood sentinel by her bed. The extra egg at breakfast and a tuneless mangling of the birthday song had started her day well. The mock GCSE exam had, surprisingly, been a welcome distraction. Physics. Not her favourite subject, but then, were any of them anymore?

She knew she was slipping, and couldn't bring herself to care.

She was capable of so much more, she knew that, but somehow, as the hope for a different life had ebbed away, so had her motivation and determination. All that angst and fervour – to prove what? And to whom?

The envelope felt light in her hands, yet weighed her down with its potential.

Good and bad.

The postmark alone hardly boded well, but for a moment, Anna allowed herself to believe: early release, time served, a date in the diary for when Graham Wilson would be allowed back into the population at large. Reformed.

She tore at the adhesive strip and held her breath.

Forever Friends bears stared back at her, two holes in the cardboard where a birthday badge must one day have been secured. Its removal was not lost on her: in prison – however low-security – a pin was a weapon in waiting.

Her father's familiar scrawl inside was like turning back the clock, to *Blue Peter* after school and being carried aloft on his shoulders. She bit hard on her lip, trying to resist the overwhelming urge to rip away the soft, tender skin inside.

> You're sixteen!! How did that come around so fast?
> Happy birthday, Anna. I miss you. Every day, but
> especially on your birthdays – when I feel you growing
> up, getting older, living your life without me. You're
> sixteen now and I've been moved to a different set-up.
> Less intimidating for you, if you wanted to visit? No
> pressure, sweetheart, but I'd love to see what my little
> Anna looks like now she's all grown up. With love, Dad.

Expectation sat on her chest.

As her teeth tore through her lip she could only wonder what the right thing to do could possibly be. And, perhaps more tellingly, whose feelings took priority in this situation.

She shoved the card under her pillow, ripping it slightly in her haste to get it out of sight and out of mind. All those years she had longed, ached, for contact from her father and now this . . .

It didn't feel anything like she had imagined it would. And it didn't feel good.

Instead, she felt almost manipulated, as though her own equilibrium was of no importance.

Even at her massive comprehensive, where half the school qualified for free lunches and possession of a two-parent family placed you firmly in the minority, they had spoken again and again of the importance of this year. This, her GCSE year.

And, even though she'd allowed herself to coast, investing less and less of her energy into her studies and her dreams, she was still confident that she would manage a handful of Bs and perhaps the odd A.

Avoiding drama and turmoil was something they spoke about at school – being selective about where you focused your attention.

But her dad – after nearly a decade – thought *this* would be a good time to get in touch. Apparently.

As she'd got older, she'd revisited her memories of him over and over again, looking for clues and understanding. They all did it. At night, the air in the corridors positively hummed with crackling emotion.

With the benefit of a little life experience of her own, one thing was now clear to her that had eluded her worshipful six-year-old eye: her father was a selfish man.

A simple statement, but years of soul-searching had brought her to that realisation and with it – dare she consider it? – a small scrap of sympathy for her mother.

Her father had done as he pleased, to please himself. His choices, his priorities, were never those of a father or a family man – he was too interested in the next big thing, being the centre of the room, or indeed the centre of attention. His charisma and bonhomie bought him entry wherever he went, however ill-advised.

And he loved it.

How Anna and her mother could ever have competed with that compulsion she'd never know, but she could be fairly certain that he hadn't given *her* circumstances much thought before penning that birthday card.

And then, just like that, the tears began to flow, filling the hole in her chest where the anger had been. Because, deep down, whether she liked it or not, she still longed to see him, to be swept up into his arms and the warm security of his conviction that better things were on their way for them. He had a plan . . .

Anna, on the other hand, just wanted a hug. She'd adored the light of his pride as she'd sat on his knee, reading way above her grade, and showing him how smart she was, how clever.

'The apple doesn't fall far from the tree,' he would say, ruffling her hair and smiling deep into her eyes.

Graham Wilson, with his three O levels and buckets of egotism would lay claim to her talents, as his wife prepared supper, hands raw from another cleaning shift to pay the bills, while her degree certificate only gathered dust on the wall of the downstairs loo.

Yes, at sixteen, there were things that Anna could see more clearly now, even if she still struggled to understand.

Yet, at sixteen, the thought of seeing her father at long last still pulled tightly at her closed-off heart, threatening to overwhelm her with thoughts of what might have been.

Anna sat at the back of the school gym the next morning, the cloying smell of sweat and trainers emanating from the changing rooms behind her. Rows of desks were laid out in a grid and bored teachers patrolled like Pacman as the minutes ticked by.

'*Q1: Discuss the use of imagery in* An Inspector Calls *and how it adds to the mood and impact of the piece.*'

She read the question again – for possibly the twentieth time – but her brain stubbornly refused to engage with the words, let alone their meaning and what they might be asking of her.

So far, she had written precisely two words: her name. And her candidate number, which had taken more effort to recall than one might have imagined.

The birthday card from her dad though was fully memorised, a visual stamp on her brain that seemed to be blocking any other function.

She turned the page, leaving the answer lines blank.

'*Q2: Is Mr Birling a bad man? Discuss.*'

Two seats in front of her, Lara Maxwell burst into tears. There was always at least one crier in every exam and, for the first time ever, Anna felt empathy rather than exasperation.

How easy it would be to fold her arms on her desk and simply admit defeat; a good sob might even be cathartic, even though her throat and eyes were still raw from the night before.

'Anna. Anna?'

She looked up to see Mrs Holt looking down at her in concern. 'Is everything okay? It's just – well, we're halfway through the exam and you haven't started yet.' She laid a hand on Anna's shoulder and it was the kindness of her favourite teacher that was her undoing.

'No,' Anna gulped, her shoulders shaking. 'I'm not okay, actually.'

Supporting her as they left the hall, Anna could see heads craning in voyeuristic delight. She might have dropped the ball, but English was the one subject where Anna still held her own.

There would be gossip now, and speculation.

She could lay odds that none of it would be halfway near the truth.

Settled in Mrs Holt's little study across the corridor, Anna struggled to get her breathing level and was only grateful that Mrs Holt didn't see fit to quiz her, focusing instead on making a mug of hot chocolate and pressing it into her hands.

'It's only a mock,' Mrs Holt said simply, her care and compassion going apparently far beyond her class's grade average.

She pulled open a desk drawer and unearthed an open packet of Hobnobs. 'Times like this call for carbs and a chat, Anna. So, once you've caught your breath, why don't you tell me what's going on? You know all that stuff inside out and back to front, but you were staring at that paper like it was written in Ancient Greek.'

Anna just nodded, shoving a biscuit into her mouth, suddenly ravenous. And even though she recognised it as that hollow, emotional hunger that no amount of hot chocolate and Hobnobs could ever fill, they still made her feel better. Warmed, from the inside out.

'I heard from my dad yesterday.' There was no point beating around the bush; Jackie had taught her that. Hiding the main issue behind a house of cards and complaints until your hand was on the door knob was a fool's errand she'd run too many times.

'The first time since he walked out, when I was six.' The words were matter-of-fact but Anna's staccato delivery hid a world of pain.

'Wow,' breathed Mrs Holt, her hands folded neatly on her tweed skirt, like a cuddlier version of Mrs Tiggy-Winkle. Whatever she'd been expecting Anna to say, it clearly hadn't been that.

'Not the birthday present I was expecting, to be honest,' Anna said, attempting a wry smile, but feeling her resolve collapse as she saw the kindness and sympathy on Mrs Holt's face.

'How does it feel, hearing from him again? I'm guessing you've a few conflicting emotions on that front?' Mrs Holt leaned forward, gently taking Anna's hands in her own. 'And in case nobody has mentioned it, that's okay too.'

Anna looked up sharply. These weren't empty words of commiseration, there was a resonance in her words that spoke of personal experience. 'Did you—?'

Mrs Holt nodded. 'My dad never left us, Anna. More's the shame. He was just a serial womaniser who ground my mum's self-esteem down into nothing. And there's nothing like loving a person and hating them at the same time to make you feel utterly lost and confused.'

'Ye-es,' breathed Anna. 'I don't know what's wrong with me, but it's like there's an argument running in my brain all the time and there's no room for anything else. Am I going to be a doormat if I agree to see him, or would I be missing out if I stand my ground and say no? This is supposed to be *my* time, to take my exams . . . And right now, I couldn't even name one character in *An Inspector Calls* if there was fifty quid and a jam doughnut on the table.'

'Oh and now you go mentioning jam doughnuts, which means that's all I'm going to be thinking about when I'm trying to teach the year tens iambic pentameter after break,' Mrs Holt chided her, a warm smile encouraging Anna to share.

'He's been moved to an open prison, and since I'm sixteen now, apparently he feels ready to have a visit. Notice I said that *he* feels ready. Just gave me the choice, said it would be nice to see me "now I'm all grown up"!' Anna felt the anger heating her cheeks just quoting his words. 'No mention of how I might be feeling about spending most of the last decade without so much as a postcard!'

'Well then, I suppose you ask yourself this – what's the rush? Put him from your mind and do your mocks. And do your best, because it's *your* future that's in the balance, not his. And then, if you've questions to ask, or just things you want to get off your chest, then you go see the man. With no expectation of happy ever after, just a chance to talk.'

'I'm guessing it's bad form to scream at a prisoner?' Anna said, a twisted smile lighting her face.

'You wouldn't be the first and you won't be the last . . .' Mrs Holt said. 'But you have to think about what's best for you. Would you really feel better venting your anger, or would you like answers, maybe even closure?'

Anna shook her head. 'If he's looking for forgiveness then he's barking up the wrong tree.' She paused. 'What if he's found God in prison and he's all about making amends?'

'Then you have to decide if a relationship with your father is what you really want,' Mrs Holt said calmly. 'But either way, Anna Wilson, you owe it to yourself to put your studies first. You are an exceptional student – and don't think I haven't noticed you slacking off. You are capable of building a wonderful life for yourself. From nothing. With nothing except your God-given brains. You'll regret it if you don't.'

Chapter 29

Coventry, 2004

Her mocks had been a bust; a train wreck that brought derisive schadenfreude from others in her class and disappointed looks from her teachers.

Still, that was what mocks were for – a dress rehearsal for the real event in a few months' time.

And throughout the long hours sitting in the gymnasium, her thighs pressed against the hard plastic chairs and the nervous tapping of pencils on desks like nails on a blackboard, her thoughts had never strayed far from Graham Wilson.

'Are you sure about this?'

Anna wound down the car window, a gust of fresh air diluting the heavy scent of Shalimar.

'No,' Anna replied. She swivelled in her seat to face Jackie, who was frowning at the road signs directing them to the visitors' centre at HM Darwent Open Prison.

'Well then, let's sit in the car until you are,' Jackie said firmly.

Their relationship had evolved as Anna got older, less prone to holding her social worker responsible for every problem in her life, with her school, with her placements. They talked now, properly talked. As though that day, waiting for bus after bus to arrive bearing her mother, had somehow forged a bond of understanding between them; Anna finally got that Jackie was looking out for her best interests without bias or agenda, and Jackie seemed to grasp that Anna's mind didn't allow her to be fobbed off or left out of the loop.

'Hope you haven't got plans to be somewhere else after this then,' Anna said.

There was a slight dig in there somewhere but Jackie let it go. She was always chasing her tail; overcommitted and under-resourced, she worried constantly about letting her charges down. Or, worse, making them feel rushed, as though their conversation was simply something to be ticked off a list.

It was only when she'd explained this to Anna that the tension had truly abated.

'It'll take as long as it takes,' Jackie said, turning off through the hammering rain and pulling up in front of a nondescript grey building that could just as easily have been a warehouse or office block, were it not for the cameras clustered on every corner and the uniformed guards in the reception area. 'But you can't put the genie back in the bottle with stuff like this. So I want you to be sure.' She hesitated. 'I also want you to remember that he's just a man.

'Yes, he's your biological father and you have some fond memories of a long, long time ago. But he's just a man. And whatever he says, even if it's something that feels hurtful, you don't need to believe it, or buy into it.' She frowned. 'Look, Anna, I would never dream of talking to another child like this, but your mind – well, it sees things and remembers things that other kids your age would miss. Just, don't let Graham Wilson rewrite your history.'

★

Anna struggled to pull her belt free of its loops on her jeans, feeling sweaty and under scrutiny as she went through the security protocol with the burly man in uniform. Not that he was unkind, quite the contrary.

'First time, is it, love?' he said in a broad Midlands accent.

Anna nodded, a ball of tears already wedged in her throat and she hadn't yet made it past the form-filling stage. She emptied her pockets and placed her mobile phone into a grey plastic tray, watching as he locked it into a pigeonhole with a bright blue door.

For a second a wild surge of laughter threatened, as Anna found herself reminded of her locker at primary school. All that was missing was her animal sticker. A for Aardvark. Not the easiest to spell, but certainly the coolest – who wanted to be Freddie the Frog?

She glanced over at Jackie, sitting in the waiting area, and wobbled for a moment.

Anna was here to listen.

That had always been her plan, but it genuinely hadn't occurred to her until they were sitting in the car outside, that Graham Wilson would tell her anything other than the truth.

Hesitating in the doorway, as other prisoners greeted their spouses and their children, Anna couldn't help but wonder whether Graham had made the right call.

Some of the children threw themselves into their father's arms, laughing happily, delighted to see them and hardly drawing breath in their quest to share everything. 'And then, Mum got my jeans out the tumble drier and the snail was still in the pocket!'

Another little boy, sensitive, quiet, and in possession of the worst haircut that Anna had seen in a very long time, clung tearfully to his mother's arm, eyes fixed on the exit and refusing to engage with anything his father said.

It was different for everybody, it seemed, but oh how nice it would have been to be consulted.

She looked around the room, seeking out the dark glossy hair and wickedly laughing eyes that were her abiding memory. Her heart thudded into her throat – he wasn't there.

She looked back over her shoulder for Jackie but she was three locked doors and a world away. The tears threatened to fall just as she felt the guard's hand on her shoulder.

''S'a lot to take in, love, the first time. But you get used to it. Come on, I'll walk you over.'

She opened her mouth to contradict him, to point out that even imprisoned, her feckless father had managed to stand her up, when she saw where he was pointing.

A man in a blue denim shirt and jeans stood up, his face a mask of surprise, his greying hair receding back from a pale, lined forehead. No sparkling amusement, just a tired resignation of his state. 'That's my dad?' Anna said in disbelief, willing him to correct her.

Who was this man?

She waited for a connection, a memory, anything that would make this stranger morph into the man she had so missed. But there was nothing.

She gave an awkward smile, tugging at the orange plastic chair to sit down opposite him, before realising that it was bolted to the floor. The guard gave her an encouraging nod. 'I'll be just over here, okay, bab?'

'Okay,' said Anna, remembering her manners just in time. 'Thank you.'

'I can't believe it's you,' said the man. Dad, she reminded herself. Graham possibly.

'I don't know what to call you,' she said quietly, watching him flinch and wondering whether the hurt was genuine or for show.

'I'm your dad, so I guess we can stick with that for now?' he replied. 'And you – Anna – you look so different. So like your mother actually, it's uncanny.'

'Not really.' Petulance slipped into her voice. 'We are related.'

'Sure, sure you are. But still, it's nice for an old man to know he has a beautiful daughter.'

Anna stilled. The whole concept made her uncomfortable. He didn't know her; what she looked like really was the very least part of what made up Anna Wilson. She tried to be generous and believe that he simply had nothing else to say to her. Not yet, not before they'd got to know each other again. But she had a sinking feeling that being beautiful was all he actually needed from her.

'How long are you here?' Anna asked.

He shrugged. 'How long's a piece of string, love. There was a misunderstanding at my old place, said it was a parole violation and pulled me back in for another five to seven, but they're all bent. I was tricked, really.'

Anna simply nodded, his words only familiar to her from bad TV dramas. Any minute now he'd talk about the 'screws' giving him grief, or doing a 'stretch'.

'What did you do?' She had no need to look at the list of questions she'd written on her hand.

'Anna, do we have to talk about that? I haven't seen you in forever. It would be nice to catch up, wouldn't it?'

She nodded. 'Eight years, nine months, five days, in case you're wondering. One grammar school place. Six sets of foster parents and three group homes. But yeah, let's catch up.'

Her words were snide, but she felt snide. She wanted him to know what she'd been doing while he'd been licking his wounds inside.

His face seemed to crumple, the flesh of his cheeks literally sinking into his face as he stared at her. 'You're kidding me?'

Anna shook her head and waited.

'But your mum? I mean, I know she was struggling, needed some help once I wasn't around . . . Anna – she said, she *promised* you were being looked after.' He looked pained and angry.

Too little too late from where Anna was sitting.

'Yeah, well, that's what it's called now. You're not "in care"' – she made the quotation marks with her fingers in the air – 'you're a "looked-after child" so she was right, I guess.'

Graham Wilson shook his head, jowls wobbling in a weirdly gross and fascinating way, a mere deflation of the vibrant man he'd once been. Except, it appeared that nobody had told him that. He still tried to work it, a twinkly glance only hollow, an indulgent smile marred by prison dentistry.

Still a chancer, but without the tools of his trade.

'I can't believe she would do that to you, Anna. To her own child. We all knew she had issues – addiction, depression, mood swings – but I just thought she'd get help, you know? That sending you away was temporary . . .' He shrugged, happy to confer the blame entirely onto his absent wife.

Anna found herself almost speechless with the injustice of it all. There was nothing that Graham Wilson had just told her about her mother that she didn't already know, hadn't already judged and found wanting; it was the fact that he seemed to absolve himself of any role in Anna's abandonment.

'I had two parents, you know,' she said.

'Anna, Anna – you know I had no choice, love. The whole thing was a botch from start to finish. I should never have been inside. You know how much fun we had together, love. Do you honestly think I would have given that up for anything?' He shook his head fervently, again with the jowls, and a waft of stale coffee on his breath. 'When a man gets put away for something he didn't do, it's always the family that pays the price, but your mum couldn't handle it.'

He nodded, as though that was that, and they could now put the past behind them and move on to talking about the weather and the state of the roads.

'What's the saying? Fool me once, shame on you; fool me twice, shame on me?' Anna said quietly. 'I know, Dad. Social Services keep track. So the whole innocent routine isn't going to work on me, because I know that this is your third sentence. I know that you were out on bail for a few months, but you couldn't even stay straight long enough to pick up the phone.'

He sat there, outlined against the thick glazed windows, his mouth agape.

Were they bullet-proof, Anna wondered, her mind adept at providing distraction.

'We deserved better than the life we had,' he said. 'I was just trying to make our lives better. This wasn't what I wanted.'

'Funnily enough,' Anna replied, 'I could say the same thing.' She forced herself to look at him, really look at the man who was her father, and felt nothing but a nauseated shame that she had wasted so many years putting him on a pedestal, believing the hype he'd been so adept at building around himself.

She stood up. 'Thanks for the invitation,' she said. 'And good luck. It seems okay here.'

He remained seated. 'This wasn't what I wanted,' he said again, never one to take responsibility for anything he'd done in his life. Some things never changed.

But it wasn't until Anna was waiting for her phone and her wallet to be returned to her that she realised one disturbing thing: in the whole conversation, with all its revelations, he hadn't once said sorry.

Chapter 30

Bath, 2019

Ignoring the concerned looks from Jack at the next table and the waitress heading over with her food, Anna had shoved a tenner under her saucer to cover the bill, and left the café, Norbert protesting every step of the way.

She wasn't sure if she was angry at herself for failing, or for trying in the first place – if the very definition of insanity was to repeat behaviours over and over again while expecting a different result, then surely she now qualified? When it came to writing, at least. Creativity was a fickle mistress, yet she craved its comfort constantly. That feeling of flow, when time had wings and meals were forgotten, carried a seductive pull that she had never forgotten, even as she spent months trying to capture it again.

But the last thing she needed was to be in a public place while she felt so raw and exposed. She should have known better.

The fresh air lifted her from the furious haze that had driven her from the café and she looked around, a little disorientated, a part of her mind still caught up in the short story she'd been writing – the story with a mind, and memories, of its own.

Across the road, illuminated by the morning sunshine, was a bookshop, its livery well-aged, but its display windows packed with beguiling covers and the promise of distraction. Tugging on a reluctant Norbert's lead, she strode forward with singular focus.

A car horn blared at her as she hopped up onto the pavement and she waved a hand distractedly in apology.

It was only when she reached the bookshop, pushed open the door so that the tiny brass bell rang out to announce her arrival, that she realised Norbert might not be welcome in this treasure trove of literary delights.

'Morning!' called a young willowy woman from behind the cash register, her boho look somehow elevated in muted layers of linens – Bath style. 'Oh, hi Norbert,' she smiled. 'It's okay, he can come in. He's one of our best customers!' The woman laughed and turned back to her order book, and Anna felt a moment of ambivalence . . .

She looked so lovely – kind and insightful – that Anna had half hoped to chat, to pass the time of day, maybe ask for a recommendation. The other half of her, the half that was still reeling from reliving her past, albeit in fiction form, was grateful to be left in peace to browse. Norbert snuffled around, dragging Anna over to a small side table where a bowl of dog biscuits sat next to a nest of china cups and a tea urn.

'You really do know your way around, don't you, Norbs?' Anna said, passing him down a small bone-shaped treat.

And just like that, Anna felt at home.

Bookshops, books, libraries – they had been the constant of Anna's young, turbulent life and she'd lost count of the number of times she'd sought refuge there. And today was no different.

She picked up copies of Elizabeth Strout, Elena Ferrante and Alice Hoffman, sitting down cross-legged in a corner, with Norbert snuggled in her lap. She felt her heart rate drop and her breathing steady just from the aroma of the printed pages; like an addict, she inhaled.

Running her fingers over the shining heron on the Hoffman cover, she wondered again whether her own dreams of being published were simply unrealistic. Like being an Olympic athlete, or a Nobel Prize winner. Were they simply the naive dreams of youth?

But she looked around her, at the crowded shelves and tables laden with books, and simply couldn't allow herself to concede the notion.

It was possible.

Certainly not outlandish.

And she had talent – even if her own self-doubt made that difficult to believe sometimes. Surely her professors at Oxford wouldn't have been so liberal with their praise simply to spare the feelings of the girl from the foster home?

There had been a time when she'd truly believed that to be the case though, as if every A grade was a bolstering vote of sympathy. Until she'd grown a little older, a little wiser, and realised that very few people on the planet actually cared where she came from. And if they did, it was more likely so that they themselves could have a clearer idea of their own place in the world, in the social hierarchy.

Once you refused to engage with the 'Oh, you must know Charlie?' and the 'The Shaws, from Cheltenham – you must have crossed paths?' then life became a lot simpler.

If nothing else, Anna had allowed herself to be judged on her own merits; there was little chance of nepotism or advantage. She had to live and die by her own efforts.

Cradling the deep-blue Hoffman in her arms, the shiny heron already a symbol of hope and resilience, she could see the rest of her day more clearly. Eleanor's chaise longue, looking out over the rooftops of Bath, with a book in her hand and Norbert on her lap.

There were worse ways to spend a day.

She leaned back and began to read, Norbert's snores gently vibrating against her denim-clad thighs. From time to time she glanced up at the shop manager, ready to signal her intent to purchase, to see off the almost standard 'this is a bookshop not a library' type comment she'd heard over the years. But the woman seemed equally as chilled as Anna herself was beginning to feel, offering only an indulgent smile when Norbert's snores ratcheted up a level.

The tiny brass bell above the door rang and Anna glanced up instinctively. A woman with sleek, expensive highlights, a fancy designer handbag and an immaculately dressed child walked into the shop, her flawless face marred only by the petulant look of boredom. Sharp suit, sharper tongue. She seemed to have forgotten that independent bookshops danced to a different beat than the boardroom where she obviously held court.

'Can you tell me where to find the book about those foreign women who hunt with birds?' she said, not bothering with hello or, apparently, please. She simply stood there, tapping her foot impatiently as the manager finished up on the phone.

'It's a children's book,' she added tightly, as though surely that should have been obvious from her sketchy description alone.

'And do you happen to know the title, or the author?' The woman with the softly spoken voice and gentle smile held her ground behind the counter.

'It's blue,' the little girl chimed in, with equally clipped vowels, yet an apologetic tone suggested that, even at that tender age, she knew her mother was being incredibly rude.

'I'm afraid,' the bookshop manager said helplessly, 'without a little more information, I don't know the book you're talking about. It's a novel, I'm assuming, so why don't we go and look in the children's section? Perhaps you'll recognise the cover when you see it?' She directed all her words at her customer, the small girl, who clearly had her heart set on a special, particular book.

The mother sighed, clearly put out. 'We don't have time for this today, Aria.' She tugged at the little girl's hand, ready to leave. 'We can order it online when we get home.'

Who were these people, Anna thought, that they could behave this way with no thought or consideration for the woman standing right in front of her? Stylish, attractive, clearly loaded – yet her unshakeable belief in her own self-importance made her ugly. It was a strange kind of epiphany, hot on the heels of Liza Lyndell, as the cogs in Anna's brain rearranged: finally, irrevocably, convinced that shouting louder, or with more confidence, did not in fact make you a better, or more successful, person.

She had no desire to be like that woman at all; she would so much rather be cross-legged on the floor in her scruffiest jeans with a dog on her lap and a book in her hand.

Anna's heart went out to the small girl whose face had fallen in disappointment, her longing so obvious, even to a passing stranger. And Anna would wager that she would far rather have a stack of lovely new books than the designer booties she wore that clearly cost more than an armful of hardbacks.

Feeling all Kathleen Kelly, and smiling as she remembered one of her favourite scenes in *You've Got Mail*, Anna swallowed hard and found her voice. 'It's called *Sky Song*,' she said. 'The book about the eagle huntress, it's called *Sky Song*.'

It was worth the filthy look she earned from the mother with one foot out of the door just to see the little girl's face light up.

'Of course! And if I recall, we even happen to have a very special copy signed by the author.' The bookshop manager shot Anna a grateful smile.

Anna could only hope there was a chunky mark-up on a signed hardback. It would go some way to ameliorating the rudeness from earlier.

With the mother still standing in the doorway, there had been no bell to alert her to a new arrival and the first Anna knew of Callie's presence was when she plonked herself down on the floor beside her. School skirt riding up her thighs and laddered tights, Callie's purple hair was luminous.

'Aren't you supposed to be at school?' Anna said. 'Not that it isn't lovely to see you, of course.'

Callie grinned. 'Would you believe it if I said I'd been sent on an errand by my English teacher?'

'Probably not,' said Anna, as Callie scooped a dozy Norbert into her arms and gave him a flurry of kisses. 'But then, it's hardly my place to say, is it?' She frowned. 'Although I'm a bit confused about why you'd play hookie and then fight about your right to stay at school. Are you just being contrary?'

'Callie, I've got your parcel for Mrs Redfern almost ready – give me five minutes to find the study guides too?' the bookshop manager called across.

Anna laughed. 'Okay, now I believe you.' She stood up and walked over to the till, the Hoffman coming home with her for an afternoon of decadent reading and relaxation.

If Kate couldn't be proud of her writing again, perhaps Emily would be thrilled that she really was taking a break?

Walking out of the shop with Callie, the flurry of panic from earlier that morning already felt like a thing of the past, an over-reaction at best. 'If you want to hang out at Eleanor's to do your homework this evening, that's fine by me,' Anna offered. Callie's easy conversation was fun, hardly taxing, yet somehow eye-opening to how a different generation saw their place in the world.

'Only if you let me cook. I do a mean carbonara. Or a Thai curry?' Callie countered, looking so much younger in her delight at the invitation.

'Deal. Now bugger off back to school, okay, because—'

There was a sudden loud bang and a shriek, and Anna turned just in time to see an older lady thrown to the side of the road, her walking stick snapped cleanly in two, where she'd been clipped by a large red bus. The hot smell of scorched rubber filled the air, although it was obvious that the driver's emergency stop hadn't been quite fast enough.

Anna thrust her new book and Norbert's lead into Callie's hands and ran across to the old lady, talking to her gently the whole time, as she knelt down in the gutter beside her. A flurry of passersby were calling 999, but for Anna her entire focus was on soothing the distraught old lady, who was clearly confused, possibly concussed, and grabbing out her hands in an attempt to climb up.

'The ambulance is on its way,' Anna said several times. 'Stay still if you can, you've taken quite a tumble.' She reached into her pocket for a sealed packet of tissues and pulled a wodge out, gently pressing them against the free-flowing wound on her temple. 'I'm Anna.'

'Oh. Oh, really? *I'm* Anna too,' said the old lady, their

momentary connection distracting her from the blood running down her face. 'Annabel, officially.'

'They'll be here in a minute,' Anna said, hearing the sirens echoing off the Georgian buildings as they surged ever closer. She smiled, reassuringly. 'It's lovely to meet you, Annabel.'

The lady bit down on her lip, seemingly suddenly aware of how prone and distressed she must look, lying in the gutter, battered, bruised, possibly broken. 'I wish it were under better circumstances.'

'Me too,' Anna replied.

Watching the care and gentleness of the paramedics as they soothed Annabel and settled her onto a gurney made Anna feel better about stepping back. It was funny to think that this lady, her namesake, had lived her whole life under the same moniker yet a world apart. Still, it wasn't lost on her that amongst the belongings tumbled into the dirt of the gutter was a canvas bag filled with library books. Picking them up, she handed them to one of the ambulance crew and stepped back to rejoin Callie.

'You were great,' Callie said. 'So calm. I was all panicky and freaked out by the blood and stuff, but you were – well – you were brilliant.'

Anna attempted a smile, but didn't think it would help to say that she'd been equally unnerved by the pulsing headwound. Her overriding emotion, though, had been empathy for the old lady, for Annabel's complete and total vulnerability.

A young constable walked over to where they were standing, folding back the cover of his little black notebook and eyeing Norbert warily as though he were a trained attack dog. 'Ma'am? If I could just ask you to step away from the dog for a moment? I gather you were first on the scene? Quite the hero, I'm told.'

'Not really,' Anna said, sharing an amused look with Callie at his obvious discomfort. 'But I was with the lady – Annabel her name is – while we waited for the ambulance.'

'So, your name and address to get us started then, please?' he said officiously.

'Anna, Anna Wilson. And I'm staying at Flat—'

'Er, no, Ms Wilson. Your address. Your permanent address, if you please.'

Anna paused, watching the flicker of irritation on his face, a face still mottled by youthful acne and insincerity.

'Well, I'm staying at—'

'Ma'am,' he said sternly. 'I need your *permanent* residence if I'm to take your statement as a witness.'

'Right,' said Anna, glancing back over her shoulder, seeing the concern on Callie's face. 'The thing is, you see – well – I don't have one.'

The pitiful look he gave her made Anna feel sick. Barely out of school, in all likelihood, who was he to make judgements about her life, yet judge her he did. He gave her a quick once-over, no doubt taking in her smart trainers, her blow-dried hair, and the clean, well-groomed dog he apparently so disliked. Disdain and confusion clouded together as he looked down his nose at her, all mention of her earlier good deeds forgotten.

'No address?' he clarified. 'Right,' he sighed. 'I'll just put you down as "homeless" then, shall I?'

Chapter 31

Bath, 2019

She shouldn't have let it get to her.

Callie's take on the situation was probably more whole-some, if a little disrespectful; she'd so easily dismissed the young constable as a 'snot-nosed little prick' and got on with her day.

But still his look of derision and determination to categorise her had irritated Anna beyond reason. She'd stayed behind, insisting that he change the word 'homeless' to read 'no fixed abode.'

A distinction without a difference, in all probability, but it meant something to Anna.

It also seemed to mean something to her that she not only shared a name with the poor lady, but that only an hour or so before, Anna herself had blithely, distractedly, crossed that same busy junction, to a cacophony of horns. She pulled Norbert into her arms and muttered apologies into his fur, that sickening lurch of what might have been suddenly a very real possibility.

For a mad moment, she was tempted to pick up the phone and call the hospital, check on Annabel, reassure herself that all was well. It really was none of her business, yet the thought persisted, until she was almost grateful when her phone rang in her hand.

'Henry? Now that's a lovely surprise. How are you?' she said, genuinely pleased to hear from him. No matter what she'd told herself about the joy of texting, it was truly lovely to hear his voice, to hear Oscar chuckling and the seagulls' evening crescendo in the background.

'I'm alright. The Lyndells are being a pain since they got back, obviously. My grandparents much preferred having you as a neighbour, I can tell you.' He paused. 'I didn't mind having you here either.'

Anna swallowed her laughter, Henry's studied nonchalance failing to convince. 'It was a good week,' she said.

There was a slightly awkward pause. 'I know we said we'd just text, but it was my grandpa who asked me to call actually. He wanted you to have a photo to remember us by – Hang on.' There was a crackling, fumbling sound on the line. 'I'm sending it over now and he said to tell you *carpe diem*, whatever that means. It's not a carp in the picture obviously, but I guess you might know what he's going on about?'

A picture message pinged onto Anna's phone and a crisp image of a peregrine falcon filled the screen, yellow talons outstretched, wings swept back, having clearly just plucked an iridescent fish from the waters of a fast-flowing river.

'That's stunning,' Anna said. 'Did he take it?'

'Yup,' said Henry. 'He's good with a camera, but better with a fishing rod. He was well narked that day, because all the trout took cover once the falcon had been.'

Anna stared at the photo again and wondered at the accompanying message – seize the day? What exactly did Arthur think she should be seizing?

Henry coughed and when he spoke again, he sounded even more uncomfortable. 'Grandpa said you had some big decisions looming and this might help . . .'

Anna thought back to their conversation on the beach that night, about travelling and exploring and writing. And his belief that all of those things were actually better – easier – when one had a base to return to. He'd gone so far as to suggest Dittisham might be the perfect solution. Certainly one that his grandson would appreciate.

There were no flies on Arthur.

'Will you thank him for me?' Anna said, truly touched that she'd been remembered. Not just that, it seemed, but considered as well.

Arthur, Kate, Emily – perhaps even Henry . . .

How was it that they all seemed to know what she needed better than she herself did?

How was it that none of them saw the inherent difficulties for Anna in their supposedly simple solutions?

Yet still, this nascent bond with Henry felt like progress. A proper grown-up friendship. No deadline or exit strategy in mind. 'How's the beach this evening?' she asked, closing her eyes and sitting back with a smile, able to visualise exactly where Henry was standing to make this call.

A bang and crash from the floor above startled her from her reflections. Doors slamming, raised voices – and possibly even a scream of pain? Disbelief?

She leapt to her feet, and shut Ulysses in the sitting room – that damn cat had got into the habit of making a bolt for the front door every time she opened it.

'Jesus! I'm sorry, Henry – I have to go.'

'Stay!' she said to Norbert, as she ended the call but kept her phone still clasped tightly in her hand in case she needed to summon reinforcements. So long as it wasn't the 'snot-nosed little prick' again . . .

Opening the front door and stepping out into the stairwell, she was almost knocked off her feet by Callie barrelling down the stairs, her face tear-streaked and her anger vibrating in every jerking movement. 'I hate you,' she screamed up the stairs, only to hear the sound of snide laughter and the front door slamming on the floor above.

Without a word, Anna ushered her inside.

'Do I need to call somebody?' Anna said helplessly after a moment, having settled Callie onto the sofa and unearthed a box of tissues to stem the flowing tears. Her entire body seemed to reverberate with each sob and it showed no sign of abating.

She had zero experience with teenagers, short of having once been one herself, but even then, she'd felt like an old person in a youthful costume; her brain had a way of making her consider everything like a middle-aged woman. The voice in her head not so much hers, as a mash-up of Marjorie and Jackie and their experienced pearls of wisdom and ability to predict the outcomes before they even occurred. Like a game of chess, thinking several moves ahead, but instead of kings and queens, it was feelings and consequences.

'Callie. Where's your mum, love? She'd want to know you're this upset, that Liam's being this unreasonable?'

Eyes filled with tears and with a yelp of slightly hysterical laughter, Callie looked straight at her. 'She's on the sofa upstairs watching *Neighbours*.'

Anna felt blindsided. She'd assumed, well, she'd just assumed . . .

Callie shrugged. 'Nothing new. She just lets us slug it out, now. I think she's bored by the whole debate.' She reached into the bag that was slung across her body and pulled out a mangled copy of *The Great Gatsby*, torn completely into two pieces, and the hiccupping sobs began again.

'It's Eleanor's,' she sobbed. 'It's one of her special set. She said I could borrow it, but now I can never replace it.' She nodded towards the bookshelf by the fireplace.

Standing up, Anna walked over and saw what she meant. Along four shelves, in different colours but the same leathered livery, were Eleanor's collection of classics, spanning everything from *Moby Dick* to *Anna Karenina*, with a little Hemingway in between. And there, on the second shelf, was a gap in the perfect serried row, like a rotten tooth in a model's flawless smile.

'Shit,' she breathed. Not knowing Eleanor, not knowing how obsessive she might be, she had no way of knowing how badly this news would be received.

At the end of the day it was a book, and surely Callie's health and wellbeing were more important. But still . . .

'Let's make you a hot chocolate,' Anna said, 'and then work out what to do. You'd be amazed what I can find online when it comes to books.'

Callie brightened instantly, whether at the promise of a hot chocolate or a possible solution, it wasn't entirely clear.

'Shit day all round really,' Callie sniffed, climbing out of the sofa cushions. 'Confirmation that my mum has truly terrible taste in men as if it were needed – the one upstairs is not only a control freak but also possibly a psycho-in-waiting.' She held up the savaged book soulfully. 'I mean, seriously, who *does* this to a book?'

Callie slumped down on one of the kitchen chairs, her limbs seemingly too heavy to support actually standing. 'And then that cheeky copper called you homeless. I suppose we've just got to be grateful it wasn't us who were hit by a bus.' She gave a twisted smile. 'Although my mum's face would have been a treat if she thought I'd been rushed off to hospital wearing boxer shorts rather than a ladylike "brief".'

Anna snorted, suddenly assailed by a vivid memory of Marjorie talking about the importance of always wearing clean underwear – just in case you were hit by a bus.

'Wouldn't it be a hoot if that old lady was rocking stockings and a basque under her tweed waiting-for-God outfit?' Callie laughed.

Anna shook her head. 'Oh don't, she was a lovely old lady.'

'You don't know that,' said Callie seriously. 'You're only saying that because you kind of have the same name; she could be the madam in a local brothel.'

Anna's face split into a grin, not because she could imagine anyone on the planet less likely to corral the local sex work-ers, but because she'd missed this back-and-forth banter with a fellow storymaker. It had been the glue that held their student house together, back in the day, no tangent too obtuse to be ignored, no backstory too bland to be embroidered and elaborated on. And, of course, the number one rule: never let the truth get in the way of a good story.

'I've been thinking about her all afternoon,' Anna said, surprising herself with the confession. 'I even thought I might phone the hospital and see how she is.'

'Do it,' encouraged Callie. 'At least that way you can relax in the knowledge that she's okay, and that I was right about her dodgy corsetry.' She picked up the landline and waved it towards Anna.

'I don't even know her surname,' Anna protested, longing to call, yet still feeling as though she might be overinvested on the strength of a name.

Yet within a few moments she found herself listening to 'Greensleeves' on speakerphone and waiting to be put through to A&E. 'Hi,' she said. 'I'm calling about someone who was brought in by ambulance this morning. Annabel. I'm not sure of her surname.'

'Can't talk to anyone about a patient who isn't a relative, I'm afraid,' said the nurse on the phone.

'Oh no, I don't need details,' Anna was quick to clarify. 'And I know I'm not a relative, it's just that I was with her, while she was waiting for the ambulance. I suppose I just wanted to know that she was okay? And not, erm . . .' 'Dead or anything' seemed a little harsh, so Anna just allowed the sentence to dangle.

The nurse's tone softened immediately. 'Of course you do. That's very kind. Now look, let me have a check on the system and maybe I can put your mind at rest without breaking any confidentiality. I happen to know she was still talking about you when they brought her in. Bit confused she was – absolutely convinced she'd met her younger self in the gutter. Was asking to see her again, but I guess that was you. Bear with . . .'

There was a flurry of typing and Anna held her breath. She hadn't realised for a moment that's what the old lady had been thinking the whole time she'd been staring at her face with such concentration and clasping her hand.

The nurse came back on the line. 'Now, well, the thing is, it actually turns out that she doesn't have a next of kin, so I reckon it's okay for you to know. She's a few broken ribs and a lot of bruising. Ironically mainly from the fall. They think that her shoulder bag full of books actually took the worst of the impact from the bus's wing mirror. Funny world, eh? But they're going to keep her in for a few days, deal with the shock and manage the pain. She'll be up on the wards already. Annabel Armistice. But you didn't hear it from me. Now isn't that a name of a generation?'

A loud alarm sounded in the background. 'Thank you so—' managed Anna before the nurse was called away to a code.

'Annabel Armistice,' she said to Callie. 'I'll bet she was formidable.'

'Probably still is – and we can find out for ourselves,' Callie said, draining her hot chocolate and plucking the bunch of tulips from the vase on the kitchen table. 'Let's go and visit her. You heard the nurse; she's got no relatives.' Callie picked up her satchel and slung it across her body. 'She'll be glad of the company, and I can ask her questions for my history project. Win win.'

Anna blinked hard, slightly thrown off balance by the resilience of youth and Callie's enthusiasm. 'Okay,' she said. 'I do hate the idea of her being all alone after such a horrible day.'

No next of kin.

The phrase rattled around in Anna's head all the way to the hospital: it was uncomfortably close to her own reality. Right up there with 'no fixed abode'.

Striding down the long, bleach-scented corridors, trailing in the wake of Callie's boundless energy, she wondered what to say to someone who was lonely and frightened.

She needn't have worried.

The moment they stepped into Bay C on the second floor they saw Annabel, her bed surrounded by visitors.

'Oh,' said Anna in surprise, attempting to retrace her steps, but she'd already been spotted.

'I thought she didn't have any family?' Callie said loudly, intensifying Anna's embarrassment.

'Come and say hello,' Annabel commanded, looking surprisingly spry. 'These are my neighbours. Aren't they wonderful to come and settle me in? I've been telling them all about you.'

Chapter 32

Bath, 2019

Anna and Callie exchanged confused glances; the lonely elderly patient they'd come to visit appeared to be safe and secure in the bosom of her friends and neighbours.

Even as Annabel introduced them all, Anna was struck by the variety of these friends – old and young, wealthy and struggling, yet with one thing in common – they all lived within three doors of Annabel's small terraced house.

'Aren't I lucky to have such wonderful neighbours,' Annabel sighed, as she tucked into a box of Terry's All Gold.

Anna simply nodded, even as Callie enthusiastically joined in with tales of Eleanor and Richard's kindness and generosity.

The simple concept of 'neighbours' hadn't even made it onto Anna's radar, if she were honest, let alone as something else to aspire to including in her life choices.

Once more, her own elegantly efficient way of living seemed to pale by comparison; a little hollow and empty if she were to allow herself a brief moment's brutal honesty.

'Our Anna thought you were the ghost of Christmas past, you know?' said one of the neighbours with a smile. 'And I can see why she might have thought it – she was quite the looker in her day.'

The compliment was subtle, yet strangely heartfelt, and Anna felt welcomed into the little group. 'And I gather she's a bookworm like me, as well.'

'I'm right here, you know,' Annabel said crossly. 'You don't have to talk *about* me when you can talk *to* me.'

'Sorry, yes, of course. I was just about to say that I gather your library books took the brunt of the collision?'

'Tell that to my ribs,' said Annabel. 'But yes – isn't that lovely – the pen being mightier than the sword, and the bus it seems.' She smiled. 'The power of a good book is not to be underestimated.'

Callie leaned across and tugged open the canvas bag, eyes widening when she saw the chunky, glitzy hardbacks – Shirley Conran, Jilly Cooper and Judith Krantz.

'I'm old, not dead,' Annabel said, before Callie could express the shock that was written all over her face. 'And it's nice to get your jollies from a lovely book, rather than a needy bloke with high blood pressure and a crêpey bottom, when you get to my age.'

The neighbours laughed, unfazed. 'Annabel's been saucing up our book club this year, haven't you? No more *The Kite Runner* or *Ducks, Newburyport*; we're getting an education in escapist fiction.'

Callie frowned, looking to Anna for reassurance, but Anna simply shrugged.

'Don't knock a good romance 'til you've tried one, love,' one of the neighbours chimed in with a cheeky grin.

'Which one's best then, Annabel? Where should we start?' Anna asked, partly to play devil's advocate and wind up Callie's literary sensibilities, and partly because she was a little bit intrigued.

'*Lace*,' the book club chorused with throaty chuckles. 'And then *Riders*, obviously.'

Annabel sighed from her pyramid of pillows. 'And if you haven't had a filthy dream about Rupert Campbell-Black by the time you get to the last page, ask for your money back.'

Hours later, back at the flat, Anna paced the bookshelves that seemed to line every room, in search of some escapist reading as Annabel had prescribed. There was no shortage of Lawrence or Hardy, a fair few indecipherable tomes in Latin and Ancient Greek, but not a glitzy paperback in sight.

It was a shame really.

Anna had half wondered whether these books might be the answer to a happier life – for Annabel, at least, with her coterie of book-loving chums.

Happiness.

And not a literary analysis or Booker Prize in sight.

She thought of her own putative works, the stories she began and abandoned, for fear of falling short of her literary heroes. Would it be so very wrong, she wondered, if her writing sounded like she did – tentative, questing, and, despite everything life had thrown at her, just a little bit naive?

It was certainly something to think about.

'Supper's ready,' Callie called from the kitchen – happy to have traded cooking detail for an evening without admonishment. The only caveat being that she go upstairs and tell her mum.

Anna still shuddered at the cold, dismissive tone she'd overheard from the open front door.

Mothers came in different shapes and sizes, a fact to which she could personally attest, yet surely the very basic tenet of the relationship had to stem from caring? If loving was, for some reason, beyond them, then the very minimum had to include a desire to do what was best – unselfishly, and with interest.

Hearing the complete lack of interest in where Callie would be spending her evening, possibly even coloured by a little relief, had hit hard for Anna.

She'd written the story of Callie in her mind already, where the boyfriend was the bad guy and Callie's mother a conflicted dupe. Yet she'd been wrong.

She could all too easily identify with the closed expression on Callie's face when she walked back down the stairs. 'Told you she wouldn't give a shit.'

Was there anything worse than maternal disappointment?

Yes, they were just people. But they were *your* people.

You couldn't drive a car without a licence, but any fool could raise a child. Or attempt to.

But that feeling of never being good enough, once that primary bond had failed? Well, it made you question everything and everyone. That sense of hollow worthlessness, that you had to prove yourself constantly just to earn respect or affection – it never went away.

And Anna would know.

But it was probably the first time she'd seen first-hand that a mother didn't have to be physically absent, in order to be absent. She frowned as the thought occurred to her, turning it over in her mind and trying to make sense of it.

'My God that smells amazing,' Anna said as Callie scooped a delicious-smelling Thai curry into two bowls. 'How did you learn to cook so well?'

Callie shrugged. 'You learn when you have to, don't you?' She sprinkled some coriander on top and offered a sheepish smile. 'And Eleanor taught me a thing or two. She was worried about how much toast I was getting through, not to mention those cans of—'

'Condensed milk?' Anna finished for her. 'Cheap but filling and utterly sickly and delicious.'

Callie just nodded, their mutual understanding of what might lead a person to eat a tin of the thick, gooey confection absolute.

'Shall we download a movie and eat on our laps?' Anna offered, suddenly exhausted and unable to contemplate a mealtime with conversation.

'Yes, please,' said Callie tucking her feet underneath herself in one corner of the sofa and looking very much like the child that she still was.

'Something trashy?'

'Yes, please.'

Eleanor's phone call came just as the credits rolled and both of them were discreetly wiping a tear from their eye; you really couldn't beat *The Devil Wears Prada* for a feel-good roller-coaster of emotions.

'How're you getting on, Anna? Is Ulysses still sulking that we left him behind?' she said, her voice crystal clear and carrying across the room without the aid of speakerphone.

'No – but I am,' Callie called across and Anna heard Eleanor laugh appreciatively.

'Oh! You're there together – how lovely!'

And she genuinely sounded as though she meant it.

'Anna, thank you. I know Callie can be a handful – and yes I know she can probably hear me – but I do appreciate you being there for her.' She paused. 'I should probably have told you more about the whole situation, shouldn't I?'

'It's fine,' Anna said automatically. 'Although, obviously, knowing there was the option of an in-house chef could only have sealed the deal.'

Eleanor laughed again, obviously relieved. 'Well, insist she makes you my famous pad thai if she's a nuisance. One dog, one cat, one teenager – it's not really what you signed up for though, is it?'

'It'll be fine,' Anna replied. 'And, actually, she's been fabulous company. Nice to get a different perspective and a little youthful enthusiasm.'

Eleanor scoffed. 'You're hardly ancient yourself, young lady.' She hesitated. 'Now, not one to fuss, but can you pop Norbert on the phone so I can hear his little snuffles before I go?'

Anna couldn't help but smile, feeling herself relax at the honesty and affection in Eleanor's voice. She might well be the world's authority on Divine Aesthetes, but oh how she loved her little dog. And that was one of the things that made Anna's job so worthwhile: without people like her, would people like Eleanor ever dare to go away?

'Before you do,' Callie said across the room, 'can I have a word?'

Anna passed the phone over and tried not to eavesdrop, but with Eleanor's echoing tones it was almost impossible.

'Hi,' said Callie. 'I'm so sorry, but I damaged one of your special books – the classic collection by the fireplace.'

There was a long pause. 'Well, these things happen.' Eleanor was clearly trying hard to be magnanimous, then, more quietly, 'Dare I ask which one?'

'*The Great Gatsby*,' Callie whispered. 'I'm so, so sorry and of course I'll replace—'

'Thank God for that. If it's only Fitzgerald you can stop worrying, darling girl. All that angst and flamboyance can get a little depressing if you ask me.' Eleanor was firm, if not overly convincing; yet it seemed enough to reassure Callie.

'Just, maybe, stay away from my Chaucer? Or read it at my house.'

There was an awkward pause that told both Callie and Anna that Eleanor knew exactly who the real culprit was.

'I'm so sorry,' Callie said again. 'But please say you're having a lovely time in Rome?'

Anna popped next door to load the dishwasher so they could catch up properly, Ulysses deigning to follow her in case of leftovers and Norbert stationed at Callie's side waiting for his turn on the telephone.

'Eleanor really is one in a million,' Callie said, ten minutes later, still clutching Anna's phone and hovering in the doorway, as Anna filled the kettle and set out mugs for tea. 'I don't know where I'd be without her living downstairs.'

Anna nodded. 'I'm not going to say you're lucky to have her, because that always used to wind me up as a child.'

'Oh my God, *yes*! Why do people say that? Your life's gone to shit and there's one ray of sunshine illuminating the whole dung heap, but lucky, *lucky* me . . .'

Anna laughed. Some things never changed. 'Eleanor worries about you, and she cares about you, and she offers you some respite from the chaos. In my book, it's okay to appreciate that without editing out the situation that threw you together in the first place. I mean, if everything was hunky dory at home, you'd hardly be hanging out with the OAPs in the building.'

'I don't know actually,' Callie said, considering it. 'They're pretty cool and we're kind of into the same stuff – books and history and politics. So, in a way, they're like my grandparents.

Not *my* grandparents obviously – they like bingo and booze. But you know, like—'

'Mentors?' Anna offered.

'Yeah. Mentors. But really, just grown-ups to look up to and whose advice you trust.' She sighed. 'I'm going to be so fucked when they leave.'

Anna frowned. 'They're leaving?'

'Soon. Three months or so. They want to be closer to their kids in Cambridge so they're relocating.' She sighed again. 'Lucky kids.'

'Right?' Anna agreed, pausing for a moment before continuing. 'Do you think they have any idea how truly lucky they are? The kids?'

'Not a sodding clue,' Callie said, shaking her head.

'Well, you know, mentors come in all shapes and sizes. I adored my English teacher at school; Mrs Holt was the only person to call it like she saw it. It was her pushing me to do better that gave me the nerve to even attempt to get into Oxford. She wasn't taking anything less than my best.' Anna smiled at the memory. 'She used to say that the only inheritance I had was between my own two ears, so I'd better make the most of it.'

'Life really isn't a level playing field is it?' Callie asked sadly.

'Nope. But then, if you asked me now whether I would rather have had a cushy life and no clue, or a shitty time with a thinking head on my shoulders, I wouldn't have to think twice.

'And, you know?' Anna thought about the vile woman in the bookshop earlier. 'I'd have to say that I would rather be the quiet voice of reason in the room than the confidence-filled idiot who shouts the loudest. And that's something I'm only now coming to terms with.'

'But you're a grown-up.' Callie frowned.

'I'm a work in progress,' Anna corrected her. 'I'm constantly surprised by the difference some inspiration, a mentor, or a little timely insight into how the world works can make. I guess I try to keep an open mind and hope the answers present themselves.'

'Okay,' Callie said, taking it all in. 'Fate, then? Or serendipity?'

Anna nodded, weighing up how honest to be. 'Both, I think. Besides, I'm still trying to work out the right questions to ask. For me, it feels like sometimes the answers come first.'

'Eleanor says you should never go into a conversation or discussion without knowing the outcome you want. I have to assume she means with the universe as well.'

'Eleanor is very wise. And she believes in you, Callie. So, wherever she ends up, you need to hold onto that – like I did with Mrs Holt – if you're buoyed by her belief then it really does only take one person to change your life.'

She hesitated, the phone call with Henry earlier still fresh in her mind. 'I'm no Eleanor, but we could always keep in touch, you and me?' She held her breath for a moment, unaccustomed to reaching out, but before she could regret or rescind the offer, Callie's face lit up.

'Do you mean that? Or is that just something you say?'

'It's something I very, very rarely say,' Anna admitted.

'Then can I be ridiculously uncool and say a huge yes please?' Callie said, almost embarrassed by her own eagerness. 'I mean, you actually went to Oxford. You are, in fact, the only real, live person I've met who's done that. Maybe we could call your old college and get a prospectus? You'd know who to ask, right?'

Anna smiled, remembering all too well that feeling that Oxbridge was a fantasy that happened to other people. A secret club with confusing rules about who was allowed entry. She held out her phone. 'Type your number in for me, then we can't forget.'

Colour suffused Callie's pale complexion. 'I kind of did that already. Before, when I was talking to Eleanor.'

'Oh.' Anna blinked.

'And don't take this the wrong way but you seriously need to cull your inbox,' Callie tapped at the red lozenge on the screen showing thousands of unread emails. Of course, she wasn't to know that so many of them were from Anna to herself. A cleansing of her mind. The perfect repository of half-formed ideas and unprocessed emotions.

Hardly ideal mentor material, if you thought about it, when she herself still had so much to learn.

Chapter 33

Oxford, Jesus College, 2007

Anna stood in the middle of the quad, clutching her newly printed accommodation chit, and wondering what on earth she'd got herself into.

In all her conversations with Mrs Holt about studying at Oxford, they had talked about the lecturing staff (second to none apparently), the history and magnificence of the architecture (undeniable) and the thrill of studying in the Bodleian library (as yet untested).

Not once had they talked about the other students and this suddenly felt like a foolish and alarming oversight.

It was safe to say that Anna was the only fresher on parade that morning wearing ancient Green Flash trainers, and with a scant forty quid in her bank account to see her through all the week zero revelries.

She wasn't sure if it was the ease or familiarity of how everyone spoke to each other that so unnerved her, so much as the overwhelming sense of privilege and confidence. She tightened her grip on the A4 page, crumpling it slightly, as she slowly breathed out.

'Waiting for your rentals?' a boy with blonde, tousled,

surfer-dude hair asked her. Although his neatly pressed trousers and expensive striped shirt were as far from the beach bum look as it was possible to get.

'Rentals?' Anna asked, confused.

The boy grinned. 'Rentals, as in parentals? Are you waiting for your folks to bring your stuff?' he said, his voice getting ever slower at the look of incomprehension on her face. 'The parking's the absolute worst. They'll be forever. Come and get a proper drink?' He waved a half-empty bottle of grapefruit Snapple disdainfully. £1.89.

Who knew what a 'proper drink' might cost.

'I'm fine,' Anna said. 'Thank you. I just need to take my stuff up to my room and get sorted.' She nudged the large holdall beside her with one foot. 'I was just taking it all in.'

He frowned, staring down at the bag. 'That's it? That's all your stuff?' He nodded towards well-dressed grown-ups guiding fully laden, and apparently unwieldy, luggage carts into the college grounds. 'What about the rest?'

Anna shrugged. 'I like to travel light.'

Comprehension dawned. 'Right, okay. You've been travelling, yeah? Gap year made you see the error of our materialistic ways? That's cool.'

He sauntered off, waving a greeting to three other boys who shared the stylistic anomaly of preppy clothes and surfing locks. 'Miles, Angus! Alright, you wankers?'

'Well at least they're self-aware enough to realise it,' came a dry voice from just behind Anna, making her smile, as she turned.

'I'm Kate,' said the girl, scruffy in that way that suggested it was a considered choice not a necessity. 'And this is some kind of madness.' She smiled, and the tiny gap between her front teeth made her seem immediately approachable and normal. None of this cloying perfection and privilege in her self-deprecating laugh. 'Please tell me that bag isn't some incredible capsule wardrobe?'

Anna shook her head. 'I had zero clue what to pack so you could call it a scattergun approach.'

'Or boho chic?' Kate suggested. 'Nobody gives a fuck about fashion here anyway, it's just so the cliques can recognise each other. And you don't strike me as someone who buys into all that. So we can be friends. What was your name again?'

'Anna. Anna Wilson,' she said.

'Okay then, Anna, Anna Wilson. Let's find out where you'll be living for the next nine months and then we can find out the best vantage point to take in all the crazy. How does that sound?'

It sounded good to Anna's terrified ears, even better when it turned out they were on the same corridor.

We can be friends.

Just like that, this girl called Kate had apparently decided it would be so.

Confident but funny, unfazed by all the one-upmanship and posturing, scathing and eloquent, Kate embodied everything that Anna could hope for – both in a friend and in herself.

'I'm glad you came along,' she confided quietly, as they hung out of her bedroom window watching the chaos in the quad below. 'I was just wondering what the hell I'd got myself into.'

'I refused to get up this morning,' Kate replied with a sigh. 'I'd probably still be in bed if my mum hadn't bribed me with pancakes. And reminded me that this was something I'd actually worked my arse off for, something I actually wanted.' She grinned at Anna. 'I guess I forgot that it would involve so many *people*.'

And so they did what freshers up and down the country were doing that week: they traded A level grades, interview horror stories and, as the night grew into early morning, their own anxieties about what studying here might actually be like.

Day in, day out, with some of the brightest minds of their generation.

It wasn't until they saw the gaggle of boys, with their pants on their heads and not a stitch of clothing on their bodies, running through the streets that they began to reassess.

Brightest minds might not be so daunting after all.

It was, in all likelihood, their proven pedigrees and inherent belief in their own superiority that would be harder to overcome.

As the weeks passed, it became harder and harder to hold on to the script she'd been running in her head: a combination of Mrs Holt's absolute faith and pride in her abilities, coupled with the ever-running question of what-would-Lucy-Graham-do? Although she'd been unable to track Lucy down, she still relied on all those conversations years ago, as she had throughout her exams. Lucy seemed to embody the spirit of what she herself wanted to achieve: to leave it all behind and rely on her own wits and abilities. And certainly, this was the place to do it.

Daunting though it was.

Lectures were overwhelming, not just in terms of content but also the posturing as other students attempted to find their place in the new intellectual pecking order, now the goal posts of A levels and school had been removed. It was a new world order.

Tutorials were nicer, simply because they were a more intimate setting and gave the quieter students an easier platform to share their understandings and analyses of the texts.

For here, at Oxford, Anna was quiet. Not shy, so much as biding her time; like trying to catch a wave, she waited until she understood the ebb and flow of the social life here before even attempting a toe in the water.

Kate, it seemed, for all her concerns on the first day, was unfazed and amused by most of it. 'I've joined the societies I like, and I've got the course I want. With you across the corridor, Anna, I'm sorted. Besides, trust me when I say it's easier to wait for all the silverbacking and hair-flicking to settle down.'

And Kate would know.

She didn't even make any secret of it – her mother was faculty. Not here, not in Jesus College – but she warranted a page of her own on the social anthropology website and she was apparently both esteemed and popular at the same time. Oxford – the town, the university – had been Kate's playground all her life. Any novelty long since eroded, yet her respect for the institution remained.

She was exactly the mediating presence that Anna needed, even without her knowing it. She was calm, friendly and focused on her studies. Most of the time. But on Friday nights she refused to take no for an answer, and tugged Anna into the JCR – the Junior Common Room – to mingle and socialise. Even if they never joined the groups 'going on' to somewhere more racy, it was the bridge that Anna needed to feel safe.

'I'm so glad I met you on the first day,' Kate said to her one Friday night a few weeks in, as three of the girls they'd been chatting with left to reapply make-up and head for the nightclubs in town.

It so closely echoed Anna's own thoughts that she couldn't help but laugh. 'I definitely think I got the better end of the deal.'

Kate shrugged. 'Maybe it was just meant to be. Hey, maybe we'll end up being friends for life? You can be my children's godmother and we'll embarrass them on their twenty-firsts with tales of debauchery and derring-do.'

Anna tried not to flinch at the very thought of becoming a parent herself. That conversation could wait until their fledgling friendship had taken a firmer hold, for she personally had no intention of becoming a mother. She would lie, she'd long since decided, and say she couldn't have children. Blame some vague biological impediment to reproduction perhaps? Certainly better than admitting the truth: the absolute fear that she had inherited the 'rubbish parent' gene that left her ill-equipped to care for anyone unconditionally and selflessly.

'Of course,' she said, by way of distraction, 'then we would actually need a few memories to call on – and I'm not sure derring-do is right up my street.'

Kate grinned. 'Give it time. You've got three years to find your feet and find your groove. I'm honestly not sure why this lot are in such a hurry.' She waved a hand around to encompass the packed JCR, little clusters of bravado and flirtation all somehow reeking of urgency and desperation. 'I like a slow burn, not an inferno.'

'I had no idea it would be like this,' Anna said, sipping at her Diet Coke and trying to make it last. £1.20.

It wasn't just the cost of being sociable that had astounded her, even as her meagre bank account dwindled, it was the priorities. Hadn't they all studied and sacrificed to get here – and yet now here they were, lectures were being skipped, deadlines missed, all in favour of a great night out or a cheeky hook-up. Relationships didn't happen. They were fluid and flexible, as shown by the number of tearful girls Anna had seen, who apparently hadn't received the memo until it was too late.

Oxford was – for want of a better description – a jungle. A jungle where all the animals were eloquent, intelligent and driven. Though without the restrictions of parents and school, it was already clear that decency and consideration were no longer a given. It really was a little David Attenborough, if you sat back and watched.

And thankfully Kate and Anna, together, were able to do just that.

The resilience that had carried Anna through the last decade now held her in good stead: she had no need to find herself, or express herself; she just wanted to explore her own abilities and potential. Hardly the stuff of popularity, yet she didn't care. With Kate and a few girls from her English tutor group around her, she was never lonely. She was never adrift on the seas of uncertainty that seemed to ebb and flow through the colleges and bars.

If there was one small spanner in the works, it was in seeing how she was perceived by others.

Her clothes were old. Unfashionable.

Her budget didn't stretch to make-up and rounds at the bar.

And whilst, yes, technically, Social Services and a lifetime of shit meant that she was getting – or possibly had earned – a free ride through university, she couldn't bring herself to get into debt to buy camaraderie or friendship.

Popularity would have been a stretch too far, whatever her means.

So, instead, she worked hard, she was pleasant and polite

– she would have to settle for respect.

Until, just after Easter of her first year, she met Max Howard.

And then suddenly, just like that, little Anna Wilson understood that frenetic drive to conform, to be approachable, desirable. And yes, for a little popularity to underscore that she wasn't just the star of the English Lit program, she was also someone to be singled out and worthy of his attention.

Chapter 34

Oxford, 2008

It was hard to put into words the effect of Max's tawny eyes on hers. Let alone the surreal feeling of being the only girl in the room when the full focus of his attention fell on her. It was as though the breath merely held in her chest, stilled to inaction, waiting on his words.

'So, you're the girl everyone's talking about – the one to watch,' he said, slipping into a chair beside her in the library, his voice necessarily quiet, leaning in close so that she could hear him without incurring the wrath of the indomitable librarian.

She'd had no answer to that one, had even been a little freaked out – it was a fine line between complimentary and creepy after all. As she pulled the air into her protesting lungs, she felt the colour rise up her neck, and any hope of a witty comeback desert her.

'I mean,' he continued, clearly bemused by her reaction, perhaps used to a little more fawning and flirtation, 'that the assignments are back and you beat all of us by a head and a half, Anna Wilson. You really are a dark horse.'

He studied her, as though the answers to her success might be found in her tousled ponytail, or the cheap, over-the-counter reading glasses from Boots that stopped the headaches that had appeared from studying long hours. He reached out and flicked her books closed. 'Come on, I'll take you out to celebrate. It's not every day you become the darling of the entire English department, is it?'

And, to her amazement, against everything she thought she knew about herself, Anna had gone with him. Sitting in a small bistro in Turl Street, Anna had allowed herself to listen; mopping up sumptuously vibrant olive oil with hunks of warm sourdough, she had allowed herself to be that girl – like the ones she had seen around town, hanging on the arms of the rowing squad or the rugby team.

The girls that she and Kate had looked down their noses at for dulling themselves down just to be seen as a catch.

'Where did you say your people were from again?' Max said, refilling her wine glass.

Her 'people'? Had she tumbled into one of the arcane novels they'd been studying?

But the part of her that wanted to mock was completely overruled by an insistent desire to watch his lips as he spoke, to imagine running her hands through the unruly mop of hair that was highlighted by long summers in the sun.

'We moved around a lot,' she said easily, the lie only really a half-truth.

'I can't even imagine that,' he said with a smile. 'We've literally lived in the same house my whole life. Well, technically, my mum has too. And she's sixty. We Howards like a steady home base.'

'Sixty years? That's amazing. And you – you've never been away from home before?'

He gave her a weird sideways look. 'Well, apart from boarding school since the age of six and, you know, sailing, skiing and stuff – I guess not.'

'Boarding school at six?' Anna said, probably missing the point of his super-casual allusion to his wealth and privilege. 'Isn't that, well . . .?'

She wanted to say 'cruel'. She wanted to say 'a travesty of parental obligation'.

But then who was she to talk? Only twelve months older when she'd been entirely alone, but for Social Services stepping in. No fancy trunk full of uniform, or tuck box full of treats.

True, her knowledge of boarding schools was more Enid Blyton than Anthony Powell, but she liked to think she had a little idea of how he must have felt, shipped off from the family home.

Instead, he simply shrugged. 'Duncan was already there, so it was hardly a stretch. Couldn't lift my bloody trunk for the first two years though.' He laughed, and for a fleeting, vulnerable moment, Anna saw the boy behind the carefully curated façade.

It made her *like* him just a little bit more.

Attraction had never been in doubt. There was an almost visceral pull towards him that she'd last encountered in a library at Hinchworth Comprehensive, and, just as Lucy Graham had pulled Anna into her orbit, so too did Max Howard. Drawn in by his conviction and his absolute sense of where he stood in the world. Grounded. Secure. At ease in his own skin.

Even if she didn't entirely agree with a lot of what he was saying, or indeed how disdainfully he treated the waitress rushing from table to table. Even if his life was so different from hers as to be unrelatable.

Her heart seemed determined to overlook these minor inconveniences, simply for the promise of one touch, one kiss, one more moment of his undivided attention.

★

'You do know he'll break your heart,' Kate said one evening, as they sat huddled together on the parapets of the college, well and truly out of bounds, but also away from the mad revelries below them.

Prelims were finished, the end of term approaching, and the sun had obligingly cast their small city, their small college, into a honeyed phase of blissful ease. All the stresses and revision seemingly forgotten as cafés and restaurants tumbled their patrons onto patios and pavements and Oxford itself felt like an idyllic haven.

Anna sipped at the sickly bottle of cider, still uncomfortable around alcohol, but softening in her willingness to settle in with the status quo.

'I know,' she replied quietly. 'But somehow that doesn't feel like enough of a reason to step back.' Tilting her head backwards she squinted her eyes against the Oxford skyline and breathed slowly out. 'It's just another rite of passage anyway, right? A little heartbreak?'

Kate scowled, her opinion of Max sinking further with every interaction they shared. 'He's a buffoon, though, Anna. All that intellect, all that potential and privilege and he's too lazy to put in the work.'

'He's not lazy; he's just relaxed,' Anna defended him. 'He's not like us, you know, stressing over every detail and deadline. He just goes with the flow and – annoyingly – he always seems to land on his feet. So, he can't be entirely wrong. Even if I have no idea how he manages it.'

'Hmm,' Kate replied sceptically, as though she suspected exactly how he managed it. 'He takes advantage of your good nature, Anna. He knows you'll never say no when he wants to borrow your notes, or needs you to proofread his essays. And by proofread, we're talking rewrite. I just – well, I don't get what you see in him.'

'Really?' Anna gave her a look that made it all too clear where the attraction lay.

'Argh, just let me know when you start thinking with your head again, then, okay?' Kate laughed. 'And maybe we'll have to implement some house rules for next term?'

'Good idea,' Anna replied, distractedly, still thinking about Max and the insatiable desire he had stirred up in her. Their afternoons lazily spent in his bed seemed to make the summer more vibrant, her body more alive and the small tendrils of hope for her future seemed to have finally taken hold.

She was living again.

Out in the world, as a normal student, doing normal everyday things.

Like falling in love.

She took a slug of the cider, wincing at the cloying sweetness, but needing something to offset the very idea.

Was that it; was she in *love* with Max Howard?

Was he actually – possibly, maybe – the person she could build her life with? Together?

'It's not love, it's just lust,' she said out loud, as much to placate herself as Kate.

'Good to know,' Kate laughed. 'But I'm serious about next term. We've got really lucky with our house and sharing with Hannah and Nicola is going to be epic. We all get on so well and we're all on the same song sheet when it comes to partying and studying and stuff. Just – let's not fuck up the dynamic from the get-go with Max Howard loafing his way through our lives.'

Anna frowned. 'Are you saying he's not welcome?'

'No. But I am saying he can buy his own food, and not leave chaos in his wake. You know what he's like, Anna. He's never washed a dish or picked up his crap in his whole life.

He's so used to having a cleaner, or a housekeeper, or a nanny to do his bidding that he's barely even house-trained.'

'Point taken,' Anna said. It was hardly something she could disagree with. Even she had been shocked by the state of his room in College, even though he paid cash to one of the housekeeping staff to come in twice a week to sort it all out.

One room.

And yet still he needed a cleaner.

She couldn't pretend that she hadn't judged him for that.

Just as she couldn't pretend that Kate's take on Max was fair: if Anna didn't *almost* love him, she probably wouldn't even like him.

It was confusing at best.

Yet still, day after day, the fascination of those few hours in bed with their limbs entwined overwrote any concerns her imagination could formulate. Hope, it seemed, had finally got the upper hand over the catastrophising lizard part of her brain that had been running the show for so long.

'If it comes to it, I'll stay at his place,' Anna said, unable to disguise the tightness of disappointment in her voice.

'Oh for fuck's sake, Anna. That's not what I was saying and you know it. And why would we knowingly send you over there, so you can become their unpaid skivvy and cook? Don't be daft.' Kate sighed. 'And please – let's agree never to let any bloke, no matter how foxy, come between us? Promise?'

Anna nodded. 'Promise.' She took another slug of cider, feeling distinctly nauseated, the courtyard now somehow looking further and further below them. 'And anyway – it might be a moot point by October. He's travelling all summer, Kate, so let's not kid ourselves that he'll be saving himself for me.' A small sob escaped her and she thrust the half-empty bottle of Diamond White out of reach, as though it were to blame for her rollercoaster of emotions.

'Ah, shit, Anna. Come here, I didn't mean to make you cry!' Kate said.

'It's not you.' Anna sniffed, wiping her nose on the back of her hand and not even caring in that moment how disgusting that was. 'It's me. How on earth did I fall for *this* guy, Kate? He's so far out of my league it's laughable. He'll be off sailing with the Sophies and Lucys and Camillas, and I'll be here all summer, pulling pints and walking dogs just to get enough cash for next year.'

The thought of money was never far from her mind. It wasn't so much a question of class, as survival. Even with her life here so heavily subsidised – possibly the one benefit of a 'looked-after' childhood – she was constantly aware that there was no buffer, no Bank of Mum and Dad if she overspent.

'Look – I'm not listening to this crap,' Kate said, taking her hands. 'If you ask me – or anyone in our tutor group actually – we would all say that *he's* out of *your* league. Everything you've just listed comes from his parents' achievements, his parents' bank account. Hell, he can barely scrape a Third without you holding his hand. Can we look at this logically and say that by any measure: independence, resilience, talent, ability? Good old-fashioned hard work? *He's* the one that comes up wanting, not you.'

Anna blinked hard, thrown by the ferocity of Kate's words. They made sense. They did. And yet still she couldn't bring herself to believe them.

Max Howard carried with him an emotional cushion from a life well led – his confidence so absolute it was alluring. As though, simply by being at his side, just a little of that patina might rub off on her. As though, simply by sharing his bed and their mutual attraction, it made Anna herself a little more worthy of this gilded existence at Oxford University.

And even if this thought deeply offended her very sensibilities, it was nothing compared to the allure that Max Howard wore like a cloak of unshakeable belief.

Chapter 35

Oxford, 2008

Anna stood in the recess of her dormer window, her top floor bedroom feeling a little like the writer's garret she had so often dreamed of, even if it did come with an avocado bathroom suite, generic magnolia walls and beige carpeting. This was her space – one of four bedrooms in this student terrace on the Cowley Road – and hers alone for the next two years.

Although, of course, should she choose to share . . .

She thought of Max, his occasional texts increasingly infrequent from the hotspots of Europe – cities, beaches, mountains – he certainly seemed to be making the most of his summer vacation. She thought of their last call, late at night, his clearly having knocked back one too many Stella Artois, and it still made her feel uncomfortable. She wasn't a prude; she just didn't feel okay about what he'd been asking her to do. Talking dirty to get him off in some anonymous hotel room didn't feel right to her. The pretence of a loving relationship was wearing thin.

Somehow, over the course of the summer, working long hours and setting up the house with Kate, Max had receded from her thoughts. Without his very presence making her mind abdicate responsibility to her body, she struggled to remember what it was about him that made all rationale leave the building.

'Can I come in?' Kate said, tapping at the door and piling in with an armful of towels before Anna could even respond. 'So, Mum says we should save our money for fun stuff, not domestic crap, and she's given us these.' She tossed the bale of soft, navy bath sheets and flannels and hand towels onto Anna's bed. 'Personally, I think it's because she saw some beautiful cream ones in The White Company and wanted an excuse to update, but never look a gift horse in the mouth.'

Anna reached out to touch them, their sumptuous softness belying any attempt to write them off as hand-me-downs.

'They're from the guest bathroom, so I guess they haven't been used much,' Kate said, watching her face carefully.

'Tell your mum I said a huge thank you,' Anna said, despite the tiny demon on her shoulder stamping his feet and raging about not being a charity case. Yet. 'They're lovely.'

Kate visibly relaxed. 'Cool. So that means we've got the kitchen and bathroom sorted, we can hit IKEA and get a desk each, maybe even a comfy chair to go with it – let's face it, we're going to be spending more time studying than anything else.'

'Are we though?' Anna smiled. Her stellar results at the end of the first year had not only brought her acclaim and confidence but a scholarship from her college towards this year's expenses. She half wondered if she could dare to slack off a little, join a few societies, expand her horizons beyond the Bodleian.

'Well, obviously, you'll need to schedule in some shagging with that eejit Max,' Kate teased her, still trying to keep an open mind about Anna's boyfriend. 'Just try and keep it down a bit, yeah. Who knows how sound travels in this house!'

Anna chucked her pillow at Kate's head, laughing, feeling wonderfully, blissfully at peace with their new living arrangements. 'I might dump him actually. Absence doesn't always make the heart grow fonder, you know.'

'At last, she sees the light!' Kate cried, a smile lighting up her face as she held her arms aloft like an evangelical.

'Oh shush,' Anna said, frowning. 'He's not all bad. He's just a little, well, light on character and heavy on charm.' She shrugged. 'It's easier to say that when he's hundreds of miles away, obviously. He's almost impossible to say no to in person.'

Kate's eyebrow shot up. 'Is that right? I'm not sure I want to hear more, to be honest. I just want somebody who treats you right, rather than an intellectual booty call.'

'A what now?' Anna said, flinching instinctively.

'Well, he turns up for help with his assignments, or to borrow your notes, and then when he's had a lovely shag, he buggers off back to his rooms. Am I in the right ballpark?'

Too accurate for comfort actually, but Anna didn't say that. She hadn't felt disposable, or used. She'd felt as though she could bask in the warmth of his attention for the rest of her life. Until he left to go travelling and, without that glow, without the intimacy making her feel so special, it just felt a little – well – cold, actually.

'Well, let's not sully our fresh start here with talk of old boyfriends – let's go to IKEA and buy hip Scandi duvet covers and weird serving bowls we will only use for popcorn, deal?'

'Deal,' said Kate, reaching across to shake her hand, her face a picture of relief.

IKEA had been a revelation. So much stuff – all brand new – so many make-believe room-sets that Anna had been unable to resist the urge to play *Through the Keyhole*.

'Now, who would live in a house like this?' she'd intoned, making up stories and lives for each mock sitting room that had Kate in stitches and, at one point, a stern security guard urging them to 'cool it'.

Kate had been amused by Anna's enthusiasm, but also, it seemed, rather touched. 'You know, I can't think of anyone I would rather be setting up house with. I've never moved house before and you've been round the block a few times, sure, but this place will be *ours*, won't it – just for a little while. Our house, our rules, our friends. I'm so stoked we get to do this.'

'Me too,' Anna had said, tucking her arm tightly through Kate's, feeling as though every addition to the trolley in The Marketplace was another building block in their friendship.

Pushing open the front door with her hip, Anna deposited the vast blue and yellow bags inside as Kate tried to find somewhere to park. She couldn't wait to pull apart the packaging and start making over her bedroom with the lamps and bookends and cushions, not to mention the soft striped duvet cover that seemed so luxurious – and for her very first double bed. Decadence indeed.

She had big plans this year, having finally, finally found her feet. There was so much to explore and enjoy, there was hardly enough time in the week. Somewhere around the lighting department in IKEA, she'd decided that breaking up with Max had to be first on her agenda.

It was time to be herself.

Until this summer, she hadn't even realised how many friends she had in Oxford. And not of the shouting-hoarsely-across-bars variety like Max had, but real conversations in the library, in the coffee shops, even just on the benches of Christ Church Meadow on a sunny day. She may not know if they took their vodka straight up or with ice, or how many shots they could down before puking their guts up; their conversations were about their lives, their loves and ambitions.

In short, friendships nerd-style.

She grinned. Finding her tribe made being herself so much less of a challenge.

Kate pounded on the front door. 'I haven't got my key and you've got visitors.'

Shoving up the sleeves on her oversized green jumper above her elbows, glasses sliding down her nose as she moved some of the bags out of the way, Anna tugged open the door.

All her resolutions deserting her in an instant.

Bronzed, buff and smiling at her as though she were the centre of his world, Max Howard held out his arms. 'Surprise!'

Anna looked to Kate but saw only her poker face giving nothing away.

'Wow. You should have said you were coming—'

'But then it wouldn't have been a surprise.' Max grinned, clearly thrilled with himself. 'You didn't seem yourself last time we spoke, and it felt like we'd been apart too long, you know? I missed you.' He stepped inside and pulled her into a deep, searching kiss, smiling confidently as he released her. 'So this is the new pad, huh? Nice digs.'

Anna was simply speechless, watching as he dropped his luggage in the hall and looked around. He gave her another devastating smile. 'Nice jumper, A – you look like a scrumptious Granny Smith.'

Anna stilled, knowing from his smile that there was a compliment in there somewhere, yet suddenly feeling rotund, as she pulled off her glasses and tucked them out of sight.

A cough from the doorstep caught her attention. 'Er, were you going to introduce me to your girlfriend, or are you too busy catching up?'

Anna blinked at the man standing beside Kate, a strange facsimile of Max, yet without the radiant glow of conceit. Smaller, wiry and with neat tortoiseshell glasses, he was obviously embarrassed to be standing on a stranger's doorstep without so much as an introduction. 'I'm Duncan, the older brother,' he said, holding out his hand politely to Kate. 'As always, I can only apologise for Max. I did say we should have called ahead and you're obviously busy.'

Kate smiled. 'No need to apologise.'

'Let me help at least,' he said, picking up the larger of the three boxes that were stacked outside. 'Depending on how long Prince Charming here needs to persuade Anna that he's not a bounder and a cad, we could probably get most of this built.'

Anna looked from one to the other in confusion. 'You brought your brother to meet me?' she asked, softening. She'd never been invited to join Max's family on any of their previous trips to Oxford. He'd also never directly referred to her as his girlfriend before.

Duncan laughed as he carried Kate's flat-pack desk up the stairs. 'Needed a lift from the airport more like.'

'Are you all moved in then?' Max asked, ignoring him and gently stroking the underside of her arm, edging ever closer to the strap of her camisole. She hadn't even noticed him slipping his hands up under her jumper, but as his eyes grew dark and his focus on her face remained unbroken, she knew exactly what he was asking.

She hesitated. Yes, her bed was here and yes, her body had immediately forgotten all thoughts of breaking up with him, but she felt a certain reluctance to leap straight into bed. He'd been gone for weeks, sharing a bed with God knows who.

'I'll put the kettle on,' she said firmly. 'And you can tell me about your trip.'

'Tea?' he said. 'Wine o'clock surely, Anna? I missed you. Let's celebrate being together again.'

She felt herself give a little more, thrown off balance by his insistence that he'd missed her and yet bizarrely feeling more dull and pedestrian than she had in weeks.

He swooped up her hair from the back of her neck and kissed the delicate skin with increasing urgency. 'Don't make me wait for a reunion while I bore you with stories of all the vapid eejits on the Euro-trail.'

'Tea. Talking,' Anna said firmly, ushering him through into the kitchen just as Kate ran back downstairs, cheeks flushed and eyes bright.

'Listen,' she whispered urgently. 'I know you had big plans for a break-up, but can you at least wait until I've got Duncan's phone number? He's gorgeous. Like a lovable geek. And seriously cute. Please, Anna?' She dashed upstairs again, casting a smile back over her shoulder that Anna had never seen before. A sure sign that Kate was actually serious in her request.

She walked into the kitchen to find Max opening and closing all the cupboards. 'You can totally tell this is a girl's house – look, it's all so organised and everything matches.' He held out his hands to her and pulled her in close. 'And look, as much as I'm enjoying the grand tour of domesticity, I guess I was hoping we could have a little privacy. I've been away from you for far too long, A. I'm sorry.'

He dipped his head and kissed her once more and, whether it was the apology or the gentle insistence of his lips on hers, in that moment, Anna couldn't remember a single reason why she'd been protesting.

Chapter 36

Oxford, 2008

Anna fiddled with the intricate silver bracelet on her wrist, confusion and longing mingling into one swirling mass of uncertainty. All the clarity she'd gained over the summer seemed to have deserted her the moment Max turned the spotlight of his affections on her again. He was certainly easier to ignore in theory than in practice.

'Beautiful bracelet,' Kate said, walking through to the sitting room with two steaming bowls of pasta. 'Expensive too, by the look of it.'

She was fishing.

She must have heard their laughter – not to mention their somewhat noisy reunion in Anna's new bedroom – yet she hadn't said a word. Distracted by Duncan? Possibly. But there was also a hint of disappointment in her voice that Anna simply didn't feel up to addressing.

'Please say you didn't stay with Max just because I asked you to?' Kate said as she snuggled down beside Anna and passed her the carbonara.

'No – don't be daft – of course not,' Anna said. But she couldn't deny that even that momentary delay in the kitchen had snapped the last thread of willpower holding her back. Was it possible to be addicted to another person? Or to what they represented perhaps?

She couldn't deny anymore, even to herself, that on some level she loved Max, but she didn't actually seem to *like* him very much and that was significantly more troubling.

'Nice pasta,' she said, her hand emerging from the duvet to hold her fork, twirling the ribbons of tagliatelle into a neat parcel and popping it into her mouth.

Kate laughed. 'My God you're like a little pea in a pod, so cosy. Are you intending to hibernate generally, or is it just a reaction to the afternoon's events?'

Anna chewed, buying time. 'I don't know. But you have to admit that it's sweet that he missed me – that he cut short his trip just to spend time with me?'

Kate froze, her carbonara suddenly requiring her undivided attention. 'Sure.'

'Kate?' Anna's appetite deserted her. 'Spill.'

'Oh feck it, Anna. I can't do this – I can't watch your disappointment and know that *I* caused it. Ask your boyfriend.' Kate stared down into her bowl again. 'We've got the most amazing year ahead of us and Nicola and Hannah are moving in next week. Can't we just enjoy this time without stupid boys ruining our vibe?'

'So, he didn't in fact come back just to see me, is what you're saying?' Anna held up her hand. 'Sorry, *not* saying.'

Kate sighed dramatically. 'Duncan said he screwed up his medieval lit prelim and had to come back and re-sit before the start of term—'

'Which he would have known about since June,' Anna finished for her, pushing away the bowl of carbonara, the glistening strands making her stomach twist uncomfortably. A strangely vivid memory of rhubarb crumble, the colour of Pepto Bismol, crept into her mind and with it the overwhelming emotion of disappointment.

It was a feeling that she was all too familiar with, and yet this time it felt different. Because this time she was disappointed in herself.

'Well, that's a real boost for the self-esteem, isn't it?' She shook her head. 'Kate, why do I have such lousy taste in men?'

'Honestly?' asked Kate, her expression serious. 'Or is this one of those conversations where I tell you what I really think and then you and Max carry on dating and things get really awkward between us, real fast?'

Anna shrugged. 'Hit me. I can handle it.'

Kate's beautifully shaped eyebrow disappeared under her fringe. 'I'm going to need the promise of immunity here.'

'Oh for fuck's sake, Kate. Spill.'

'Well, if you ask me, you have no frame of reference for what a good man looks like. Or acts like. Or how he might talk to you.'

Anna frowned. 'But that's—'

'So on the money? Let me give you an example. I don't think it's okay when Max teases you for being a super-brain, says you wouldn't enjoy the parties with his mates, but still constantly borrows your notes.

'I don't think it's okay every time he calls you "sensitive" for having an opinion that doesn't tally with his wonky views.

'And I *really* don't think it's okay the way he negs you all the time, subtle little digs that make you shrink before my eyes.'

'But . . .' Anna began and then stopped, so many conversations suddenly cast into a different light. She swallowed hard.

'But that's just how they talk, isn't it? Boys, I mean. Young, stupid boys. They're just full of bravado and everything's a joke?'

'But is everything a joke to you?' Kate said quietly. 'Would you be friends with a girl who spoke to you the way Max does?'

Anna shook her head. 'But then I wouldn't feel that way about a mate, would I? All the other stuff . . .'

'The shagging?' Kate said curtly. 'Is that what this boils down to?'

'No! I mean, partly, maybe? It's not *just* the shagging is all I'm saying . . . I like the way he's so certain about everything—'

'Even when he's wrong,' Kate interrupted. 'Look, I get that life is confusing and that maybe you're exploring being away from the system and everything, but Max Howard does not live a normal life. He lives a life of absolute privilege and as a result, to slightly misquote Hermione Granger, he has the emotional range of a teaspoon.'

Anna laughed despite herself. 'It's true. He has. There's never been a hurdle to overcome or a challenge he couldn't buy his way through. But, Kate – I think I'm a lost cause because all of that? It intrigues me.'

'Then study anthropology. Go see my mum and swap courses. Because a proper loving relationship shouldn't be about one-upmanship and power games. He's got you doubting yourself and chasing your tail. Seriously – all summer, you've been like Anna-Plus and it's been heavenly. Six hours with Max Howard and you're all Anna-Lite again.'

Anna was speechless. She'd known it; she'd felt it. She just hadn't realised it was noticeable to anyone else.

Orange squash – diluted.

'Do you think this is just going to be it for me then? Stuck in old patterns, bending myself round like a pretzel to fit into whatever lifestyle catches my eye. I'm like a fucking magpie – anything sparkly, or easy, and I'm there, with my little beak pressed against the window.'

'I'm going to forgive your horrific mangling of your metaphors, and say no. No, I don't think this is how it will always be. But I do think that you need to take a step back and look at your motivations. Maybe Max Howard isn't just your catnip because he's fit and confident; maybe it's more about the family weekends, and the family dinners and the house that gets passed down from generation to generation? None of which, by the way, you have been invited to.' Kate shrugged. 'I'm not saying you're a gold-digger, by the way. I think it's just the allure of a close-knit family that has you hooked.'

'Fuck,' breathed Anna, her mind whirring with the implications of what Kate had just said.

'By that token, it probably explains why you're friends with me too,' Kate said. 'But I won't judge you for it, because I'm fabulous. I mean, seriously, who could resist?'

Anna laughed. 'You know I love your mum and dad. I mean, I could live without your annoying little brother. But honestly, *you* had me at hello. That first day, when you just decided we would be friends.'

Kate looked astonished. 'I was just trying to hide the fact that I was bricking it – I knew nobody and I hated how lost I suddenly felt, in a place where I'd always felt at home.'

'Are you serious?' Anna asked, laughing. 'Well that puts the whole thing into a new perspective.'

'Well, to be fair, you looked plain terrified too, so I was thinking safety in numbers,' Kate said.

'Safety in numbers,' Anna echoed, liking the sentiment and the warm feeling of belonging that filled her chest. 'I like it.'

'We should get T-shirts,' Kate said, draining her glass of wine, the carbonara long abandoned and congealing. 'And maybe go out and get kebabs?'

'Going out for kebabs' was Kate-speak for wandering the streets of Oxford, occasionally stopping for food or a drink, or a chat with friends they bumped into. It was Kate-speak for just drinking in the glory of this beautiful city, the pot of gold at the end of the A level rainbow.

And it was every bit as wonderful and inspiring and fulfilling as Anna had dreamed it would be.

Mainly, she had to confess, because of her friendship with Kate. It gave her an anchor.

But she had to disagree with one part of Kate's incredibly astute assessment. It wasn't Kate's family that drew her in, it had been Kate.

Kate herself was enough. More than enough to make Anna feel loved.

She'd never had a proper friendship like this before and the wonder and novelty of it had yet to tarnish. She'd never known that somebody had her back so completely, as to even risk angering or offending her with a few home truths.

It was, in short, a revelation.

'Max's a twat,' Anna said, as she wrangled her kebab back into its pitta bread sleeve. 'And I'd like to say that it's just a sex thing. That I was the kind of girl who could divorce emotion from all the shagging, but I don't think I can.'

'Okay then,' Kate said, nodding. 'So, it looks like you have a decision to make.'

Anna sighed, thinking of the long June nights she'd spent entwined with Max's golden limbs and the complete release she'd discovered with him in the small hours of the morning, naked and uninhibited. Wondering, still, if she could shelve her concerns and just enjoy the fun.

Beside her, Kate's mobile vibrated and she glanced briefly at the screen, a small smile quickly extinguished as she tucked it away in her pocket.

'Duncan?' Anna asked, watching closely.

'No. Well, yes actually. He just wondered if I – if we fancied meeting up for a drink.' Kate shook her head. 'But I'll tell him no. Definitely no.'

'Is he lovely?' Anna asked. 'Is he kind and thoughtful and switched on without being arrogant? I'm just saying that if we judged everyone by their little brothers then you yourself would be a sketchy proposition.' She pulled Kate into a hug. 'You should go. Go meet him and see if he's the real deal. If nothing else, we've established that I need a role model to guide me.'

Walking back to the house on the Cowley Road, Anna knew she'd made the right call. The selfless call. Yet still she felt adrift without Kate's certainty and reassurance: all her decisions felt less resolute.

Finding Max sitting on her doorstep, complete with flowers and Prosecco, threw all her good intentions to the wind.

Even as he kissed her neck and pulled her upstairs to bed, even as he gently teased her about the pallor of her skin against his golden tan, she felt herself slipping. Falling in love – or lust – with Max had been a huge emotional risk for her. And, even though it was at last clear to her that it wasn't working out, it felt like she was already invested.

It felt as though she couldn't walk away.

'I love being here with you,' Max breathed, running kisses down her naked body and making her ache with longing. The closest he ever came to saying those three little words. She ignored the insistent voice in her head that called comparisons with Zermatt and Cannes and Rome, where he'd been whiling away his summer as she pulled pints to pay her bills.

She wanted to believe him.

And even when she woke the next morning, tender yet replete, to an empty space in the bed beside her, she tried to think back to when she'd last felt this close to being loved, simply for being herself.

Not by somebody who was paid to care, but with free will and no agenda.

She couldn't believe it would be possible for them to have shared such intimacy through the night if the feelings weren't there all along, whether they vocalised them or not.

She stretched languidly, wondering how Kate's drink with Duncan had gone, smiling at the thought of the four of them, double-dating, hanging out. Their own little posse like a TV sitcom.

It was only when she got up to get showered that she noticed the gap on her bookshelf.

The gap that, until last night, had housed all of her notes on early medieval literature. The very same module that Max would be re-sitting next week.

Suddenly shivering, she pulled her robe tightly around her and tried not to cry. Could she actually say that she felt used, she wondered, when she'd clearly been so complicit in their all-night shagathon?

Or was she, in fact, just a desperate fool?

Chapter 37

Bath, 2019

The more time she spent with Callie, the more Anna was forced to analyse her own shortcomings and insecurities. The girl was a force of nature and woe betide anyone who stood in her way.

It felt strange to admit even to herself that Callie was inspirational, yet for the first time in a long time, Anna had conversations about The Big Picture. About hope and ambition and where she saw herself in five years' time.

'Do they teach you this stuff in school these days?' Anna asked, as they drove up towards the hospital again the following day, Norbert on the back seat panting by an open window as all the sights, smells and sounds made his ears quiver with delight.

Callie grinned. 'Nah. I was just born feisty.' She popped one of the Starbursts from Anna's glove box in her mouth, puckering her face in disgust. 'Ew the green ones! When will I learn?'

Anna snorted with laughter, her stomach still aching from the YouTube marathon the night before when Callie had introduced her to all the up-and-coming comedians and their 'fresh take' on life in Gen Z.

They had been almost inseparable the last few days. It was

an unusual arrangement, to be sure, but every time Anna thought of Callie's mother sitting watching *Neighbours*, turning up the volume while Liam belittled and raged at her daughter, she couldn't bring herself to turn the girl away. It was presumably the same approach that Eleanor had been taking before she went away – and what was her role as house-sitter if not to bring a little continuity of care?

She couldn't deny that there was a payoff for herself too, though. Without Kate at the end of the phone, the last few weeks had dragged on a little. Without Henry's company in Dittisham, she would have been hard pushed to keep the demons in her head at bay.

It was as though those demons could sense that their end was nigh, that a change was brewing. There was only so much of her life that Anna was prepared to step away from, in a failed quest to 'find herself' – or more specifically – to find the life she wanted to lead.

But being with Callie had finally shone a spotlight on the flaw in her plan: she could only ever be a pale imitation of somebody else, if she used their life, their home, their passions as her template.

'Be yourself, everyone else is already taken,' read the Oscar Wilde quote on Callie's locket.

It was a sentiment that deserved consideration.

And, despite some initial misgivings, Anna had tried very hard to be herself around Callie. To give herself permission to just 'be'. She wasn't there to be a role model, or a mentor. And although it had been hard to admit that the years between them should have been a barrier, the simple fact that Anna's adult life had been on pause for so long meant that they really weren't that far apart. In thinking, or in working out what they wanted from the world.

'Do you think Annabel would notice if I pinched one of the mini muffins from the basket?' Callie asked, her constant teenage hunger already a running joke between them.

'I think she would,' Anna replied, easing the Mini into the stream of traffic heading up towards the RUH. 'I also think she'd be very impressed with our purchases this morning.' A bookshop carrier bag slid up and down the back seat, filled with chunky, glossy novels that had never once troubled the A level syllabus. 'But I dibs the one that says "feminist bonk-buster" on the cover.'

Callie laughed. 'Fine by me. I'm starting with *Riders*.' She tipped her head back against the headrest and smiled. 'You know, Anna. You're kind of weird, like, the least grown up grown-up I've ever met – but I've had more fun with you in the last few days than I have in ages.'

Anna pressed one hand to her chest, properly touched. 'Me too,' she said seriously. 'And you're so annoyingly motivated about life, it's given me a little kick in the right direction as well.'

Callie beamed. 'What can I say? I do what I do.' She reached for the Starburst packet again, before remembering that only the green ones remained. 'Are you going to stop talking about writing a book and start writing a book then? 'Cause it's about damn time.'

'Well, yes actually,' Anna said, feeling sick with nerves at just the thought. 'Emily's lined up a wonderful apartment in Paris for next week. It's the perfect place to get started – just around the corner from Les Deux Magots – you know, the café where Sartre and Hemingway used to hang out all the time? Although obviously not together.'

'Paris?' Callie said. 'Why do you need to go to Paris to write a book? Why do you need to go anywhere, come to that?'

Anna stilled, her hands perfectly placed at ten and two on the steering wheel. 'Well, you know, for the vibe – for the inspiration.'

'That's bollocks and you know it,' Callie said bluntly, unwrapping another sweet on autopilot. 'The only thing you need to write a book is between your own two ears.'

A lump in Anna's throat stopped her replying immediately as her mind ricocheted between past and present, trying to pin down where she'd heard those words before.

Mrs Holt.

Mrs Holt, who had made so much sense, yet had still left Anna strangely ill-prepared for what life at Oxford would be like. Indeed, who'd probably had no idea of the insecurities and hurdles that would block Anna's path along the way. Her own foolish need to be accepted overshadowing any of her hard-won common sense and savvy attitude to life.

'I guess I've just waited so long, that a little cultural catalyst is no bad thing. All things being equal,' Anna said quietly, deftly reversing into a miniscule space and yanking hard on the handbrake.

'Is this like when I can't possibly do my coursework until I've got the perfect pen, or the perfect notebook?' Callie said gently, obviously realising that her flippant comment had been more barbed than supportive. 'Because if you need professional procrastination advice, then I am clearly your girl.'

'Oh, honey, you are still firmly in the amateur stakes when it comes to procrastination, avoidance, denial – I have a master's in self-delusion at this point.'

'But at least you're self-aware enough to realise it,' Callie countered, unable to stop the burst of laughter that followed.

*

Seeing Annabel looking so much better, seeing the whole of sunlit Bath laid out below them as they drove back down from the RUH a little later, brushing the chocolate muffin crumbs off her top, Anna could honestly say that she hadn't had a happier day in a long time.

And it wasn't because the day had been decadent or blissfully vacation-like; indeed, it was the sheer ordinariness that had touched her so deeply.

Life in Bath, without any glamour or Frette sheets, held an appeal that went beyond bookshops, pavement cafés and glorious Georgian architecture. Her stomach ached from laughing – and possibly a surfeit of muffins – and her mind felt free and unstymied.

The appeal of Paris as the springboard for the next phase of her life had been so logical, but right now, the notion of needing such a catalyst felt naive. It was, as Callie had so astutely pointed out, exactly what teenage Anna would have done: make sure everything was in place before even beginning. Despite the obvious flaw that had been her undoing on so many occasions – the 'perfect' situation just didn't exist.

And yet, nearly ten years later, this salient point was only just sinking in.

'You know,' said Callie as they squeezed the Mini into a ridiculously small space across the road from the flat, 'I think we make a good team, you and me.'

'We do,' Anna agreed, cranking the steering wheel hard left and willing the Mini to oblige; the Tesla SUV parked behind them probably cost more than she dared contemplate.

'So, I've been thinking that, if you set up home somewhere – like, properly bit the bullet and committed to your writing for a bit – then I should come with you.'

Anna's foot slipped off the clutch in surprise and the Mini gave a nerve-wracking leap forward, barely missing a glossy BMW. 'Say what?'

Callie simply nodded, as though they were discussing the benefits of getting take-out for supper. 'Yeah. I mean, I'm not really a child. I just need an adult willing to be my guardian while I do my A levels. You wouldn't have to adopt me or anything. And, if I'm honest, Anna, I am all out of options. This is kind of a Hail Mary pass for me.' She swallowed hard. 'So no pressure or anything.'

'I—' began Anna and then stopped, the naked hope and vulnerability on Callie's face cutting short her immediate, instinctive refusal. 'Look, I get that sounds attractive, but I am seriously not *parent* material, Cal. I'm barely capable of taking care of myself. The Avon and Somerset Police agree, remember – homeless. Might as well read "useless". I'm sorry.'

'You're "homeless" by choice though, aren't you, so you can go travelling around wherever you like. Footloose and fancy-free. Yeah? But you've also spent the better part of the week talking about writing, thinking about writing but barely actually picking up a pen.'

Anna breathed out slowly, wanting to protest, but knowing that her abortive efforts in the café the other morning hardly counted as committing to the process.

'So,' Callie continued, undaunted, 'you could hole up somewhere for a bit, and I could come too. It sounds complicated, but it really isn't, is it? We would just have to decide to do it and then – well, you know – actually do it.'

Anna reached out and took her hand, her focus distracted for a moment by the puzzling enigma that Callie seemed to be – so forthright and focused, yet still so clearly adrift and looking for an anchor. She was almost winded by the surge of empathy; her teenage self so similar to Callie she felt the emotions as keenly as though they were her own.

'You know I'll help, Callie. When I leave on Friday, it really isn't goodbye and I will honestly be there, at the end of the phone, or whenever you need me. But I am not the right fit for this. I'm too – well . . .' She sighed. 'Look, I don't think it's especially healthy for someone who's essentially a bit broken to delude themselves that they're in a position to help anybody.'

'That's bollocks and you know it!' Callie burst out, turning in her seat, hemmed in by the confines of the Mini, her voice echoing loudly. 'I have never met ANYONE,' she shouted, 'who understood what I was feeling like you do. Because you've been there. Kind of. Eleanor hasn't, Richard hasn't – they're lovely people who want to help me and I appreciate it, but they have no fucking clue how deep the hurt runs. How fucked up this whole situation is, when someone like me has no chance of choosing a different life, because I'm thwarted at every stage by ignorant bastards. The kind of people who don't want anything more in life than somewhere to live and enough cash to get drunk at the pub or head to the bookies on a Saturday morning.

'Anna,' she pleaded. 'I want more!'

Anna simply nodded. 'And the very fact that you do is something to be proud of, Callie. And you *know* that I think you're right. Mrs Holt was right too. Education is the silver bullet – it's the way to change your life. And okay, yeah, I'll be the first to admit that I hit pause for a bit too long and lost my way, but getting to university, getting a degree . . . These are the things that make a difference. And I will help you any way I can.'

'Except the way I want?' Callie finished, visibly slumping in her seat. 'I get it. You don't owe me anything. Hell, a week ago you'd never even heard of me. And I know that. I just – well, I just thought it was better to ask than spend every day of the next two years wondering "what if?".'

Callie grabbed her bag from by her feet and paused for a second, before getting out of the car and just walking away, leaving the door wide open behind her and Anna's mind in turmoil.

Chapter 38

The guilt sat heavy with Anna that evening, unable to muster the enthusiasm to cook a solo meal. Even delicious Stilton crumbled onto crackers, slices of a ripe, fresh pear and some densely rich Medjool dates failed to lift her spirits, as she munched them, perched on the deep Georgian windowsill, The Circus swooping away from her into the twilight.

Tonight – her last night in Bath – was supposed to have been so very different.

And it wasn't that Anna was unaccustomed to saying good-bye and moving on, although it was never easy. But this week, here, in Bath? It had been such a different experience – mainly due to a grumpy teenager and a redoubtable pensioner taking on a bus.

It wasn't the kind of thing one could predict, yet it seemed to be exactly what she'd needed.

She had felt part of something; useful, appreciated.

Progress.

She'd made great strides on other fronts too. Ulysses now allowed her to stroke his dense, lustrous fur as he slept in the evenings, without lashing out and drawing blood, although he would still offer an occasional warning hiss that kept her on her toes.

And with the flat so compact and pristine, she'd even stepped back from the endless loop of locking up at night. Half tempted, in fact, to leave the front door ajar in case Callie should need her.

She'd also been sucked into Annabel's parallel universe of reading; Eleanor's leather-bound classics ignored in favour of glitz and glamour. If only she'd realised sooner how easy it would be to travel the world and experience the highs and lows of other lives, *contemporary* lives, through the medium of books, then all her choices might have been so different.

While the classics had fed and nurtured her soul for so long, it was these novels – the kind she'd always eschewed – that now lifted her spirits, offered her companionship and also a certain kind of hope.

Hope that came from knowing that she wasn't alone. Hurdles came in many forms and she was fortunate in having managed to scale so many, but not without cost.

Her self-esteem was in tatters. Losing a few pounds and buying a killer outfit, as the women in these books tended to do, was hardly going to be her personal salvation. And yet . . .

And yet, there was something to be said for getting up off the mat and saying, 'Enough. Hear me roar.'

There had been far too little roaring in Anna's life since she left Oxford.

She'd actually been hoping that she and Callie might proverbially 'roar' together, but it seemed she couldn't offer what Callie needed, and so that was that.

There was no arguing or shouting from upstairs – a reliable indicator that she wasn't at home – so who knew where the girl had disappeared to. Call after call, text after text, went unanswered, even the ones offering as much remote support as Anna felt she could possibly commit to.

Packing her bag so that she was ready for an early departure the next day, Anna realised that watching Callie stride away from her car might really, truly be the last time she ever saw her. It wasn't as though their paths would ever cross again, no matter how many times they'd bumped into each other in Bath this week. Small city, it was bound to happen, yet Anna had come to rely upon it, to relish the prospect.

Saying goodbye was never easy, in fact Anna had been dreading it, but apparently Callie was choosing to say goodbye her own way, on her own terms, by cutting off contact altogether.

Anna's newly packed notebooks suddenly felt hollow, her fresh determination to get words down on paper a little self-indulgent.

Fiddling while Rome burned.

Yet, however Callie's plight spoke to her, Anna knew that she owed herself something too: an opportunity to follow her dream, her ambition, her own silent roar onto the page.

With the Mini left somewhat forlornly at the long-stay car park and Eleanor and Richard delightedly installed back in their West Country lives, tanned and happy after their Roman holiday, Anna found herself taking shallow, jerky breaths as she walked across the concourse at St Pancras. Her small bag thumped against her thigh with each step and she looked down, rather than be overwhelmed by the crowds surging around her.

The contrast to the golden hues and calm serenity of Bath was not the only issue.

Even treating herself to a beautiful new polished silver pen with which to begin her 'fresh approach' hadn't given her the rush of serotonin she'd expected. Instead, she heard Callie's disparaging comments in her head about needing the 'perfect set-up' before she could write: 'That's bollocks and you know it.'

Of course she knew it.

Yet old habits died hard and somehow it was vital that if she was going to take this giant leap of faith, then the setting was almost as important as the inspiration. She wasn't doing this lightly; in fact, she was slightly terrified that, after all these years of procrastination and prevarication, she might still fail. It might have been more efficient to discover years ago that ambition did not eclipse a lack of talent.

The fear was real, but the drive was compelling.

Something about the last few weeks, the people she'd met and the stories she'd heard, had fired up the dormant part of her brain that had bundled itself into a protective coma for all these years.

And Callie was at the forefront of that. Her insouciant determination that she could make a better life for herself, despite so much blocking her path, had been like a jolt of caffeine to the system.

It was just a shame they weren't in this together.

Anna sighed deeply, closing her eyes for a moment, convinced she'd made the right decision about Callie, yet regretting it nevertheless.

A hard shove from behind jolted her forward, her bag slipping from her shoulder onto the concourse with a dull thud; the new pen jerked from her hand, rolling away across the polished marble floor as a crowd surged around her towards the platform. The suited man cast her an annoyed glare and carried on striding forward, as though it were her fault for simply existing in his day. Bending to retrieve the pen, she was knocked nearly sideways by the corner of a leather suit carrier and another sigh of exasperation.

She watched as the silver barrel rolled further out of reach, her own small bag now another hurdle for the passengers to step over – never around, she noticed. Their haste, their pent-up irritation and rage drove them forward. A platform had been announced. Ten minutes until departure, yet still they drove forward; time was money, perhaps?

'Just get out of the way,' someone hissed at her as she looked around, her breath coming ever shorter and unshed tears clogging her throat. She instinctively checked her possessions: wallet, watch, passport, phone, wallet, watch, passport, phone, wallet, watch, passport, phone. In lieu of anything else, her old rituals gave her a perverse kind of comfort.

The surge had passed.

Anna scrambled to pick up her new pen, the barrel scuffed and crushed. She felt disproportionately broken by its mangled silver remains, ink leaking out onto her palms as she cradled them. It wasn't a stretch to imagine herself tram-pled underfoot, disposable, useless, nothing more than an impediment to the ordered flow of their ordered lives.

Glancing up at the information board overhead, she forced herself to drag oxygen into her lungs and blink away the tears. She wasn't some country yokel overwhelmed by the big city, she reminded herself. She was simply overwhelmed by life, and those people who seemed to know instinctively how to live it.

Wiping her ink-stained hands on a tissue, she wrapped the pen up with a certain reverence for its aborted role in her life and placed it in one of the bins. Even as she did it, she could feel her sense of reality warping slightly.

What was she even doing here?

Wallet, watch, passport, phone.

She hefted her bag back onto her shoulder, the hordes already jostling to board the train, despite the assigned seating printed on their tickets.

It was times like this when Anna knew for certain that her brain functioned in a different way. And it wasn't the age-old introvert, extrovert chestnut. This was about how all it took to change a life – hell, to save a life sometimes – was a little kindness. A little consideration.

She felt nauseated by the very thought that she herself might have missed that opportunity with Callie.

She clambered aboard the train, each table already bristling with laptops and righteous indignation, should she dare to take the empty seat opposite.

Her phone rang out loudly, demanding her attention. Perching on an armrest, she took the call.

'Are you on the Eurostar already?' said Emily curtly.

'Well, hello to you too—'

'If you're on the train, get off. Get off now. The booking's been cancelled.'

Anna's heart rate ratcheted up and she grabbed at the handle of her bag, snagging on each and every headrest she stumbled past. She heard the sound of the whistle just as she reached the door and leapt out, just as the guard stepped forward to wave her back on board.

She felt her ankle give, and the bag swung forward, striking the side of her face. The impact was so unexpected that it took her breath away, even as the guard yelled at her for her lack of consideration.

The irony was not lost on her at all.

Crumpled in a heap of mixed emotions, Anna held the phone to her other cheek.

'Well, I'm not on the train anymore.'

'Jesus, Anna! Are you alright? That all sounded – well – *are* you alright?'

Anna took a shuddering breath, her ankle throbbing, her hands ink-stained and now raw from her awkward landing. Her cheek felt wet, possibly with tears, or possibly blood.

'I'm fine,' she said. 'It'll be fine.' She made no move to stand up, merely sitting crumpled like a baby giraffe as the train sped away from the platform and the tannoy announcements echoed overhead.

The guard gave her a filthy look and walked away, no offer of help forthcoming.

'Look,' said Emily. 'I'll sort all of this out and come back to you, but the booking's been cancelled. Last minute. Like, literally a minute ago, so I didn't get any details – I just wanted to make sure you didn't get on that train. I'll call you back in a minute.'

It hadn't even occurred to her that Anna now had nowhere to stay. That she might as well have had nowhere to stay in Paris, as in London. That she could have walked along the Seine and sipped café au lait and scribbled in her notebooks or journals in a pavement café. That she might have wanted to be given a say . . .

She quietly gathered her things together and walked out into the grey mizzle of a London afternoon.

The rust-red façade of the St Pancras Hotel filled her eyeline.

Somewhere she'd always wanted to stay. Somewhere she'd always thought was beyond her budget. Hobbling along, her ankle screaming in protest, she wiped her hands clean and tucked her hair smoothly back behind her ears.

Something good had to come out of this.

It had to.

The thought that leaving Bath, leaving Callie, missing out on steak frites on the Left Bank had all been for nothing, was more than she could bear. She had to find some method in all of this madness.

'Hi,' she said, an unusual calm and confidence filling her voice as she approached the gilded and ornate reception desk. 'I'm unexpectedly in London for the night,' she shrugged with an unknown Gallic charm, 'when I should be in Paris.' A gentle smile. 'I don't suppose you've a last-minute rate for a single room?'

Chapter 39

St Pancras, 2019

The fronds of indoor palm trees brushed against Anna's shoulders as she lingered for a moment in the grand foyer, its plush decadence almost overwhelming. It was certainly a far cry from the Premier Inn across the road where she often made base for early Eurostar departures. And yet . . .

The same towering façade and indulgent décor that had captivated her imagination for so many years hardly offered comfort. There were small groups of guests, immaculately attired, polished and pristine taking sips of cocktails and champagne even at this hour. Their conversation and laughter seemed to buzz with energy and only served to highlight that Anna was here alone.

In a beautiful room for an absolute steal.

But alone.

She slipped into the Art Deco elevator and closed her eyes, as the swooping vertigo told her that she was up in the gods. Alighting on her floor, where the imposing corridors swept away on either side, punctuated with mirrors and foliage and the odd chaise longue should the endless walk prove too taxing, she began to feel like Alice in Wonderland.

Indeed, she would not have been surprised if a white rabbit bearing a pocket watch had rushed by.

Her phone rang in her pocket, and she pulled it out to stare indecisively at the screen.

Emily. Again.

So many missed calls, yet she was still unable to formulate an appropriate response. She knew perfectly well that Emily had her best interests at heart in pulling her off the train, but – house-sit or not – she could also have been on the banks of the Seine right now.

Still, the Renaissance was hardly sloppy seconds.

She limped the few yards to her door, the phone ringing impotently in her hand, denied attention as she juggled with the electronic key. The small bag from the pharmacy at the station rustled on her wrist and she tried to keep her focus.

Rest, ice, compression, elevation.

Her ankle positively thrummed with inflamed heat. She couldn't begin to tackle a rational conversation without first taking care of herself. Washing back two ibuprofen, she sat down in the winged armchair by the window and began the painful but necessary job of removing her Converse hightops. Biting her lip and breathing through the nauseating waves of agony she half wondered whether she should have skipped the five-star hotel and gone straight to A&E. She flexed her foot gingerly and winced. Surely she wouldn't be able to do even that if it were broken?

With the ice from the mini bar wrapped in a soft monogrammed napkin and her foot balanced on a stack of silken cushions on the coffee table to get height, she leaned her head back and looked out at the view, at the birds swooping across the rooftops.

Forcing herself to breathe slowly and her taut limbs to soften, she felt as though she'd been fleeing some invisible aggressor from the moment she'd fallen to the floor. As she began to shiver now, her teeth chattering against one another, she recognised that, yes, she probably was in shock a little. Even scrambling through the crowds to rescue her belongings had shaken her up, but her expedited exit from the Eurostar had given her no time to think, only act.

Staring blindly out of the window, Anna was forced to admit that today's events alone were probably not the issue; they were simply compounding something she'd staunchly denied, even to herself.

Andrew Fraser had done a real number on her at Gravesend Manor and then she'd simply carried on. Unwilling, or perhaps unable to admit that the actions of one man were enough to derail her fragile détente with her own psyche.

Fight. Flight. Freeze.

Those three words summed up decades of Anna's life and, however much she liked to assert her own independence, her freedom, her very flexibility, she was also hemmed in. Limited by fear in general, yes, but also the very specific anxiety about 'getting it wrong'. Setting up a life, a career, maybe even a home, only to then realise that she'd made the wrong choice.

Keeping moving kept that spectre at bay.

Even if only as a temporary measure; a measure it seemed that had now outlived its usefulness.

Her phone rang again, Henry this time, and yet still she ignored it.

And that was okay. Jackie of the awful perms and Shalimar obsession had taught her that. And, whilst as a teenager she had been slow to learn the lesson – the dread of being thought selfish far outweighing any personal benefit – as an adult she had valued that nugget of advice enormously. You could not pour from an empty cup and Anna had been running on empty, on adrenaline, for weeks now.

Instead, she opened her email and began to type. Survival came in many forms.

Ordering an omelette and frites from room service, with a chilled chubby bottle of Orangina to wash it down, was Anna's last concession to the lost dream of the Sixth Arrondissement. Yet it still felt like a necessary closure to attain.

Paris was to have been the catalyst, the inspiration to kick off her writing. The end, in fact, to nearly a decade of self-doubt and procrastination.

And no matter that Callie's words still echoed, knowing that she did in fact have everything she needed right there between her ears, it still felt like a wrench to let go.

She listened to Emily's increasingly worried voicemails and hit 'call'.

'Hi,' she said. 'It's me.'

And then she simply listened, sipping her Orangina, as Emily furiously made it clear how concerned she'd been. In rather more detail than was strictly necessary, in Anna's opinion.

'Em – Em! Look, you're very sweet, but I'm fine. I sprained my ankle leaping off the train, but I'm checked in to a nice hotel for the night and it'll be fine. I just needed time to sort everything out. I was supposed to be Paris, you know, not limping around King's Cross looking for a bed.'

'Shit, Anna. I'm so sorry. That client was such a flake from the outset, changing his dates and his plans – I should have known.' She paused. 'Anna, when did all this start unravelling? Did you break a mirror or something?' She gave a nervous laugh. 'Seriously? I mean, for years, your diary has run like clockwork and all of a sudden – well—' She sighed. 'I'm starting to think you're jinxed.'

'I'm tempted to agree, actually,' Anna said. 'Maybe it's time to take a hint.'

There was a long silence at the end of the phone, then, 'Are you saying that you're done?' Emily sounded completely choked up at the very suggestion.

'Maybe?' Anna replied. 'I really don't know. But I do know that you were right and I needed more time to get over the Oxford debacle.' For a moment her mind split focus, between that hideous night of Kate's wedding and Max Howard's complete and utter betrayal a decade earlier.

Oxford, it seemed, was destined to be the venue for both the best and the worst moments of her life so far. Or maybe that was just 'life' – she was beginning to wonder whether the location actually played any part at all in the existential rollercoaster.

'But Bath went well, you said? You had a break – made a few friends?' Emily's doubt was almost voluble, as she clearly revisited every conversation they'd had over the last few weeks.

'It did, I did. Actually it was mostly pretty wonderful. I just think maybe that I'm still off balance a bit.'

'Do you think that's why you hurt your ankle?' Emily asked seriously.

'I think it had more to do with leaping from a train seconds before departure while a crazy person shouted "Get off the train!" over and over in my ear.'

'Sorry about that,' Emily said guiltily. 'I was just in such a panic that you'd be halfway through the Chunnel before I could tell you there was no place to stay at the other end.'

'Ah, yes, Paris – renowned for its total lack of *pensions* and hotels,' Anna replied, a smile creeping into her voice and replacing the annoyance that had buzzed around in her head for the last few hours. 'I know you were thinking of me. I just didn't have time to think about where I wanted to be.'

'You know,' Emily said, 'I think that applies more often than just today. I've lost track of when you last asked me to send you somewhere specific. Do you remember, when you started out, you had that list of all the places you wanted to go and see? And you used to check off each country, each city, like you'd "done" it? Now you just go where the nice houses are . . .'

Anna blinked away the wave of memories as they crashed over her.

The List.

How on God's green earth could she have forgotten about The List?

All those hours with Kate in pub gardens that last summer, writing out all the destinations she'd longed to see with her own two eyes, not via the Discovery Channel. All the cities, coastlines, countryside vistas, mountains, fjords . . . The List had been nothing if not comprehensive.

And where was it now?

Was it tucked inside an old journal, not yet completed but already obsolete?

She sipped the Orangina again, her lips puckering against the pithy tartness. So much hope, ambition and thought had gone into making that list: a genuine reward for all her hard work and resilience and a little celebration that she'd made it through to twenty-one unscathed. Or so she'd genuinely thought at the time. Back when psychological scars were not only invisible, but also denied and disregarded.

The List was to have been the gateway to her new, independent, adult life. It was not supposed to have been a way for her to play ostrich and put her life on hold.

'Do you need me to sort somewhere for the next few days? I mean, it sounds like you'd be better off clearing your head, but I know you like to be busy . . .' Emily sounded completely wrong-footed, as though she were walking on eggshells.

Anna looked around, taking in her stash of pristine notebooks, her swollen ankle and the plush brocade curtains framing the breathtaking rooftop view.

'You know, Em? I'm good here actually. I'm going to rest this ankle and maybe take a little time to work out what I want to do, where I want to be.' She pushed aside the thought that this was exactly the same intention she'd jettisoned in Bath.

'Good idea.' The relief in her voice was obvious. 'And just in case it needs saying, you do know that this house-sitting gig isn't an all or nothing arrangement? I mean, most people just do it for a few weeks or months each year when they fancy a change of scene. You're the only nutty nomad who never stays still. And God knows, I've loved working with you, but I'd be just as happy – happier, actually – to be your friend rather than your ena— I mean, booker.'

Anna laughed. 'Were you just going to say "enabler", Emily?'

'No! Well, maybe. But you have to admit you have some serious ants in those pants of yours. You're like that dog on the TV – *The Littlest Hobo* – do you remember? He was always moving on too . . .'

'Have you been smoking something? Be honest – I'm asking as your friend. Interventions work both ways you know,' Anna laughed.

'Google it!' Emily said. 'The resemblance is almost uncanny.'

'If you say so. And seriously, Em? I know I was a little pissy earlier, but thank you for looking out for me. Like you say, things aren't going so smoothly at the moment.' She didn't mention that this was throwing her back into the well-worn grooves of her teenage years, shuttled from pillar to post and in a constant state of uncertainty, but she didn't need to. Emily cared. Even without the grisly backstory, she was a good friend to Anna and it bore saying once in a while. 'I really appreciate it.'

'No thanks needed. I just wanted to be sure I hadn't abandoned you somewhere.'

Anna looked around the luxurious hotel room. Her own personal cocoon for the next few nights. 'I'm fine here, Em. Truly.'

She hung up the phone and picked up her pen. There was no time like the present to test Callie's theory. Perhaps Callie might even respond to one of Anna's text messages if she thought that her opinion, her thoughts, actually mattered to someone. And not just anyone, Anna thought, as she picked up the hotel's branded biro – hardly the stuff of Hemingway – Callie mattered to her.

Chapter 40

Anna awoke with a vague confusion about where she was. The painkillers had given her a few good hours' sleep, but she was now groggy and disorientated, even as her swollen ankle positively pulsed in protest under the weighty bed linen.

Breakfast and then a plan – that was what she needed.

She sat up and her notebook slithered to the floor with a thump, many of its pages torn loose and crumpled into angry balls. Testament to her late-night attempts to corral and crystallise her thoughts. It seemed that writing really was like a muscle and hers was weak from neglect. Tenuous ideas for her long dreamed-of novel eddied through her mind but they were stubbornly evasive and uncooperative. She could only see the scale of the task ahead of her.

Gone were the days of easy productivity at university when she could nail two thousand words before lunch on a Saturday and go to the park.

Gone were the days of direction and focus.

She was utterly rudderless.

A gentle tap at the door and Anna hobbled over, her

stomach grumbling in anticipation of the full English she had ordered the night before.

'Morning, miss.' Ah, that Italian accent! 'I've your breakfast here for you. The concierge also thought you might need to borrow this for your stay, shame to stay cooped up on such a beautiful day.' The young man handed her a handsome walking cane with a silver top and smiled at her shocked reaction. 'It's been in lost property for months, miss, so nobody will complain for your borrowing it.' He laid out the silver dome and tray of coffee and juice, smoothing the weekend papers into a fan shape beside them. 'He also said, that if you've to see the doctor about your ankle, it would be better this morning; the afternoons get busy after all the sporting injuries turn up.'

He paused and she panicked for a moment that she'd forgotten the tipping etiquette in a place like this. 'Are you sure you're okay, miss? You don't want us to arrange transport for you, or call anyone?' His eyes skittered around the hotel room, taking in the medical supplies strewn across the coffee table and the carnage of papers littering the bed.

'You're very kind, but I'll be fine. And thank you for the walking stick. Very thoughtful. If you could just wait while I—' She hobbled towards her bag and wobbled as she reached down to pull out her purse.

'No, no, miss. Really not necessary. You take care now. Ciao.' And he was gone. Taking with him his sparkling Italian eyes and that warm flirtation instinctively imbued into every interaction. The room felt a little emptier, a little lonelier, for all its sumptuous decadence.

She certainly hadn't realised when she'd wandered in through the door last night, battered, bruised and on the off chance that a room might be available, just what an incredible deal the receptionist had offered her. A pity deal, she now recognised. But that didn't mean she wasn't grateful.

Just as she was grateful for the cane, which made lurching across the room towards her bacon somewhat safer and easier than it had been.

And just because she couldn't stride around the streets like she always did, didn't mean she couldn't go outside and enjoy London at its finest. Hop on an open-top bus and play tourist? And maybe, just maybe, it might be worth seeing a doctor too, since the distorted size of her ankle this morning perhaps explained the widening of that poor chap's eyes far more than her fleecy pyjamas might have elicited on their own. Although the penguins doing yoga *were* an absolute eye-catcher, in her own humble opinion.

She sat down and poured herself a coffee, feeling grown up and in control of her own day. Yes, this was decadent. Expensive too, no doubt, as London breakfasts go. But there was a pleasure to be had in knowing that this was something she herself had paid for, no services traded.

A simple transaction.

And when was the last time her travels had given her that?

She snapped a photo for Kate – take that, octopus curry – and then nibbled at the perfect toast triangles initially before the call of the full English overpowered any restraint and she ate with gusto and a lack of inhibition she hadn't felt in a while. Poached eggs, grilled halloumi, crispy bacon and two tiny chipolatas. She wouldn't need to stop for lunch.

Swallowing two more painkillers with the freshly squeezed orange juice, she flicked through the newspapers, skimming headlines and squinting at photos of celebrities she didn't recognise. And then she came to the book reviews – where a small neat box on the opposite page caught her eye.

A short-story competition.

Two thousand words. What was that? Like three, maybe four pages of A4?

It wasn't a novel, but to Anna it was something more significant.

Somewhere to start.

Several hours later, Anna sat on the rooftop terrace of the Ham Yard Hotel – why swap her run on luxury now? She'd crossed London by bus, the sun warming her face as she'd taken in landmark after landmark, vista after vista. A London she'd never really bothered to see before had lifted her spirits.

The doctor, it turned out, had already been in the hotel seeing another patient. He'd given her ankle a quick once-over and decreed in dismissive tones that if the swelling got worse an X-ray might be in order, before suggesting a little codeine and rushing on his way. For free advice, it had really only offered reassurance.

And so, with a cafetière of dark roast and a club sandwich in front of her, she sat with her foot elevated and the torn-out page from the newspaper in front of her.

Two thousand words.

How hard could that be to get her literary muscles flexing again.

And then she thought of Annabel's words back in the hospital in Bath. Books didn't have to be classics, they didn't have to be great literary outpourings of sentiment and insight. They could also entertain, comfort, arouse even.

She could write from the heart and with conviction and nobody could question it, because it was her story, her words, her truth.

She stilled for a moment, the very idea of sharing truths anathema to her usual reticence.

Kate would encourage it, she knew. Kate, who viewed writing as therapy, as much as anything else.

And perhaps that was where she was going wrong. For everything she wrote these days took on a life of its own. A direction already decreed. Whatever the topic, or the angle, Anna seemed destined to write the same story over and over again.

Her own.

Sure, it wasn't always immediately recognisable as such. Names, places, relationships were always different, but the sentiment remained.

They were stories of loss and of abandonment. Stories of pain and denial.

She glanced at the newspaper page again. 'Food must be at the heart of the story.'

And whilst most people might think of fine dining, or harvesting luscious crops in exotic locations, Anna's thoughts went straight to a bright yellow laminate kitchen and a double-slot toaster, to a slice of claggy white bread that would serve as dinner. Sugar sprinkled on top.

She put down her club sandwich, the avocado and egg suddenly rich and intense, and picked up her phone.

'Are you shagging? Because I can call back later?' she said, earning a surprised look from the ladies who lunched at the next table.

Kate's laugh echoed down the line. 'We're doing couples yoga on the beach. And yes, you can shoot me now.'

'Shoot me first,' called Duncan from the background, and the two of them laughed together, in unison. Adorable. But also annoying if Anna were honest.

'What do you need, Pod? Are you coming to pick us up from the airport tomorrow? I can cancel the car if you feel like a natter all the way back to Oxford.'

'She's sick of me already,' Duncan called. 'I'm no match for you on the conversation front, it seems.'

Anna grinned despite herself. 'No change there then,' she said. 'But no. You'll have to wait a few days to catch up with me. I'm in self-imposed purdah in a smart London hotel, with a sprained ankle and a slightly mad plan that might force me to drink. Or possibly cop off with the hot Italian room service guy.'

'What happened to hot, strapping fisherman guy?' Duncan called, before being shushed by his wife and Anna clocked that in fact, she was on speakerphone and the whole beach could probably hear her every word.

'Okay, let's break this down. Nice job on a lovely hotel. Invite me next time. How's the ankle? And what's the mad plan?'

'Yes. It's fine. And I think you were right.'

Anna heard a thump and a grunt. 'Fuck. Sorry. Was in downward dog and I must have misheard that. Did you, Anna Wilson, finally admit that I was right?' Her voice was filled with laughter and affection, like a hug from the Indian Ocean. 'And what exactly was I right about?'

'The writing thing. Or rather the lack-of-writing thing. Oh, and the life on hold situation too, in all probability,' Anna said quietly.

'Wow. Big day for me,' Kate replied. 'So what's going on – are you going to send your book to Sarah? She's dying to see it, you know. Messaged me again the other day.'

'Not quite,' Anna said. 'It's just, well it might be tricky. Seeing as the book is only in my head, not on the page exactly.'

'She won't mind seeing a partial, or a synopsis—'

'No, Kate, seriously. I have to say this now, before the codeine buzz wears off. There is no book. Not a page.

Nothing. Just an idea, and a dream of being a writer. That's it. That's all I've got.'

A long silence stretched out and Anna knew that she'd been right to do this with a few thousand miles between them. It felt honest and real and long, long overdue.

'Anna,' Kate said. 'Why didn't you say something sooner?'

'Because I didn't know how. Because it meant admitting I'd pissed away the better part of a decade being crap.'

'Oh hang on,' Kate cut in. 'I'm not buying that. Have you written anything? No, apparently not. But have you travelled and seen the world and seen life from all sorts of angles you would never have known as a tourist? Well, hell, yeah. Do not sell yourself short.'

'Maybe,' Anna said.

'But I don't get it – what was I right about?' Kate said, curious.

'That sometimes the only way out is through.'

The realisation earlier had dawned like a punch to her solar plexus, almost winding her with its intensity and strange familiarity. A kind of déjà vu.

'Ah, that wasn't me, that was Robert Frost, kind of. But I'll happily take credit.' Kate's voice was gentle, concerned, but without a hint of judgement and Anna felt herself relax a little.

The first step was admitting you had a problem. Possibly the bravest step. And whilst this wasn't alcohol or drugs or gambling – God knows there was a veritable buffet of dysfunction in her DNA – maybe denial carried its own addictive qualities?

'Every time I write, I end up writing about my childhood. And if not my childhood then the emotions that it triggered, or the feelings that never leave. It's like the soundtrack to every story I've ever attempted.'

'Of course it is,' said Kate calmly, kindly. 'It's your story. It's the filter through which you see the world, Anna. And maybe it's time to stop fighting it?'

'The only way out is through,' Anna said again.

'I think so,' said Kate gently. 'But I'm guessing it won't be easy.' She paused and there was a mumble in the background with Duncan. 'Listen, when we get back, wherever you are, I'm coming to you, okay? Next weekend. I'm yours.'

'Yes please,' Anna said simply, choked with gratitude and love for this wonderful woman in her life.

As she hung up, she heard a gasp from the lunching ladies beside her and looked up, following their gaze into the sky. From their vantage point on the roof terrace, only the taller buildings rearing up around them, they had a unique view of the London skyline – and, in this case, a bird's-eye view of a single, yellow-clawed peregrine falcon, swooping down from the gods and plucking a hapless pigeon from the air, mid-flight.

It felt like a sign.

It felt as though Henry's gentle acceptance of the circle of life was a lesson she herself needed to understand.

This second sighting could only be a clarion call.

The yellow claws flashed and feathers flew as the falcon bore its prey to a nearby ledge.

No sentiment, just doing what needed to be done to stay alive.

Rare. Beautiful. Unforgettable.

She reached for her journal, sketching the roofline onto a fresh cream page, determined not to forget this feeling. Then she picked up her phone and dialled. 'Henry? It's me.'

Chapter 41

Oxford, 2010

Anna leaned back in her chair and looked around the scrubbed pine table happily, cementing the moments in her mind, never wanting to forget what this felt like.

'Another roastie, Anna?' asked Louise, with a knowing smile. Even with the silver streaks that twinkled amongst the tawny brown of her bob, she was still the spitting image of her daughter.

'Mu-um,' said Kate. 'She's not foie gras. Stop feeding the girl!'

Anna laughed. 'Is it poor form to admit I was about to say yes, now you've said that? You know I can't resist them.' She held out her plate, Louise's roast potatoes like crack cocaine for her soul. The perfect combination of soft potato inside and glorious golden crunch on the outside. It was worth dragging herself out of bed and into proper clothes on a Sunday for these alone.

Kate's little brother, Alex, snorted with delight. 'My record is twelve. You won't beat that, because you're a girl.'

Kate and Anna both drew an annoyed breath to respond, neither of them taking kindly to any aspersions on their roastie-scoffing abilities.

'Lad, if there's one thing I've learned,' Kate's dad cut in before war broke out, 'it's to never tell a woman she can't do something. Even if she didn't want to do it before, you've thrown down the gauntlet and you can bet that there's every chance you'll lose. Not always the challenge, but you'll lose one way or another for even having doubted her.'

'Quite right, Simon,' said Louise with a loving smile down the table. Theirs wasn't a marriage of hearts and flowers, indeed they seemed to live somewhat independently of one another for most of the week, their own spheres of academia calling on their time and attention, but these Sunday lunches were sacrosanct and the affection between them almost palpable.

The bantering, the bickering, the political debate, and daft competition for Darwin Student of the Week from amongst Louise or Simon's students. This ritual had become the part of the week that Anna looked forward to the most, especially with the pressure of finals looming. The days sped by, the weeks gathering momentum and Anna had almost, *almost*, forgiven herself for the debacle at the beginning of her final year.

A moment's weakness, a drunken slip that had thrown all her good intentions and hard work into jeopardy.

Without Kate, without this bolthole, she might never have made it through.

'Ta-da!' said Louise with pride in her voice, startling Anna from her thoughts.

She looked up to see Alex – all five foot nine of awkward, gangly teenager – blushingly, proudly carrying in his contribution to this week's meal.

'It's pineapple upside-down cake,' he said, as the single glacé cherry nipple rolled off the side of the luscious yellow dome.

'Very retro, darling,' said Louise proudly. 'Cookery club was a wonderful idea. It looks delicious.'

'It really does,' Anna agreed. 'I didn't know you were into cookery though.'

'Girls. He's into girls,' Simon said with a knowing smile. 'Although, not literally yet I hope . . .'

Kate snorted with laughter and Anna found herself joining in, only pulling up short at the look of abject discomfort on the poor boy's face. Colour swept up Alex's neck and into his hairline, the only blessing being that his acne was now camouflaged by his blushes.

Alex looked at his father imploringly. 'Da-ad, seriously stop! We have guests.'

'Nonsense,' Simon said, his eyes twinkling with mischief and thoroughly enjoying winding up his somewhat serious and bookish son. 'Anna's not a guest at this point; she's family.'

Anna caught her breath, touched beyond measure as Louise nodded her agreement. She pressed her hand to her chest to soothe the pounding of her heart and swallowed hard. 'You are so lovely,' Anna said, not to anyone in particular, more to the moment, the emotion of that simple message of acceptance simply overwhelming.

'Never unloads the bloody dishwasher though, does she?' Alex grumbled half-heartedly, making her smile even more.

Acceptance, good food, excellent advice and, it seemed, her very own truculent surrogate brother. 'No, but I'm a whizz with a tea-towel.'

Alex just shook his head, but his eye roll was as close to genuine affection as a fourteen-year-old boy might ever achieve.

He carved up his pudding into five large wedges – little point in pretending they wouldn't demolish the whole thing in one sitting – and gave Anna first pick. Virtually a serenade in sibling statements.

Anna hefted the vast blue and white striped custard jug and poured, its weight familiar and comforting by now. The 't' and the 'd' had long since worn away and there was a chip in the rim from where Kate had flung a spoon at Easter as she'd gesticulated wildly in support of some half-arsed political debate. Little pieces of history that Anna had been a part of.

And that, in itself, was new.

She herself would never have the markers of family life that were barely noticed in this house by anyone but Anna – like the cheese platter with baby handprints on it that was simply a piece of their everyday crockery, or the serried ranks of primary school photographs, replete with wonky fringes and gappy teeth, gathering dust on the bookshelves. They were just background to the family who lived here and yet they fascinated Anna in a way that eclipsed her studies.

And just as she held tight to the memories of Marjorie's Tupperware jug and the tart crispiness of her favourite Heinz Sandwich Spread on the last crust of bread, she was determined to hold these new memories tight as well, to weave them into the story of her life.

For around Louise's dining table, absorbed into their Sunday routine, there was a beguiling sense of who Anna herself might like to become. The temptation to stay on and do a master's was enormous. She could make this her life. Stay here in Oxford. Make this her home – well not 'here' per se, but somewhere that filled her heart the way this ramshackle home did.

A home where Classic FM burbled constantly in the background and the washing machine was never knowingly empty.

With a bedroom like Kate's perhaps, with her Scouting for Girls posters still on the walls, the Blu Tack ageing and yellowed, alongside her certificates for being basically brilliant at everything – ballet, gymnastics, spelling bees, maths challenges . . . Only the photos of her deplorable attempts at home-dyeing her hair for her sixteenth birthday made it clear that Kate was in fact a mortal. Fallible.

And yet, there was no entitlement with Kate; she was aware of her good fortune to the possible point of embarrassment. Her easy instinctive urge to share it with Anna made any potential envy a moot point. These special Sundays, the use of a tumble drier, even heading home as they would be later that night, with softly scented clean clothes, foil parcels of leftovers and the residual happiness and warmth of belonging that money could never buy. Kate was more of a friend than any person could ask for.

Standing at the sink drying glasses as Alex loudly stacked the dishwasher, Anna tried not to think about the hours of study awaiting her at 44 Cowley Road. The pressure of finals was ramping up and she knew that it wasn't her memory that was likely to let her down. The nerves could easily be her undoing.

'So, Anna, any plans falling into place for next year? Kate seems to have the next five years of her life mapped out already, but she always was an exhausting child. The other girls were playing shop and Kate was wafting around the house in a gown and hood lecturing her teddy bears.' Louise laughed, the nostalgia softening her face. It apparently hadn't occurred to her that the very presence of not one but two sets of academic robes in the house may have been a contributory factor.

'I'm considering staying on for a master's actually,' Anna said shyly.

'That's fabulous news. We need more bright young women lining our halls.' She paused. 'Just make sure you're doing it for the right reasons, that's all.'

She filled the kettle and lifted down a box of After Eights, holding them out to Anna to tackle the cellophane, Louise's frustration with packaging a family joke.

'What would be the wrong reasons?' Anna asked, intrigued, as she slid a perfect square of dark chocolate from its sleeve.

Louise leaned back against the kitchen counter and thought for a moment. 'Well, learning for the sake of learning isn't ideal. Expensive too.' She gave Anna a gentle smile, a hint of sympathy colouring her words. 'Sometimes it's just a way to procrastinate about making the real decisions. The big decisions about what you want to do with the rest of your life.'

Anna looked downwards. 'There are good reasons too.'

'Oh, darling, I'm sure there are. I just thought – well . . .' She reached over and plucked an After Eight from the box, chewing slowly and deliberately, buying time. 'Well, you may not have anyone to talk this through with. A little bit of advice from someone old and crumbly?' With her neat tailored trousers and soft orange jumper bringing out the tones in her silvered hair, Louise was anything but old and crumbly. But she was kind and, apparently, insightful.

'What do you want to do with your life, Anna? What's your burning passion?'

Anna blinked away the immediate and confusing image of Max Howard from her mind's eye. The answer was surprisingly simple. 'I want to write,' she said.

'Books? Articles? Are we talking author, journalist or scholar?' Louise said, nodding. None of the sceptical derision that Anna was always braced for. After all, didn't every second English undergrad want the same thing? Weren't they all secretly pining for a creative life?

'Author?' Anna replied, and Louise smiled.

'Then you'll need to lose the question mark, darling girl. From what I've seen, it's often the case that perseverance and belief can carry one further than natural talent alone in that business. But tell me, why do you need a master's degree to write? Is it because you need the skills, or the approbation? Validation of your talent? You don't need a certificate to tell you that your opinions are worthy of attention and consideration?'

Anna frowned, genuinely considering the question. It was a talent of Louise's to get straight to the heart of the matter.

'I don't know,' she said, two After Eights and some hurried soul-searching later.

Louise smiled. 'Then maybe that's what you need to consider before you make any commitment. And you know . . .' She reached for another chocolate, deep in thought. 'I'm sure Simon wouldn't mind if you wanted to move in here for a bit? If it's having the space to write that's an issue . . .'

'That's very kind,' Anna said, 'but I couldn't possibly.' The refusal was instinctive, yet the offer so enticing. 'The master's would be a good reason to stay in Oxford. Otherwise I should maybe broaden my horizons a little, you know? Work out what I want, and where I want to be?'

Louise nodded. 'That makes sense, but the offer is always open, Anna. Whenever you need us.' She picked up the tray of tea and walked through to the sitting room, leaving Anna munching After Eights on autopilot as she considered Louise's words of wisdom.

Learning for learning's sake.

That one had hit home.

It was telling that Anna always talked of 'a master's', yet never dwelt upon which specialty attracted her. In that moment it occurred to her that it was almost immaterial.

Chapter 42

Oxford, 2010

Back at 44 Cowley Road, Anna couldn't motivate herself to study. And, despite the vast Sunday lunch she'd consumed, she was disproportionately ravenous. Beating an egg into a few spoonfuls of butter and sugar in a mug, she chucked in some cocoa powder and flour and shoved it into the microwave.

Cake. Well, cake or toast. The only answer to emotional hunger.

Watching the little green LED digits count down, she felt as though her time here in Oxford was slipping away from her too. Her time with Kate, in this house. Her time as a student, real life on hold for those few precious years while she worked out what she really, truly wanted.

'Oh, cake. I'm starving,' Kate said, walking into the kitchen behind her. 'Why do we get the munchies so badly on a Sunday night?' she asked, unfolding the foil packaging from her mum and whittling away at the donated risotto. 'I've eaten enough for a family of four today but I still feel—'

'Hollow?' Anna said, just as Kate finished her sentence with 'Snackish.'

An awkward pause as they both took a moment, wondering whether to address Anna's accidental revelation.

'You okay?' Kate asked. 'I mean, I know my mum was ladling out her legendary life advice again, but she's not your mum. You don't *have* to follow it.'

'But maybe I should. What if she's right?' Anna said, opening the microwave door and smiling at the perfect dome of chocolate in her mug. A modern miracle for the munchies. She wandered into the sitting room and wrapped herself in a blanket, going full hermit.

'Look, my little Pea Pod. I can't lie to you; the woman is a savante. Uncanny, annoying, but often so on the money it drives me to distraction. So what did she say to get you all swirly?'

Anna dug her spoon into the melted fudgey chocolate cake and sighed. 'That there was no point staying on for a master's just for the sake of it.'

'Ah,' Kate said and sat back on the sofa beside her, the opened foil parcel balanced on her knees as she carved off large forkfuls, the risotto standing no chance of survival for tomorrow night's supper. 'She did that number on me too. But, you know, I told her my plan and how I needed the research creds to do it justice. That I wouldn't just be doing a master's but a PhD too, all being well.'

Anna blinked. 'What did she say?'

'She just nodded and accepted it,' Kate said, frowning as she tried to recall the conversation exactly. 'Made some comment about earning my way through and not relying on the Bank of Mum and Dad and then made me unload the dishwasher.'

Anna shovelled a huge spoonful of cake into her mouth to buy her some thinking time. 'Whereas when we were talking about it, I couldn't give a single reason why a master's was a good idea, other than that I wanted to stay here in Oxford. With you. With our life.' She shrugged. 'I'm happy here.'

'Mostly,' Kate replied. 'Not a good time for rose-coloured glasses.'

They ate in silence for a moment, their futures stretching out ahead of them, beyond the pressure of their finals, beyond graduation, into what?

'You don't have to leave Oxford if you don't want to study anymore. You could get a job here? But in all honesty, I don't see the downside in buying a little more time to work out what you really want from life. And you'd be even more employable with a few more letters after your name.'

They both knew that wasn't necessarily true in the current job market, but a delusion was more effective when shared. They both also knew that Anna's dedication to studying and research didn't hold a candle to Kate's instinctive passion and drive.

'She would know though, right? I mean, she's spent her entire career in academia. She would recognise a flake if she met one.'

'You are not a flake!' Kate protested. 'Flakey, sometimes, sure. But who isn't?'

Anna shrugged. 'I'm thinking that I should take a little time and go travelling or something. Widen my horizons. Genuinely start writing, rather than talking about writing, you know?'

'You'd actually go travelling without me?' Kate said, looking hurt.

Anna fixed her with a stare. 'Come with me then. And don't say you will, because we both know you won't – you're hardly going to leave Duncan, or your studies, or your family. Your whole life is here.'

'Shit – you're not talking about a holiday are you? You're talking about picking up and fucking off. Like – gone.'

'It had occurred to me, yeah. I mean, three years is the longest I've ever been in one place, you know that. And it's the only place I've lived independently. Maybe there's somewhere out there that suits me better. Maybe I need meadows or beaches, or a dog of my own.'

'Or maybe you don't and you're giving up on a wonderful life here that you know is real and possible, for the dream or the promise of something that might not even exist,' Kate said, leaning forward and waving her hands in frustration.

Anna scraped the last of the mug cake away and swallowed hard. Kate's words hit home in a way that made her uncomfortable, simply for being quite so transparent.

'Pea Pod? Anna? Look at me – is this about something else? Is it money? Because I know there are grants and things . . .' She frowned. 'Or is it Max?'

Anna shook her head. 'Neither. Truly. I mean, it does seem a slightly expensive boondoggle, yes. And it's not exactly easy with you dating my ex's brother. But I wouldn't change that for anything because you and Duncan are just so perfect together. Truly. I just . . .'

'Finish the sentence, Pod.'

'I just don't know who I want to be.'

'You mean *what* you want to be?' Kate clarified, her forehead wrinkled as she desperately tried to understand.

Anna shook her head and breathed out slowly. 'Nope.'

'Anna? An-na?'

A smattering of tiny pebbles clattered against her bedroom window later that night. Well technically the next morning, as Anna stared blearily at her alarm clock. 3.28.

Too early, or too late. Either way – 'Fuck OFF,' she mumbled crossly into her pillow.

'Anna!'

She stumbled from her bed, struggling into a jumper against the chill bite of the early hours and yanking up the sash window that overlooked the street.

'Let me in.'

'Max, would you seriously just fuck off,' Anna hissed down at him. The very last person she wanted to see, and yet still her heart lurched like the traitor that it was.

'But I need to see you.' His face looked up at her, tousled, sun-kissed hair tipped back. His clothes rumpled and his arms held wide. 'I need you.'

'Got another paper due? Need something to plagiarise?' Anna's anger with Max was never far from the surface.

'Mate! Go home and sleep it off!' came the shout from their next-door neighbour.

'Let me in? Anna? Please?' Max looked so forlorn, so far from his usual polished self that she found herself softening, just for a moment. The little devil on her shoulder insisting that maybe he had changed. Maybe, *maybe*, he'd even come here to apologise?

'Fool me once, shame on you,' Anna murmured to herself, as she often did when it came to the thorny issue of Max Howard. How much heartache could she have saved herself if only she'd had the courage of her convictions? If she hadn't fallen for his charm over and over again? If she hadn't been so fucking needy . . .

'Fuck off, Max!' she said firmly and slid the window closed, turning her back to his remonstrations.

Sitting on the end of her bed, she wondered how different her final year might have been if she had been a little more settled within herself. She'd been so different here at Oxford, her confidence growing, her sense of self evolving and solidifying, and with it – finally – some confidence in her own worth.

And yet there was Max: her first – urgh, it pained her to admit – proper love.

Her first experience of the blinkers and justifications one can find to excuse appalling behaviour.

Her first insight, actually, into her mother's life and the string of excuses that kept that marriage together against all better instincts. No wonder it had broken her in the end. What might Anna's life have been like if her dysfunctional parents had loved each other a little less? She was reminded yet again of that uncomfortable truism: the children of lovers are orphans. Well, that seemed pretty spot on from where Anna was sitting and she was determined to break this toxic cycle with Max once and for all.

He'd lied to her.

He'd stolen from her.

And one notable Friday night last November he'd persuaded her into bed, passionately, convincingly, lovingly even . . . Then left her all over again two weeks later with a sour taste in her mouth and a positive pregnancy test.

Taking the lion's share of her self-esteem and her dissertation plans with him.

She put her hands over her ears to drown out his voice now.

She had nothing more to give to the Max Howards of this world. God, she'd rather be alone than in a relationship that broke her down into the very smallest pieces of herself. She'd rather be anywhere that didn't remind her of her own mistakes.

Because wasn't that at the heart of all her uncertainty now?

She'd spent the last decade firm and confident in the belief that she would be *better* at this, better at being an adult than her parents had been. How hard could it be to do the right thing, earn a wage, pay the bills and still be true to your own convictions? She saw people doing it every day. Grown-ups, making grown-up choices.

And yet, here she was, twenty-one years old – an adult in every sense of the law and she too was fucking it up. Perhaps it was genetic? Or maybe it was simply harder than it looked – like juggling, or making sushi, or leaping off the high diving board.

She gave herself a shake. She shied away from any suggestion that her parents might just have been young and flawed individuals, doing the best they could in tricky circumstances. Because then she would have nobody to blame. And somehow, even after all these years, it was often the blame and recriminations that had kept her going.

The adrenaline of getting her A levels, carrying her into the rush of a university degree.

And not just any degree – but a place at Oxford. Thumbing her nose with every personal achievement at the very people who should have believed in her the most.

This doubt – it was corrosive. For it brought a hint of understanding.

She couldn't stay here in Oxford, she realised. It had been the best of times and the worst of times – that Dickens wanker really knew his onions, she thought, a slightly hysterical giggle escaping her.

She may have gained so much over the last three years, but it hadn't been without loss. Loss of her innocence, certainly. Losing Max's baby before she could even make a decision about a termination might have been a blessing in disguise, but that didn't eclipse the pain.

Although, if she were honest with herself, it wasn't the pain of losing a child. It was the pain of knowing that she was just as fallible as the next person. As her mother had been.

To make mistakes was human.

Yet it had still been a crushing realisation to Anna that her life was, often as not, beyond her own control.

And no matter how tempting Louise's offer to stay here and write, or Kate's urgings to stay here and study, maybe it was time for Anna Wilson to go out into the world, on her own terms, and grow up a little bit?

Chapter 43

Bleary-eyed the next morning, Anna lay in bed and stared at the stack of revision notes and past papers that demanded her attention. She slammed the pillow over her face and groaned. Now was absolutely not the time to drop the ball. So close, and yet her conviction that an elusive first would also give her the freedom and closure she needed didn't make the pressure any easier.

All around town, final-year students were drinking, smoking, knocking back Red Bull and Pro Plus. All around town, people were making plans.

Yet for Anna, even with the prospect of academic success within reach – the one thing she had been working towards for so many years – she still felt bound by her circumstances. As though her history might yet eclipse her present when it came to planning for the future.

'I brought coffee,' Kate hammered on her bedroom door and walked in without waiting. 'Double-shot latte and a contrite apology for one?' She sat down and one side of Anna's bed dipped suddenly.

'I'm so sorry, Anna. I must have sounded like a properly entitled bitch last night and I completely understand if you hate me – "what's the downside in doing a master's?"' She parroted herself with a tone of disgust in her voice. 'Here, take the coffee at least, while you consider my fate!'

Anna struggled upright in bed, her hair sticking out in all directions and, she now noticed, her pyjamas misbuttoned. She held out her hand for the takeaway cup from the deli round the corner. Serious coffee. She took a long, grateful sip and then smiled. 'You're such a drama queen this morning.' She drank again. 'And I'd say no apology necessary but if it gets me coffee in bed . . .'

Kate just shook her head. 'The apology is as much to appease my guilt as it is to make you feel better, to be honest. No such thing as a selfless good deed. And, *of course*, you must do what feels right to you. Not everybody wants to spend their entire lives poring over musty documents. That's what works for me, sure. But it's not the only way.' She looked sheepish for a moment. 'And you can hardly shoot me for wanting you to stay?'

'It's not a good enough reason though is it?' Anna said resignedly. 'Just wanting to be with my best friend?'

'People stay for less. And arguably, I'd say it made more sense than staying for a boyfriend. At least we *know* we'll have each other for life.'

Anna felt herself blush. 'Oh, you.'

Kate just looked smug. 'You see. I know you. And I'm probably the only one around here who does. Let's face it, you've done a pretty good job of reframing yourself while you've been here.'

Anna scowled. 'You just got in under the wire, that's all. Before I realised that fresh starts were do-overs just waiting to happen.'

'Then I can only be grateful that I met you on the very first day. Because now I get to know the real you. Warts and all.'

'I've told you,' Anna said, laughing as she clapped her hand over her collarbone. 'It's just a really weird freckle!'

But Kate made a valid point. Within weeks of her arrival, as the freshers shared A level results and school stories, their families' lives edited to create the impression they wanted to share, Anna had realised that this was a golden opportunity to be whomever she wanted to be. Even her own writing evolved and developed, borrowing from her new friends' lives and experiences. From their anecdotes and even their understanding of how the world turned.

With each passing term, Anna stepped further and further away from her own experiences, her own life story.

Denial was effective, rewriting her own personal history even more so.

Had she lied, she often wondered. Or was she simply reframing the truth to make it a little more palatable and to avoid the head tilt of pity she'd endured for so long?

Yet it was Kate who predated the gradual transformation, while in so many ways having also been the catalyst for it.

But with each misdirection, Anna had diluted the truth in all her other relationships, until it became but a shadow in the back of her mind. Ready with a reason she had no childhood photos for T-shirts in rag week. Ready with a quip about carbon emissions being more important than gap years. Ready to be the confident high achiever with a lively bunch of mates and the perfect houseshare.

But in Anna's heart, it seemed the truth had never really left her, or that caustic feeling of simply not being enough. For her parents. For herself. For anyone.

'I think we should blow off revision this morning and go out for breakfast,' Kate said, half dozing from having lain down beside Anna in the warm nest of her duvet. 'A proper artery-clogging fry up at Greasy Joe's. And then, while we're there, you can fill in this.' She reached into her pocket and pulled out a pristine Moleskine notebook.

'We can make a list of all the places you've ever wanted to go. And it'll be just yours. You can put the John Lewis haberdashery department on it, if that's what floats your boat. And then you'll have a plan.'

Anna nodded, speechless and properly touched. A plan. That was all she needed. GCSEs, A levels, university. Stay alive. Stay safe. Stay solvent. She'd been buoyed along by these milestones for so long, eclipsing the other worries and baggage in her life.

So now, she just needed a new one.

As Kate had apparently recognised. Anna took a quavering breath in, her emotions all over the place at this act of true understanding.

'And,' Kate continued, 'we'll put an asterisk by the places I can join you. I'll have holidays, you know. So if you can't be here, then I can be wherever you are.'

Kate sat up, unnerved it seemed by Anna's silence. 'Ah, don't cry about it, ya daft sod. It's only a notebook.'

They eschewed Greasy Joe's in the end in favour of tomato and mozzarella paninis in the sunshine watching the college Eights working on their stroke on the Isis.

They sipped peach Snapples and dipped into bags of salty crisps, their tableau the epitome of the Oxford dream. Revision folders lay littered around them on their rug, more as a sop to the process than any likelihood of their being opened.

The Moleskine notebook on the other hand was already filling with handwritten notes: Venice, Iceland, Oslo perhaps more likely than the Galapagos Islands or—

'Look, this isn't a blueprint – you're not legally bound to go to these places, Anna. If you want to go to Madagascar, write down Madagascar!' Kate laughed while Anna blushed.

'It's just – well, I really like the movies . . .' Anna carefully added the island to The List.

'You do know, though, that there won't be actual penguins there, right?' Kate snorted. She had a particular affinity with 'Little Anna' as she liked to call her, whenever small childhood dreams or ambitions surfaced. Late, sure, but nonetheless compelling.

Anna just smiled. 'Maybe we should add Antarctica too. That's the penguin one, right?'

Kate, however, was still following a thought. 'You should have another list in the back of that notebook, you know? Just for your eyes. Make a list of all the things you never had the chance to do growing up, all the rites of passage you missed out on.'

The idea lay between them for a moment, heavy with significance. Not only that Kate knew Anna so well, but that those gaps in her youth might yet account for her Emmental existence.

'So, you learned to ride a bike when you first got here – there must be other stuff like that?' Kate persisted.

Anna simply shrugged, her brow furrowed. 'I can swim, I can ice skate, I can play a little piano, a little clarinet, a little hockey . . . I am basically a dabbler. I guess it's normal to try and adapt to wherever you are. And I have form on the beginner's luck front too – I pick things up easily. I just never had the opportunity to take anything further.'

'Except literature,' Kate pointed out. 'Or you wouldn't be here.'

Anna turned on the rug to face her. 'Yes, but I could take books anywhere. And I didn't need anybody else to make it happen.'

'Self-sufficient.' Kate nodded.

'I suppose. But actually,' she smiled, 'it wasn't the big stuff like learning to ride a bike that sprang to mind when you suggested another list. It was all the little things that were missing – having a photo album, knowing my first words for a project at school, knowing stuff for my medical history.' She paused. 'Actually does it make me really shallow that after all these years the thing that bothers me most is never knowing if anyone was really proud of me?'

She swallowed hard. It was one thing to carry that in the back of your mind, it was another entirely to voice it. Out loud. To Kate.

'Anyone in particular?' Kate asked gently.

Anna gave a strangled laugh. 'Well, anyone would do.'

'Shit,' Kate said, pulling a horror-struck face to break the tension. 'I was kind of thinking more getting your ears pierced or having a Barbie birthday party.'

'Ah, how well you know me.' Anna snorted, the laughter and emotion twisting her face as she attempted to rein in a sudden attack of the giggles. 'It should be perfectly obvious that I was more Ninja Turtle than Malibu Barbie.'

They both looked out across the river, shouts from the cox in the boat echoing along the water. 'But did you ever think you'd end up here?' Kate said.

Anna nodded. 'I had to believe. It was the only thing that kept me going sometimes. I mean, everybody knows what "Oxford" means, don't they? You can't argue with a degree from Oxford – it says something about a person.'

'It says you deserve a little pride and appreciation.' Kate nodded, taking in the subtext to Anna's words. 'Actually, it says more than that though, about *you*, Anna. It says that you're resilient and intelligent and driven. It says that anyone who's lucky enough to have you as a friend has won the lottery. And anyone who has missed out on having you in their life is really the one who's been missing out.'

'Oh you,' Anna said for the second time that day.

'Have you thought any more about inviting your dad to graduation? I mean, they might let him out on day release or something?' Kate paused. 'It might be nice to know he's sitting out there, marvelling at your achievements. Maybe feeling a little guilty?'

Anna gave a wry smile; hadn't that been exactly what she'd been thinking when she'd mailed the invitation? 'I did already. I wrote to him at the prison.' She reached into her backpack and pulled out a crumpled letter. 'They sent it back.'

Kate looked shocked. 'He wouldn't even read it?'

'Couldn't is more accurate. He got out a few months ago, apparently. He just hadn't thought to, you know, let me know that.' Anna nodded repeatedly, still struggling to process the excruciating rejection. Not so much a rejection of their relationship as a total lack of consideration that they might even have one. 'Fool me once . . .' she said with a shrug.

'I guess some people never change,' Kate offered apologetically.

'Yet, it seems that pigeons learn faster than me.' Anna stared out across the water. 'I seem destined to attract loser men into my life. But isn't that the pattern? Loser dad, loser boyfriend . . . Should I hold out hope that one day I can have my very own loser husband too?'

Kate shook her head. 'Not if I have anything to do with it! Besides, why on earth would we ever get married? I mean, this is not the 1970s is it? I don't need a man to make my life work. I like boyfriends – scratch that, I like Duncan. I like our friendship and I really like the shagging, but I cannot honestly see a day when I would need a piece of paper to make it valid.'

'I suggest we make a pact then,' Anna said with a grin, 'but I think, on this one, we're both in agreement. You can still have the kids though, okay? I would be excellent auntie material.'

'Deal,' Kate said, holding out her hand and shaking Anna's firmly.

'You know, though, you might have actually hit on something before,' Anna said, her smile lighting up her face with mischief. 'There was one thing I always wanted to do as a child.'

'It's never too late,' Kate said. 'I'm up for a challenge.'

Anna shovelled their folders and notebooks into her backpack and leapt to her feet. 'No time like the present then.'

Chapter 44

Oxford, 2010

'I think maybe the lady at Paint a Pot was right and we should have come back for their ladies' night,' Kate said, picking little flecks of paint from her hair. The exuberance of the birthday party at the table beside them had been remarkable to see, not least for the size and extravagance of the birthday cake.

Anna laughed, still feeling vaguely nauseous from the enormous slice of cake that the embarrassed mother had pressed upon them. 'Oh, I don't know. I think it was the perfect way to get an authentic tenth birthday experience. And I have to say, my mug will be a masterpiece.'

'It's true, if the whole writing thing goes tits up, you could always go all Emma Bridgewater. In fact, I think we should swap mugs – like, as a memento of today. Then every time you have a cup of tea, wherever you are, it'll be like—'

'Like I'm drinking from a shit mug covered in creepy goblins?' Anna teased.

'They are not goblins!' Kate protested. 'It was supposed to be you and me. Dancing in the kitchen with a glass of wine. It's not my fault it looks like an *X-Files* massacre.'

'Then, I think it was choosing *red* wine that was the mistake,' said Anna drily, before dissolving into laughter, high on sugar and elation at their ridiculous, stupid, wonderful afternoon.

It had been exactly the tonic she'd needed – the perfect distraction from thoughts of finals and the future. And Kate, as always, was the perfect companion. Assuming you ignored the private smiles that seemed to grow wider with each successive text from Duncan.

'You know,' Kate said, shaking her head and trying to maintain her faux indignation, 'there are other ways to have a proper "birthday party experience". Like, we could actually *have* a party. A belated one. For you.'

Anna shook her head instinctively. 'Nooo. Too weird. And anyway, you know me, I'd still spend half the night hanging out in the kitchen while the cool kids snogged and got high in the sitting room. I can't seem to help myself.' She smiled. 'It's like I'm so used to being the outsider looking in, that I've given up fighting it.'

'You know other people feel like that too, though, right?' Kate said, frowning. 'It's not a unique reaction to your – er – situation.' She gave Anna a squeeze. 'Sometimes I think it's part of a person's DNA.'

'Like extrovert, introvert?'

'Nah – more like self-belief, or possibly a complete disregard for what other people think. Or consequences,' Kate said. 'Like maybe there's a "good at parties" gene?'

'You'd think they could test for a thing like that. Put us all out of our misery.' Anna sighed. 'And look, I get what you're saying. I'm not the only person in the world to feel like I've got my face pressed against the window, looking in. But I don't think it's the same.'

'Okay. But nobody's experience of anything is exactly the same, is it? I mean, when I was at school, I would literally feel like an alien on my own planet some days. Or as though we were all speaking the same language, but there was a subtext, or a dialect or something, that I just didn't understand. And it wasn't because I didn't want to – I just couldn't *compute* how these girls would think – their priorities and interests – their total lack of ambition or self-worth. And so, I stepped back. Because being on the outside of a social group looking in was actually being kinder to me than reducing myself to fit.'

Anna slowly blinked, blindsided a little by Kate's heartfelt revelation.

'Diluting yourself. Like Kate-Lite?' Anna said quietly.

'Exactly,' Kate replied, nodding. 'Like, I'd rather be me – full-sized and a bit quirky – than a poor approximation with a packed social calendar. You know?'

'I do,' Anna replied. 'I really do.' Wondering how it had taken them three years to have this conversation. This moment of complete empathy. But that in itself came with issues. 'But *now* you've left me with a quandary – or possibly a life crisis. Because *now*, I'm wondering how many other hurdles I've ascribed to my start in life, when they were in fact just a part of life.' She looked up at Kate with wide, confused eyes and slowly shook her head.

'Look, would it be incredibly insensitive of me to suggest that, maybe, it's time to stop looking back and start looking forward?' Kate said, pulling an awkward face as if to suggest that she knew exactly how thin the proverbial ice might be beneath her feet with that proposal. 'I mean, you're about to graduate from Oxford and probably, let's face it, with some ridiculous over-achieving first. There are myriad jobs you could apply for, and despite what my well-meaning mother says, there's a master's on the table to buy you some life-planning time. You don't have to go all Greta Garbo with your notebook for a year.'

'Greta what now?' Anna said.

'You know, the actress. "I vant to be alone" – that one.'

Anna wrinkled her nose. 'Do you think there was lead in the paint at the Paint a Pot?'

Kate shook her head. 'You really are the queen of evasion, aren't you? Is that what this new house-sitting idea is about then? Because really, if you want to see the world, there are other, more sociable ways to do it. I'm just worried that you're essentially going to become a travelling hermit.'

Anna was rather wishing she hadn't even mentioned the idea now, but there was something of the confessional about sitting side by side painting mugs while ten-year-olds at the neighbouring table told ridiculous jokes and mainlined Party Rings. It was just an idea. A concept. An article she'd read online the night before when she couldn't sleep.

And to her, the notion of cost-free accommodation and a carousel of dream locations while she worked out not just how to write, but exactly *what* she wanted to write, had seemed like a dream come true. No shabby hostels, or room-mates, or backpacks. Just a little bit of time to breathe after the insane treadmill that had carried her this far.

But Kate's interpretation had clearly been a little different. 'I guess I just don't understand the logic.'

'I want to write,' Anna replied simply. 'I want to see if I actually can, as opposed to just talking about it conceptually, you know. I just want to write, to try and make sense of what's going on in my head.'

'So, what's stopping you doing that here? I mean, go travelling, take a holiday, but why the need to take yourself away from everyone who can support you? You know, my dad would say that a goal without a plan is just a wish,' Kate said, her tone suddenly serious, as though convincing Anna to see her point of view was of vital importance.

'Then what's a plan without a goal?' Anna replied, taking her hand and willing her friend to understand that she was operating blind on this one.

Kate shook her head resignedly. 'Research?' she offered with a gentle smile.

Back at the house, Anna sat on her bed, flaking the last remnants of paint from her hands and trying to find the energy to revise. Her first was by no means a done deal and she couldn't afford to drop the ball now. Tugging her notebooks of useful quotes and references from her backpack, her father's letter fell onto the duvet beside her.

At least this time, she couldn't blame the appalling timing of another rejection on him. After the whole GCSE debacle, she'd sworn that she would keep her distance. But, as her housemates began talking about graduation, about their families, she'd been powerless to resist that insistent tug of hope.

But, of course, he hadn't changed. Always taking short cuts through life, the line of least resistance, or at least a line that enabled him to blame any failure on somebody else – why would his parole this time be any different? That visit to Darwent Prison had redrawn all Anna's memories of the funny, caring bear of a man who had read her bedtime stories, even using special voices for the various characters. The shutters had dropped from her memory the moment he'd assigned blame to her mother for Anna's situation, and a convenient lack of culpability on his part for her childhood in care.

And with each year that passed, it seemed that Anna remembered more, not less, of the shouting, the anger, and the lying that had characterised his final years at home with her. Gambling her mother's wages – the same hard-won money that was supposed to pay for food and heating. Until, in her mind now, she was unable to separate the gnawing chill and hunger of that last winter from his confident, blasé bragging about how life was going to be when his plans came together.

She gave a shudder as that last thought formed in her mind.

She had never known what exactly those 'plans' were, but the echoes of that sentiment still had the power to make her feel cold and abandoned all over again. It wouldn't take a psychologist to work out their subliminal part in Anna's absolute aversion to making a solid life plan moving forward, would it?

And, while Kate made a valid point about looking forwards, not back, there was still the open wound of neglect that coloured Anna's every relationship, that still cried out to be cauterised. Perhaps she could break the cycle of self-critical beliefs, the conviction of never being good enough? And, if not healed, then perhaps at least she could hope to find a little closure on her year of discovery.

She picked up the Moleskine notebook and reread The List.

She could feed her soul and explore the planet at the same time as pursuing her dreams, couldn't she?

And then, when she knew who she was – Anna Wilson in her own right – well, then, *then*, she could settle down and enjoy a future of her own making. Where she could be her best self – no dilution required.

Chapter 45

Oxford, 2010 – Graduation

Anna clutched the printed-out page in her sweating palm like a talisman, hugging the knowledge to herself. Her secret, her success. The anticipation and nerves of the day were making everyone around her a little skittish, desperate to impress their guests, bidding farewells to friendships and, indeed, their privileged undergraduate lifestyles.

Life would never be the same again.

For any of them.

Proud conversations eddied around her: a veritable alphabet soup of graduate positions with KPMG, PWC, GSK, GCHQ or the BBC. And so, in the pocket under her graduation robes, that single printed page gave Anna the boost she needed. The boost from knowing what came next, courtesy of a company called Home Network and a sweet Yorkshire girl called Emily.

Her very first placement as a house-sitter, references approved.

A mews house just off Kensington High Street. Small, but perfectly formed, and eye-wateringly expensive, if the internet was any guide. Immaculate living spaces and three bedroom suites – not bedrooms, she noted, bedroom *suites*. She supposed that she'd discover what that actually meant when she arrived tomorrow to take possession of the keys, her instructions and the care and feeding of two wire-haired dachshunds for three full weeks. There was the use of a Smart car at her disposal but the very thought of driving in central London brought Anna out in a cold sweat.

She would take the bus.

The warmth of this quiet win was not to be underestimated today, a surety to her madcap plan to step away from the certainty of the milk round of recruiters and forge her own path. And, yes, there had been a buzz from explaining her plan to the sweet, enthusiastic Emily – her request to be a full-time house-sitter for a whole year so that she could write.

'So you're like one of those lady novelists?' Emily had sounded a little in awe, which was nice in a way because it took the edge off the fraudulent feeling of being a slightly pretentious imposter.

Time to write. But what to write?

She could only hope that a little time, space and inspiration would solve that particular riddle. It seemed the height of self-indulgence to let on that her writing, until now anyway, had always been a cheaper and more accessible version of therapy. Her ambition simply to hold a book in her hand, bearing her own name, as testament to her talent and hard work. Despite everything life had thrown at her.

Around her the crowds of people in identical black robes, bedecked with coloured hoods and pointed mortarboards, surged forward. Deep breaths required, as she silently offered up a prayer to anyone that was listening. A prayer of thanks for this experience, but also one of hope, moving forward.

★

Taking her allocated seat, Anna fought the wildly inappropriate urge to laugh. Whenever they'd studied certain writers, often of the male and self-aggrandising variety, Anna had a tendency to roll her eyes; caricature and cliché left her cold and irked, as a rule. She'd written numerous essays and book reports on the subject, unable to jump blindly on board with the notion of 'classic literature', simply because an imprint or editor had labelled it so. But here, today, amongst the excited hubbub of the Sheldonian, costumed in this – let's be honest – slightly ridiculous mortarboard and robe, she began to wonder whether that bastard Hemingway actually knew what he was talking about: it was sometimes lonelier to be surrounded by people than to be on your own. Although, to be fair, she considered, most of the time he'd been off his head on booze and pills, or the electro-shock therapy they seemed to dole out back then with such abandon.

Looking around, she wasn't the only one craning her neck to take in the spectacle of the Sheldonian before the degree ceremony commenced; the only difference being that her friends and classmates were seeking out their families and guests, to wave, to smile, some nervously looking for approbation.

Anna, on the other hand, was simply trying to drink it all in, notice every little moment and foible. Imprint this achievement on her memory. She had nobody in the invited audience to cheer when she received her degree, or to snap a photograph as she tossed her mortarboard into the air with her classmates.

Three years of study, of laughter and belonging, over with one flick of the wrist.

She thought of the beautifully inspiring, yet ultimately disappointing letter from Mrs Holt that had arrived, complete with a ten-pound book token that brought tears to Anna's eyes. It had felt a little strange to invite her, but after her father's ignominious disappearance, it had actually made more sense. After all, who better to share this day with than her sixth form English teacher? It had been those crucial years of support and encouragement that had made this very day possible, but Mrs Holt had new commitments at school, and most likely a new protégé to urge towards greatness. And rightly so. Yet still, it was hard not to feel a little slighted, a little more abandoned, on this momentous occasion.

But really, who else could she have invited to fill the void?

Those who populated Anna's childhood had been, in the main, paid to care.

Whether you called yourself a 'foster child', or simply a 'looked-after child' – as the forms always insisted on delineating her – it was still sobering to realise that money had changed hands, a bargain had been struck. Maybe recognising *that* was just another part of growing up, of gaining a little more perspective, of leaving the system that had carried her this far?

And she had been lucky in so many ways. Sometimes there had been affection, respect, maybe even love – but she was under no illusion that those relationships held any of the permanence or dedication she saw in these families around her today.

There really was nothing like a big event to highlight such a glaring absence. Her grip on the page in her pocket tightened.

Kate twisted around from the row in front of her, the alphabet keeping them apart on a day when it would have meant so much to sit together. 'You *are* coming for lunch afterwards aren't you?' she whispered. 'I think my dad's more excited about your first than he'll admit. And it honestly wouldn't be the same without you.'

Anna hesitated. All of her housemates had issued similar invitations and she'd quietly declined every single one. This was their big day too; the last thing they needed amid such a familial rite of passage was an interloper.

'And before you say no – or say yes and then duck out at the last minute – can I just say that we wouldn't invite you if we didn't actually *want* you there, Anna Wilson. Like it not, you're stuck with me on your team now. And one last lunch with my folks is really the very least you could do. If you're committed to flaking off to write – making my mad mother inordinately proud of you, by the way – then don't abandon me now.' She grinned, before turning back to face the front, as the music swelled and the Vice Chancellor took to the stage to begin his address to the Class of 2010.

Kate was taking no chances, and wended her way through the crowd towards Anna the moment the ceremony was over, tucking her arm through Anna's tightly and tugging her forwards. A table at Quod was booked, awaiting them.

Alex stood with his parents, gangly and gruff, yet clearly very proud of his big sister. He held out his camera to Anna and she instinctively removed the lens cap, assuming he was asking her to take a family photograph. 'Come on then, Porters – smile for the camera,' Anna said, even as they bundled together, with Kate at the centre of the photograph, embarrassed to be so banal as to want this quintessential image, yet equally delighted to have the moment they were all together captured on film.

'Thanks for doing that,' Alex said. 'I'd actually forgotten and it'll mean the world to Mum.'

'You gave me the camera, take the credit.' Anna smiled, loving the slightly dorky, but incredibly kind young man he was becoming. Three years was almost a lifetime in teenager years after all.

'Actually,' he blushed, 'I was showing you these. If you want to pick your favourites, I can get them printed with the others and send them on. Wherever it is you're off to.' He held out the weighty SLR towards her again, the screen folded back for viewing.

He'd taken photographs of Anna and Kate, flushed with nerves and excitement before the ceremony, looking incredibly young and yet so worldly at the same time. You could almost see the bonds of their friendship holding them together in the artful way their images were crisp and sharp and the crowds behind them softened out of the frame.

'Alex! These are beautiful. I had no idea you were such a photographer.' She flicked through the images like an old-fashioned movie reel, love and laughter filling the screen. Then on, past images of Kate up on stage, receiving her degree and capturing to perfection the pride on her face as she turned to the crowd, her gaze seeking out her family, and by extension this very lens.

And then . . . Then there were the photos that Anna never dreamed she would have. A series of beautifully framed images mirroring those of Kate, but only focused on Anna on stage, shyly overwhelmed, reaching out her hand, her face a picture of awe.

'This is the best one, I think,' Alex said, reaching across and zooming in.

Anna simply nodded, the lump in her throat preventing her from speaking. Instead, she simply reached up and impulsively kissed his cheek. 'Thank you,' she said, clasping his hand

and trying to communicate how very much this thoughtful gesture meant to her.

He grinned goofily, flushed bright, bright red. 'Well, you know, it's a big day, right?'

Anna nodded, unable to take her eyes off the tiny camera screen.

Bizarrely, it was hard to say which meant more to her, the degree certificate in her hand or the photograph of her receiving it.

In her life there were so few photos, so few tangible mementos – and there was no way that Alex could have realised the significance of his kindness. 'Thank you,' she said again, his bemused smile confirming that suspicion.

'Did Alex tell you?' Louise said, walking over and tucking her arm through Anna's as they walked as a pack through the cobbled lanes by the Radcliffe Camera towards the High Street. 'He's signed me up to Facebook so I can track your travels.'

She seemed inordinately proud of this foray into social media. So much so that Anna didn't have the heart to confess that she had yet to do the same. Or that it simply hadn't occurred to her to document her travels online. A journal perhaps . . .

'It's so exciting, isn't it, Kate? The thought of not knowing where one will be a month from now, six months from now. All those new horizons. All that glorious inspiration.'

Kate raised an eyebrow and looked at Anna. 'I told you she was overly invested in your plan,' she said drily.

'Oh, you, with your library fixation. I never dared dream you'd be so frivolous as to take a gap year, but this – well, Anna darling – this is something else. A year on the road. A year of discovery,' Louise insisted.

'Have you been at the gin, Mother?' Alex laughed, teasing his mum as he made the most of his new height and leaned on her shoulder gently.

'Ah come on,' Louise protested. 'Let me applaud the adventure. The very idea of being technically homeless for your art wouldn't occur to either of my cossetted offspring, Anna. And I think it's fabulous. Hello *Brave New World* and all that.'

Kate rolled her eyes. 'Mu-um, Anna isn't the next Aldous Huxley. She's not on a quest for danger, poetry and sin. She's an original.'

Alex looked from one to the other in confusion. 'Homeless? I thought she was just looking after people's dogs?'

'It's all part of the *adventure*, darling boy . . . While Anna writes her book.' Louise's face was pink with delight as she explained to Alex what was afoot.

Anna was just grateful for the distraction; Louise's easy and cavalier use of the word homeless had, quite literally, brought her out in a cold sweat. Is that what she was now? Homeless? And voluntarily at that!

She had means, and qualifications, yet nowhere to be and nobody to be with.

This nomadic adventure had seemed like the perfect bridge from her chaotic student digs into the adult world. At least until she worked out what the adult world held for a person with few career aspirations and even fewer commitments.

Homeless. The weight of the word was disproportionate to its two meagre syllables.

Her plan – her much-vaunted voyage of discovery – suddenly felt foolish and ill-advised. Saying she wanted to write somehow both naive and arrogant at the same time.

She was only twenty-one years old. Barely an adult. Really, truly, what could she possibly have to say?

All of those around her were moving on to pastures new, seemingly graduating with a clear idea of who they were and what they wanted. Or so it seemed to Anna. And how very lightly they took that privilege.

Envy was never pretty and Anna worked hard to avoid it, but in that moment it unfurled within her, cloying and corrosive.

'Hey,' Kate said, catching the change in mood from the expression on Anna's face. 'I know Mum said you could move in with them whenever you liked, but does the offer go both ways? I mean, can I move in with you when you're somewhere remote and fabulous and in need of company?'

Anna felt tears feather her eyelashes, unusually emotional. 'I'd really like that,' she said.

Chapter 46

The Mews, Kensington High Street, London, 2010

Sophie Knightley was everything that one might expect from such a name. From such an address.

It was a baptism of fire from the very first moment. A first for both of them, it seemed.

'Mummy normally takes Dixie and Dalai when I'm away, but she's a little under the weather. So a friend told me about you. Not you, per se, obviously. But this Home Network situation. So, I guess I have to trust you,' Sophie said, her forehead weirdly smooth and sheeny, in contrast to the obvious concern in her eyes.

'Would it help to speak daily? I can update you on the dogs, or anything that might be on your mind. Just tell me what you need.' It was easy for Anna to be accommodating; she had no plans and no real frame of reference for how this might work. Emily had talked her through the usual parameters over the phone and impressed upon her that this was supposed to be a mutually beneficial arrangement. Anna was not "staff". She was not there to clean, organise or handle secretarial matters. She had one job: to keep the house and the dogs safe and well.

Period.

But somehow, Anna still felt beholden to this woman for the leap of faith she was taking. Anna had no reviews online as yet. She had no credibility as a house-sitter at all. And a First in English, albeit from a prestigious university, hardly qualified her as the perfect canine companion. She swallowed a bubble of nervous laughter, as the thought occurred to her: it hardly qualified her for anything at all!

But, seemingly, it was enough for Sophie to hand over her house keys, her car keys and detailed instructions for the care, feeding and entertainment of two incredibly fortunate dogs. Their life was apparently one of ease and luxury, even if they did look totally unfazed by their owner's imminent departure.

And so, as she waved Sophie off to some Scottish country estate, despite her mother's inconvenient 'teeny tiny heart attack', Anna found herself wondering as always whether anything in life that was easily acquired meant even a fraction of what it might.

She clipped on the dogs' leads and decided to make the most of the sunshine. Storms were forecast and, in this first rush of diligence and excitement, she determined to make the most of every moment in this, her vicarious new life.

Even stepping out of the mews into 'Ken High Street' – as Sophie had called it – was a shock to the senses. The quiet oasis of monied calm immediately gave way to crowds of tourists and shoppers; multilingual, multinational, multitudinous. The dogs weren't bothered. They trotted neatly to heel, following it seemed a well-worn path to the parkland where they were allowed a little freedom and time with their frisbee.

Anna smiled to herself, already feeling more like a local than the map-touting tourists who seemed both driven and confused as they marched along the pavements. She stopped for a coffee at Bean-o, Sophie's recommendation taken seriously. And sipping the perfect cappuccino, she tilted her face to the sun.

Everything felt new and different and way, way out of her comfort zone, but the fact that she was staying in a house, not a hostel, and carried with her a detailed breakdown of all Sophie's favourite haunts, gave this adventure a legitimacy and credibility that was encouraging. In her satchel were the fresh new notebooks that Kate had given her, wrapped into a bundle with blue ribbon and a multipack of Fruit Pastilles. Brain sweets – the revision pick-me-up of choice for the slightly dull and drug-averse.

She would walk the dogs every morning and jot down ideas as they came to her, as she'd heard other writers discuss on various forums and festivals. Then in the afternoon, her time was her own and she would write.

Live like a local, enjoy the dogs' company and start her new career.

At least that was the plan.

It took four days for her naivety to be fully revealed.

As the fifth day of filthy weather whipped down the mews, the icy rain not giving a shit that it was summertime, Anna found herself twitchy and on edge. Predictably, Sophie hadn't logged in once, or responded to Anna's question about the leaky roof on the top floor. Number 3 was apparently a triumph of smoke and mirrors. Once you looked past the address and the winning pastel blue façade, it was faded and ageing and in need of repair. Who knew what a new roof for a place like this might cost, but Anna would wager that it might put a dent in Sophie's global gallivanting.

There were framed photographs on every horizontal surface – sailing with family, skiing with friends, beach barbeques with an incredibly good-looking boyfriend. Not the same boyfriend as in the other photographs, but still. There was no shortage of narcissism in the photo array – not one single image anywhere that didn't feature Sophie's broad, unfettered smile of glee.

In fact, if Anna hadn't been forced to relocate the sodden file boxes on the landing as the rainwater gushed down – if she hadn't seen with her own two eyes the heap of job rejection letters and wince-inducing credit card statements, then Sophie Knightley might almost be the kind of girl one might resent.

But those blonde highlights – £209 at John Frieda of Mayfair – were just a distraction.

Along with this house. It was not just her father's aquiline nose that she'd inherited.

And Anna hadn't meant to snoop. In fact, her very first commitment to herself on taking this job was that she would be beyond reproach – the kind of house-sitter that could be trusted and relied upon. The kind of person in whom you could be confident looking after your beloved pets and your privacy.

But for the flood.

Anna had been torn, as Sophie's mobile rang out again and again – should she leave the box files to turn to papier mâché on her watch, or should she attempt to rescue them? She'd opted for the latter, draping sodden pages over radiators around the house. But the cost had been confidentiality.

Another bang outside the front door as the bin rattled along the mews in the wind. Another window slamming next door. Voices, muffled but in heated debate on the other side of the party wall.

Day five and already Anna's nerves were wired to breaking point.

Five days, four nights and not a soul for conversation or company.

The dogs were adorable, yet mostly self-sufficient and independent. They had each other and Anna was merely the means to food and outings. To be tolerated perhaps, rather than appreciated.

For the first time, it dawned on Anna that a year was a really long time to be alone. Not alone, in the sense she'd always known it – surrounded by people – but actually, I-can-hear-my-own-heart-beating alone.

Another crash outside in the mews roused Anna to her feet, as she once more went methodically from room to room, checking doors, checking windows.

Old habits died hard.

But she was damned if she would pick up the phone after only a few days and admit that this was a mistake.

She just needed to focus on her words, on her characters, on the parallel universe she was constructing out of thin air every afternoon as she sat at the kitchen table with a pen in her hand.

Six pages was all she had to show for her efforts.

She would need every week of the year to have something concrete at the end of it.

So losing her nerve now was hardly the answer.

If it turned out that house-sitting was just a different way to procrastinate with a wider geographical reach and fewer deadlines, then she might have been better off doing a master's with Kate after all.

It wasn't too late.

But even that calculation felt like an admission of defeat and pride had carried her this far.

As though summoned by the very thought of her friend, her phone bleeped with a text from Kate, somewhere in Greece with Duncan as a last hurrah before they knuckled down to the fresh term.

> Write me a letter? I've been reading this biography of Eleanor Roosevelt and she reminds me of you so much . . . That's a compliment by the way . . . So, if the words don't flow, start small and write me a letter. Then invite me to stay somewhere wildly glamorous that we lowly academics will never afford in a million lifetimes.
> Kxx

She didn't want to write letters, she didn't want to start small, but Kate's text was a timely reminder that in the wobbliest of times, there was normally a book that might hold the key to sanity. She clicked open her phone and searched for Kensington Library.

It was a small thing, but it was somewhere to start, and that was all she needed right now.

If anything was to come from this house-sitting plan, Anna realised, then above all, it had to feel like the *start* of something.

Chapter 47

Chipping Norton, 2019

'And you're quite sure it's okay if a friend joins me for a few days?' Anna clarified, not sure if Mrs Loseley could even hear her above the sound of squabbling and tuneless singing in the background.

'Yes, yes, it's fine. Now I'll leave the key in the key safe – I told all this to the girl at Home Network.' The poor woman sounded stressed and as though her attention were being pulled in three different directions at once. 'Let yourself in, make yourself at home, and honestly just ignore the mess.'

'No problem. I hope you have a lovely holiday.'

Anna could have sworn there was more than a hint of irony in Mrs Loseley's reply. Three children under five couldn't be easy, whether there was a beach involved or not. Even the logistics of airport security and sunscreen application defeated Anna. And it certainly sounded as though Mrs Loseley was in need of a well-earned break.

The less maternal side of Anna's brain supplied the notion that a holiday without her offspring might actually be more conducive to relaxing, but she knew all too well how the families that left home stressed, exhausted, and with relationships at the point of fracture, would all too often return two weeks later renewed, ready to embrace the new school year. Easy smiles, tender touches and conviviality for the price of a fortnight in the sun.

Apart from the ones who headed straight for the divorce lawyers, of course, and she'd seen a few of them in her time as well . . . High days and holidays as always the perfect litmus test for life, loves and litigation.

She pulled over into a lay-by and looked across the rolling Cotswold hills. She was early. In fact she'd been up before the dawn broke, ready and willing to move on. To collect her dust-spackled Mini from the long-stay car park and head west, away from the somewhat suffocating confines of a hotel room, however luxurious.

Back on schedule, back on track.

And if she so wished, she could almost erase the last month from her mind.

Perspective. That was what was required here.

And not just the patchwork of fields and hedgerows laid out below her in shades of chartreuse, asparagus and emerald.

Perspective she would hopefully find in the four file boxes crammed into her boot. An idea that arrived in her head, fully formed and insistent at three that morning was now already one step closer to exploration.

It had been a somewhat major detour to drive to her storage locker and it was possible she should have prepared herself for a few uncomfortable moments. Not least, the bloodstained silk dress balled into the corner from her last visit.

But there had also been a moment of clarity, as she boxed up all her travel journals and clippings and her Home Network files and photographs, and looked around at the wire racking and plastic boxes that housed all her worldly possessions.

She needed to take stock. A fresh start. Another new beginning.

And in the charming market town of Chipping Norton, with the space of a four-bedroomed house and no real calls on her time outside the care and feeding of Mr Loseley's extensive tropical fish collection and an enormous and apparently somewhat elusive grey Ragdoll cat called Spook, Anna now had the perfect opportunity.

And, whilst she could now see clearly enough that this was hardly the first such opportunity, it was the only time she had ever felt ready to tackle such a project. The only time, in fact, it had even occurred to her as she bumbled along from placement to placement, so close to the daily calls on her time as to have missed the big picture altogether.

Driving through the marketplace of Chipping Norton, Anna smiled as she saw the double-fronted windows of an independent bookshop, followed by cafés and boutiques that were welcoming and just the right side of quirky. After a few days in London, the cheery greetings as residents passed each other on the street were almost jarring as she tried to adjust. You could travel the length of Oxford Street some days without so much as a smile, discounting the builders, of course – who never missed an opportunity to exhort the benefits of cheering up. Apparently, it might never happen.

She smiled despite herself, wondering what it was that they imagined worried her. Women like her. Were they really convinced that women's anxieties were all fictional and forthcoming and never in the here and now?

She pulled over again and checked the directions, even the road names reminding her that she was in the countryside again now: Spring Street, The Cattle Market, Cotswold

Crescent . . . She flexed her swollen ankle, the long drive having taken its toll. Still, the distractions around her were plentiful: beautiful dogs were being walked almost everywhere she looked, and there was no small number of chiselled, tousled men with their tattersall check shirts rolled distractingly to the elbow; several cliques of women with strollers and toddlers on unwieldy scooters gathered outside a hall advertising a music group for children, half looking peppy and exuberant, the other half simply exhausted and resigned.

Anna wondered which category she herself would fit into, before dashing the very thought from her mind. Motherhood was not now, and never would be, on her agenda. Even as she put the Mini into gear again to pull away, though, she couldn't help but wonder which group of women was more authentic – and how many tears were hidden behind the bouncier ponytails and Sweaty Betty outfits.

Finally pulling into the designated bay outside number forty-two The Lea, Anna struggled to remember why, all those months ago, she had chosen this particular assignment. This sweeping cul-de-sac was hardly high-lux, even if the brand-new Cotswold stone homes here seemed to be selling for a small fortune if you looked on the internet. Everything was so new. Squeaky, shiny, *Desperate Housewives* new.

Even the key in the key safe was barely scuffed.

There were no hand-me-downs here. No compromises.

Any sacrifices to live here, in The Lea, were apparently those of the parents. And probably their bank accounts.

It was a way of life that Anna had always secretly wondered about, yet simultaneously avoided. Even as the sunshine lit up the rolling hills beyond the rooftops and dried the last drops of rain from the various plastic climbing frames and bike stores, Anna still felt strangely ambivalent about being there.

Perhaps it would come to her, over the next few days, why exactly she had sought out this little slice of family life to be her base in the Cotswolds.

An hour later and she was none the wiser. The whole house was exactly as Mrs Loseley had described. Organised chaos.

The grey Ragdoll cat had retreated, as predicted, to the top of the kitchen dresser, its tail swaying back and forth. Large and beautiful, its intense blue eyes watched Anna's every movement, taking her measure. Once approved, Anna could apparently look forward to Spook dropping silently and without warning onto whichever pillow or cushion she might choose to doze upon. Still – at least this time, she'd been warned.

Walking upstairs, Anna was struck immediately by the three smallest bedrooms. They were like a movie set, with their miniature beds, and miniature wardrobes. Everything new. Everything clean, even amongst the deluge of toys. The pink, the dinosaurs, the Lego – absolutely everywhere, as advertised – and then there were the books. Shelf upon shelf of tiny books with stiff cardboard pages and appealing illustrations of Gruffalos, dragons and witches, and of course aliens flaunting their underpants.

Anna was entranced, wandering from room to room, wondering what a childhood like this would *feel* like. Could it possibly be as magical as the brush-strokes of the murals painted on each bedroom wall, the trompe l'oeil doorways and arches leading to other worlds of fairy gardens and grottos?

And for a moment, she tried to imagine her own child in a room like this. Even knowing that he – or she – would have been a little older than this age by now. And just the very thought made her chest tighten.

Maybe, she thought by way of distracting herself, this was what Oscar's bedroom looked like too? Had Henry lovingly painted his name on the bedroom door; did he curl up at night and read him a story? She would find out, she realised, with a nervous intake of breath, when she went to visit next month. She could still hardly believe that she'd suggested it. Something about that peregrine falcon in London had made her long for such strength and beauty in her own actions – although ideally without collateral avian casualties.

Well, at least Arthur couldn't fault that she was following his advice to seize the day. The postgrad prospectuses in her handbag alone carried a ring of progress about them. No regrets for not exploring this sooner; she simply hadn't been ready.

But she might be now.

Anna paused, noticing that each bed was adorned with a much-loved teddy bear from the Hundred Acre Wood. Winnie the Pooh, Piglet and Eeyore sitting confidently on each pillow, as though to mark ownership. Despite herself, Anna couldn't help but wonder about the child allocated the doleful Eeyore though, and whether this was a prescient marker for her future mental health. And, also, why each slightly mangled bear wasn't allowed to go on holiday too.

Nitpicking.

Determined to find fault with this family home. This home where the rooms were still stylish and modern, but without detriment to comfort or ease. Indeed, bizarrely, the clutter seemed to add to, rather than detract from, the welcoming palette of sand, teal and eau-de-nil in the sitting room.

Aspirational.

It was a word that was bandied about all too often on the Home Network website. And yet, to Anna, it had lost all meaning. Too often, it was coupled with thread counts and wet rooms and marble-countered kitchens stuffed with unused appliances.

An aspirational life.

What did that even *mean*? Was she supposed to long for the luxury that had left Liza so lonely and insecure in Dittisham? Or the promise of inherited wealth that made Andrew Fraser so dissatisfied and entitled? While the Henrys and Callies and Annabels of this world in fact offered so much more, just by being themselves? Who they were, rather than what they could flaunt to the world?

And yet, hadn't she herself spent the last decade leapfrogging from one decadent bolthole to another, drawn like a moth to a flame by the promise of well-stocked libraries, waterfall showers and overstuffed sofas?

She looked out into the garden, framed by smart bifold doors covered in sticky handprints. The landscaped garden was again a scene of casual disorder: a plastic sand tray studded with dinosaurs in danger of drowning in the small lake of rainwater that filled the quarried trenches; a set of tiny deck chairs arranged in a huddle, as though for miniature pensioners on a day out at the beach . . . And then there was Anna's personal favourite: a wooden playhouse with window boxes stuffed to the gills with flowering plants and scented herbs.

These children were loved.

These children were adored.

She picked up a tiny jewellery box, cardboard carefully adorned with painted macaroni, a heart picked out in glossy red poster paint, smudged by tiny fingers, and sighed, her mind chasing itself in loops of contradictions and judgements.

She had never owned anything as precious as this small box and she felt an overwhelming surge of emotion that she couldn't identify. Envy? Perhaps. Or maybe simply the hollow recognition of missed opportunities.

As a child.

But also – dare she even think it? – as an adult. She shuddered at the very implication.

She was here to observe.

And with that thought, the memory returned. The moment she had clicked on this placement, filled with certitude and conviction that it was the right place to be. The right time to be looking beyond her own carefully curated corridor of placements that always, always fell into the beautiful yet shallow category.

She could almost physically recall the sense of urgency that she had felt as she read the outline from Mrs Loseley, the sudden and uncharacteristic desire to peek behind the curtain and dare to see how families – real families in Middle England – lived their day-to-day. God knows, Anna herself had spent the last three decades between extremes: she'd wanted to know what normal – what ordinary – felt like. Looked like.

Not her own early childhood of scarcities and fear, nor those she visited with untold privilege and wealth, but how those parents in the world in between managed their lives: prioritising their children, their families and more often than not, going without . . . These were the families where a week in Devon or Cornwall was the height of their summer extravagances, carefully saved for. These were families where the children's happiness was the only currency that mattered.

Anna replaced the jewellery box tenderly, reverently.

Two weeks. Two weeks to gain a little insight into the life in between. Not her own childhood. Nor the borrowed luxury with which she had so effectively distracted herself. But a little reality, or at least one kind of the many.

She thought of Callie, of how her life might be so different were she to grow up in a home where she was truly heard and supported. She dared to think of herself.

So many what ifs and maybes.

So many versions of the truth.

She sat down on the sofa, the cushions squashing beneath her, and picked up a large stuffed elephant, its sumptuous softness dented in places by tiny arms and insistent fingers. With the weight of him against her chest, she allowed herself to imagine, for a moment, a life like this.

Chapter 48

Chipping Norton, 2019

'How many fresh starts can one person have?' Anna asked, barely giving Kate time to get out of her car that Friday. Jittery with caffeine and a long few days alone with her thoughts, Anna's urgent need for an answer seemed to override any decorum.

'Well hello to you too, darling girl!' Kate laughed, her tanned face radiant and serene, despite the mammoth flight from the Seychelles and her return to work. Married life obviously suited her.

'Sorry,' Anna said, duly chastened, yet still looking expectantly at her best friend, waiting for an answer.

Heaving her weekend bag onto her shoulder – all Anna's attempts over the years to advocate the freedom of travelling light falling on deaf ears – Kate looked around. 'Do you mean *here*?' she clarified.

'Here, anywhere. You know, in general,' Anna said. 'Seriously, though, how many times can you have a do-over without just seeming like the biggest flake in the world?'

'Umm, Flakes.' Kate grinned. 'I could actually murder some chocolate—' She broke off in her teasing, suddenly seeming to realise that Anna needed a serious answer. 'I think,' she said, looping her arm through Anna's and looking around the cul-de-sac, 'however many times you need. I don't think it's a finite thing, Anna. In the same way that I don't believe there's only one Mr Right for each person, or just one chance to make a first impression. I think,' she paused, furrowing her brow in an attempt to get the words right, 'that if you're honest and authentic and keep grafting, then you get as many shots as you need.'

Anna nodded, considering. 'And the flakiness?'

'Well, for what it's worth, I actually think it's braver to admit to making a mistake and make a change, than it is to stay stuck in a situation that isn't working. Whether it's a job, or a relationship, or even a family.' Kate watched Anna's face carefully to gauge her reaction. 'And I'm thinking that, maybe you, Anna, deserve a few on account. A few U-turns, a few false starts? So what? Who are you trying to impress? You have only yourself to answer to, so maybe it's okay if you stumble around a bit . . .'

'Trial and error?'

'Better than error then trial,' Kate said, the riposte instinctive. The comfort, though, in their long-standing jokes, from their shared history, was never to be underestimated.

'I'll do my best, but there's form in the family,' Anna said, shrugging off the host of challenging feelings that instantly crowded in whenever she so much as referred to her parents. So many questions about what her DNA might be carrying, waiting for the right time to blow up her existence more effectively than TNT. Lousy parenting, criminal tendencies, addictive personalities? Harder to quantify than blue eyes and brown hair, but nonetheless a possibility.

'Before we dive in to the whole nature versus nurture debate, can I have a pee and a cup of tea?' Kate asked apologetically. 'And since, by the look on your face, you've been up all night going batshit crazy, maybe I should be the one to tackle the kettle. Oh, and—' she turned and reached into the passenger footwell, balancing a precarious foil package on the palm of her hand. 'Alex sends his love and his signature pineapple upside-down cake. He thought it might make you smile, apparently.' Kate handed it over with a knowing look. 'He does like a bit of nostalgia, my little brother.'

'I knew I liked you Porters for a reason,' Anna replied, truly touched, her smile genuine and her relief at Kate's reassuring presence almost overwhelming.

'Well, why wouldn't you? We are fabulous,' Kate said easily, her eyes widening as they stepped inside. 'Jesus, this place is huge. Can you even imagine having this much space in Oxford?'

Anna shrugged. 'You'd have to sell your firstborn to afford it, which kind of negates the point of a family house then, right? Actually, I think the husband commutes in from here. It's all a trade-off isn't it, once kids get involved.'

Kate wandered around, having seemingly forgotten the urgent call of her bladder. 'How on earth do they keep everything so organised though? I mean – for God's sake – the Lego bricks are colour-coded.'

Anna pulled an awkward face. 'Yeah, uh, that was me actually. Couldn't sleep.'

Kate turned her head slowly, with the focus and poise of an eagle owl alighting on her prey. 'You stayed up all night, sorting someone else's Lego? Oh, honey . . .'

'Not *all* night,' Anna protested. 'And besides, don't knock it 'til you've tried it. It's strangely soothing, like meditation, but you know, actually useful.'

Kate shrugged. 'Well I suppose it's less addictive than Valium.'

'And cheaper than vodka.'

Kate stepped forward and pulled Anna into a hug. 'God I've missed you, you tiny eejit. Can we please agree that a month is far too long?'

'Agreed,' muttered Anna into her jumper. 'No more honeymoons for you, okay?'

'Ah shit.' Kate sighed. 'I forgot to bring the wedding photos. I'm so sorry. I've got a few of the island on my phone but all the fancy ones from the wedding photographer are sitting by my front door.'

'Useless girl,' Anna breathed, choosing to stay in her friend's embrace and hide the instinctive sigh of relief from her reprieve. It had been the only cloud on the horizon of their long weekend together: the necessity to relive every moment of one of the worst days of Anna's life, thanks to Andrew Fraser.

'Oh,' Kate pulled away, 'and I have news. Try not to gloat, but Max got sacked. Duncan's furious with him, but I can't help a little schadenfreude on this one. You'll never guess why.'

Anna blinked, waiting for the glee to kick in at his demise, yet strangely feeling nothing bar a mild intrigue. 'I'm going to go out on a limb and say he'd been drinking and he passed a colleague's work off as his own?'

Kate nodded happily. 'Long time coming, but still, it has to be sweet?'

'Is it weird that I just can't bring myself to care all that much?' Anna said, pulling an embarrassed face. Max-bashing was one of their favourite rituals. Max's various dumpings, demotions, and even the first signs of his receding hairline had all brought a little vicarious entertainment over the years. Yet this one – arguably the most salient hiccup in his otherwise gilded existence – left Anna cold.

'Mate! I am so proud of you. If you can't get excited about a little reckoning then I'm happy to say that you finally have closure. Maybe it was seeing him at the wedding? Was it the apology – I know it was long overdue . . .' Kate slowly petered out, waiting for a response from Anna. A word, a sign, anything really to show that she was engaged in the conversation.

Instead Anna simply shrugged. So much had happened since she'd seen Max at Kate's wedding, she'd honestly almost forgotten about it. And all the ups and downs of the last month had seemingly reconfigured the filing system in her brain.

All these years, constantly moving around, everything running smoothly, she'd returned to those old thoughts and grievances again and again, a well-worn groove in the vinyl of her life. Yet all the upheaval and soul-searching since that night at Gravesend Manor, all the abrupt changes in plans and the people she'd met, were now front and centre in her mind's eye.

Fresh, new experiences and hopes, finally, at long last, eclipsing the old.

'Poor Max. His mum will be furious,' Anna said eventually. 'Now, about that cup of tea?'

'This place is amazing, like it's built with families in mind and the world here revolves around them,' Kate said, standing at the bifold doors with a mug of milky tea in her hand and staring out across the gardens, rooftops and fields beyond. There was a cheering soundtrack of children laughing and splashing in their paddling pool next door, while a small yappy terrier attempted, by all accounts, to join them. Across the way, you could hear two other neighbours talking about delphiniums over their fences, a little local gossip thrown in for good measure.

'Maybe,' Anna said. 'It's exactly what I wanted when I was growing up, for sure. But now? I don't know – it feels a bit full-on, doesn't it? Everyone so sociable, so friendly. Three of the neighbours already introduced themselves. One of them had muffins, Kate. In a basket. We're going to yoga on Tuesday, God help me.'

Kate frowned. 'But isn't that what you do, as you move around? You always seem to be gathering new friends, new acquaintances, getting the lie of the land?'

'It's *exactly* what I do.' Anna nodded, frowning. 'And that's why I can't quite put my finger on why this feels different.'

Kate slurped her tea, deep in thought. 'If you asked my mum she'd probably have some fancy anthropological reason, but if you're asking me – well, I reckon it's because this feels real. It isn't some fancy apartment in Chelsea, or a brownstone in Brooklyn, or even that shiny uber-glazed place down by the sea the other week. This isn't a rarefied life. This is just life. A nice one, don't get me wrong, but it's all so ordinary isn't it?' She paused for a second, weighing her options. 'And, if I didn't know better, Pea Pod, I would hazard a guess that it's exactly the reason you chose it.'

She reached out a hand, their fingers only inches apart. 'Maybe you had a point when we spoke last week – maybe you *are* finally ready to think about the kind of life you want. Realistically. Not through the portal of Home Network's fancy clients.'

'Maybe,' Anna mumbled.

'And maybe,' Kate ploughed on, 'it's a good thing to look beyond the smoke and mirrors of a place like this. Beyond the muffin baskets and yoga?' She put her hands on Anna's shoulders and turned her to face eastwards, towards the town. 'Somewhere in there, a man is leaving his wife' – another small turn – 'and another wife is cheating on her husband.' Another turn. 'A woman is crying because she can't handle her toddlers and her job, and another is crying because she can't get pregnant.' Ten more degrees towards the sun. 'There's a couple celebrating their engagement, and another one thrilled with a longed-for promotion.' Kate let go and shrugged. 'There's probably a few people shagging, or dying, or bored out of their skulls too—'

'Although hopefully not at the same time,' Anna cut in drily. 'I get it, I do.'

'Do you, though, Pod? Do you see that there is no such thing as a straightforward life? It's not all about where you are. Life happens anyway. The good and the bad. I just want yours to be filled with lovely people and a fulfilling job – whatever that may be. Wherever you land.'

Anna nodded, the depth of Kate's emotions almost tangible in the echoing kitchen.

'You only get one pass at this, Anna Wilson. I think you have to start making it count.'

Anna smiled and Kate hesitated, thrown for a second. 'Are you mocking my attempt to be your Yoda?'

'Nope,' Anna said, the air flowing freely into her lungs for the first time in a long time, without the constrictions that held her together so often. 'It's just that you're pushing against an open door.'

'Since when?'

'Since last week. Or actually since about twenty-four hours ago.' Anna mirrored Kate's actions, turning her towards the lengthy table strewn with her scrapbooks and travel journals and photographs. 'I wasn't just doing Lego all week, you know. I've been doing this. I've been taking stock.'

Chapter 49

Chipping Norton, 2019

'You know,' Kate said as she twirled spaghetti around her fork, as she continued to flick through Anna's journal of last spring in the Hamptons with the other hand, 'I have a confession to make. And possibly an apology.' She deftly transferred the laden fork to her mouth without flicking the pesto anywhere; a feat that Anna had yet to manage herself despite their ritual pasta consumption.

'All these years,' Kate continued, turning page after page of handwritten notes, interspersed with sketches and doodles, postcards and souvenirs slotted and pasted into place, 'I thought you were just dodging reality, mooching around, and then you show me this.'

She sat back in the chair and stared at Anna, unblinking and appraising. 'I never knew you were really seeing life, experiencing the places you stayed. These notes, these journals – I just never knew.'

Anna shrugged. 'I think you were probably right the first time, to be honest. I'm kidding myself by calling it research, aren't I? Research of what? For what? Surely it's only research if it has a purpose in mind?'

Kate blew out her cheeks, allowing the air to gradually deflate with a slow whistle. 'I think I have to beg to differ. Call it researching the human condition. Call it a travel journal from the inside out, but don't dismiss this, Anna. For all my worrying, and all my nagging to commit to a career and do something tangible . . . Well, I think you might have been doing that all along.'

'So I shouldn't just throw it all out, then?' Anna smiled. 'Because I have to tell you that around 3 a.m. that was a definite possibility. Hence, you know, the Lego.'

'No! Shit – is that what you meant by a fresh start? Do *not* throw this away.' She pulled a face. 'Not that I can tell you what to actually do with it, either, but this is not something to be discarded.'

'My lost decade – how I had to get lost to find myself!' Anna said dramatically, holding the back of her hand to her forehead in a swoon.

'Bloody hell, I'd read that. And I know you're only taking the mickey, but seriously, I can get Sarah on the phone right now and she'd agree. Surely there's a market for vicarious therapy and travel – sort of wanderlust porn for the mind and the senses?'

'And that, ladies and gentlemen, is why my friend does not work in marketing,' Anna snorted.

'Oi,' Kate said, inadvertently flicking spaghetti against her cheek and ruining her perfect twirling record. 'Just because I'm an academic doesn't make me entirely clueless, you know. Besides, I'm pretty certain you've the basis for a master's in social anthropology right here. Seriously, if you don't want it, my mum would bite your hands off for this little stash.' She paused and sat upright in excitement, nearly upending the bowl balanced so precariously on her lap. 'Or you could actually come back yourself. Come back to Oxford and do this!'

Anna's heart flipped uncomfortably in her chest. A simultaneous longing to be back with Kate in Oxford, paired with a fearful lurch of what analysing these journals might reveal. Beyond her lapses in judgement and her nomadic clamourings.

Psychologically speaking.

There was a willingness to be vulnerable that was inherent in any original research, of course, but the very thought of being so exposed left Anna utterly cold.

'Or maybe we can just entertain ourselves with a few Top Fives?' she hedged, tugging a battered leather journal out of the heap. 'And I think we can start with the Summer of Giovannis to get the ball rolling. Tuscany 2016. Pisa, Siena, San Gimignano, before ending up on the banks of the Arno. Four Giovannis in one month – you can't say that every day.'

Kate's eyes widened. 'You slept with four Giovannis in one month?'

Anna shook her head, frowning. 'No! I slept with zero Giovannis, but went on lovely dates with all of them.' She sighed as she reminisced. 'I love first dates. All the anticipation, no rules, just the promise of possibility.'

Kate laughed. 'So you've been flirting and teasing your way around the globe on a promise? No wonder you're so frustrated with life. Everyone knows it's the third date where things get interesting.'

Anna shrugged. It was hard to put into words, but it never felt that way for her. The moment there was an expectation, a call on her emotions, she felt herself backing away. And that instant reserve did not lend itself to uncomplicated flings, wherever the setting. God knows she'd failed to have sex in some of the most romantic places in the world. The Maldives, Cap Ferrat, Edinburgh, Venice . . . The list went on.

She couldn't help but smile to herself, though, with the memory of her most meaningful connection in years. A month in the Lofoten Islands last year where the long, long summer nights and lack of sleep had gradually worn down her defences against the utterly gorgeous and insatiable Birger. 'One who helps.' And, yes, he had certainly lived up to his name.

'What are you looking so smug about? And why do I get the impression that there is so much you're not telling me?' Kate persisted.

'Well, there's loads you're not telling me,' Anna countered, suddenly nineteen again. She leaned forward, pressing her hands together. 'Like what it's like being married, for one thing. What it's really like.'

Kate paused, taking her time to very slowly twirl another forkful of spaghetti, comfortable in the routines of their student days: pasta, intimacy, friendship. She shrugged. 'You know how when we moved into Cowley Road, it just felt right? After all that time in halls the year before, we suddenly felt at home, like we could properly relax?'

Anna nodded. 'Like we could breathe . . .'

Kate shrugged. 'It's a bit like that, right now. But with more sex. And presents.' She laughed. 'Don't get me wrong, the presents are nice, but actually I just feel like we're on the same song sheet. Like *committed* to be on the same song sheet. Is that weird? Am I officially the worst feminist ever?'

'Yup – you're a rubbish feminist these days – we can't ignore that fact, K. I mean, the moment you mentioned pink jobs and blue jobs, I worried for you.' Anna couldn't resist teasing her. 'But actually, if part of feminism is having the life you want, then aren't you just honouring that?'

'Oh that sounds so much better than what Gilda said at work. She thinks I'm selling out to the patriarchy.'

'Gilda with the impressive moustache and wonky eye?' Anna clarified. 'Hmm, well it's one opinion. But you haven't taken Duncan's name, have you? Or given up your job to look after him?'

'Nope, and it makes me indecently happy that I out-earn him two to one and can refuse to take the bins out with a clear conscience.'

'Well there you go then. It's all about what works for you. Like, each person needs their own version of life that respects their beliefs and their politics and, you know, loving who they want to love,' Anna said seriously. If you put it like that, then there was no failure in the choices she herself had made.

They had felt right at the time.

And even if they no longer resonated with her, and at times made her feel a little ashamed of the time she had wasted, then she had only to remind herself of one of Marjorie's favourite maxims: time you enjoy wasting is never really wasted time.

'Pod? You do know that you can tell me anything, right? I mean, if you secretly long to be an accountant, or have fallen for the gorgeous Gilda, or you're pining for the Arctic Viking chappy from last summer—'

'Birger,' Anna supplied.

'Right, that one. Just know that I'm here. Unconditionally,' Kate said, her gaze still searching Anna's face as though trying to read the tea-leaves in the bottom of her cup.

'I know,' Anna said, a slightly tearful smile catching her unawares. 'I really do know, actually. And I also know that it sounds mad to admit it, but having you there, even miles away, is actually what gave me the confidence to get out there and get on the tiny ferry to nowhere and the little seaplane – oh, and that road in America that frightened me shitless.'

'One hundred miles and not a single car.' Kate nodded.

'Route 50. No people, no bends – enough to drive a person crazy.'

'Too late for that,' Kate said. 'You've been bonkers for as long as I've known you, anyway. Just a quiet simmer of nutjob beneath the surface.' She grinned. 'It's one of the reasons I love you actually. Perfection is so suffocating.' She stood up and dumped her bowl in the sink. 'I mean, seriously, look around this town. Could you live here? Really? Even though we know it's all smoke and mirrors, wouldn't you need a little more – well, a little more *grit* in your life?'

She stood over the table and flicked through the journals again, each beautifully labelled and bursting with extra photos and enclosures. 'You're very good at editing to the heart of things. You always have been.' She picked up the notes from Anna's aborted short story, the bare bones sketched out on napkins and notepaper from the fancy London roof terrace last week. 'Why is it so much harder when it's your own words, I wonder?'

'Because you get too close,' Anna replied simply. 'Two thousand words was all they needed and look, I've got at least three thousand right there – half-formed thoughts and senti- ments without a single clue how to pull it all together.'

'So you gave up?' Kate asked, intrigued, skim-reading the notes and glancing up. 'This is good though, Anna. Really good. Can you not fillet it down to the core and just send it off?'

Anna plucked it from her fingers and crumpled the pages into a ball, tossing them into one of the storage boxes on the floor. 'No point. The deadline's probably already passed.'

'Jesus!' Kate flinched as Spook silently appeared in pursuit of the balled-up paper. She bent down to rescue the pages, barely avoiding an angry swipe, and then stopped dead. Standing up slowly, she had a strange expression on her face. 'Can I just ask – all this stuff here? It's all so beautifully organised and curated . . .'

Anna nodded. 'You kind of have to, or you lose track of where you've been, you know?'

'Makes sense,' Kate replied, before bending down again and lifting up the carrier bag she'd spotted. A bag haphazardly, almost violently, stuffed with crumpled letters and envelopes. An A4 folder was bent double in amongst it all. Something had been worthy of filing. Once.

'So, my little Pea Pod, dare I even ask what this little monstrosity represents?'

She plonked the bag on the table, a small tear in the side widening with the impact, the handles stretched thin, almost to breaking point. Whatever Anna had been carting around had apparently deserved no respect or attention whatsoever, as though she couldn't bear to look at it, let alone handle it. Toxic.

'Put it away,' Anna scowled. 'It's nothing important.'

'But—'

'Put it away!' Anna stood up, her good mood evaporating as an all too familiar wave of shame and anger overtook her. She made to snatch for the bag, but Kate was too quick and she only caught the edge of the handle, this last affront too much for its fragility, as the bag tore and its contents spilled across the table. 'What the fuck, Kate?'

'Sorry,' Kate said, her face blanching even beneath her tan. 'I didn't mean to rip it. I just thought—'

'You didn't think,' Anna hissed. 'Not everything needs to be analysed to death you know.' She began grabbing at the papers, her actions suddenly jerky and out of control. All thoughts of happy reflections eclipsed in a moment by the logo on the headed paper.

Kate stepped away from the carnage and caught Anna's hands. 'Stop. Stop now. We can tidy it away again in a moment. No reading required. But right now, I'm more concerned by how one carrier bag of paperwork can trigger a whole Jekyll and Hyde situation in my best friend.'

Anna sank back against the wall, her breath uneven and the red heat in her face gradually abating. 'Read it,' she said. 'Then you'll understand. But then I don't want to talk about it. Ever.'

She gave Kate's hands a reassuring squeeze and then walked out of the room.

Chapter 50

Chipping Norton, 2019

Anna came back downstairs, slightly shame-faced at her teenage flounce from the room a few hours earlier. 'I'm sorry,' she said from the doorway.

Kate looked up from the table, her hair skewered into a tousled bun with a biro and a distracted expression, the same expression she wore in the Bodleian when she was detangling one of her historical tomes, teasing out its secrets and subtexts, immersing herself fully in the life and times of some bygone feminist.

'Oh God.' Anna smiled. 'I've left it too late to apologise and you've gone down the rabbit hole, haven't you? I'm one of your case studies now.'

Kate said nothing but simply pushed back her chair and walked across the room, wordlessly pulling Anna into an enormous bear hug and dropping a loving kiss on the top of her head. They stood together for a moment, framed in the double doorway, the house silent around them, save for the muted purring of the cat, no doubt draped across the top of a cupboard somewhere, elusive and still piqued by Anna's presence.

'I'm not going to do the sympathy thing, okay,' Kate said eventually. 'I mean, you've always told me that you had a tricky time growing up. But, honestly? I had no real understanding of what that meant – you know, in actual day-to-day life.' She paused and squeezed Anna's hand. 'I do now.'

Anna just nodded. 'It's all in the past.'

Kate pulled a face. 'Is it though? Because, Anna Wilson, apart from being incredibly bloody impressive – I mean, how many kids come back from that kind of start in life, to end up where you are?'

'Unemployed and unemployable? No sense of direction and with a deep-seated fear of commitment? I'm going to go out on a limb and say quite a few,' Anna said with a sigh. 'See, I'm not totally oblivious to my shortcomings.'

Kate swatted at her, with no small amount of force. 'Argh! You will literally be the death of me! I mean, seriously – only you could reel off all your challenges and gloss over all your achievements. I'll begin shall I? You have a First from Oxford. You've had the same – rather unique, slightly strange – job for nearly a decade. You have a strong and lasting friendship with me – that's a commitment whether you realise it or not. And' – she let out a hard breath of frustration – 'to the very best of my knowledge you're not broke, or addicted to anything. You're also bright, articulate and bloody gorgeous. If the four Giovannis didn't convince you of that though, then heaven help us all.'

Anna wrinkled her nose. 'Please stop.'

'I will not. I'm going to keep going like a broken record until you appreciate that we all have strengths and weaknesses. You are not the sum of your failings.'

'How come I feel like this then?' Anna said quietly. 'As though I'm stuck and can't move on?'

'Because you're stuck, and you can't move on,' Kate said gently, slowly pulling Anna over towards the table, travel journals now catalogued neatly by year at one end, and the contents of the Co-op bag stacked across the table. Sorted, it seemed at first glance, by placement. Which in itself was pretty sobering, when you realised just how many stacks there were.

A catalogue of Anna's childhood in care.

'Have you read them all?' Anna asked, her voice a shadow of its usual self.

'No. There's a couple of sealed envelopes. But I had a field day with your psych evaluations and your school reports though,' Kate said gently. 'Have you? Read them?'

Anna shook her head. 'I don't need a psych assessment to tell me what's in my head; I have to live with it every day. I know who I am and some shrink's opinion is never going to change that.'

'Shame,' said Kate, placing a smart blue folder in front of her, its cover dog-eared and stained from being shoved into the mix with the other documents. 'This one might have given you a boost actually – you're charming and well adjusted by all accounts. Gifted too. Empathetic. Resilient. Ambitious. But then I knew all that already.'

'You see?' Anna managed a smile. 'Money for old rope.'

'They also said you were struggling to get closure on any of this. Cited a visit to your dad during your GSCEs as a flash point. They recommended ongoing therapy actually, once you left school.'

'Yeah, well, I was a bit busy if you recall.' Anna couldn't help the instinctive prickle in her voice, the snide bite. She stopped herself. 'Sorry. It's kind of weird thinking that you probably know me better than I know myself now.'

'No worries. I think I'd be a bit tetchy too if my entire teenage experience had been catalogued and analysed. Can you even imagine what they would have made of my comfort blanket 'til I was fourteen? I mean, seriously, how much comfort does a person need?'

As if Spook could sense the atmosphere in the room, he dropped down from his perch on the dresser, draping himself across Anna's lap, limp and pliant, his moanful purring more soothing than one might imagine. 'Bloody hell,' Anna said with a small yelp of laughter, 'I must be a sad sack, if even the mad cat has deemed me worthy of attention.'

'We had words,' Kate said seriously. 'I briefed him while you were upstairs. Although he is a weird little fucker, isn't he? Just sat and stared at me with those huge eyes for like an hour straight.'

'Spooky by name,' Anna said, stroking his long, soft fur and feeling her heart rate settle. One half of her was strangely relieved that Kate now knew where she came from, the other half was still battling a mortified humiliation at the whole sorry picture.

'Well, look, while you're sedated by the enormous cat, do you think maybe it's time to open these? They're postmarked on your eighteenth birthday.' She gave a small nervous laugh. 'And to be honest I can't quite believe you never opened them.'

Anna picked up the two envelopes, both with the same date on the postmark: a sliver of an official-looking letter and a square cardboard envelope, pink and tired, with a typed address sticker incongruous on the front.

'I don't need to,' she said. 'This one is my "you're-eighteen-now-and-you're-on-your-own" kiss-off, and this one' – she tapped the pink square – 'is possibly the saddest kind of birthday card you can ever receive as a child. Think of it as a really pathetic version of a telegram from the Queen, a soulless box-ticking exercise from the local authority.' She picked them up and was about to toss them into the bin when Kate reached forward and snatched them.

'Did you learn nothing at Oxford? Every source is valid. Now open the sodding envelopes, Pod,' Kate said, the soothing tone eclipsed by her shocked frustration. Never one to delete a voicemail half played, or discard a movie or book before the end, Kate needed completion. And couldn't really understand those who didn't. 'Please? If they're what you think they are, then fine, you can chuck them.'

'Jesus,' Anna said, again with the petulant tone, but this time on purpose. She shook her head. 'Give them back then.' Kate handed her the pink envelope first, warily, as though Anna might not be trusted not to shred it instantly.

Anna teased gently at the flap of the envelope, the glue already yellowing and fragile. She slid the predicted card from the envelope, poised to wave it in Kate's face and show her the emotional punch of an anonymous hand on a token card. Brutal. Every year. Whoever thought it was a good idea for morale needed to experience it on the receiving end.

But instead she paused, a lump in her throat at the tiny sketch on the cardboard. Benji, Jasper and Nitwit instantly recognisable even after all these years. Marjorie's swirling handwriting a blast from her past that brought tears to her eyes. And to think, how close she'd come to—

'Are you okay?' Kate said, leaning forward in concern, confusion writ large on her face.

Anna nodded, the tears overwhelming her. 'It's – they're Nitwit. From the—'

'Well that's crystal clear,' Kate said gently. 'Jesus, Anna. What is this?'

But Anna barely heard her voice, as she opened the home-made card and saw Marjorie's writing inside. Tremulous rather than bold, perhaps written as she'd grown weaker after Anna's enforced departure. Even towards the end, she'd been thinking of the future. Anna's future. Her words filled Anna's heart as they had so often in their brief time together, bringing love and hope and a sense of possibility. The final line however nearly broke her.

'It's a bequest,' Anna said aloud. She looked up at Kate. 'And you can say "I told you so" now. Look.' She passed Kate the card, and buried her hands in Spook's fur. 'She wanted to leave me something to get me started in life, but it wasn't allowed until I was eighteen. She wanted me to have enough to set up home somewhere, or to go travelling. She wanted me—' Anna inhaled sharply with emotion and the tears clogged her words. 'She wanted me to be happy.'

'Oh Pod,' Kate said, tenderly passing back the card, folded closed so that Jasper, Nitwit and Benji were looking out, beneath the little banner saying Happy Birthday. The absolute antithesis to the sterile missive Anna had been braced for.

'Bloody hell,' Anna breathed. 'I can't believe she did that. So much money, Kate. I can't believe I so nearly—' She dashed away the tears with the back of her hand and then steadied herself. 'You know though, that's not strictly true. I can absolutely believe that Marjorie did that – it's exactly the kind of person she was. Always paying it forward, always hoping for the best and expecting an adventure. Looking for an adventure.' She breathed out slowly, an image of Callie suddenly popping into her mind and a determined thought accompanying it. Be more Marjorie, she thought to herself for a second, doing sums in her head.

This kind of money, not to mention the thought and – yes, love – behind it, was utterly life-changing. A deposit on a flat maybe? Or even enough for her master's degree?

Marjorie, she knew, would be proud either way. Because Marjorie, for all her love of adventure and of travel, had been the first person in her life to offer Anna something she had so desperately needed: security.

And what better security right now, albeit belatedly, than to put down a few roots?

Anna breathed in the thought, her conviction building. The bequest in her hand a catalyst for all the changes to which she had been so hesitant to commit. For herself. And yes, if she was feeling truly brave enough, for Callie too.

'Anna? Anna? Maybe you should open this too, now you're on a roll?' Kate held out the second envelope eagerly.

'You open it,' Anna said. 'I can't cope with any more emotion tonight. And I don't want to ruin my Marjorie buzz with some dreary discharge papers.'

She picked up the card and read and reread Marjorie's words until they were imprinted on her heart. It wasn't just the size of the bequest awaiting her in this savings account; it truly was the thought that mattered to her the most. Knowing that right until the very end of her life, Marjorie had kept her promise that they would be family to one another.

Build your life, build your family, find your home.

Marjorie's last words to her had been filled with love and hope for the future. And here in this weird, peachy-pink envelope, she had been making sure that would be a possibility.

Although, she smiled, of course, Marjorie hadn't accounted for Anna's stubbornness. Or perhaps how very bruised and broken she would be as her eighteenth birthday came around. But Marjorie was ever the optimist; she would have filled this envelope with faith.

Anna was literally breathless, blown away by how much that absolute belief meant to her, would mean to her life moving forwards. A financial cushion which would give her that elusive, audacious independence she had only known from afar.

'Fuck,' breathed Kate from beside her, the second, slender envelope slit open to reveal a single typed page on headed paper. 'I don't even know where to begin with this one.'

Anna shrugged, still distracted. 'You get used to it. Official language, box-ticking. They have a job to do. Just chuck it.' She had no desire to read the empty words sending her off into the world as an adult. And who was truly an adult at eighteen, for God's sake? Looking back, she'd still been a child. Off to university with a head full of literature and not a freaking clue. She had zero desire to read their platitudes and empty promises.

Box ticked.

'No,' Kate said, pulling at Anna's arm. 'This isn't what you think, Pod. I mean, it *really* isn't what you think. You have to read this; it might change everything.' She held out the letter and Anna instinctively, childishly, closed her eyes, as though if she couldn't see them, the words would no longer have the power to disrupt her life still further.

'Anna – Pod – there's letters waiting for you. They were holding them for you until you turned eighteen. God knows why – you probably understand the legal stuff more than me – but Anna, they're from your mum.'

Chapter 51

Mostly on the M5, 2019

'Jesus Christ, Anna! Your driving hasn't improved.' Kate's knuckles turned white as she gripped the handle beside her, Anna darting deftly between lanes, the rev counter straining between each gear change.

'I was just avoiding him – boy racer!' Anna countered with a nod of her head, as a pimped-up BMW in pillar-box red surged erratically through the packed lanes behind them. 'So technically, they're evasive manoeuvres.' She gave a tense, apologetic smile. 'Sorry if I scared you.'

'It's all been a bit of a whirlwind the last few hours,' Kate said gently. 'And I know it's tempting to rush—'

'I'm not rushing; I'm driving. And you know I don't believe in fate and serendipity and all that, but even you have to admit that the whole morning has been a bit surreal. It's a Saturday morning. The solicitor was in the office to pick up his gym kit, for God's sake, or he wouldn't even have answered the phone.'

Kate nodded, her expression anything but soothed. 'I just don't want you to get your hopes up.'

'Kate, if I don't go and get these letters today, and I mean right now, I cannot promise that I will ever summon the nerve again. There are just too many what ifs and maybes in my head right now. And, yes, it is entirely possible that I will not like the answers I get. But at least I'll know what she was thinking, rather than what my dad *says* she was thinking.'

'Just as long as you remember there are three versions of the truth in every scenario, Anna. In this case, his version, her version and what actually happened.'

'Yes, professor,' said Anna with a wry smile. 'I will keep an open mind. And please don't judge if we drive all this way for nothing.'

Kate frowned. 'But I thought he just needed photo ID? He did confirm the box was there, waiting for you. I thought he seemed excited actually. Sounds like they'd all but given up trying to track you down.' She cast a sideways glance at her friend. 'God knows how many of his letters you've ignored over the years, Anna.'

Anna scowled, remembering the second shoebox stuffed with unopened correspondence, high on a shelf in the storage locker. Anything that looked vaguely official pushed out of sight and out of mind: dusty and forgotten, exactly the way she liked it. Protecting herself from the past, from the system that raised her, the only way she knew how. 'The letters may be there, Kate, but I genuinely don't know if I'll be brave enough to read them.' She paused, concentrating as a large articulated lorry blew past and buffeted the tiny Mini in its lane. 'I mean, there's no way of knowing if finding out the truth will solve the problem, is there?'

'What problem?'

Anna shrugged. 'Me.'

'Oh love,' Kate said, reaching across to Anna's hand on the

gearstick. 'You are not the problem in this scenario. The survivor? Yes. The injured party? Very possibly. But never the problem.'

'Well, let's see, shall we? Because all the arguments I can remember were about me. Who was going to pay for things I needed, or look after me while my mum was at work . . .' Anna wrinkled her nose. 'And these are things I haven't thought about in years, so I guess I'm a little pissed off at having to relive them now.'

Not strictly true, Anna knew that. Being with Callie in Bath, hearing the raised voices on the floor above night after night had brought back that sickening sense of familiarity and distrust in a moment.

'I guess I'm just intrigued to hear how she justifies walking away. What excuse she's prepared to put into writing, you know?'

'Explanation,' Kate said, seemingly unable to help herself, her analytical skills well honed. 'What *explanation* she's prepared to write down, because whatever the circumstances, there really is no excuse.'

Anna blew out her cheeks in frustration. 'If you'd told me that at eighteen, I would have said it was a distinction without a difference, you know? But I guess I'm that bit older and wiser now: being a grown-up is hard – God knows what it's like being a parent – and I have to assume that she was doing the best she could at the time.'

Kate was silent for a moment, her hand still flexing instinctively on the door handle, her face a blanched shade of apple-white. 'You're right, of course.'

They veered off towards the M32 skirting Bristol, Anna trying to ignore the lure of the airport signage and an easy escape. 'I'm so glad you're with me,' she said quietly. 'Seriously,

I'd still be reading that letter over and over, frozen with indecision. Thank you for giving me a nudge.'

Kate still said nothing, staring out of the window at the wooded hillside that framed this next stage of their journey. 'Do you mean that? About your mum just doing the best she could? Enough to forgive her?'

'Whether I forgive her or not is kind of immaterial,' Anna said. 'It's too late to do anything about it. I'm *thirty* years old, Kate. I can't ever promise to forget the choices she made, but I'm also not kidding myself – understanding why she made them might really help put it behind me.'

'So you wouldn't want to see her? Try and build a relationship?' Kate ventured.

Anna shook her head. 'I don't think so. I think – well, I think she abdicated any right to play Mother Dearest a very long time ago. I think that, if anything, I'm looking for answers not absolution.'

Kate simply nodded, still staring out the window. Several junctions flew by in silence, both of them wrapped up in their own thoughts. The satnav on Anna's phone chimed an occasional reminder, but otherwise the only sound was the monotonous thrumming of tyres on tarmac.

'I want you to consider something,' Kate said suddenly, making Anna jump with her intensity. 'I want you to move into our house in Oxford. As a tenant, as a guest. Whatever you like. But I want you to think about it. Properly.'

'Kate, you're adorable and I love you, but you've just got married. You do not need some mad spinster living in your house. You've been reading too much Brontë.'

Kate laughed. 'No, you mad bat. We're moving out, is all I'm saying. We get the option of lovely married quarters through the university now, nicer than anything we could ever afford to buy. And we want to keep the house. We've been looking for a tenant, to rent it out. Can you honestly think of a better arrangement than you moving in?'

'You don't need to do that,' Anna said tightly. 'I'm really not homeless. And I don't need charity.'

'Oh for fuck's sake,' Kate burst out, uncharacteristically. 'It's hardly charity if you're family, is it? I got a little help buying the place and it's a good investment to hold on to it. Let me pay that forward and offer you a base to take stock. Mates rates on the rent. Please, Anna. We all talked about it — my mum really would be over the moon. Oxford's currently sadly lacking in waifs and strays in need of her own peculiar brand of life advice, and she misses you. Even Alex is on board. And that's saying something because he just got dumped by Little Miss *Love Island* and has been in a foul mood for months. Just think about it. That's all I'm saying.'

Anna nodded. 'Am I allowed to be totally freaked out by the idea of your whole family sitting around the table talking about what a sad sack I am?'

'You can if you like,' Kate said magnanimously, 'but that wasn't the conversation we had at all. Much more along the lines of who would make the perfect tenant. And who might truly benefit from a base in Oxford. But, you know, you can fill in the blanks however you like.'

'Were there roasties?' Anna said, images of Sunday lunches at the Porter house filling her mind and making her stomach rumble.

'There were.'

'And Leah really dumped Alex this time? It's actually over?' Anna clarified.

'Political differences, I gather. But more likely the fact that he woke up one morning and realised that however amazing she is between the sheets, it's no substitute for having nothing between her ears. I mean, the boy's an idiot of the highest order, but Leah takes ignorance to a whole new level. She just doesn't care about anything. Except maybe *Love Island* and fake eyelashes.'

'Poor Alex,' Anna said. Despite all six-foot-two of his rower's build, her image of him was still very much the blushing fourteen-year-old, proudly bearing his pineapple upside-down cake to the table. A pineapple cake just like the one they had been gradually devouring for the last twenty-four hours. 'Doesn't *he* need somewhere to live, before you start handing out your front door keys?'

'Nah. He's fine. Oddly excited about even the prospect of having you back in town actually. But you would have to take on Gary though, if you decide to move in. He's kind of a fixture,' Kate said.

'Oh my God, Gary is still alive?' Anna laughed. 'How is that even possible?'

'Well, to be fair it might be son-of-son-of-son-of Gary, but the sentiment's still there.' Kate grinned, their proud purchase of their very first potted plant together – a spider plant named Gary – had been another of their shared rites of passage. Their first taste of responsibility.

'So now really isn't a good time to confess that Gary isn't Gary at all.' Anna pulled an embarrassed face as she concentrated on avoiding the vintage Austin going deadly slow in the middle lane. 'I bought a replacement when I forgot to water him that first Easter. Shit. I'm so sorry, Kate. I genuinely didn't think you'd still be nurturing him all these years later.'

Kate gave a filthy laugh. 'I dropped him. Replaced him and then accidentally watered him with hot water. Replaced him. And that was all in the first three weeks.'

They grinned like teenagers for a moment, the innocence of their youthful mistakes so much easier to laugh about. 'Well then maybe "Gary" is more of a moniker than a descendant – he is still a spider plant though, yes?' Anna said, their daft conversation exactly what she needed to distract her.

'He is. I mean, really, we're not so much talking about taking on a house, as becoming Gary's legal guardian . . .'

'Because I did such a bang-up job the last time?' Anna shook her head. 'What is it with everyone wanting me to be their guardian this week? I mean, sheesh.' She slammed on the brakes as the Austin cut right across in front of her, sailing over to the exit without so much as a backwards glance.

'Anna?' Kate said, bracing herself against the dashboard, as the satnav chimed its countdown to the exit they needed. To the solicitor they needed. And maybe even a little closure. Long overdue. 'Who else needs you as their guardian?'

An awkward silence descended.

'Nobody. Well, I mean obviously somebody. But it's nothing. You don't know her. Hell, I hardly know her myself. It was just a suggestion. Well more of a request. But she's gone now. And I couldn't – I mean, how could I possibly – because, I'm no parent. And she needed – well, she said she needed me. But then, she hardly knows me either – you know?'

'I really, truly don't,' Kate said firmly. 'And what the hell was that for a monologue? I half expected your head to start spinning round.'

Anna looked back and indicated, swooping up the slip road away from the motorway. 'Callie. A girl called Callie. Asked me for help. And I said no.'

'Why?' Kate asked, intrigued by Anna's flustered response. 'Why did she ask? Why did you say no?'

Anna cast a sarcastic glance sideways. 'I'm not parent material. But she thought that we shared a lot of common ground. That I might understand what she needed.'

'Do you?'

Anna nodded. 'Probably. But I couldn't help her in the way she wanted. I'm just not equipped to help her. So she left.' A shrug belying how much that simple fact had wounded her. No calls, no contact. Not even a monosyllabic teenage text. Hell, she would have settled for that ridiculous 'K' that Callie so often employed with such lazy insolence.

'You know, sometimes the intention to help is enough. Don't overthink this,' Kate said gently, watching Anna's face carefully, no doubt seeing the hurt and regret scud across her features.

'The road to hell is paved with good intentions,' Anna bit back, 'and I can personally attest that not everyone is cut out to be a foster parent.'

She swallowed hard, Henry's conviction about 'making it work' ringing loud in her ears, almost drowning out that long-held belief. A growing part of her willing to take a chance, play the odds, and dismiss any lingering doubts. Willing and ready, in fact, to offer Callie the springboard into adult life she needed. Longing, actually, to take that leap together.

If only the girl would answer her bloody phone.

Anna navigated her way around another ridiculous roundabout, counting down the exits until they were heading into the heart of St Pauls. The rows of shuttered shops and tatty terraces hadn't really changed from the memories of her youth. There was still the vague sense of disquiet, clusters of youths hanging around, bored, looking for something to fill their day. No sign of the promised gentrification that had spread throughout the other wards of Bristol.

Anna shivered, despite the cloying heat in the Mini.

'Well, isn't it fun taking a trip down memory lane?' She waved a hand to the left at a nondescript government building, the signage faded and defaced. 'Signing-on money here, and then – oh so conveniently – bookies and pub here.' She indicated and turned right, the satnav squawking in protest. 'Arguments and brutal rows two hours later – here.' She stopped the car in the middle of a narrow street, the tiny houses butted together to almost block out the light. 'Home sweet home.'

'Drive on and return to your route as soon as it is safe to do so,' intoned the satnav with no idea of its uncanny insight.

Anna shook her head. 'I thought everything would feel smaller, somehow. Or different. It's kind of sad that nothing has changed.' She put the car into gear, on familiar ground now, weaving her way through identical streets until she reached a strip of office buildings. Tired but clean.

'You have reached your destination,' said the satnav.

'Deep,' said Kate with an encouraging smile.

Chapter 52

Chipping Norton, 2019

Barely half an hour later the letters sat on Kate's lap in a faded blue box file, and it took all of Anna's concentration to keep her eyes on the road. There had been no grand reveal, no momentous ceremony to mark the occasion. Just a photocopy of her passport, her driving licence and a signed chit to acknowledge receipt.

And now, merely inches away, a ticking time bomb.

'Look, why don't you pull over somewhere and just read them? Or read one?' Kate said, watching her closely, making no secret of her concern both for their safety and for Anna's mental health.

Anna shook her head. 'Nope. I'm just going to read them all in one sitting once we're home. By myself. Try and process whatever she's chosen to share and then get on with my life.'

'Well it's a plan,' Kate said tentatively. 'And for what it's worth, I heartily approve of diving in. Drives me mad in movies and books when they tease it out for weeks, months, years even. I mean, who even does that?'

Anna shook her head. 'Weird people, Kate. Weird people with self-control.'

'Another Hobnob?' Kate said, plucking one from the nearly empty packet and passing it across.

'Don't mind if I do.' Anna smiled, comforted by their easy familiarity. As though she could just relax and be herself, warts and weaknesses and all. She paused in her chomping, crumbs tumbling down, wondering if that was how other people felt when they went home for the weekend. Was that the pull, more than roasties and hugs? Was it the opportunity to drop the exhausting façade that modern life seemed to demand, even if just for a few hours?

'I'd be lost without you,' she said, eyes on the road. 'Whatever those letters say, Kate, you've been more like family to me than she could ever be.'

'You can have both, you know. You never ever have to choose. I'm not going anywhere.' Kate gave her shoulder a squeeze.

'And I'll get used to sharing you with Duncan. I will. I just, well, I hope he knows how bloody lucky he is.'

'He does. And it's kind of handy that he loves you too, you know. He's always so proud of everything you do, like you're his sister and Max is just an embarrassing cousin he got lumbered with.' She laughed, drumming her fingers nervously on the box file. 'Have you thought about what you're going to do if she wants to meet up?'

Anna shook her head. 'Nope. I can't even – no. I'm just going to read them. With an open mind if I can.'

Her phone trilled on the hands-free cradle and Emily's picture filled the screen. They were overdue a conversation, but Anna had simply no headspace to spare to talk about house-sitting and feisty felines in need of her attention. She pressed decline and stared straight ahead, incredibly aware of Kate's appraising look from the seat beside her.

'I'm beginning to think that I should meet this Emily of yours,' Kate said.

Anna shook her head. 'I'm not sure that hearing your opinions in stereo is helpful for any of us.'

Kate laughed. 'Ooh, now I am intrigued. Don't tell me that lovely Emily and I agree that your random house-hopping is *waay* past eccentric and bordering on bonkers?'

'It's her business,' Anna reminded her.

'But you didn't say no.' Kate nodded with a smug smile. 'Tellingly.'

There was a pause – not so much a comfortable silence as Kate realigning her advance.

'Did I mention, by the way, that Duncan and I converted the third bedroom into a study? The one in the attic with those little dormer windows?'

'Subtle,' Anna replied with a smile.

'One room for you, another for your writing and then a lovely spare . . . For guests, or friends.'

Anna simply shook her head. 'You'll get so much money renting that out on the open market. It'll be snapped up in a heartbeat.'

'And what if money isn't my only motivation? Hmm? Had you even considered that?' Kate said crossly. 'You of all people can identify with how little a full bank account means if you're still not fulfilled or happy.'

Anna frowned. 'You didn't tell me you were unhappy.'

'I miss my best friend,' Anna replied simply. 'I know she misses our life in Oxford. And I'm the kind of spoiled brat whose parents helped them get a foot on the property ladder. You, Anna Wilson, are the salve to my middle-class conscience. Please help me—' She couldn't keep an entirely straight face.

Anna shook her head, smiling. She slowed as they drove into the web of narrow lanes leading into Chipping Norton. 'You know I'd do anything for you, you daft muppet. But this – it still feels too much like charity.' She held up one hand to ward off Kate's interruption. 'As though you've given up on me making my own way in life and you're staging an intervention.'

'Well that's just stupid. A little bit true, but still stupid,' Kate huffed. 'But it's mainly for my benefit though. Look, don't make a big thing with Duncan, will you? But I had a lot of time to think on that island and there were very few changes I wanted to make in my life but one of them was undeniable. I am deeply in love with my husband but I love *you*, Pod. I'm my best self with you – and when we talk things through it puts everything into perspective. So yes – I got married – but that doesn't stop you being the love of my life.' She managed a teary, twisted smile.

Anna allowed the car to glide to a halt at the entrance to the cul-de-sac, twisting in her seat. 'And you know I feel the same way about you, right? Our friendship is the most meaningful relationship I've ever had. The only relationship that's ever lasted. Or made me feel safe. You are my rock.'

There was so much more she could have said, but emotion never sat comfortably out in the open. Safety and stability were huge in Anna's world – ironic really for someone who made a conscious choice to continually seek out the unknown.

Kate sniffed, a little hiccup of acknowledgement making her smile. 'Bloody hormones,' she said.

Anna leaned over and pulled her into a hug. 'Should we have stopped and bought chocolate?' she offered, Kate's emotional rollercoaster of PMT almost legendary on occasion.

'Always. But in this case . . .' Kate sat back in her seat, hands resting squarely on the box file. She hesitated. 'Actually, one

thing at a time. Let's get you inside to read these letters while
I cook up a feast.' Her stomach growled in appreciation of the
suggestion and she shrugged. 'I'm starving. And then we'll
play Big Picture.' She bent down and tugged her handbag
from the footwell, reaching inside and pulling out a notebook
identical to the one she had given Anna all those years ago.
The depository of the infamous List. 'Time to start a new
plan, I think, Pod, don't you?'

Anna simply nodded. Her best friend, a box of the past and
a blank page. All they needed now was a bowl of risotto.

Anna pulled into the driveway of the Loseleys' house and
immediately slammed on the brakes. 'Jesus!' Kate said, grabbing for the dashboard. 'What the—?'

Anna stared at the porch and blinked for a moment, as
though to confirm that her eyes weren't playing tricks on her.
'Callie,' she said simply, before pushing open the door and
running across the lawn, leaving Kate strapped in, weighed
down by the box of letters and none the wiser.

It was as though their conversation earlier that day had
summoned her physical presence and Anna struggled to
compute what she was seeing. Snuggled against the front
door was Callie, fast asleep and tousled, one of her eyes
blackened and swollen, a coat clearly pulled on in haste
over what looked like her pyjamas and without even a bag
at her feet.

She crouched down. 'Callie? It's me – Anna. Callie, love,
wake up.' She gently shook her shoulder and felt winded by
the lost expression on her face, as Callie drowsily gathered her
bearings.

'Hi,' she said simply, falling into Anna's arms for a hug.
Never the most touchy-feely of people, Anna surprised herself

by drawing the girl in close and whispering reassuring nonsense into her hair.

'Please don't be cross, but I didn't know where else to go,' Callie said quietly, her voice plaintive and dejected. Nothing like the confident, outspoken young woman that Anna had left behind in Bath.

'I'm not cross, I'm worried,' Anna said. 'And that eye looks really painful.'

'You should see the other guy,' Callie joked, tears welling up. 'Seriously. I might be in really big trouble.'

'How big?' Anna said, her mind running on and evaluating all kinds of scenarios. The only solicitor she knew was the flakey one back in St Pauls and that thought alone didn't exactly fill her with confidence.

'He hit me, so I hit him back. Hard,' Callie said, a shadow of her previous grit in her voice. 'And then I left.'

'And your mum?' Anna asked, ever hopeful.

'Stood and watched the whole thing,' Callie said, choking up again. 'Then screamed at me when I stood up for myself.' She paused. 'Although to be fair, I didn't expect him to just go down like a tree trunk.' She looked seriously worried. 'I just hit him back, Anna. It was a decent punch but I didn't mean anything.' She bit her lip and her whole face seemed to flinch with the movement, the bruises across her cheekbone and around her eye already darkening to deep Professor Plum purple. 'It was just one good punch.'

'With a year's worth of pain and frustration built in,' Anna said, her empathy for this girl almost suffocating. 'And nobody would judge you for that. It's called self-defence for a reason. And it's okay.'

There really were worse ways of being an absent parent than being physically absent, Anna decided, biting down on the impulse to pick up the phone to Callie's mother and let rip.

Callie pulled the coat more tightly around her, shivering despite the heat of the afternoon. The laughing shouts of children playing in their gardens utterly incongruous to the very real drama playing out on this doorstep. 'You said I could call if I needed you, so I pinched Mum's emergency cash and got in a taxi. I mean, this counts as an emergency, yes?' she managed, and then the tears began, the shuddering, wrenching sobs of a girl at the end of her tether. Afraid and alone. The concept of picking up the phone before it came to this obviously beyond her.

And Anna, knowing all too well how those feelings pulled your very soul apart, sat down on the doorstep beside her, tucked her body in close and began to re-evaluate everything she thought she knew, her priorities realigning in an instant.

Chapter 53

St Pauls, Bristol, 1995

Anna flinched as her father swung around in the doorway, his tattered holdall like a heavy pendulum. A brutal version of the swingball game she so adored.

She looked to her mother, frozen in fury in the kitchen, bleeding hand wrapped in a tea-towel, broken crockery scattered across the linoleum floor. Her precious Peter Rabbit mug lay amongst the broken shards and seeing his little blue coat in pieces brought a wave of fury that Anna could barely contain.

Why weren't they listening to her? Or to each other?

This argument they had went round and round in circles, but never truly went away.

She didn't understand all of it, but even she could recognise that her father's furious accusations were some kind of madness.

Although that didn't make her mother's immediate leap to anger any more helpful.

'Well – you got what you wanted, Jenny,' he said, his eyes black with fury, focused so intently on his wife that it was as though Anna, caught in the middle, simply didn't exist. 'Try life as a single parent for a bit if you think you're so bloody capable.'

'How will I notice the difference – you do fuck all around here,' her mother said tightly. 'Maybe we'll even have a bit of money left over each month without you pissing it away down the bookies. Or on another one of your idiotic get-rich-quick schemes. Does it not occur to you that even a small wage is better than an empty promise? Why does it always have to be all or nothing, with you? Be a *father* for once, why don't you?'

Anna wiped her clammy hands down her dungarees, her head swivelling back and forth as they argued. But nothing was ever resolved.

Two ears and one mouth – that's what Mrs Joseph said at school. God's way of making sure you knew your priorities. Her mum and dad didn't seem to know that.

'Please!' she shouted in the end, her hands clamped over her ears. 'Just stop!'

And to their credit, silence fell for a moment, and Anna felt her lungs fully inflate for the first time since her dad had walked through the door that evening, jittery and looking for an argument, his pupils large and his words all fat in his mouth.

'Look what you're doing to her—' Her mum was the first to pick up the baton. 'Look! How you're upsetting your daughter.'

And then they were off again, blaming, accusing and picking holes in each other, as though Anna were too young or too stupid to understand what was happening here.

Because there had always been rows, for as long as she could remember.

Thursdays were always the worst.

Thursday was when her dad went to sign on and yet still came home with empty pockets.

Or when one of his 'plans' went wrong. And they were worse off than they'd been before. Empty promises were his currency of choice – that's what she'd heard her mother say, but Anna had no idea what that meant. She just knew that life with Graham Wilson was either feast or famine. And that he would 'rather die' than have a steady job like her mother's.

But today's fight felt worse. Much, much worse. Because of the holdall swinging over her dad's shoulder and because her mum stood still in the kitchen, watching him gather his things without taking a single step to stop him.

She blinked for a moment, another silence taking her by surprise, even more so when her dad crouched down in front of her. 'Listen, kid.' His aftershave was woody and spicy and oh-so-familiar and Anna couldn't help but throw herself into his arms, almost knocking him off his feet.

'Don't go,' she said, her face buried into his shoulder, the soft, worn fabric of his T-shirt against her cheek.

'Kiddo, your mum's had her say. She doesn't want me here right now. But you'll be okay.'

'But why? Why can't you stay?'

Her dad looked up and across at his wife, his mouth twisting as he spoke. 'Ah well, your mum's full of big ideas with her new job, isn't she? Your old man's not good enough for her anymore.'

'Big ideas?' Her mum's voice was cold, sharp and pointy. 'Big ideas like paying the rent on time and dodging the bailiffs? Go to hell, Graham.' And she turned her back.

It was like when the sun went behind a cloud, and the whole room felt colder for a moment. Darker without her mum's protection. 'Mummy? Mummy? Say something. Stop him,' Anna shrieked, panicking now as her dad strode towards the front door.

'Daddy? Stop. Please.' Anna looked back and forth and ran after him, hanging on his arm even as he strode away down the pavement, stubbing her bare toes on empty cans and filthy, sodden food wrappers.

He stopped for a moment, looking almost embarrassed to have a small, snot-bubbling child clinging to him. 'Anna. Enough. Go home to your mum. You'll be fine and you don't need to worry about me. I've got a plan.'

'But – I can't,' Anna managed. 'I don't understand.' How could she say that it wasn't *him* she was worried about? Was it selfish that her only thoughts right now were for herself?

'Look, Anna, she doesn't want me here,' he said coldly.

'Then stay for me?' Anna begged, her eyes sticky and her breath coming in short, stabbing gasps as she fought against the tears overwhelming her.

He paused for a second, as though to consider her request, her heart leaping in her chest at the possibility he might, just for once, have truly heard her.

'It's not enough,' he said, shaking his head, as he untangled his arm and walked away, leaving Anna on the pavement, shivering in disbelief.

For those weren't the words that her six-year-old brain had heard.

'You're not enough.'

The only legacy from her father that would last a lifetime.

Chapter 54

Chipping Norton, 2019

It seemed both urgent and vital to Anna that Callie understood that her mother's mistakes were not her own, and yet somehow, even as she busied herself making an ice pack for Callie's swollen eye, she struggled to find the words.

Maybe it really was the last taboo? To accuse someone – someone she barely knew – of being a lousy mother. A dangerous mother, really, if you considered that passivity could be its own form of cruel abuse.

Standing by and watching – saying nothing, doing nothing. The choice not to act, to intervene as your child suffered in any scenario surely equally damaging to the bond of trust as any physical blow.

And God knows, Anna could empathise.

'How did you even know where to find me, Cal? You never answer your phone. And I've been calling—'

'I know you have,' Callie said sheepishly. 'But I was really pissed off when you left and I didn't want to say anything I might regret.'

'But how did you—?'

Callie reached across and took Anna's phone, tapping at the screen until a map was visible, complete with two pulsing blue dots on the outskirts of Chipping Norton. 'I might have installed an app. You know, Find My Friends?' She looked up at Anna apologetically, flinching as even the small movement caused her pain.

'Try this,' Anna said, passing Callie a bag of frozen peas wrapped in a soft linen tea-towel the colour of bluebells as she tried to process what she'd just heard. All those 'coincidental' meetings in Bath suddenly made a lot more sense. And yet, she didn't have it in her to be angry, only relieved that Callie had had the foresight to plan for a rainy day. 'And when this one melts there's a Mr Bump ice pack poised and ready,' Anna said, mustering what she hoped was a reassuring smile, gratified by the relief on Callie's face that a bollocking wasn't incoming.

'Not to mention Savlon, arnica, and more sticking plasters than Boots,' Kate said, still rummaging through the kitchen cupboards. 'Having kids is obviously a hazardous occupation.' She held up the boxes. 'Do you want Barbie, Peppa Pig or Minions? Ooh and ginger biscuits.' She ripped open the package with enthusiasm.

She hovered slightly nervously, not yet introduced, yet feeling as though she knew Callie already. Anna's description of her had been so spot on, so insightful. 'I'm Kate by the way.'

Callie nodded. 'I figured. The posh one. From Oxford.'

Kate frowned and looked to Anna for guidance.

'My friend from Oxford, yeah,' Anna said, pulling up a chair beside Callie and repositioning the ice pack to cover most of the bruising. 'But don't call her that.'

'Posh?' Callie sulked. 'Why, is that an insult now?'

'It is the way you're saying it,' Kate bit back, unable, it seemed, to restrain herself.

Callie chewed her lip, staring down at her fingernails, bitten to the quick. 'Yeah, must have been awful for you, growing up in Oxford with your mum and dad still together, studying and getting all the support you needed . . . Bet you're one of those families that love fancy-dress parties too.'

Anna looked from one to the other, trying to work out why they seemed so determined to wind each other up. Both so important to her – in different ways, of course – she had simply assumed they would get along.

'When I was about seventeen,' Anna began, seemingly apropos of nothing, 'my social worker Jackie told me a story. They had to do some professional development or something and they were given a case study. Alcoholic mother, neglected kids, absent father. Debt. Adultery. Nothing new or especially shocking, just another heartbreaking story of kids not being looked after, or feeling safe or even being fed properly. And so they all discussed it and agreed that the children should be taken away from the family home. For their own good. And then the examiner told them that the case study was based on Princess Margaret.' She shrugged, slightly gratified to have elicited a shocked response from both Kate and Callie. 'Privilege and wealth don't always make for happy families or protect vulnerable kids is all I'm saying.'

There was an awkward pause.

'Sorry,' Callie said, looking up at Kate for the first time. 'Jealousy is an ugly thing.'

'No need to apologise,' Kate said, her cheeks colouring slightly. 'By any measure, I've been incredibly fortunate. But you know, it wasn't until I met this one that I ever felt right in my own skin. I was always a bit of a weirdo – more interested in books than gossip.'

Callie's face broke into a smile, making her wince as her swollen eye screamed in protest. 'Seems perfectly normal to me.' She paused, a sideways glance at Anna. 'She has that effect on everyone maybe? 'Cause I was feeling pretty low when she moved in downstairs.'

'Well, when she's not being a veritable tonic, she's a right pain in the arse, I tell you.' Kate pulled up a chair and leaned forward. 'Have you ever seen the mess she can make getting one simple meal in the oven? Talk about making a mountain out of a moussaka.'

And so Anna sat back, knowing that was her cue to let these two women – these incredibly special women – find their common ground. And if it had to be at the expense of her catering skills or her dating apathy, then so be it.

Her eyes travelled as though magnetically drawn to the box file on the kitchen counter, dumped there hurriedly as they'd handled Callie's unexpected arrival. She breathed out slowly, calming her racing heart. The letters would have to wait. After a decade forgotten on a shelf somewhere, what was another few hours until everyone else was asleep? She needed the time and the space to give them her undivided attention. To possibly do justice to her mother's inner thoughts and feelings about walking away from her only child.

Kate and Callie were here, right in front of her, flesh and blood, and they deserved her focus right now. The three of them together, in this carefully curated family home, so bizarre as to be unsettling.

'Is this your way of saying that you don't want me to cook supper?' she said when they had eventually tired of ragging her foibles and quirks.

'I'll cook,' Callie said. 'If you don't mind spaghetti?'

'Spaghetti always works,' Kate said. 'I'm beyond starving.' This despite the now empty packet of ginger biscuits on the table.

'Cool.' Callie offered a smile, an olive branch of sorts, her gaze falling on the travel bands on each of Kate's wrists.

'Oh!' she said involuntarily, as the penny dropped. 'Can I ask, is it weird eating for two? Or is it a lovely excuse to just pig out?'

'Jesus, Callie. A little tact,' Anna leapt in. Sure, Kate had piled on the pounds on their all-inclusive honeymoon, but it was hardly endearing to have it so blithely pointed out.

Kate stilled for a second before turning her attention squarely to her best friend in the whole world. 'About that, actually . . .' She reached into her handbag and slipped a small black and white picture across the table towards Anna. A small black and white printout in fact.

'But,' Anna managed, looking down at the incontrovertible proof in her hands and at the quietly serene expression of hope on Kate's face. 'Are you—?'

Kate nodded. 'Twelve weeks yesterday. I've been dying to tell you, but stuff kept happening. The wedding and life and then last night it didn't seem quite— Well, it wasn't the way I'd envisaged sharing the news.'

'Fuck,' breathed Callie. 'I'm so sorry. I've blown your cover.' She looked simply mortified and Anna allowed the briefest of irritations to pass. Sure, in an ideal world this would have been a momentous announcement for the two of them to share, but sharing seemed to be the key word here. Not just with Duncan, now. But with this little soul who would no doubt change the landscape of their friendship for ever.

She'd thought about this moment, almost as soon as Kate had showed her the neat solitaire diamond on her left hand. But not for one second had she expected to feel this wave of anticipation and inclusion. Was it possible that there was more room in her life, in her heart, than she'd allowed herself to believe? The arbitrary boundaries suddenly seemed so foolish and narrow-minded.

Anna swallowed hard and leapt to her feet, pulling Kate into an enormous hug. 'I'm just so freaking over the moon for you. And you're feeling okay? Not too pukey and all that?'

Suddenly Kate's green, nauseated face in the car earlier that day made a lot more sense.

'Pukey, chubby, teary, sleepy – it's like an alternative universe of *Snow White and the Seven Dwarfs* in my body right now. But honestly, Pod – I'm truly happy.' She laid her hand on the tiniest swell of her normally taut stomach.

'Can I be a surrogate aunt? Or something?' Anna's voice trembled with the hope and vulnerability of the suggestion.

'Godmother, aunt – take your pick. But promise me you'll be involved. I need you. I'm genuinely thinking that old saying about it taking a village might be right on the money.' She paused, glanced briefly at Callie, who was now ostentatiously rummaging in the larder, trying to give them some privacy and space. 'And obviously *wherever* you're living' – she gave Anna a hard look – 'I just want this little bean to really know you. As a part of the family.'

More Tetris blocks dropping into place in Anna's mind: the rush for the bigger house in Oxford, the offer of a tenancy for her. Even Kate's renewed interest in Anna's job choices and prospects. Was this like a kind of nesting – getting not only her own proverbial house in order, but that of her family too? Certainly, Kate hadn't held back on weighing in with Alex and *Love-Island*-Leah's break-up.

'You're going to be an amazing mum,' Anna said, meaning every word. 'Simply because you will love this little bean more than anything or anyone. Even Duncan. Even me.' She smiled. 'And I can't wait to watch you juggle all the squeamish bits.'

Kate shook her head and flung a napkin at her. 'Not just me. Duncan. And my mum. And you. It's the only way forward.' She paused. 'I guess I've seen too much about what happens when all the parenting eggs are in one basket.'

'So now I'm a cautionary tale?' Anna shook her head, still smiling, but unable to deny the smart of pain at how on point Kate's assessment had been.

'More of an inspirational one, to be honest. But yes, being your friend has rather focused my mind on the kind of parent I want to be.' She paused. 'What you said the other night, about your mum being fallible, you know, just a person doing her best? Well, I get that. And actually, I think it's great if you truly feel that way. But I can't get past the thought that, once you're a parent, your words, your actions – well, they just carry so much more weight, don't they? The ability to inspire, just as much as the capacity to wound.'

Callie laid a bunch of cutlery down on the table beside them, and instinctively nodded at Kate's words. 'Valid point. Harsh words from a parent have serious longevity. Exhibit Number One.' She held up her hand.

Anna breathed out slowly, her mind filled with discarded comments from her youth: some uttered in anger, some with no thought at all, yet all of them filed away and still undermining her self-esteem by stealth.

As Callie dished up three huge bowls of carbonara, Anna sat back and listened as they talked. About books, about Callie's study plans.

'I'm going to Oxford too,' she said with such conviction that Anna had no reason to doubt that this gutsy girl would make it happen. Somehow. 'I want to be a writer. Like Anna.'

'Don't say it,' Anna cautioned her friend, Kate already taking a breath to drop her in it.

Kate grinned. 'Now why would you think I would judge? I mean, it's only been a decade.' She stuck out her tongue.

'Some people might have rustled up a few chapters . . . But you know, writing is tricky.'

Callie frowned. 'But she's written tons. Not just those journals but all those thousands of emails. I mean, there's practically enough material for *War and Peace* in there alone.'

Anna stilled, eyes wide, shocked into silence by Callie's casual confession. It wasn't so much the invasion of privacy as the realisation of how many emails might have accrued. How many half-formed thoughts and truncated loops of introspection and self-analysis.

Callie looked at Kate for guidance as the silence lengthened. 'Should I not have said?'

Kate gave her a supportive smile. 'More likely, you should not have *read*.'

They both turned to look at Anna, waiting for a response, but somehow there was only one question she wanted to ask.

'Well,' she said to Callie after a moment. 'You've read them. Were they any good?'

Kate shook her head, laughing. 'Oh my God, some things never change. Do you know, Callie, when we were students, Anna would be so obsessive that she would go and sit down with her professors and analyse every single dropped grade or percentage point. One by one.' She twirled her finger against her forehead.

'Well, I'm giving up on being a perfectionist,' Anna countered. 'Too exhausting; too limiting.'

'So you don't really want to know what I thought about your writing?' Callie asked, a little confused by the back-and-forth banter. 'I mean, am I in the shit for snooping or not?'

'I think that depends on whether you're prepared to offer fair literary criticism,' Kate cut in, giving Anna a warning look.

'Or, you know, therapy – depending on what horror show you've unearthed in my favourite person's subconscious.'

'Didn't you *just* get married?' Callie was still bemused. 'Like, isn't your husband your favourite person?'

'God no.' Kate shook her head. 'But he is a very healthy second, and he will have to be grateful for that.'

Anna pressed her hand to her chest, suffused with a warm feeling she couldn't quite name but utterly adored. It felt a little bit like acceptance.

Unconditionally.

She squeezed Kate's hand and paused, wondered for a brief second whether it would ruin the mood to ask what else Callie had been looking at on her phone, wondering whether it actually mattered. Perhaps her slightly obsessive need for privacy was yet another habit she could learn to live without?

Especially if it led to moments like these.

And as the shadows lengthened and the evening mellowed, Anna tried to put her finger on why this felt so natural, so different, to any other supper party she'd attended since her undergraduate days. Impromptu or otherwise.

As Callie leapt up to get Kate another portion, the conversation carrying on between the table and the counter-top, she smiled. Three women listening, empathising, caring. There was no male voice at the table trying to advocate a solution; the debate itself was enough. Action was not necessarily required; it was enough to feel heard, to feel validated, to feel cared for.

And not for one moment did Anna feel as though any of them were destined to carry their individual burdens alone.

All this time, Anna had cleaved to the belief that choice was power.

That so long as she was the one calling the shots and setting the boundaries – choosing her destinations for adventure and flexibility – then she was winning.

Looking around this table tonight, in laughter and heartbreak and uncertainty, she couldn't help but wonder if she had misread adult life entirely.

A little vulnerability, it seemed, went a very long way.

A little community, even further.

She bit her lip and dared to wonder if she was brave enough to commit.

Not just to Kate and her burgeoning family. Or to Callie and her thwarted educational aspirations. Or even one day to an insane ninja cat like Spook.

But to herself. And the promise of a settled and meaningful future.

She glanced again at the box file on the counter and considered whether Kate might be right about this, as about so many other things in Anna's life. If she was truly stuck in a pattern of evasion, might these letters be the long-overdue catalyst for change?

'This,' Kate said, holding her PAW Patrol beaker of apple juice aloft as though it were finest Cristal, 'is exactly what I needed. Thank you both – this evening – the company of fine minds and wonderful women – is everything the Seychelles couldn't offer. Thank you. Truly. My hormonal little heart is full.'

And, as Anna raised her own glass, she found that watching Callie's tired, sore face light up at the compliment meant more to her than she could possibly have foreseen.

'To new beginnings,' she said, and slowly took a sip.

Chapter 55

Chipping Norton, 2019

Anna checked that the bifold doors were locked for the third time, following the rooftops with her gaze, out beyond the cul-de-sac. Kate had been spot on in her assessment and it was somewhat galling to realise that Anna herself had fallen for the oldest trick in the book: it was so very easy to imagine that nothing bad could ever happen in a place like this. But where there were families and marriages and, well, people really, there would always be heartbreak. And the good stuff too, obviously. But it was easier to focus on the downside.

It was also a little sobering to accept that finding her own 'perfect' place to call home had very little to do with the bricks and mortar, or the view, or an abundance of chi-chi coffee shops where she could pretend to write. Because, if she was entirely honest, there was more pretence than productivity when it came to her grand ambition.

'You still checking every door a thousand times before bed?' Kate asked quietly, catching Anna unawares.

'I thought you were asleep?'

'Hungry,' Kate said apologetically. 'But seriously, do you want me to lock up with you so you know it's done and you can relax?' She deliberately looked away from the box file that was now open on the table. Its contents not yet fully revealed.

'It's fine. Honestly. Even if you do, I'll still be doing the rounds again later. It's kind of soothing in a way.' Anna attempted a smile but it faltered. 'Plus it makes me the best darn house-sitter.'

'But—' Kate started, before Anna held up her hand.

'Honestly, it's just something I've come to accept. And the more stressed I am, the more loops I do. So today – well, let's just be grateful I'm staying here rather than one of the yawning stately piles I've been to in the past.' This time the smile was real. 'But then it certainly keeps me fit.'

'Oh, Pod. You really don't need a Fitbit, do you?' She looked around, the low illumination from the giant fish tank lighting up the sitting room beyond with a ghostly green light, Spook once again draped across the top of the French dresser. 'Don't you ever – I mean, isn't there even a part of you that wants to be somewhere familiar? Somewhere that's yours? Somewhere your Wi-Fi connects automatically? And your things are all around you, rather than packed away somewhere?'

Anna nodded. 'There really is. And that feeling just gets stronger. But then – every single time – I get caught up in wondering, what if I make the wrong choice? What if I choose somewhere and I hate it?'

'But doesn't that also apply to every choice you make in life? Jobs, husbands, pets even?'

Anna just gave her a look.

And then suddenly the penny dropped for Kate, as she realised that her lovely friend had been unable to make those choices and commitments either. 'Oh, Pod. Thank God you have me.'

Anna returned the hug, the reassuring scent of vanilla so comforting that she daren't imagine her life without it. 'Ah, but you're forgetting. You didn't give me a choice. You were just there – every day, no question – you made it so easy for me to be your friend and by the time I realised, I was all in.'

'Well, *stay* all in, will you please?' Kate said, looking at her strangely. 'I could do the same with the rest, you know. Just make the choices for you.'

'Isn't that what you are doing with the house in Oxford?' Anna smiled.

'Maybe, just a little bit. But I'm not fixing you up on dates or presenting you with a puppy or setting up job interviews.'

'Yet.'

Kate shrugged. 'Just say the word and I can be your fairy godmother. Although you'd better make it soon before my brain turns to mush and all I can think about is snacks. Because I tell you, it's happening already. The paper I wrote on Wednesday was about Simone de Beauvoir and I wrote Simone de Biscuit. I kid you not.'

Anna laughed, not quite sure whether to buy into the myth. 'Well, at least you're writing. I'm stalled beyond reprieve at this point. I think I need to go back to school and relearn everything I've forgotten.'

'Am I allowed to say something? I mean, I wouldn't normally, but there's just so much to unpack in your life right now – even if you do insist on living out of a holdall that wouldn't cover me for a one-night stay. You're stuck in chrysalis stage, living with ideas in your head, rather than on the page. Honestly, I've seen it happen to so many people at work. You have to get them out of your head in whatever format you can, give them space to breathe and evolve on the page.'

Anna nodded. 'You're right of course, but when I was in London it kind of dawned on me that there's a huge difference between *wanting* to write and actually having the idea for a novel. Not just a notion for any old book, you know, but the Big Idea for my book. And I'm stuck with this conflict between the kind of literary creation I've longed for and the themes that have somewhat insinuated themselves into any creative mind space.' She paused. 'Do I sound like a literary twat, yet?'

'Getting there.' Kate smiled. 'But you know, maybe you should just listen. Maybe those ideas are trying to tell you something, or,' she gave Anna's shoulders a gentle squeeze, staying, leaning against her, 'maybe they're helping you to *process* something. Because fiction is not the only way to write. Maybe you're not a novelist at all. Maybe you're a biographer, or a satirist, or a political commentator. You have a way with words, Anna Wilson, that puts me to shame. But novels are not the only way to communicate. So, then you have to decide, what are you trying to do? Are you aiming to entertain and elevate, or educate and illuminate?'

Anna said nothing. The only characters in her outlines and synopses insisted on morphing into versions of herself. Sometimes with more bravery, or resilience, or that mixed and elusive blessing: objectivity. Yet nevertheless, there was no denying the tenacious themes that asserted themselves over and over again.

And, as much as she had been enjoying her foray into Shirley Conran's oeuvre, she couldn't ever imagine herself having the guts to write about such intimacies and physical longings without sounding like an awkward spinster.

Non-fiction.

What would that even look like?

But, standing there in the quiet darkness, with Spook's low insistent purring matching that of the pastel-coloured fridge, Anna felt a shiver of illumination.

For sure, real people didn't live like characters in novels, their story arcs mapped out in advance for maximum impact or the most rewarding outcome. But still, every now and again, in an astute turn of phrase, Anna would find herself. Would see herself – her own worries, inhibitions and hopes – and she would feel a little less alone. Centuries, even, did not alter the human condition; the intrinsic desire to be accepted, to be successful and, in so many different ways, to be loved.

Books had never been simply a pastime for Anna – they were a manual for living, if you only allowed yourself to look.

But what if she allowed herself to truly open her own eyes and look? Not at what was written on a page, but what was real in the world around her?

Writing the truth was still writing. It was just called non-fiction.

'Do you want me to mix up all the Lego bricks again?' Kate offered kindly. 'I'll stay and help you sort them.'

Chapter 56

Chipping Norton, 2019

It was hard not to be a snob, but two letters in and Anna found herself flinching at the naive and obsequious tone of her mother's letters.

She'd sorted them by date.

One letter each year, set to arrive on her birthday and one other envelope, penned in a different hand, which Anna had set aside with an inexplicable irritation. Somehow it felt intrusive in this most intimate of moments between mother and daughter.

The first letter had been written with her eight-year-old self in mind, adorned with doodles and a recipe for her favourite shortbread. Almost as though it carried on a conversation and with no reference at all to the abject abandonment that had separated them. Reading between the lines, Anna could only hope that, at that point at least, her mother had seen their separation as temporary. Necessary. While her mother apparently was 'poorly'.

Poorly.

What did that even mean?

To an eight-year-old. To her now. Thoughts of cancer treatment and debilitating disease flickering through Anna's mind as she attempted to fill in the gaps in these coy and unrewarding missives. Excuses by the plenty. But no shortage of 'take care darling, Mummy loves you'.

But with the fourth letter, an abrupt change. Almost accusatory. The guilt fairly seeping from every pore of the cheap, flimsy paper. One single side.

A relapse it seemed. And the definition of 'poorly' became clear, because suddenly there was talk of rehab. No censoring of language for eleven-year-old Anna.

Anna sat back, pushing the letter away from herself, hearing only the excuses over and over again.

'Without your father . . .'

'Too much for me to cope with . . .'

'I know you'll understand . . .'

That last one brought a hot wave of anger through Anna as though she'd been doused in boiling water. While she'd been wedging chairs under door handles to avoid the attentions of Dave, her mother had been travelling, 'to find herself'. Well how very lovely for her.

Was there a more bitter pill to swallow than maternal neglect? That deep-seated disappointment in the person who gave you life, yet was entirely incapable of managing their own?

Simply knowing, deep down, where nobody could hear you cry, that you were not a priority. You were not enough. That, maybe even on some level, your very existence scared or intimidated? Or even that, without that primary bond, it was impossible to ever truly value yourself or to believe in your ability to be loved.

And then there was the shame . . . Unrelenting and stubborn. Colouring the world.

Anna swallowed hard, unaware even of the tears that were flowing until the taste of salt on her lips brought her back into the present. Brought with it some small understanding of her mother's pain between each written line.

Vivid memories of loneliness, even as they'd been together, in those last few months. The acid smell of cheap wine. The lingering stench of tobacco. And the turn-on-a-sixpence fury.

Maybe it had been a blessing that Jenny had simply failed to collect her from school that day?

You needed a licence to drive a car, she thought – and not for the first time – but any selfish fool could attempt to raise a human being.

Anna slowly ripped open the next letter, realising even as she did so that each envelope bore only her first name. No address.

She frowned in confusion, but any thoughts as to their delivery were immediately eclipsed by the contents of the letter.

A small photograph. Faded in the vintage hues of Kodak but the resemblance unmistakable. Anna and her mother. That last hot summer, when they'd eaten strawberry Mivvis and dangled their feet in the paddling pool. Sun cream smudges and burned noses. Together. And smiling.

Anna cradled the photo as though it were priceless.

Which of course, it was. The only image she had of the two of them together and with it something still more precious.

A happy memory.

Folding her lips in together, she tried to stem the emotion but her chest ached with the intensity of the feelings.

She unfolded the letter: warm, caring, apologetic.

These were the words of a sober woman. Not yet confident in that sobriety, to be fair. But the honesty rang through and for the first time, Anna could see herself in these words.

Could identify and empathise with the struggles of this woman who felt like a familiar stranger.

She read on and on, her eyes smarting with tiredness, but her hunger for understanding only growing more rapacious.

This woman who had found a new life, leaving Dublin behind for a new home in the States. This woman who seemed to be under the misapprehension that Anna would be happier with her foster parents. A bucolic picture that bore so little resemblance to the truth it was almost laughable.

Had she been lying to herself for convenience or did she genuinely believe her own logic?

It was hard to say.

But in her mother's conviction, in her stubborn affiliation to the situation that she herself had created, Anna saw more and more of herself.

There was pain and there was anger, but Anna could not deny the connection.

Parents were just people.

Fallible.

Human.

Imperfect.

And yet their legacy carried such a weight.

Her mother's misguided decisions – whether taken lightly or not – had affected so many lives.

And continued to do so.

Returning the card wishing her luck in her GCSEs – a year too late, but the thought was there – Anna turned to the stack and stilled when she realised there was only one envelope remaining.

The interloper.

Her hands trembled as she tore it open, jarring slightly at the pages inside. The handwriting was tight and neat. Controlled and unmistakably masculine.

She skimmed the first paragraph and could not contain the small exhalation of pain that escaped, as her heart seemed to rip itself from her chest. She blinked as she attempted to read on, but as her body instinctively folded in on itself, the letter trembled too much for her to focus.

This man. This William Davies. A name she had never heard and yet now with the power to topple the precarious house of cards these few letters had built.

'I cannot imagine how difficult it must be to read these words,' her mother's husband wrote.

Selfish even in death, Anna thought furiously for a moment, glancing at the date on the front page.

Six weeks before her eighteenth birthday.

A childhood in limbo. No adoption a possibility as she waited for Jenny to return.

She breathed out slowly, feeling small and cruel for even allowing the thought. Settling her breath so that she could at least take in the enormity of William's words. Of the life they had built together. The children they shared. And of this box of letters he had discovered on her passing.

Unposted.

'It's hard not to feel as though I hardly knew her,' he wrote, and for a moment, Anna's heart went out to him too. His wife, the mother of his children and, apparently, the keeper of secrets.

Anna.

The biggest secret of all in their otherwise All-American life. The photograph of them together lay facing upwards on the table and Anna couldn't bring herself to touch it. As though by even holding it she would make the betrayal more real.

Instead, she pushed the letters to one side and picked up her pen, eyes streaming and her knees pulled tightly to her chest, as though some security and comfort might be derived from not baring her heart.

So, instead, she bared her soul.

'Dear Mum,' she wrote, 'I know now that we will never have the conversation I need. The chance to ask you the simple question why. But I need you to know how I feel . . .'

It was hard to say how many hours had passed. Anna's hand cramped uncomfortably and the table was littered with page after page after page – her thoughts, her feelings, her anger, her understanding – purged into this one letter.

In so many ways it felt like the most important thing Anna had ever written.

The *only* important thing Anna had ever written.

A letter that would never be received. Would never be read by the one person, it seemed, who had shaped Anna's entire life.

Long overdue but somehow the richer for it.

Even imagining how Anna would have felt as a fragile, nascent adult – still raw and unformed – had she read these letters at eighteen, made her keen with pain for what might have been. Relief, at last, for her procrastination and stubborn commitment to evolve her own life in her own way.

So much better that she read these now, with a little idea of how challenging life could be. Pitfalls waiting at every corner. How vulnerable even adults could feel, none of them perfect and each bound to make their own mistakes. And how terrified her mother must have been.

Alone. An addict. A single parent.

Forgiveness would come. Somehow Anna was sure of that.

But before that came resolve: resolve never to be that person. The person who put themselves and their insecurities above all else.

She pushed her chair away from the table and switched off the single light, noticing as she did so that the sun had already risen. She took a deep breath and steadied herself, walking quietly upstairs.

She could hear Kate snoring deeply from behind the closed door of her bedroom and smiled. The sound itself a reminder of happier times. Of security and comfort at 44 Cowley Road.

Peeking into Callie's room, the door left ajar and the night-light on, she smiled to see Callie curled up in the dinosaur bed, her arms wrapped tightly around a furry stegosaurus. So worldly wise and yet still so young. Her lashes lay long and fluttering on the smooth curve of her cheek and Anna had to resist the urge to straighten the duvet, to tuck her in more tightly.

If this evening had shown her anything, it was that she owed so much to the women in her life, whose only connection to her had been one of choice rather than biology.

Marjorie, in her own inimitable and influential way. And Jackie, paid or not, had always been there when it mattered.

Kate too. Even Kate's mum had played a role in helping Anna through to graduation.

Quite how that momentous landmark had served to throw Anna off track, rather than smooth the path to adult life, still confused and eluded her. But here she was. Still alive. Still with the ability to care and engage.

Not least the ability to hope.

She leaned against the doorway and allowed herself a moment to dream. To dare to dream.

She breathed out slowly.

Could one ask for a better family of choice than the women in this house right now, if she finally allowed herself to face life head on? Without blinkers. Bravely, without anger and regret holding her back. Was there better company anywhere for the emotional apocalypse she might yet have to embrace in order to come out the other side?

She smiled to herself. At the very idea of a life in Oxford, of Kate's new baby and of sitting in the Bodleian library once more.

Home was not an address on a piece of paper, or dependent on a solid foundation.

She could build a home, the way Marjorie had intended, by filling her life with people she loved, allowing herself to simply be just that – herself. This was no time to shy away from her innate talents and experiences; this was the time to embrace everything she had learned and to finally have the courage to share it.

She tiptoed forward and perched on the edge of Callie's bed, the urgency to share her decision eclipsing all thoughts of waiting until morning.

'Callie,' she whispered. 'Callie. Wake up. What do you think? Do you still want to take a chance on your mad plan together?'

Callie's eyes flickered open, her sleepy face infused with hope. 'Are you serious?' she managed.

'How do you feel about a little house in Oxford?' Anna said. 'You and me and an indecent amount of books.'

Acknowledgements

It is no small miracle that this book has landed in your hands and I truly hope you have enjoyed it, perhaps been moved at times, and maybe even picked up the phone and called your best friend to tell them they are loved.

I wrote *Home*, for the most part, during 2020: the strangest and most challenging of times to attempt creativity. Without some very wonderful doctors – chiefly the fabulous Arnold – there is every chance this book wouldn't even have been finished. And whilst we can never fully express our gratitude to the healthcare workers who continue to go the extra mile, for all of us, I nevertheless want to say a huge thank you to each and every one of you out there.

Likewise, to my amazing publishing team at S&S – an enormous vote of thanks and appreciation for your kindness, your insightfulness, and your hard work, not to mention your patience! I truly wish we could have credits rolling now, as they do in the movies, to acknowledge all the effort that goes on behind this glossy cover, but to Clare, to Sara-Jade, to Alice – my utmost appreciation for trusting in this new concept and supporting me all the way.

To Jess and Sarah, my deepest gratitude for always spreading the word and the book love.

To Laura and Jenny and Pip – thank you for polishing and creating and bringing the whole manuscript together, wrapped up in this gorgeous cover.

And then, to so many of the team whose work is so crucial in bringing a book out into the world – to Francesca and Gail, Rich, Maddie and Joe, and to Dom and Rachel – yet more thank yous to all of you for your help and your support.

Appreciation and thank yous, of course, are also due to Cathryn and Jess and the rest of the Curtis Brown team – it's been no small thing to shepherd this book, my fifth novel, out into the world, not least during the most difficult of years. Here's to brighter days ahead.

And there is another person who deserves a cheer and a special mention – and who will probably be bashful about the vital role she played in bringing such resonance and empathy to this book – Nicki, I could not have done this story justice without your time, your insights and your experience. Thank you!

I have always felt that, once a book leaves the author's hands, it becomes something other – released with trust (and not a small amount of faith) to readers, bloggers, reviewers and booksellers out in the big wide world . . . I am incredibly grateful for each and every one of you. Your enthusiasm and support are truly invaluable. Please never forget how important you are: each thoughtful review, or rating, or hand sale makes all the difference in this industry. Not least to the author behind the words, holding their breath and hoping.

And now lastly – because such is the way of these things – yet always, of course, first in my mind, let me say one last huge and heartfelt thank you to my family and my friends, for putting up with the crazy rollercoaster ride with this book over the last year or so. To Sam, Rosie and Bertie – you are my world. To Emma and Emma – always. To Milly, Bernie and Jane for wisdom, advice and laughter. And to the wonderful AJ, Katie, Kate and Caroline for being there, even when we couldn't actually be anywhere.

P xx

The inspiration behind the story of *Home*

The story of *Home* began with an idea that wouldn't leave me alone, this notion that the word 'home' means different things to all of us – is it where we live? Who we live with? Or perhaps how we present ourselves to the world? I believe it's become such an intrinsic part of our identity, whether it happens to be an accurate reflection of our lives or not ...

Even the act of writing this novel, though, challenged those beliefs, as I had no idea starting out that I would be approaching this idea from the concept of absence. And how that absence might shape a young life. Then, perhaps more importantly for the purposes of this story, how those ripples might continue into adulthood and future relationships.

So, as the character of Anna grew in my mind and her role as a nomadic house sitter evolved, it became clear to me that, in all her travels, Anna had actually been seeking out a template for the kind of life she wanted – somewhere she wouldn't have to dilute herself to fit in. Anna had become very skilled over the years at reframing her life, making it more palatable for those around her as she moved from foster placement to placement as a child, becoming the ultimate chameleon.

And it still surprises me, to be honest, how many of us still do this to a certain extent – whether it be at work, with the in-laws or in certain social settings – giving away our own agency and authenticity. So, this was something I really enjoyed exploring in this story, guiding Anna towards letting go of her inner pretzel and her people pleasing, and suspecting that this might resonate with quite a few of you.

But of course, there was also another, deeper layer to Anna's experience growing up and I could not have done her years as a 'looked-after child' justice on the page without a lot of real-life input and experience from an amazing professional in social care – who shared her insights with me. This went on to shape the story, the narrative and indeed the outcome of this novel. Writing this story quickly became one long lesson in adaptability and humility, and I hope that Anna's story is all the more relatable for it.

Whilst this story is by no means a romance, there is of course, one pivotal, inspiring relationship in the book and it was an absolute joy to write – the love story, if you like, between Anna and her best friend, Kate. Because, ultimately, this whole novel is about friendship and I wanted to write a love letter of sorts, to that enduring platonic love that also has the power to shape and even validate one's adult life and choices. I wanted to give Anna her family of choice, and to acknowledge that, whilst she doesn't really know what having a home feels like, there's an absolute conviction within her that she'll recognise it when she sees it.

For Anna, as for all us, working towards the realisation that it isn't where you settle down that matters, but the people you have around you when you do.

With love

Px

Reading Group Questions

1. Which characters in the novel did you find yourself drawn to the most and why?

2. Are there any passages that you underlined, or that particularly resonated with you?

3. What are some themes or issues that came up for you whilst reading this book?

4. 'Anna just smiled. Words eluded her; it confused and intrigued her in equal measure that her staunchly feminist friend was taking vows at all. It had seemed like the one thing they had both always agreed on – they didn't need to belong to anyone.' Do you think that getting married might affect the views of a feminist?

5. Did you know much about the foster care experience before reading? Were there any of Anna's childhood experiences that surprised you?

6. As you were introduced to Anna's experiences as a child, could you see how her past had shaped her life? Were there missed opportunities for her to build a more stable foundation as an adult?

7. 'Home was not an address on a piece of paper, or dependent on a solid foundation. She could build a home, the way Marjorie had intended, by filling her life with people she loved, allowing herself to simply be just that – herself.' Where do you consider to be your home and which particular aspects truly make it feel like home for you?

8. Have you ever considered travelling long-term? If you have travelled for a long time, what have you ended up missing the most? And were they the things/people you might have anticipated?

9. Did you find the ending of Anna's story satisfying?

10. What's something that scares you that you'd like to do in your life, just once?

Out of Practice

Penny Parkes

WINNER OF THE RNA's ROMANTIC COMEDY
OF THE YEAR AWARD 2017!

Meet married mum of two and successful GP
Holly Graham as she relocates her family to join the team
at The Practice at Beckerford, hoping to find the peaceful
life she craves, despite the chaos that comes with her two
year old twins and the troublesome state of her marriage. It
will certainly be a challenge to keep her private and
professional lives separate in such a tight-knit community.

Her colleagues have their own issues to contend with. The
gorgeous **Dr Dan Carter** is struggling to focus on work
and the last thing he needs is any more stress; having his
ambitious ex-girlfriend **Dr Julia Channing** working
alongside him isn't really helping. Thankfully, the rather
delectable **Dr Taffy Jones** is on hand to distract
Holly from the escalating situation at home.

Feisty octogenarian and resident celebrity, **Elsie Townsend**,
is Holly's favourite patient and saving grace. Elsie's
inspirational Life Lessons come at the perfect moment,
as The Practice is suddenly under threat of imminent
closure and Holly rediscovers her voice and
her priorities just in time . . .

OUT NOW IN PAPERBACK, eBOOK AND eAUDIO

Practice Makes Perfect

Penny Parkes

WINNER OF THE RNA's ROMANTIC COMEDY
OF THE YEAR AWARD 2017!

The Practice at Larkford has suddenly been thrust under the spotlight – and its nomination as a 'NHS Model Surgery' is causing the team major headaches. **Dr Holly Graham** should be basking in the glow of her new romance with fellow doctor, **Taffy** – but she is worried that the team is prioritising plaudits over patients, and her favourite resident, the irreverent and entertaining **Elsie**, is facing a difficult diagnosis. Add to that the chaos of family life and the strain is starting to show.

Dr Dishy Dan Carter's obsession with work is masking unhappiness elsewhere – he can't persuade girlfriend **Julia** to settle down. It's only as Julia's mother comes to stay that he realizes what she has been hiding for so long.
Alice Walker joins the team like a breath of fresh air and her assistance dog Coco quickly wins everyone round – which is just as well, because Coco and Alice will soon need some help of their own. Can they pull together and become the Dream Team that the NHS obviously thinks they are?

'If dishy doctors, cute dogs, hilarious OAPs and idyllic country settings are your thing, you're in for a treat with this second novel set at a GP practice in the village of Larkford. Funny, moving, romantic and full of characters you'll love – it's perfect in every way' *Heat*

OUT NOW IN PAPERBACK, eBOOK AND eAUDIO

Best Practice
Penny Parkes

Love and laughter with the residents of Larkford
is exactly what the doctor ordered!

Dr Alice Walker has become accomplished at presenting a
façade to the world – to anyone watching, she is the
epitome of style, composure and professionalism. But
perhaps it was to be expected that the cracks might begin to
show at some point. Thankfully Grace is on hand to offer
both friendship and support when it's needed most.

Meanwhile, **Dr Holly Graham** has her hands full both
professionally and personally. Planning a wedding with Taffy
Jones is challenging enough, even before some surprising
news changes everything. At least beloved Larkford resident,
Elsie, still has a few tricks left up her sleeve!

Dr Dan Carter, on the other hand, has decided
to throw himself into his career – the best antidote he's
found to unrequited love. When tragedy strikes in the heart
of Larkford, Dan makes it his mission to help the
community.

'The characters are crafted with love, the plot grips
throughout and you turn the final page feeling like
the world's a lovely place after all' Isabelle Broom

OUT NOW IN PAPERBACK, eBOOK AND eAUDIO

Snowed in With You
Penny Parkes

Previously published as Snowed in at The Practice

Larkford Surgery is the heart of a tightknit community in the Cotswolds, as well as a hotbed of drama, rivalry, resentment and romance – and that's just the doctors ...

Dr Holly Graham has just had twins and is finding life exhausting. Even with husband **Dr Taffy Jones** and devoted friend Elsie by her side, she is completely outnumbered. Making the transition back to work will be no easy feat but then an unexpected job offer changes everything.

Her maternity cover, **Dr Tilly Grainger**, has arrived in from South America to cover but it seems that she isn't finding life in the peaceful Cotswolds valley as rewarding as she'd hoped, and she is causing chaos.

Then widower and former rock star Connor arrives in Larkford, ready for a new start. He's not sure how he will fit in with his new tightknit community. Has he made a mistake leaving his old life behind, or will he find exactly what he's looking for in the beauty of the Cotswolds?

Curl up with this wonderful festive novel from the bestselling author and winner of the RNA Romantic Comedy Award 2017.

'Full of humour, warmth and characters you care about – this is a festive read you're sure to love' *Woman's Weekly*

booksandthecity.co.uk

the home of female fiction

NEWS & EVENTS | **BOOKS** | **FEATURES** | **COMPETITIONS**

Follow us online to be the first to hear from
your favourite authors

booksandthecity.co.uk

@TeamBATC

Join our mailing list for the latest news, events and
exclusive competitions

Sign up at
booksandthecity.co.uk